"What if I want to make a pass at you?"

With both hands free, Jen wreathed Matt's neck.

To her disappointment, nothing.

"What if I want to kiss you...." She rose on tiptoe, and with lust pouring through her, brushed her lips ever so briefly across the scruff on his jaw. "Just like this..."

Matt remained still as a statue, the only hint he was affected by her outrageous ploy was the heat emanating from his body, the thudding of his heart and, lower still, the unmistakable imprint of desire.

"You really want to find out?" he asked hoarsely.

Did she? Jen tilted her head, her heart—and temper—raging. She studied his battle-weary eyes.

Maybe not...

She stepped back slightly, telling herself that she had made her point.

Then, to her shock, Matt made his. His arms clamped around her, tugging her closer still.

Dear Reader,

Crisis—in the form of illness—eventually strikes every family, and Matt Briscoe and his father, Emmett, are no exception. Matt's mother's death profoundly affected him and his dad. Although they sought very different remedies for their broken hearts….

Since then, Matt has tried to control everything he can in life. He goes the extra mile to protect his vulnerable father. Emmett—always something of a risk-taker, and a very loving, if egocentric, man—has tried another approach. Constantly seeking to replace the passion he lost, he has married multiple times, to disastrous result. And now, much to Matt's consternation, Emmett is at it again.

Enter bronze sculptor Jen Carson. She, too, lost her mom, and dealt with the fallout from her father's crushed dreams. Now, she takes nothing for granted, and tries to control nothing *except* her own reaction to things.

There's only one problem with that. Jen can't seem to quash her fast-rising reaction to sexy, fabulously wealthy rancher Matt Briscoe. Nor he to her. Neither Jen nor Matt put their trust in the future, or dare hope that passion will last more than the moment they are in. And yet, the kind of love that can last has a way of entering the picture after all. The only question is: dare they risk all for the happiness that has always seemed just out of their reach?

Happy reading! And feel free to visit me at cathygillenthacker.com, and on Facebook and Twitter.

Cathy Gillen Thacker

The Texas Rancher's Vow

CATHY GILLEN THACKER

TORONTO NEW YORK LONDON
AMSTERDAM PARIS SYDNEY HAMBURG
STOCKHOLM ATHENS TOKYO MILAN MADRID
PRAGUE WARSAW BUDAPEST AUCKLAND

PLEASE RECYCLE
THIS PRODUCT IS RECYCLABLE

Recycling programs
for this product may
not exist in your area.

ISBN-13: 978-0-373-75416-8

THE TEXAS RANCHER'S VOW
Copyright © 2012 by Harlequin Books S.A.

The publisher acknowledges the copyright holder
of the individual works as follows:

THE TEXAS RANCHER'S VOW
Copyright © 2012 by Cathy Gillen Thacker

FOUND: ONE BABY
Copyright © 2009 by Cathy Gillen Thacker

CONTENTS

ABOUT THE AUTHOR

Cathy Gillen Thacker is married and a mother of three. She and her husband spent eighteen years in Texas and now reside in North Carolina. Her mysteries, romantic comedies and heart-warming family stories have made numerous appearances on bestseller lists, but her best reward, she says, is knowing one of her books made someone's day a little brighter. A popular Harlequin Books author for many years, she loves telling passionate stories with happy endings, and thinks nothing beats a good romance and a hot cup of tea! You can visit Cathy's website at www.cathygillenthacker.com for more information on her up-coming and previously published books, recipes and a list of her favorite things.

Books by Cathy Gillen Thacker
HARLEQUIN AMERICAN ROMANCE

*The McCabes: Next Generation
**Texas Legacies: The Carrigans
***Made in Texas
‡The Lone Star Dads Club
‡‡Texas Legacies: The McCabes
†Legends of Laramie County

The Texas
Rancher's Vow

Chapter One

"I know what he said, but it's not your artistic talent that my father is interested in."

Jen stared the unexpected visitor to her Austin gallery. Matt Briscoe was six foot four inches of incredibly determined, swaggering cowboy. As well as handsome to a fault.

Knowing it would irritate him as much as he had already irritated her, she let her glance drift slowly over his ruggedly chiseled face to his thatch of curly black hair. It was cut short in a way that wouldn't require much maintenance. His beard was another matter. He had the kind of dark, dangerous-looking scruff that never totally disappeared no matter how closely he shaved. The kind that made her suspect the man just oozed testosterone. In bed. And out. "And you know this because…?" Jen prodded.

Eyes the color of the Texas summer sky zeroed in on hers. Lingered. Just long enough to get her pulse racing in a way she most definitely did not like.

The corner of his sensual mouth lifting slightly, Matt Briscoe continued brusquely, "In the past ten years Emmett's married—and divorced—a novelist, a violinist and an actress."

Okay, so that not only wasn't a good personal track

record to have, it didn't portend well for her future dealings with the wealthy Texas cattleman.

On the other hand, Jen reminded herself, Emmett Briscoe hadn't been hitting on her—or even flirting with her—when he had made the appointment.

On the phone, Matt's sixty-year-old father had been all business, and perfectly polite.

Unlike the blunt-to-a-fault younger man standing in front of her.

Jen took a calming breath and forced herself to look around the small but respectable gallery she had leased to display her work.

She was a sculptress—and a darn fine one at that—whether Matt Briscoe chose to acknowledge it or not. So she wasn't going to let him, or anyone else in his blue-blooded, Texas ranching class disparage her.

"This leads you to believe that your father would now turn to a practitioner of the *visual* arts—for female company?"

Matt flinched. Her assumption had clearly struck a nerve. "For more reasons than you could possibly understand," he retorted gruffly. "Yes. It does."

He really thought her a gold digger?

Jen folded her arms beneath her breasts. "Well, you'll be happy to know, Matt Briscoe, that I am not looking for a sugar daddy."

He rested his hands on his hips, pushing back the edges of his lightweight summer sport coat, then rocked forward on the toes of his expensive, hand-tooled leather boots. "It wouldn't start out that way."

Unable to take the raw masculine intensity of his gaze, Jen focused her attention on the strong column of his suntanned throat, visible in the open collar of his pale blue dress shirt.

Damn, he smelled good. Outdoorsy and brisk and male. Not that she should be noticing, she thought firmly.

Indignantly, she forced her glance upward and continued as if he hadn't spoken, "Nor am I looking to get married again. Ever."

His gaze meshed with hers. Something that might have been empathy appeared all too briefly in his expression. "So you've been…?"

"Divorced." Old bitterness welled inside her, filling her heart, keeping the force field of independence up and running. "Yes." Jen nodded. She wasn't ashamed, just regretful. "I have."

Matt inclined his head, murmured conversationally, "Then you understand how difficult it can be to end something that never should have begun."

He was so close. Too close. Her heart skipped another beat.

She stepped back a pace. "I do."

"So do I," he returned softly, as if that fact somehow bonded them. Put them on the same page. With the same goals and values.

But she and Matt—and his very wealthy father—weren't joined in anything, Jen reminded herself sternly.

Any more than she and her ex and his family had ever been.

Yes, there had been instances of closeness. Moments when she had hoped—even imagined—that everything would turn out all right. Only to find out that Dex had an agenda of his own that left her in the dust. Not to mention disgraced and completely heartbroken.

Never again, Jen had vowed, would she allow herself to be used as a pawn between a wealthy scion and his family.

That was truer now than ever.

As was her goal of wanting her own financial stability.

Determined to let Matt Briscoe know where he stood with her, she smirked. "Now why doesn't it surprise me that you're a veteran of divorce, too?" She stepped away and snapped her fingers. "Oh, I've got it. Your outright charm."

He remained motionless, his expression a blank slate.

Jen noticed he neither claimed nor disavowed what she had just alleged. Which meant what? He was single? Involved? It certainly didn't look as if he was married, since he wasn't wearing a wedding ring.

"I'm trying to be forthright with you—in a way my dad likely won't be, at least not in the beginning," Matt said gruffly.

His words had the ring of truth, but it made them no less offensive and overbearing. Jen stepped closer once again and dropped her voice a notch. "What you're trying to do, Matt Briscoe, is intimidate me for your own reasons." Something else she was oh too familiar with... The alleged "good guy" who was at heart a selfish jerk.

Jaw hardening, he shook his head. "Let's just cut to the chase, shall we? I'll double whatever he's offering for you if you don't show up."

Matt really thought he could buy her off? Jen's temper flared. He wasn't the first—although she really wished he would be the last—to make that mistake. "Well, that's an expensive proposition," she drawled.

He pulled a checkbook from the inside pocket of his jacket.

Incensed that he assumed she was that easy, Jen glared at him. "Save your cash, cowboy."

"Sure about that?" he taunted, wielding a pen. "It's a one-time-only offer."

Jen was finished being polite, too. "And one I don't intend to take."

Footsteps sounded behind them.

"Trouble here?" a low voice rumbled.

Cy and Celia were suddenly at her side.

Jen stepped between her coworkers, aware that they were ready to kick butt on her behalf. Of course, it would have been ludicrous if the married couple had tried. Cy was almost a full foot shorter than their interloper. Celia was even more petite and only days away from delivering their first child.

Jen held up a hand, staving off any further intervention on her behalf. "There's no trouble, Cy," she said quietly, her eyes still on the ruggedly handsome rancher standing before her. "Mr. Briscoe was just leaving."

Matt remained where he was.

Cy glowered. "You heard the lady."

Matt dug in his heels. "I'm not going to let you hurt my father."

"And I'm not going to let you tell me what I can or cannot do." Jen opened the gallery door, grasped his elbow and pushed him through. Then she shut the door behind him, locked it and flipped the sign to Closed.

Matt's lips thinned. He shook his head at her through the glass, then stalked off down the street.

"Wow," Celia said, moving to the window to stare after him. "I wasn't expecting that."

Shaking off the dark mood that had descended, Jen ran a trembling hand through her hair and quipped, "Never a dull moment in my life, that's for sure."

"You feeling okay?"

Jen surveyed her friend's petite, pregnant form. Was

it her imagination or had the baby dropped another couple inches in the last day? "Fine. It's you I'm worried about." She led them upstairs to her studio.

"Celia is right," Cy said. "I don't think it's a good idea to meet with the senior Briscoe."

All three of them congregated around the works in progress. Jen was just finishing up a bust of the mayor, slated for city hall. Cy was making the molds for her work, as well as the dozens of baby shoes that would be bronzed at the foundry. Celia also played an integral role in the business, scheduling all the appointments and keeping the books.

"He said on the phone he wants to commission several bronzes. That's a lot of money we could all use." Maybe if they had enough coming in, they could ease out of the baby-paraphernalia-bronzing work that currently underwrote the operating costs of the gallery and the studio, as well as all their salaries.

Cy shook his head. He removed his apron and hung it up next to his own workstation. "We'll find another way to bump up profits and bring in income, Jen."

Easier said than done, when my career as an artist is just beginning to take off. Besides... She folded her arms again. "I don't care how inhospitable Matt Briscoe was. I'm not letting that audacious cowboy scare me off."

Celia ran a hand over her swollen tummy. "Jen..."

Jen shook her head, refusing the advice. "You two worry about your baby. I'll worry about me."

"ALMOST THERE?" Celia asked Jen late the next day.

Jen pressed her cell phone closer to her ear. "I can see the entrance to the Triple B Ranch from where I'm standing." The fifty-thousand-acre ranch was located on the far western edge of Laramie County. Hundreds of black Angus cattle grazed sedately in the rolling green pastures, for as far as the eye could see.

"How is the radiator holding out?"

Jen took the clear plastic jug out of her aging white utility van, pulled on an insulated leather work glove and walked over to lift the hood.

"Okay." *Considering I've just driven two hundred miles in a little over four hours.* "I've been stopping every hour or so to add water." Carefully, she unscrewed the top. Steam rose, dissipating quickly in the hot, dry summer air.

"I wish you would just get it fixed," Celia fretted.

Jen frowned at the sight of a horseman breaking away from a group of cowboys. He was headed her way. She turned back to the radiator and dumped another pint into the opening. "I will, as soon as finances allow." Finished, she set the jug on the ground, replaced the top and then shut the hood. "Listen, I've got to go." She walked back to put the water in the van.

"Call us later. Let us know how it goes."

"Promise." Jen ended the call and slipped her cell phone in the pocket of her skirt.

"Trouble?" Dismounting with easy grace, Matt Briscoe inclined his head at the engine.

Jen watched one of the other cowboys come forward and take the reins from him, then he rode back to the herd they'd been tending, with Matt's horse in tow.

Great. Now she was stuck with him.

"Nope...I'm fine."

Matt adjusted the brim of his straw hat. "I was hoping you'd take my advice."

Someone else had said that to her once, and the situation had not ended happily.

The only difference now was that she was a lot better equipped to handle the inevitable criticism doubt-lessly coming her way.

Her gut tightening, Jen slammed the cargo door with unnecessary force and gave him a challenging look.

"You're going to regret this," he predicted.

For reasons that had little to do with the man she was supposed to meet—and everything to do with the one in front of her—Jen already did.

Determined to get what she wanted out of this ar-rangement, she bantered back. "I think I can handle whatever comes my way." *Including you.*

MATT WAS USED TO beautiful women. Texas was full of them, and Laramie County had more than their share.

But there was something about this one.

He wasn't sure whether it was her delicate heart-shaped face, the gold highlights in the wavy chestnut hair, the cornflower-blue of her eyes or the full soft lips beneath her model-perfect nose, but something in Jen Carson had his rapt attention.

It didn't matter whether she was clad in a short denim skirt and a man's work shirt, or outfitted in a pretty sun-dress that bared her silky shoulders and even sexier legs. She was five foot nine inches of curvy woman, one who knew what she wanted and was determined to get it.

Matt respected ambition. Strength of purpose. And iron will.

What he could have done without, besides her show-ing up here in that pathetic old white van, was her sass.

Jen Carson had a mouth on her that just would not quit.

To the point she was already getting under his skin.

And she had barely entered their lives.

Matt could only imagine what would transpire if Emmett got his way, and Jen was soon ensconced with him.

Matt worked to rein in his disdain. Nothing would be gained by him losing his cool. He needed to stay calm to outmaneuver this pretty little protégée.

He headed around to the passenger side of her van. "I'll escort you to the ranch house, to meet my father."

Long lashes fluttered briefly. "Wow, this is my lucky day."

Matt moved the remains of a take-out lunch from Sonic, set them carefully on the floor and slid into the passenger seat. "Are you this rude to all your potential customers?"

Jen's jaw set. "You're not my customer."

Nor was he ever likely to be.

Still...

He couldn't say he minded looking at her.

Or inhaling her sweet womanly scent, a mixture of lilac, fragrant grass and summer air.

Jen discreetly tugged the hem of her dress down as she settled in the driver's seat, cutting off his glimpse of silky thigh. "Don't feel you have to stay with your father and me while we talk."

Matt ignored the tightening in his torso, the one that reminded him he hadn't had sex—or intimacy of any kind—in way too long. "Are you kidding?" he drawled, just to get her goat. "I wouldn't miss it."

Jen sent him another annoyed glance, then turned the key in the ignition. Nothing happened. Flushing, she turned it again.

Still nothing.

He couldn't say he minded her humiliation, given the havoc she was about to wreak on his life. Trying not to think how chivalrously his father would react to this situation, Matt reached for his cell phone and punched in the number for the bunkhouse.

She tried again. The third time was the charm.

Crisis averted. For now, anyway.

Resisting the urge to say something about her vehicle, he gestured toward the wrought-iron arch at the head of the drive. "The house is at the end of that."

Her eyes flashed as she slid him a look. "Good thing you told me," she quipped. "I never would have found it."

There she went with that mouth again.

Jen shifted into Drive and hit the accelerator. To Matt's surprise, the van edged forward smoothly and almost soundlessly. It glided onto the road, and then a hundred feet later, onto the paved lane.

She was silent as she drove down the shady, tree-lined drive toward the cluster of buildings a half mile back from the road. He could see that she liked what she saw. And why not? The white limestone ranch house was stately and expensive-looking. So was the adjacent glass-walled garage, which showcased all ten of his father's cars and trucks.

Jen's eyes slid to the Lamborghini.

"A memento from marriage number two," Matt said. "Dad rarely drives it anymore."

"What does he drive?"

"These days, mostly his Lincoln Navigator or his Cadillac Escalade. But that could change." Matt tilted his head toward the collection, not above testing her at every turn. "What's your favorite ride?"

Jen rested her surprisingly delicate hands on the steering wheel. "Couldn't say."

Matt wondered how she kept her hands so soft looking, given the nature of her work. He lifted his gaze back to her face. "Noncommittal, hmm?"

"About some things." She looked him right in the eye. "Others, not so much."

Meaning she had already decided she didn't like him. Fair enough, given the fact that the distrust went both ways.

He swiveled toward her on the uncomfortably worn bench seat, his knee landing just short of her thigh. For some reason he wished he had an excuse to make physical contact, see if she was actually as soft and warm and womanly as she looked. "It's not too late to change your mind, you know. And just forget it."

Jen scoffed and gave him a classic don't-mess-with-me expression. "After a four-hour drive? I don't think so, cowboy."

Matt knew it wasn't likely he'd change her mind. When big sums of money were involved, people tended to stick around. "All right then." He climbed out of the passenger seat and said a silent prayer, bracing himself for the inevitable emotional disaster that lay ahead. "Let's go. My father is waiting for you."

Chapter Two

Jen had barely stepped through the front door of the sprawling ranch house when she was greeted by a big, handsome bear of a man. Giving Jen a hint of what Matt would act like if he were actually happy to see her, Emmett clasped her hand warmly. "Miss Carson? Emmett Briscoe! Welcome!"

Jen smiled at her host. His eyes were the same sky-blue as his son's, his suntanned skin had a weathered appearance and his thick salt-and-pepper hair was cut short and combed neatly to one side. She was happy to note that Emmett was as welcoming in person as he had been on the phone. "Thank you."

When he released her hand and stepped back, Jen drew a breath and tried to get her bearings. Not easy when Matt was hovering close by.

Working at ignoring him, Jen noted the interior of the ranch house was elegant, and as expensively put together as the stately abode itself.

On the left side of the foyer was a sweeping staircase, to the right, a man-size living area. Two large brown sofas and several upholstered easy chairs formed a conversation area in front of a huge white limestone hearth. The dark oak floor was scattered with beautiful Southwestern rugs. Photos of a much younger Emmett, Matt and a woman Jen guessed was Matt's mother, graced the mantel.

Emmett walked to the bar and stepped behind it. "Please, sit down. Did you have any trouble finding the ranch?" he asked.

Matt followed with implacable calm.

Feeling anything but tranquil, Jen sank into a chair and crossed her legs at the knee. "None at all." Deliberately, she ignored Emmett's son, keeping her gaze on the older man's face. "Your directions were perfect."

As if aware that their conversation would continue to be awkward with Matt present, Emmett turned to him. "I can take it from here," he said easily.

Matt looked from Jen to his dad and back, his glance speculative. "Actually," he drawled politely, "if Miss Carson doesn't mind, I'd like to stay and hear what she has to say."

Realizing it was a test, Jen forced herself to be as gracious as the situation required. Matt wanted to pretend he was willing to give her a fair shake? Well, the least she could do was pretend to play along. "I'd be happy to speak with you both," she agreed, dipping her head.

"Then it's settled," Matt said, his eyes fixed on hers in a way that made her stomach tighten.

Emmett regarded his son for a long moment, and Jen sensed a lot more would be said had there not been a lady present. Wordlessly, the older man added ice to three glasses, topped them off with sparkling water, and passed them around.

He gave Matt another long, warning look, then turned and led the way past the sweeping staircase and down a long hallway lined with floor-to-ceiling windows. "We'll talk in the gallery," Emmett said as they passed a beautiful outdoor courtyard, which was flanked by an ivy-covered retaining wall and the rest of the U-shaped, two-story house.

When they reached a big open room, at the rear of the home, Jen looked around in awe, trying to take it all in. There was hundreds of thousands of dollars worth of art displayed, all of it set off by perfect lighting.

Momentarily forgetting the family drama, she moved from one piece to another, studying them avidly.

To her annoyance, Matt followed close behind her, as taut and on guard as his father was relaxed.

Emmett sipped his water, watching them both. "You'll have to forgive my son. He's become ridiculously overprotective in his middle age."

Matt swung back around, his irritation apparent. "Only because I've needed to be," he retorted in a low voice.

Jen sucked in a breath, drawing in the sunshine-soap-and-leather scent of him.

Nerves deep inside her quivered.

Oblivious of her reaction, Emmett arched a brow in reproach. "We've both made mistakes when it comes to matrimony, Matt."

Both of them?

Matt had indicated he wasn't divorced.

And if he wasn't divorced…what was he?

"It doesn't mean there have to be any more," Emmett continued sternly.

Matt pinned Jen with his gaze. "I don't want there to be."

Could you make it more obvious that you think I'm a threat? Jen wondered.

"Nor do I." Emmett stared at his son over the rim of his glass. "So unless you'd like to discuss this further…"

Seeing an opening, Jen stepped between them.

"What I'd really like to discuss is the reason I'm here." Certain she had both men's attention, she said sincerely, "This is an amazing collection." She walked around, inspecting the shelves holding bronze statues and figurines, as well as the paintings on the walls. She turned and smiled at Emmett. "Whoever put it together has a very good eye."

He beamed with the enthusiasm of a true collector. "It was started by my grandfather. He was an early supporter of Remington, and countless others, and my father and I have continued the tradition."

"Well, y'all have done a wonderful job." Jen moved from one to another. Some of the artists were famous, others more obscure, but each work on display was beautiful, detailed and original. "These are all pieces I would have picked."

She stopped, seeing one of her own first works, and for a second was speechless with surprise. She turned back to Emmett. "I didn't know you had any of my sculptures." Never mind this one.

Emmett inched closer, still sipping his water. "It's my favorite, to date."

Jen heard that a lot. The bronze sculpture depicted a small girl having her first horseback-riding lesson, while her doting mother stood nearby, holding the reins.

"There's a wistful, loving quality about it," he murmured.

Matt paused beside it, too. His guarded expression slipped just a tad.

"Did you know your subjects well?" he asked, eyeing the bronze, then her. "It seems like a very emotional piece."

It was, but not for reasons either Briscoe would have assumed.

Wishing he hadn't noticed that, Jen acknowledged the unexpected compliment with a nod. She was way too aware of Matt's physical presence, and turned away. So what if he had the kind of hot, powerful body no woman could ignore? He didn't trust her, certainly didn't respect her. And without that... There was no way she would let him draw her in.

"I conjured this from my imagination," she murmured in response to his question. Although she wished it had been real.

Matt studied her, as if seeing beyond what she'd said to the yearning for family she felt inside.

And maybe he did know, at least a little bit, she conceded. Emmett had said Matt's mother had died years ago. Jen had lost hers, too.

Being orphaned was hard at any age.

But although Matt and she shared that experience, it wasn't a bond she intended to pursue.

Emmett looked from one to the other. He, too, knew there was more going on than what Jen said, but was kind enough to move on to safer territory. "You often work from photographs, don't you?"

Jen nodded. "Yes, I do. Particularly with commissioned works."

These days, she stayed far away from memory lane. Focusing only on the present. Never the past, nor the future.

Inching closer, Matt said, "So you don't need to see a subject in person to be able to do justice to his or her likeness."

She acknowledged that fact with another brief nod. *Why not just show me the door now, Matt?* "Although it helps to at least hear about the personality of the person I'm depicting."

"Well," Emmett boomed, "no problem there."

No, indeed. His personality was very distinct, his ego strong.

"Dad," Matt interjected, clearly still worried his father was going to be taken advantage of, "are you sure you want to do this?"

"I have to, son." His voice was suddenly hoarse and unsteady. "Whether you understand or not." Emmett cleared his throat and turned to Jen, all business once more. "So...here's the deal. I want ten bronzes to start. All commemorating my life. And I'll pay you triple your normal rate—on the condition you set up shop here, start right away and do only my work, under my supervision, until we're done."

"YOU DON'T HAVE TO GIVE my father an answer by evening's end," Matt told Jen after Emmett had gone off to tend to other business. "Dad won't make the same offer to another artist."

She stared at him. "Are you sure about that?" she asked.

He let out a measured breath. The truth was, he couldn't figure out what his father was thinking, never mind why he was doing the things he was right now. One minute he'd be ebullient—full of dreams that had to be fulfilled right away. The next, he'd disappear, sometimes for a few hours, other times, a few days.

When Emmett did return, he usually seemed fatigued. Pale and almost shaky.

If Matt didn't know better, he'd think his dad was binge drinking. But that didn't make sense. The man could hold his liquor. He just didn't choose to drink very often.

Instead, Emmett handled stress by spending. Land, works of art, cattle—it didn't seem to matter what he bought as long as he enjoyed the wealth he had and purchased something.

The big question was what was causing his dad's anxiety lately. As much as Matt had nosed around, he still couldn't figure it out. All he knew for certain was the beautiful thirty-year-old woman in front of him was involved. And given Emmett's history of chasing younger, completely inappropriate women, that couldn't be good.

"Earth to Matt. Earth to Matt..."

"I'm still here."

Jen quirked a brow. "Really? You seemed a million miles away."

Glad he had been tapped to give her a tour of the property while she made up her mind, he shook off his unease and escorted her through the formal dining room.

He paused near the magnificently carved wooden table, which routinely sat thirty guests, determined to find out as much as he could about the beautiful sculptor. Like it or not, that meant spending time with her. "You've probably noticed my dad is a strong-willed guy, with a very healthy ego."

A hint of cynicism lit Jen's eyes as she paused by the chair where Emmett generally presided. "Seems to run in the family."

Trying not to think about how alluring she was, or what reaction the two of them might have had to each other if they weren't on opposing sides, Matt added, "Dad wants what he wants when he wants it."

Brushing past him, Jen glided along the length of the table, her hips swaying seductively beneath her sundress. She tossed him a look. "Seems the same could be said of you," she noted drily.

Matt braced his hands on the ornate scrolling across the top of a mahogany chair, trying not to be fascinated by her. "I know enough to realize when I need to slow down. And reevaluate." Like right now.

Jen eyed the huge crystal chandelier, then stiffened her spine and compressed her lips. "Your father doesn't seem likely to do either at the moment."

Something in the speculative way she was studying him, prompted Matt to be completely forthright, too. "Probably not," he said, with as much indifference as he could muster. "Which is why you need to think long and hard about just what it is Dad is asking you to do."

Jen slanted him a pitying look and folded her arms again, which plumped up her breasts. "What is it about Emmett's offer that you think I can't handle?"

Lazily, he appraised her pretty dress and sandals. Everything about her was feminine and enticing, from her dainty feet and stunning legs to her slender waist and round, perfect breasts. Nothing about her said ranch-ready. "I think the better question is what part of living out in the wilds of rural Texas could you handle?" he drawled.

She scowled. "Hey. Just because I grew up in the city—"

"And live in Austin now, where the population is a million plus."

Appearing irritated, she shrugged. "So?"

"Laramie County is thirty-five square miles with one small town and wide-open spaces—"

"Spaces," Jen interrupted, "peppered with ranches

and horses and cattle, and even, from what I saw on my way over here, the occasional donkeys, sheep and alpacas."

No doubt this area of West Texas had its share of rugged individualists, Matt acknowledged silently. And like it or not, her work as a sculptress put her in that category, too.

The problem, he thought, as he let his gaze roam her once again, was that Jen was incredibly feminine and unconsciously sexy in a way that drove men wild. Every glance, every movement of her hands, every touch of her fingers, was innately artistic, unbearably gentle and sensual.

Matt had noticed this on sight. And that was something they couldn't have. Not when it made him continually wonder how that overt sensuality would manifest in lovemaking.

Oblivious to the direction of his thoughts, she argued, "Being out here in the Texas countryside is going to help, not hurt, my art."

He would concede to that. "Even so...the ranch can be a lonely place." Which made it all too easy to establish intimacy with someone.

His observation earned him nothing but a smile. "Lucky for me, I work best when I'm not interrupted. Although all the bronzes will have to be finished back in Austin, where the foundry and my studio are located."

Sounded good, to have her back in central Texas where she belonged. Especially since he couldn't talk his dad out of this.

Helpfully, Matt suggested, "Why not just negotiate that it all be done there—except the initial consultation?"

"Wow," Jen taunted softly. "You genuinely want me off the Triple B."

Her voice seemed to ripple over him like velvet. He folded his arms defensively. No need to mince words now. "I think it would be best for everyone," he stated flatly.

"In your view," she corrected without hesitation. "Not Emmett's. Or mine."

With effort, Matt kept his distance. "You're really planning to accept my dad's offer and stay here?"

"I really am." Jen sashayed out of the dining room and into the corridor that led past the pantry to the kitchen. "So cowboy up, fella." She tossed the words over her shoulder. "And get used to it."

"JEN," CELIA WAILED, when told of the plan in a conference call one hour later. "This is such a bad idea."

"I agree," Cy added vehemently.

"Driving all the way out there in that wreck of a van was bad enough," Celia fretted, "but to stay for the next however many months…"

Jen was used to holding the hands of very wealthy, incredibly egotistical clients who were seeking to immortalize themselves for posterity. This, she told herself firmly, would be no different. Even if there was a handsome, sexy, difficult son on the premises. She could handle Matt. She'd just avoid him.

She ran her palm over the silk fabric of the comforter on her bed. "Actually, I'm hoping it will just be for one month."

"The time it will take you to complete the first statue," Celia affirmed.

Jen got up and walked to the guest-room window, overlooking the courtyard. "I think once Emmett understands my process and sees the quality of my work, he'll be amenable to granting me whatever I need to finish." Which was an environment far, far away from his maddeningly handsome, wickedly provoking son.

"And if he doesn't? If he plays the rich man card and says you have to stay and do everything his way," Celia countered, her voice rising with concern. "Then what? It's obvious father and son have issues. The last thing you need is to put yourself in a situation where you try to fix other people's problems—again."

Jen wasn't going to do that. Once had been more than enough. "Look, it's obvious Matt and his dad don't see eye to eye on hiring me to commemorate Emmett's life. But that's for the two of them to sort out. I'm concerned about the business." Not to mention the fact that Cy and Celia were about to have a baby, and Jen's van needed substantial repair. "The profit from this job will allow me to expand into the next storefront, showcase other artists and hire another employee." Which meant all their schedules would be a lot more flexible.

"Assuming it goes as planned," Cy groused, reminding Jen that he and Celia had a financial stake in this.

"It will," she promised. "You'll see." And when it did, the rent for the gallery would be paid for an entire year, and they wouldn't be living paycheck to paycheck any longer.

She looked up to see Matt looming in the guest room's open doorway, a thick accordion file in hand.

She turned away to finish her conversation. "In the meantime, I'm emailing you a list of things I'll need overnighted to me…."

After Cy and Celia promised they would get right on it, Jen ended the call and put her phone back in her bag.

"Obviously, you have been invited to stay for dinner, regardless of your decision about the offer my father made."

Jen wondered what Matt thought could have possibly changed in the last fifteen minutes, since she had already told Emmett her decision and he'd asked Matt to show her to the guest room. "You just won't give up, will you?"

He came closer, his expression grim. "I was hoping it wouldn't have to come to this."

His words had an ominous ring. Jen felt her stomach clench. For the first time since she had arrived at the ranch, she felt she was out of her league as she stared into his implacable blue eyes.

Wordlessly, he handed over the file he held. "You have a very interesting past."

His statement delivered a punch a hundred times more powerful than she had anticipated. "You had me investigated?"

He let out a breath. "I checked into the backgrounds of all the artists my father was interested in." Moving closer, he looked at her for a long minute. "Curiously enough, you were the only one who had married for cash. I guess my dad really does have a radar for fortune hunters."

Jen's temper rose. "I did not marry for money, Matt. I married for love." Which, unfortunately, had turned out to be one-sided.

His eyes dipped down to her mouth, then back up again. "His family says otherwise. They say you led their son down the garden path, and had they not intervened, you would have gone through his entire trust fund in a matter of years."

Jen knew how it looked. But how it looked and how it was were two entirely different things.

Sensing Matt Briscoe wouldn't believe her even if she did tell him everything that had transpired during the two unhappiest years of her life, she focused on the facts that would vindicate her. At least in Emmett Briscoe's eyes. She tilted her head and murmured, "Then you also must have uncovered the fact that I left the marriage exactly as I entered it. With five hundred dollars in my savings account. The clothes on my back. An armful of possessions. And the same van I'm driving now."

He looked at her for a long moment. "A smart move, if you were looking for another rich man to bamboozle."

"But what if I wasn't?" Jen swallowed hard. "What if, at the end of the day, all I wanted was my freedom? My self-respect intact?"

A devastating silence fell.

Matt didn't believe her.

He was never going to believe her.

So Jen did the only thing she could do.

She gave up trying to convince him of the truth and took another approach. One that a man like him *would* buy.

Dropping all pretext of innocence, she threw up her hands and sashayed toward him like a hussy on the hunt. "You're right." Reaching behind him, she shut the bedroom door, then swung back around to face him. "Why deny it?" Her heart pounding, she glided even closer and lifted a hand to his hard chest. "I did come out here looking for another rich husband." She splayed her fingers over his heart. "But it's not your father I want, Matt," she confessed, even more softly. "It's you."

His eyes smoldered. He caught her wrist and held her away. "Very funny."

Her instinct was to fight his grip. Instead, she relaxed into it. Pretended she wanted him to touch her. Moved closer still.

"Do I look like I'm joking?" Aware what a dangerous game she was playing, she brought her other hand up to trace his lower lip. "You're a vibrant and sexy guy." Surely, in another second or two he'd realize how ridiculous this all was.

"Tall. Dark-haired. Handsome." She continued her litany of his attributes. "What's not to like?" She let her fingers sift through his dark, curly hair, stroke the shell of his ear, feel the pulse in his throat.

"It's not going to work." He stared at her, daring her to get past his tough exterior.

"Sure about that?" Jen prodded, her ego suddenly in play. She extricated her wrist from his hand. "Sure you don't want to make a pass at me, just a little bit?"

Again he refused to budge.

"What if I want to make a pass at *you?*" With both hands free, she wreathed her arms around his neck.

To her disappointment, he didn't respond.

"What if I want to kiss you..." She rose on tiptoe and, with lust pouring through her, brushed her lips ever so briefly across the scruff on his jaw. "Just like this..."

Matt remained still as a statue. The only hint that he might be affected by her outrageous ploy was the heat emanating from his body, the thudding of his heart and lower, the unmistakable imprint of desire.

"You really want to find out?" he asked hoarsely.

Did she? Jen tilted her head and searched his eyes. Maybe not...

She stepped back slightly, telling herself that she had made her point.

Then, to her shock, Matt made his. His arms clamped around her, tugging her close again. Suddenly, she was anchored against him in a way that thoroughly outlined the challenge he presented to her.

Aware that it was her turn to call his bluff, she narrowed her eyes and declared, "You. Wouldn't. Dare."

Matt lifted an eyebrow, lowered his head and growled, "Yeah? Watch me."

Chapter Three

Matt had not expected their confrontation to end with a kiss. But as he gave into instinct and flattened one hand against her spine and slid the other through the silk of her hair, he knew that was exactly where it was headed. Trouble was, one kiss wouldn't begin to satisfy the desire pouring through him. Not when he brushed her mouth lightly with his; not when he responded to the slight opening of her lips and moved in to kiss her hard and deep. And *especially* not when he heard her make a soft, sexy sound that was part frustration, part need.

And then, suddenly, she was surprising him again by meeting his demand. Going up on tiptoe. Wreathing her arms about his shoulders once again.

Her breasts pressed against his chest. He felt the hardness of her nipples, the quick beating of her heart, the erratic rasp of her breath. And knew he had invited way more than should be happening....

Jen knew Matt was only trying to prove a point.

She was proving one, too. Not only could she handle a forbidden kiss. Or two. Or in this case, three... She could handle *him*.

Yes, he was hard and sexy. Yes, he looked really hot, whether dressed up, as he'd been the first time they'd met, or in a simple chambray shirt and worn jeans, as he was now.

Yes, he knew how to fit her against him for maximum contact, angle his head and kiss her breathless.

He tasted good. A combination of cool spearmint, warm summer sun…and man.

And he made her feel wonderful.

All soft and willing and womanly.

Even when she knew she was not going to let this go any further than it already had, for fear her knees would collapse under her and she'd lose what precious little common sense she had left.

Not when this was solely for the purpose of proving a point.

Deliberately, Jen broke off the kiss.

Ignoring the molten look in his eyes, she drew a halting breath and stepped back. Watched him get control of his faculties, too.

She struggled for calm, reminding herself this was very dangerous territory they were in. "Look. I get you trying to control everything, because there have been times when I tried to do that, too. But life doesn't work that way. You don't get to control someone else's actions or prevent their mistakes. Never mind engineer their epiphanies."

He quirked a brow but allowed her to continue.

Jen aimed a lecturing finger at the center of his chest. "You get to be the master of *your* destiny. Make your own decisions. Control your own reactions to things. And that, pal, is it."

Matt's lips compressed. "Sounds like the credo for Al-Anon," he said, in a voice dripping with cynicism.

Reeling from the verbal left hook, Jen sucked in an anguished breath. She had expected Matt to fight hard.

But this was a low blow. She scowled at him, making no effort to hide her resentment. "Nice, Briscoe, bringing that up."

Shock had him going completely still.

Jen groaned and bit down on an oath. Darn it all. He didn't know!

Working to get her pulse under control, she slid him a look. "I thought you had me investigated."

He met her gaze, his eyes dark and heated. "Briefly. Just in terms of your professional expertise and general background."

She studied him intently. "Then you know I grew up in the economically disadvantaged part of Austin."

"And that your mom died when you were three, and your dad raised you," he stated in a quiet voice.

Her stomach quivered. This was stuff she never discussed. "What else?"

Matt cocked his head, still studying her. "That your father was a self-employed housepainter who worked sporadically, usually eking out just enough to get by."

The hardships of that time still haunted her. Jen was working on being okay with it, but she hadn't quite gotten there yet.

Deciding if Matt was going to hear this, he was going to hear it from her, she moved a step closer and asked, "Do you know why?"

Matt continued watching her as if something didn't quite add up. "The investigator didn't get that far, but I can go back and see what else can be found out...."

Jen shook her head and lifted a staying palm. "No need for that," she declared firmly, forcing herself to hold his steady gaze.

Might as well get this over with.

"I'll just tell you."

She swallowed as another wave of emotion swept through her. "My father drank." Her throat closed in a way that made it difficult to get the words out. "A lot. Not all the time, but…whenever something set him off. Instead of dealing with his frustration and anger over the hand that fate had dealt him, he would self-medicate with booze."

Compassion flashed across Matt's face. "I'm sorry."

She shrugged off the sympathy. She didn't want his pity. "I wouldn't have survived my childhood had it not been for Alateen. The people there—the counselors, the sponsors, the other kids—helped me realize that my father's problem with alcohol was not my fault." Tears stung her eyes.

Matt clamped his hands on her shoulders, gave her a brief, comforting squeeze. "Of course it wasn't," he said softly, looking a little rough around the edges himself. "He was the adult. You were just a kid."

A kid with a big heart and a sensitive nature…and a hopelessly idealistic outlook on life.

Jen had worked hard to erect a hard shell around her vulnerable inner self, to put all her pent-up emotion into her artistry, where it could do some good.

The trouble was, with just one steamy embrace, and an unexpectedly gentle word or two, Matt tempted her to undo all that.

She had no intention of letting the floodgates open. "Unfortunately, I didn't learn my lessons well enough until I got a lot older."

Matt locked eyes with her. "And this caused problems."

"Oh, yes. Tons of them. In big and little ways." Jen hitched in a restless breath and resisted the urge to pace. "Because for a while there, I still chased after lost causes. Thinking if I could just make someone else's life better, it would make up for the fact that I never got through to my father. Never managed to get him to a single meeting."

Matt's expression softened. The empathy in his eyes gave her the courage to go on.

"So I got involved with someone else, someone with family problems of his own, hoping to help him in a way I hadn't been able to help myself."

"Only, that didn't work, either."

"No," Jen said tautly. "It didn't."

"Which is why you got divorced."

Jen nodded.

Pushing the turmoil away, Jen lifted her chin. "But don't worry. I am not interested in sponsoring you." Jen threw up her hands, her boundaries firmly in place once again. "Your issues are your own. And so," Jen emphasized flatly, "are your father's."

Jen spun around and made a beeline for the door, which she flung open, gesturing for him to take his leave. "Now, if you'll excuse me, I've got to get ready for dinner."

MATT HAD WEATHERED a lot since his mom died. Some of it was caused by his own grief and reaction to loss. The rest was due to his dad. So Matt didn't feel guilty about trying to prevent more heartache for all of them.

This, he figured, was his duty as Emmett Briscoe's son.

But he also knew enough to realize he was holding Jen Carson accountable for far more than she deserved. She hadn't pursued his father, as the other women had.

Emmett had evidently done his research this time

and sought Jen out for the clearly defined purpose of commemorating his life.

So maybe, Matt thought, if he let them all concentrate on the business at hand, there would be no more romantic disasters.

He sure didn't need to be acting on impulse and kissing her. Either to make a point, or to ease a natural desire that had gone unfulfilled for way too long.

What he should do, he decided, was adopt a formal attitude. Be helpful, yet reserved. Become a sort of emotional Switzerland for Jen and his dad to come to if and when they needed him. Clearly, they were both grappling with some deep-seated issues, but he wasn't exactly sure what was at the root of it all.

All Matt knew for certain was that Jen wanted the money and fame that came with this commission, badly enough to put up with the rest of the flack.

Wanted it enough to come into the formal dining room—even after he'd admitted to having her investigated—and sit down for a meal with him and his dad.

Luckily, from that moment on, Emmett dominated the conversation with talk about the Texas art scene. Jen was only too happy to oblige. When the meal concluded, they rose from the table, and Emmett, looking happier and more content than he had in weeks, led the way to the library.

More than a dozen storage boxes sat in front of the oversize mahogany desk.

"I'd like to have the sculptures commemorate my adult life on this ranch, and I'd like them all to honor my first wife, Margarite, as well. I'll leave it to you to figure out how to do this, Jen, but the bronzes should include our courtship, marriage, and the birth and upbringing of our only child."

"Sounds good."

"I don't want to look old or infirm in any of the sculptures," Emmett further stipulated. "And I don't want Margarite to ever look ill, or be confined to a wheelchair or a hospital bed in any of the bronzes. She would not have wanted to be remembered that way."

That was true, Matt acknowledged.

"Not a problem," Jen declared. "I'll make sure she appears vibrant and healthy in all the sculptures."

Matt wanted to concentrate on the positive, too.

"Too many of my fellow ranchers and friends are becoming ill or dying," Emmett continued, still on the same depressing tact. "I am not interested in memorializing that."

Seeing the conversation about to continue down a path it shouldn't, Matt interjected firmly, "Dad, you're fine."

Matt realized, of course, that Emmett was getting older. That sometimes his dad felt a little sluggish and occasionally suffered from tired, aching muscles. But these things happened to everyone when they reached their sixties. Bodies began to age and wear out. It was just something everyone dealt with at that point in their life. It didn't mean they were sick.

If his dad were really ailing, he would go see his doctor. And he hadn't. So…

Emmett harrumphed. "Life can change in an instant, Matt. Not always in ways we want. Your mother proved that."

There it went, Matt thought in frustration, the maudlin attitude that inevitably led to chaos.

He turned to Jen. "My mother died ten years ago of multiple sclerosis. She'd been ill for a long time." She'd had a difficult, depressing decline.

Emmett grimaced. "It was hard on Matt. He was just a kid when Margarite became sick."

But it was his dad who'd gone off the deep end. "It was harder on you," Matt said.

His father stared at him. "I don't know how you can say that. Since I'm not the one who eloped to Vegas with a woman who was barely even a friend." Emmett paused, letting his words sink in. "And then never even bothered to consummate the marriage."

Wow, JEN THOUGHT. *I have not seen drama like this since my own marriage ended.* She held up a hand, more than ready to excuse herself. "I really think you two should continue this discussion in private."

Jaw set angrily, Matt stepped to block her exit. "No need for that. Dad and I are done."

"We certainly are," Emmett agreed, just as tersely.

Matt stomped off.

The older man sighed and returned to the boxes. He opened one and pulled out a big stack of photographs. For the next thirty minutes, they looked through them. Finally, eager to get the conversation back on track, Jen said gently, "Let's talk more about what you'd like to see in the bronzes."

Beginning to relax, he sat down next to her.

"I want to go out—at least in the public perception— very much the way I've lived. With my boots on. If and when I ever do get sick, I am not going to put Matt through that. It's enough what he went through with his mother."

Matt reappeared in the doorway—clearly unable to stay away no matter how much he wished he could, Jen noted curiously.

Looking much calmer after a brief respite, Matt ambled in. He looked at his dad. "With the exception of your slightly elevated cholesterol and blood pressure—both of which are well controlled through the medicines you take—there isn't a thing wrong with you, Dad."

Emmett looked at him for a long moment, an undecipherable emotion on his craggy face. "The point is," he said at last, "you never know." He pressed a hand on the table and pushed himself to his feet, looking suddenly too weary to go on.

"I'm going to bed," he announced with an apologetic glance at Jen. "We'll talk again in the morning?"

Seeing firsthand how the constant bickering with his only son was taking a toll on Emmett, she nodded. Why couldn't Matt just let his dad be?

"Yes, sir. Thank you again for the opportunity."

Emmett looked at Matt, his brows lowered. "Don't you chase her away with your bad behavior."

Jen jumped to reassure him. "He won't, I promise. You have nothing to worry about on that score."

"Good to know." Emmett exited, leaving them alone.

Jen slid Matt a reproachful look. "You really don't have to stay. The silver is safe."

He slid his hands into his pockets, looking totally at ease. "Ha, ha."

Feeling way too aware of him, Jen began sorting through the photos. "All I want to do is work." *And forget about that kiss we shared earlier...*

Matt sat on the library table, hands braced on either side of him. "I know you think I'm being ridiculously on guard."

Jen hated feeling so vulnerable whenever she was near Matt. And she resented knowing how intensely attracted she was to him.

Hadn't she done the rich-man's-son thing once?

Hadn't she seen how badly that had turned out?

She swallowed and continued laying out the photos in a haphazard collage. "I understand. For whatever reason, your father is suddenly feeling the need to document the most important parts of his life in a unique way only someone with his wealth could afford." She paused to move some of the pictures around. "That sentiment leaves him vulnerable. You don't want to see him taken advantage of, monetarily or in any other way."

Matt's eyes fell on a photo of himself at two years of age, standing with his mother and father in front of the Alamo. They all looked so happy. Content. Without a care in the world.

Exhaling, he stood. Worry lines appeared at the corners of his eyes. "The disastrous second, third and fourth marriages aside…life hasn't always been easy for him."

Jen watched Matt pace the room. "Or you?"

He chose his words carefully. "I know my dad thinks this process will bring him comfort." Matt raked his fingers through his hair. "I worry all it will do is dredge up the unhappiness that sent him into a tailspin to begin with." He shook his head, still vibrating with pent-up emotion. "Which, in turn, could lead him to feel so lonely he'll marry badly again."

"And maybe," Jen said softly, as another shimmer of tension wafted between them, "you will, too?"

MATT SHOULD HAVE KNOWN that Jen wouldn't let information that volatile go unexplored.

Before he could decide how he was going to handle this, she lifted a hand. "Don't worry, cowboy. You don't have to tell me about your failed elopement." She surveyed him with something like reproach.

"I'm sure I could look it up. Or get someone else to tell me." Still laying out photos, she waggled her eyebrows at him playfully. "Maybe even have you investigated."

Ouch.

Although, Matt conceded, he may have had that coming.

He exhaled. "You want the story?"

Jen pushed back her chair. "Actually...I do."

He watched her sashay toward him, all feminine sass and confidence. He tore his eyes from her spectacular legs. "Why?"

"Because it doesn't fit with anything I know about you so far." She bit her lower lip, then said, "You seem like the last person to impulsively tie the knot."

He leaned against one of the custom floor-to-ceiling bookcases. "Which maybe was the point," he drawled.

Jen walked around the table and rested her hands on top of a straight-backed chair.

Aware that he could use some comfort—a fact that made him feel entirely too vulnerable—Matt confessed, "It was six months after my mom died. My dad was already planning to marry the novelist. It was too soon, and everyone knew that, but Dad wouldn't listen to reason. So I decided to take a page from my future stepmother's book—and bring a little more carefully scripted drama into our lives."

Jen's brow lifted. "By eloping in Vegas with a female friend you barely knew?"

Matt nodded. "I thought if I embarked in a hasty, ill-thought-out marriage before Dad went through with his own wedding, he would see how ludicrous it was."

Jen's expression gentled. "He'd learn from your mistake."

Matt swallowed. "Yes. And I thought that Elanore—the girl I ran off with—understood that."

Jen walked around the table toward him. "She didn't?"

He grimaced. Thinking some fresh air might help, he strode toward the French doors that led to the courtyard, and stepped onto the beautifully landscaped stone patio that his mother had once loved.

Darkness had fallen. There was a quarter moon and a sprinkling of stars overhead. "Apparently, she'd had a secret crush on me for a long time." Matt passed one of the gas lanterns that illuminated the courtyard.

Jen was right behind him. "When did you find out?"

He sank down on one of the cushioned chaises. "When I passed on the opportunity to get drunk on champagne and really 'show everyone' by actually consummating our foolhardy marriage."

Looking stricken, Jen sat down sideways on the chaise next to him. "What happened next?"

Matt folded his hands behind his head, savoring the warm night air. "We got on a plane back to Texas and broke the news to our folks."

And, oh, what a mess that had been.

Jen clasped her hands around her knee. "What was their reaction?"

"Dad saw it for what it was and refused to be manipulated."

Intrigued, Jen prodded, "And her parents?"

Matt frowned. "Elanore's parents knew how she had secretly felt about me all along, and were incensed. They accused me of leading her on, and insisted we not annul the marriage—that we needed to stop and think about what we were going to do next."

Jen's eyes widened. "You explained to them what had happened? How it had all come about?"

The unhappy memory still rankled. "They didn't care. They had a brokenhearted daughter who wanted to stay married to me and give our union a real shot."

"Even though you didn't love her and viewed her only as a friend."

Matt scoffed at the naivete of it all. "They felt that love could grow, given half a chance. What they didn't want was for their daughter to be any more humiliated. To have her known as a willing accomplice to fraud was not a good thing, either." He shrugged. "Her parents preferred for everyone to think we'd eloped in the heat of young love. Then if, over time, the marriage didn't work out—and they desperately hoped it would—they could save face and say that we'd given it our best shot, but that the marriage had been too hasty, after all."

"How did you resolve it?"

He grimaced. "The same way my father got out of his ill-conceived marriages—with a hunk of cash, and the opportunity to blame the whole debacle on me and my fickle heart."

Jen blinked. "And that worked?"

He let out a low, regretful laugh. "Every sad story needs a villain. In ours, I was it."

"You didn't mind."

Yes and no. "I was just glad to have my freedom. The last thing I wanted was to be stuck living a lie." The way his father had eventually. Three times.

"Hmm. Well." Jen rose from the chaise in one graceful motion. She walked over to admire the roses. "I see why you mistrust women."

Not all, Matt thought. Just the ones who stood to benefit monetarily from their association with his family. Like it or not, that included Jen.

"My point is—my dad is a lot more vulnerable than he looks. My mom's death hit him hard. He went into a life crisis when she passed, and he's never come out of it. I don't want to see him hurt."

"I have no intention of hurting him," Jen insisted.

Famous last words, Matt thought, giving her a skeptical look. Just the process of taking out these old photos and repeatedly walking down memory lane was bound to open up every old wound. And then some.

Jen glided closer, inundating him in a drift of her lilac perfume. "I'm not going to let him take advantage of me, or the situation."

More famous last words. He just hoped they were true.

Matt sighed. "Just be warned. Dad has a way of getting what he wants from people, whether they want to give it over or not."

He left her to think about that.

Chapter Four

Later the following afternoon, Jen took stock. The day had been blissfully quiet. Matt had gone off with the cowboys before dawn to move cattle. Emmett had attended a breakfast meeting of the local cattlemen's club, and had other business scheduled after that. So it had been just Jen and the housekeeper, Luz, in the Triple B ranch house for most of the day.

Which of course had been for the best, Jen mused. No interruptions. No Matt barging in—or out—for hot kisses, or learning things about the lone Briscoe heir that she would rather not know.

Like the fact they'd both lost a parent in their early twenties, then been betrayed by someone they had trusted.

Not, Jen scolded herself firmly, that any of that mattered. She and Matt Briscoe were as different as night and day. And likely to stay that way, since he tried to control everything in his universe, and she tried to control nothing in hers...except her own reaction to things.

"So what do you think?" she asked Emmett, when he stopped in to check on her progress.

He looked at the twenty photos Jen had selected. All were displayed on the big library table. All had the potential to be turned into bronze sculptures.

"This is my favorite," he said in a choked voice. He pointed to a particularly poignant photo of himself and his late wife, taken soon after they had married. Emmett and Margarite were riding side by side on big beautiful horses. Young, vital and exceptionally attractive, they were clad in casual Western riding attire, and seemed in sync emotionally and physically.

"Mine, too," Jen murmured.

Mostly because Emmett and his new bride both looked so happy. And so immune to the life challenges to come...

"I'd like you to start with this one," he continued, tearing up.

Jen turned away and gave him time to compose himself.

When she looked again, he was standing with both hands thrust in the pockets of his khaki trousers. Tears gone. No longer trembling.

"You've done a great job whittling it down," he declared in a firm, authoritative voice.

Happy to hear that, Jen smiled at him. "Thank you." She was going to enjoy working with Emmett on this commission.

"I like this one, too." He pointed to a photo of Matt and he flanking his wife's chair, at what appeared to be Matt's high school graduation. All were smiling determinedly, but there was a sadness underlying the cheer on those faces, giving the moment special poignancy. Yet Jen had pulled it out anyway, because it was definitely a milestone moment for the family.

"I wasn't sure if you wanted any sculptures of your wife when she was sick." Although Margarite was not seated in a wheelchair, Jen suspected that she had been using one at the time the photo was taken. Otherwise, she probably would have been standing with her husband and son.

"That was my initial response. Maybe I was wrong. Perhaps," Emmett said, "it's time I embraced every aspect of my life. And hers." He turned toward Jen. "Can you do all twenty of these photos? Turn them into sculptures?"

That was double his initial order!

Trying not to get ahead of themselves, Jen warned, "That would take at least a year and a half, if not more...."

"I'll give you ten thousand dollars per bronze, as long as I get a royalty on any copies that are sold."

That ego again!

"Why don't I do the first one—the one we decided on last evening—and see how happy you are with that before we go any further?" she proposed.

Emmett grinned, looking like his old self again. "Trying to raise the price on me?"

"Not at all."

"Good thing," Matt said, sauntering into the room. Ranch dust clung to his sweat-stained clothing. A touch of sunburn highlighted the handsome angles of his face. Jen figured he hadn't shaved since the previous morning, which made the black scruff on his jaw all the more pronounced. And he smelled to high heaven, yet she was ridiculously glad to see him.

"'Cause I'd have something to say about that," he continued in his lazy, provoking drawl.

"Good to see you, too," Jen murmured, rolling her eyes. *Not.*

Ignoring his presence, she looked at Emmett and continued their conversation in a crisp, businesslike tone. "Everything that was shipped to me arrived by noon, but there are still some things I'm going to need for my stay. So if it's okay, I'm going to call it quits for today and head into Laramie to do a little shopping and get some dinner."

"We'd be happy to hold the evening meal for you," Emmett said.

She lifted a hand. "No need for that."

It was time to start setting limits with both father and son.

She smiled and gathered up the photos for further study.

Ignoring Matt's intent appraisal, she headed for the door. "You all enjoy yourself this evening. And I'll get started setting up a temporary sculpting studio tomorrow."

FIVE HOURS LATER, Emmett said in a worried tone, "Jen should have been back by now."

Matt looked up from his laptop computer. He'd been doing the ranch books. Or trying. Hands shoved in the pockets of his khaki trousers, Emmett had been pacing the front of the house, looking out the windows, for at least forty-five minutes now.

"Did she give anyone a time to expect her?"

"No. But a storm is brewing. And I don't like the idea of her driving unfamiliar back roads in the dark and the pouring rain."

Matt had been thinking the same thing.

Then cursed inwardly for allowing himself to worry. Jen Carson was *not* his problem.

Except when it came to keeping her from taking advantage of his father.

"I'm sure she has driven in rain before, Dad."

"In the city. Where she probably knows the roads, and the location of all the low water crossings to avoid."

He had a point there. "If she takes the farm-to-market road straight to town, she'll be fine."

"But she won't be if she drives the shortest route, which is on the back roads. A lot of which are not well marked." Emmett grabbed his hat off the coat tree in the front hall and planted it on his head. "I'm going to go out and look for her."

Matt studied his father's wan complexion. Although his dad was loath to admit it, these days he tired easily.

Matt supposed it was to be expected, though.

After all, his dad wasn't getting any younger.

Reluctantly, Matt put his laptop aside and followed him out to the porch.

If Jen hadn't wanted to handle another stressful family dinner with the two of them, Matt couldn't wait to hear how she would like being tracked down during her "free time." Eager to avoid a situation she was likely to consider an intrusion, he asked casually, "Have you tried calling her cell?"

Emmett nodded grimly, squinting at the rural highway barely visible in the distance. Overhead, no stars were discernible. Along the horizon, there were violent flashes of jagged yellow light, and the wind had started whipping up, making the cattle nervous.

"I imagine her phone is either turned off or she's out of range of a tower."

She was fine.

It wasn't like she needed him to rush to her rescue and wrap his arms around her. Even though, Matt admitted to himself, that was a tempting fantasy.

Aware that his dad was still weighing the advisability of going after her, Matt consulted his watch and tried to talk sense into him. "It's only nine-thirty, Dad."

It just *seemed* as if she'd been gone forever.

Emmett rubbed his wrist, as if it were hurting him. "The stores all close at nine."

"Maybe's she grabbing a late dinner."

Or avoiding an early return by taking in a movie or hanging out at the Lone Star Dance Hall in Laramie. Both were pleasant ways to while away a stiflingly hot summer evening. The latter, especially, if Jen was looking for a little action....

Emmett took his car keys out of his pocket with a hand that shook slightly. "I'm going to go out and drive the road to town, anyway," he announced with typical gallantry.

Matt didn't want to think about his dad driving in the rain, with the moon all but obscured by the heavy cloud cover. The faint but distinct rumble of thunder was now audible. He shoved his own reluctance aside. "I'll go. You stay here and man the phones in case Jen is in some kind of trouble."

"Drive the entire route," Emmett ordered. "Both of them!"

Matt nodded. He would, if only to keep his dad from getting further entangled.

I SHOULD HAVE checked the radiator before I left. At the very least refilled all the water bottles, Jen thought.

But she hadn't.

She had simply hopped in her van and driven thirty minutes into Laramie, in the scorching hundred and ten degree heat. Her carelessness, coupled with the evaporation in a van that had been sitting in the full sun all day, with a growing leak in the radiator, had triggered the Check Engine light.

Halfway back to the Triple B, Jen had been forced to pull over into the nearest safe place—the middle of a field, just off the highway—and lift the hood, lest the van catch fire.

It was as she feared. The radiator had been bone-dry, the engine sizzling hot. Jen had poured the half bottle of water she had with her over both, then tried to call for help.

Only to find she was too far from a cell tower to get a signal.

Because it was already getting dark, and she could see storm clouds gathering in the distance, she had decided to climb back in the van and wait for help.

Only help hadn't come.

And now, at nearly 10:00 p.m., with the wind blowing fiercely, Jen began to think she was going to have to spend the entire night out here. The notion of being stranded inside this stifling hot van, surrounded by whatever critters lurked in the deserted Texas countryside, didn't bode well.

Worse, what had at first looked like heat lightning now appeared to be the real thing. She could hear thunder rumbling in the distance, and that made her nervous, too. In the middle of a flat field, she felt like a sitting duck.

She had read that rubber tires would absorb a lightning strike. She'd also seen Austin news reports of lightning going right through the hood of a running vehicle, decimating the motor.

Which made sense. The exterior was metal, after all.

Metal attracted lightning.

But she would be no safer outside the vehicle, because then she would have no protection whatsoever. So, heaven help her, she had to stay inside and try not to be scared witless. Wait…was that a truck going down the road?

Jen hit the horn—hard—but it wasn't necessary. The pickup had already swerved around, and the headlamps swept the van.

The truck accelerated, coming right for her.

That quickly, the lightning—which had seemed so far away—lit up the dark sky with a bright yellow flash and a simultaneous clap of thunder that was so darn loud it had Jen nearly jumping out of her skin.

Tears sprang into her eyes as it was followed by a second lightning bolt and even louder rumble of thunder. Not that it seemed to bother the driver. The pickup circled around as the sky opened up and the rain poured down in fierce sheets. The vehicle did a U-turn and came back, stopping alongside her van. The passenger door swung open.

Matt Briscoe was clearly illuminated.

Jen had never been so glad to see anyone in her life. Or embarrassed. Of all the people to rescue her…

He leaned over. "Get in!"

That would mean hopping across six feet of field, exposed to the storm. "I…" *Am scared witless!*

Too scared, in fact, to move.

Matt's glance cut to the lifted hood on her van—the age-old sign of a vehicle in trouble. "Don't argue!" he commanded, even more fiercely. "Just do it!"

Another bolt of lightning slashed down, striking a distant fence post. Fire flashed, splinters flew. A split second later, the thunder was deafening.

Jen didn't have to be told twice. She wanted out of there. Now! After shoving her keys and phone into her purse, she jumped out of the van, slammed the driver's door shut behind her and then dashed through the pouring rain to his vehicle.

Matt reached out and helped pull her inside the truck as yet another bolt of lightning struck the ground, an even shorter distance away.

Jen slammed the door.

"Hold on!" he said, shifting the truck into Drive.

Seconds later, they were bumping across the field toward the rural highway. While Jen scrambled to put on her safety belt, Matt drove through the pouring rain with a sure, steady hand.

Eventually, the worst of the lightning and thunder was behind them. He slowed.

"Might help to breathe," he said.

He was right, Jen realized belatedly. She had been holding her breath. She let it out, then sucked in a rush of air that did little to dispel the tension coiled inside her.

She blotted the rain from her face with the backs of her hands. Pretty sure her mascara was running, she reached into her handbag for a tissue and dabbed it beneath her eyes. Feeling marginally better, she dropped the soiled tissue back in her purse, then cleared her throat, still trying to calm down. "How did you know where to find me?"

Matt shrugged, his broad shoulders straining against the soft cotton of his shirt. "If you were coming back from town, I figured you'd be on this road." He paused to send her a brief, probing glance. "The question is, what were you doing parked in that field?" He turned his attention back to the road. "If you were broken down, why didn't you call for help?"

I wished I could have called you.

Aware that she felt safer than she had in a long while, being here with him, she gestured out the window. "No cell phone reception."

Matt's lips compressed. "Yeah, coverage is spotty this far out of town." His strong, capable hands clasped the wheel. "We have it on the ranch because we put up our own tower. Most don't."

"I'll remember that next time."

He looked her over, taking in her windswept hair and rain-splattered skirt and blouse. "What was wrong with your van?"

There was concern in his eyes. A protectiveness that shouldn't mean anything to her.

She feigned indifference—to both the situation and his gallantry—while she rubbed at the splatters of mud on her bare calves. "The radiator has a leak." Her voice was hoarse and she cleared her throat again. "I didn't check it before I left because I had just filled it yesterday afternoon, when I got here. But what was in there must have mostly evaporated."

He scowled. "It'll do that in this kind of weather, when there's a leak."

"Yeah, well, now I know that." Jen sighed, her emotions roiling.

She squared her shoulders and tugged her skirt down, trying to prove to him that she was one hundred percent in charge of the situation, when of course she wasn't. She didn't seem to be in charge of anything when it came to Matt Briscoe.

Swallowing, she continued weakly, "I have no idea whose property I pulled off on...."

He shot her an evocative look. "The Armstrong ranch."

Jen shivered in the cool air blowing out of the vents.

Her blouse was damp, her arms bare. She ran her palms over her skin in an effort to warm herself. "I hope they don't mind."

Matt leaned forward to adjust the controls. Then his gaze drifted over her again. "I'm sure they won't."

Jen looked away from his handsome profile, the masculine set of his jaw. Aware that her nipples had pebbled—and he had *definitely* noticed—she crossed her arms in front of her and did her best to discreetly pluck the fabric away from her breasts. "How old is this pickup?"

Matt slowed as they neared the iron gate of the Triple B. "Sixteen years, give or take."

Jen drew a shuddering breath. "It's in really nice condition." The bench seat seemed to have new leather. The dash and doors were equally pristine. Unfortunately, she had tracked mud onto the floor mat.

His large capable hands circling the wheel, he turned effortlessly into the lane. "Thanks."

They traveled up the driveway in silence. "So it's yours?" she asked when they finally reached the house, aware that—rational or not—she didn't want this time with him to end.

"Yep." Matt parked close to the porch and cut the motor. He eyed the pouring rain with a frown.

In no hurry to emerge from the cab and get soaked again, either, Jen relaxed in her seat and flashed a small smile. "How long have you had it?"

Matt released the buckle on his safety belt. "Since I got my learner's permit." With a sentimental gleam in his eyes, he admitted, "I learned to drive in it."

Made sense, Jen mused. Years ago, this sturdy Ford 250 would have been the perfect vehicle for him. Now, when he could afford whatever he wanted...

Curiously, she asked, "What else do you drive?" She tried to picture him in a small, trendy sports car, and just couldn't see it.

One hand resting on the steering wheel, Matt turned toward her. His knee nudged hers, sending another thrill pulsing through her still chilled, overstimulated body. "This is it. Unless it's in the shop, and then I drive one of the other ranch vehicles. Whatever's available. Doesn't matter."

Jen turned toward him, too.

The porch lights bathed the truck in a circle of warm yellow light, but the windows had already begun to steam up again, giving them a measure of warmth and privacy.

"I can't believe we have that in common."

He studied her, interest lighting his eyes. "You learned to drive in that van?"

"Yes." Needing something to hold on to, Jen curled her fingers around the strap of her shoulder bag. "It belonged to my dad." She struggled against the poignancy of the moment. "He used it for his housepainting business. I inherited it when he died. And now I use it for the gallery."

Matt didn't touch her, but something in the way he looked at her was at least that intimate.

"So it's sentiment rather than finances that prompts you to keep it," he guessed finally. "Even though it's clearly on its last however many miles."

"Three hundred thousand," Jen informed him ruefully, glad Matt seemed to understand what few others did about her attachment to the vehicle. "But...yes."

Another silence fell.

She noted his bemused expression and realized it would be so easy to take this to the next level and succumb to a kiss. For their mutual protection, she drew on formality to douse the spark of attraction between them.

"Thank you for coming to my rescue." She released a shaky breath, and couldn't help but add honestly, "I wouldn't have expected it." *Any more than I would have expected this flood of desire rushing through me.*

"Don't go thanking me too much." His response was polite enough, but she heard the steel undertone. "It wasn't my idea. It was my dad's." Matt grimaced. "I just didn't want him out on the roads."

If Matt meant to push her away, after just drawing her close, he had succeeded.

"Well, thanks for clearing that up," Jen said wryly as she picked up her bag and reached for the door handle. She planned to make her escape—even if it was still pouring rain. Of course, as luck would have it, the door was locked. And the button that would open it not all that easy to find. Especially in the semidarkness.

Not done with her yet, Matt caught her hand and pulled her around to face him again. His mouth quirked.

"At least that's what I told myself initially," he said softly, resting his right arm on the seat behind her. "But it wasn't the truth." His other hand came up to cup her face. "I was worried about you, too."

Jen's heart took a little leap as his words sank in.

Matt threaded his hand through her hair, and this time his gaze met hers without hesitation or resignation. "I'm glad I found you."

Chapter Five

Matt wasn't a guy who'd ever really been in touch with his emotional side. Probably had something to do with the toughness required of him as a kid, when he'd been dealing with his mom's illness. All he knew for certain was that when it came time to feel something, he usually shut down, dealt with the practical aspect, and then moved on.

That attitude had served him well. Kept him from getting entangled. Until now. Jen made him want to stick around. At least long enough to kiss her again, find out if the chemistry was as potent as the first time they'd locked lips. To see if she felt as good pressed up against him.

Because if she did—if it hadn't been his imagination—then they were both in a whole heck of a lot of trouble. The kind that could make their lives damn complicated....

Jen knew Matt was going to kiss her. Knew that if she had a lick of sense she would put a hand against his chest; shove him away. After all, it was imperative that she stick every barrier she could find between them.

Instead, she splayed her fingers across his hard pecs and sighed as he came even closer. Head tilted, eyes at half-mast, lips parting, she was already giving in.

And then it was too late. His mouth was on hers, and her fingers were curling into the fabric of his shirt as he took her to her own little corner of heaven and kept her there.

With a low murmur of acquiescence, she slid across the bench seat. Arms clasped around her, he tugged her closer, anchoring her hard against him. Together, they deepened the kiss, tongues tangling, thighs bumping, breaths meshing. He slanted his mouth over hers and took everything she had to give, and she demanded everything he had in return. He was more than happy to comply. One hand in her hair, the other brushing the swell of her breast, he kissed her deep and slow. Bringing forth all the emotions she never knew existed, the emotions that told her it wasn't too late, for her to be wanted, loved, needed. Just like this. She could be so turned on that nothing mattered but this instant in time.... And that was when the cell phone rang.

Jarring them right back to reality.

The fantasy of the moment broken, Matt swore under his breath.

Knowing this was crazy, that they were way too different...and no good would come of it, Jen tensed and pulled away.

Feeling flustered, she shoved her hands through her hair then pressed a palm to her trembling lips. What was she thinking?

They were parked in front of the Triple B ranch house! The home of one of her patrons. They'd been kissing and groping and on the verge of recklessly doing more for heaven only knew how long!

It had felt like too short a time. And yet, judging by the thudding of her heart and the way the truck windows were steamed up, that kiss they had just shared had gone on for way, way too long.

She was jarred from her thoughts by the sound of his incessantly ringing phone.

Grimacing, Matt unhooked the device from his belt, punched a button on the lit screen and lifted it to his ear. "Yeah, Dad. No. Everything is fine. I found her. We were just waiting until the rain died down a minute before coming in." He winced. "Yeah, I can see that it has. Be right there."

Matt ended the call.

Jen hadn't felt this embarrassed since she was a teenager. She summed up their predicament with one word. "Busted." Then bit down on an oath.

Matt shrugged off her concern. "He's not going to know."

"Really." Jen felt herself blushing to the roots of her hair. She slid her gaze from the implacable expression on his face to the front of his jeans.

This time Matt flushed, too.

Suddenly looking as sheepish as she felt, he adjusted his jeans. "Give me a minute."

The front door opened. Emmett stepped out on the front porch. It was all Jen could do not to groan out loud.

"We don't have a minute!" Jen muttered.

Emmett Briscoe might be Matt's dad, but he was her client, so she took the lead.

She grabbed her handbag and the things she'd picked up in town, and vaulted from the truck. Fortunately, the rain had started to let up. "Sorry if you were worried about me."

Matt rounded the front of the pickup and mounted the steps beside her.

To cover her embarrassment, Jen kept right on babbling. "My radiator quit working. I had to pull off the road…. There was no cell phone reception. Then the storm came, and there was lightning all over the field I was parked in…."

Matt stood beside her, hands braced on his waist. His expression as implacable as ever, he picked up where she left off, in an enviably calm tone. "Luckily, I found her and got her out of there."

"We drove back here," Jen continued, modestly holding her damp blouse away from her breasts. "And here we are." *Fighting to cover up what we just felt.* Which was all-out passion and lust, and a compelling need to be closer, that had stunned both of them.

Emmett was studying her face. Then Matt's. Then hers again.

"No need to pretend with me," he said finally. "I don't mind if you two feel a few sparks. In fact—" he grinned "—I'd like nothing more than to see my son get involved with a woman I know his mother would approve of."

Matt cleared his throat and slanted Jen a protective look that was oddly thrilling. "Dad!"

"It's true, son. Your mother—who I firmly believe is looking down at us from heaven—would love it if you were to marry an artist."

Jen was so startled by the suggestion that she dropped everything in her hands. The bag from the drugstore split, and the necessary toiletries went all over the porch, along with most of the items in her handbag. "Marry!" she rasped. She knelt down to collect everything.

Matt waved off his father's aid and hunkered down, too, his denim-clad knee brushing her bare one.

His glance slid to the hem of her skirt, which, thanks to the way she was positioned, hovered at midthigh.

Lazily, he picked up lipstick, perfume, van keys and her cell phone. Jen collected the hand cream and sunscreen.

"Obviously, Dad's been hitting the whiskey," Matt drawled.

Still in matchmaking mode, Emmett chuckled. "You only wish."

"Then you should." Finished, Matt stood and offered Jen a hand up. "Because you're talking crazy," he told his father.

Emmett shrugged off the observation, then turned and walked inside the house, his gait unusually slow. But he looked, Jen thought, absolutely sober.

He tossed a look at them over his shoulder as he headed through the living room to the bar. "Anyone care to join me?"

Jen shivered in the air-conditioning as she entered.

Matt looked at her, saw what she'd been trying to hide earlier. His manner matter-of-fact, he grabbed a soft cashmere throw off the leather sofa and draped it chivalrously over her shoulders.

Only the heat in his gaze told of his continuing awareness.

Jen knew exactly how he felt.

She wanted to kiss him again, too.

Matt headed toward his dad. "Whiskey sounds good," he told him, then turned back to her. "Jen?"

Maybe a drink would help ease the pounding of her heart. She nodded. "Yes, please."

Emmett got down three glasses and poured an inch of whiskey in each.

Matt brought Jen's to her.

Outside, the storm intensified, lightning and thunder coming near once more.

Inside, silence fell, more awkward than ever.

Nervously, Jen jumped in to fill the void. "So your wife was a patron of the arts, I gather?" she asked Emmett.

The silence became poignant. The older man moved to study the photos of his late wife gracing the mantel. "She was an artist herself. Most of her paintings were western landscapes, although she did some of Matt and me, when he was a baby."

Aware that she hadn't noticed any paintings when she was touring the house, Jen asked, "Do you have any of her work here?"

Emmett returned to the bar and poured himself another two fingers of whiskey. "All her paintings are here."

Matt slouched on the sofa. The worry on his face made Jen want to reassure him. "She never showed her work," he interjected, looking a little heartbroken, too.

Jen understood. Grief was a hard thing to master. It came and went in waves, often at the most unexpected times.

Emmett sipped his drink slowly. "Margarite wasn't interested in what the critics said."

"Nor did she want to put a price on her art," Matt murmured, setting his empty tumbler on his denim-clad thigh.

"I can understand that," Jen replied, cupping her glass in her hands.

There was something about bringing someone else in to judge what you had done. It could change the way you felt about your art—when it shouldn't. And Margarite hadn't needed the money to live, the way Jen did.

Still, she knew that beautiful art was meant to be shared.

It was part of the legacy Margarite had left behind.

Something else her family could treasure.

Jen sent a hopeful glance in Emmett's direction. "I'd like to see them."

He assented with a nod. "Tomorrow morning," he promised. "Now, if the two of you don't mind, I'm going to call it a night."

"Did I upset him?" Jen asked Matt, after his dad had ambled off, second glass of whiskey in hand.

Matt studied the bottom of his glass. "Talking about Mom always makes him sad. He misses her."

The whiskey that warmed her inside also loosened her mountain of inhibitions, making Jen bold enough to sink down next to Matt, still clutching the ivory cashmere throw around her shoulders. "What about you? Do you miss her, too?"

He ran his finger around the rim of his glass. "I try not to think about it."

The burn of the alcohol was nothing compared to the fire in his eyes, when he finally lifted his head.

Jen sighed. "That's not an answer."

Annoyance flickered across his face. Cocking his head, he studied her for a long moment. "Do you miss your dad?"

Jen shrugged, aware that the mixture of curiosity and pique between them seemed to go both ways. "I miss the good things," she admitted finally, aware that her grief was a lot more complicated than his.

She swallowed around the sudden ache in her throat. "I don't miss the intermittent chaos my dad's alcoholism created in our lives." She was glad that was gone.

Matt raised a brow and waited for her gaze to meet his. "That was honest."

She compressed her lips. "It is what it is." Once she had started accepting the bad with the good, and lowered her expectations accordingly, life had become a lot easier.

She wanted it to stay easy.

Unfortunately, there was nothing about Matt—except his propensity for kissing her like there was no tomorrow—that was anything near easy.

He was complicated.

Maybe the most complicated man she had ever met.

But, intuition told her, worth knowing. And knowing well.

A small smile curved his sexy mouth. His gaze roved over her mussed, rain-dampened hair. He looked at her as if he knew of her inner battle. "I like your candor."

"When it's about me." Feeling a little empowered, and a lot feistier, Jen turned toward him, her blanket-draped knee brushing his thigh. "Not," she stated bluntly, "when it's about you."

Matt chuckled and set both their glasses aside. Still grinning, he reached inside the throw to capture one of her hands. "That's because you don't know as much as you think you do."

The warmth of his touch sent a thrill rippling through her. "Then tell me something I don't know." *And need to know to understand you.*

He shrugged. "I've never been in love."

Jen couldn't say she was surprised about that. Love would have left him vulnerable. "Me, either."

"But you were married."

He hadn't shaved yet, and the stubble gave him a dark, sexy look. Memories of the way he had kissed her earlier sent a burning flame throughout her entire body. "I didn't say I never thought I was in love. Of course, I thought I loved my ex, but as it turned out, what Dex and I felt for each other was merely lust." Jen sighed, promising herself she wouldn't make the same mistake again. "And lust, as everyone knows, doesn't last."

Something hot and sensual shimmered in his eyes. "It can last."

For a moment, she let herself imagine what it would be like to make love with Matt. Not once, just to bank some flames and satisfy their curiosity, but many, many times…

"Has it for you?" she challenged, as if she hadn't been thinking about that possibility at all.

He flashed her a crooked smile. "Well, no."

"Me, either." Jen sighed, knowing that when a fantasy about someone dissolved, so did the desire. And she wasn't in the mood to have her heart and hopes crushed again. "So…"

He slid his eyes to the hollow of her throat, then her lips, then her eyes. "I think our passion is the kind that might not ever go away."

She told herself the evening definitely would not end with her kissing him again. "Now that's the whiskey talking."

He dipped his head in a gallant bow and took her in his arms again. "Or the knowledge of what it is like to kiss you."

Romantic notions bubbled up inside her, and she shivered.

He threw off the blanket and shifted her onto his lap.

"Matt…" she whispered.

"Hmm?" Eyelids lowered, he kissed his way down the side of her throat.

She splayed her hands across his chest. "This is no good."

He tunneled one hand through her hair, then pressed his lips to hers. "It's very good."

Tingling, Jen averted her head. "For what we're trying to do here." Knowing she would be lost if he kissed her again, she buried her face in his shoulder.

Matt nuzzled her neck, finding the nerve endings just beneath her ear. He stroked a hand down her back, his hot callused palm easing beneath the hem of her blouse, above the waistband of her skirt, to caress her skin. "What are we trying to do?"

Jen quivered at his touch and drank in the fragrant, masculine scent of him.

Stay on track. Stay on track....

"We're trying to make your dad happy," she reminded him thickly. "Commemorate his life and his love for your mother. Help him feel good about all he has accomplished, and all he still has in front of him."

The mention of his father had the desired affect. Matt dropped his hands, sat back. "You're going to do that with your sculptures?"

Jen nodded. She could pretend all she wanted...but Matt was right about one thing. The desire she felt for him wasn't ever going to go away.

But there was no reason he needed to know she felt that way.

She eased off his lap and turned the talk back to business. "I'm going to try."

And while I'm at it, I'll work a whole lot harder at protecting my heart.

"I HATE TO IMPOSE," Jen told Emmett, when she encountered him having breakfast in the kitchen the next morning, "but is there someone who could give me a ride over to the Armstrong ranch to pick up my van? They can't be happy to have it just sitting there in a field."

"Matt's already taken care of it."

Jen did a double take. "What do you mean?"

"He called the auto service and had it towed into town to the repair shop."

And how much was that going to cost? Could she even afford it?

"Don't worry," Emmett said, misinterpreting the reason behind her concern. "They'll get it fixed up in no time." His movements almost painfully slow, he gestured for her to sit down with him. "Help yourself to some breakfast. No eggs or bacon this morning—it's Luz's day off. But we've got pastries, juice and coffee."

Jen surveyed the rancher. Something was definitely off. "You feeling okay this morning?" He looked a little pale, as if he hadn't slept well, and his left hand was trembling slightly.

The day before, it had been his right.

He cupped both hands around his coffee mug. "I should have figured you'd notice." He winked, jovial as ever. "I'm paying for my bad judgment. I know better than to have more than one whiskey in an evening."

Jen had plenty of experience in that regard, with her dad. This did not look like any hangover she had ever seen. Both hands should have been trembling if Emmett was in his cups, not just one. Was it possible, she wondered, that something might be wrong with the otherwise healthy looking and virile man? Was that fact, rather than just ego, behind the wealthy cattleman's drive to commemorate his life?

Emmett sat back in his chair. "I see you're feeling fine this morning, however."

Jen smiled. She had slept surprisingly well. And had woken up dreaming of kissing Matt....

Flushing, she poured herself some juice from the bottle on the table. "I'm anxious to get to work on the first sculpture." Work always made her feel better. Maybe because it was a place for her to channel her emotions.

Emmett glanced at his watch. "I've got business meetings in San Angelo at ten, but I'll have time to show you the studio Matt's mother used to work in."

Jen munched on a cinnamon roll. "You're okay having me set up shop there?"

"It'll be nice to have the space used again. I think you're going to like the light in there."

Emmett wasn't kidding, Jen realized half an hour later, when they went up to the second floor loft in the wing of the house that the older gentleman now occupied.

The light was spectacular, the room large and airy.

It was also empty except for handsome built-in shelving and cabinetry along one wall, and a large wooden worktable located beneath the bank of windows.

Stunned, Jen turned to Emmett.

"She donated all her art supplies and easels to the local community college when she could no longer paint," he explained. "We had her paintings displayed on the walls in here, but after she died it was just too painful to see them, so Matt and I wrapped everything up and put them in storage."

"They should be hanging."

Emmett squinted. "Just what I was thinking." He rubbed his jaw with the hand that trembled. "Tell you what...I'll bring some of Margarite's favorite pieces up, later today."

It turned out he was as good as his word.

Only it wasn't Emmett who brought up the paintings some three hours later.

It was his son.

Chapter Six

Matt knew it was going to be tough seeing his mother's work again, never mind have them in the studio where he'd had his last truly happy memories of his mother before she had been stricken with multiple sclerosis and confined to the lower floor of the ranch house.

It was rougher still walking in with the paintings, all still carefully wrapped, and seeing Jen in what had always been his mom's arena.

Jen took it over, much as his mother had, her presence lending an air of tranquility to the large, sunny space.

In faded jeans, peacock-blue cowgirl boots and a sexy, formfitting white tank top, her hair swept up in a messy knot, she was so damn pretty she took his breath away.

And she was not glad to see him.

Not. At. All.

Because he'd kissed her and she had kissed him back? Or because their evening together had ended on a businesslike note, and they hadn't gotten around to making out again?

Matt looked in her eyes. No clue. All he knew for certain was that she blamed him for something. Luckily for both of them, he was in no mood to wrangle.

All he wanted was escape. Escape from the feelings being around Jen conjured up, and the notion that with very little effort, the two of them could have something truly amazing.

"Dad texted me that you wanted the paintings," he announced, planning to dump them and run before they were actually unwrapped.

When he did eventually look at the canvases again—and he would…at some point—he wanted to be alone.

"So." Matt propped them carefully against the wall. "There you go."

To his consternation, no sooner had he set them down than Jen was reaching for the tape holding the protective quilts over the oil canvases.

Reacting quickly, he left her to it and headed back out into the hall.

She followed. "That's all?" She caught up with him in the long corridor outside the studio.

"Well…" Matt paused, not sure why she was so irked when he'd done as asked, the moment he got back to the ranch house, no less.

Again, their gazes held for a long moment, and as always, when she gave him her undivided attention, something flashed between them and his body tensed with need.

A little unsettled by the way he kept wanting her, Matt cleared his throat. "Obviously, there are more paintings in the climate-controlled storage room where we keep all the valuables. Twenty-five more pieces, to be exact."

Jen kept staring at him.

He adjusted his posture slightly, to relieve the ache. Lowered his gaze from her face and encountered the soft, sexy swell of her breasts instead. Which to his frustration only made the situation worse. "But that was all I could easily carry at once," Matt continued, with the poker face he'd perfected at a very early age.

Jen folded her arms in that way that really got his blood pumping. And she still looked ticked off.

"I'm not talking about art." Her low voice dripped with resentment and she stepped nearer, with a drift of lilac perfume.

Deciding the farther they were from the studio, the better, Matt kept right on moving down the corridor, to the stairs. Sweaty and grimy from a morning spent outdoors in the summer heat, he wanted two things: a shower and release from the tension he'd felt ever since they'd kissed.

Well, the latter wasn't going to happen. Not if either of them had any sense.

"Then what *are* you talking about?" he demanded.

"I want to know about my van!"

Matt paused outside his bedroom door. Of course that was what she wanted. "I took it to the best mechanic in town. Naturally, because the van is so old, he had to order the parts…but it'll be ready in a couple of days."

Jen's face turned pink. "You okayed the work without even talking to me?"

Matt shrugged. "It's not going to run unless you replace the radiator and the transmission."

She sagged against the wall, hand over her heart. "The transmission!" she croaked.

Matt resisted the urge to prop her up with an arm about her waist. "Yeah." He stood with his legs braced apart and continued offering moral support—from a distance. "That's why we couldn't get it started this morning."

Jen raked both her hands through her hair, forgetting for a moment that she had it up in a clip. Her fingers got tangled. Frowning, she extricated them, then removed the clip. "Do you have any idea how much that is going to cost?"

Matt tracked the silky chestnut waves flowing about her shoulders. "Eight thousand dollars, give or take."

"Eight thousand dollars!"

"For the amount of work he's going to do, and the cost and difficulty tracking down the right parts, that's a bargain, Jen."

She moaned and bent over from the waist, as if trying not to be sick. "That's not the point." She groaned again.

Matt tried not to notice the way her neckline gaped, revealing lace and curves, and jutting nipples. Stifling a groan himself, he averted his gaze and moved past her into his bedroom. "Really." He tossed the words over his shoulder. "Because I thought getting your only mode of transportation back in order was exactly the point."

Jen followed him, closing the distance between them once again. "I don't have that kind of money right now, Matt."

Surprised to see her standing in the middle of his bedroom, he shrugged. "Then Dad will give you an advance on your commission."

Jen lifted her chin, coming closer. "How do you know?"

Matt exhaled. "Because I know him, and if he didn't...then I would."

Those cornflower-blue eyes glittered angrily. "I don't want *your* money, Matt."

Now, that rankled. "You didn't seem to have a problem taking my father's."

Jen threw up her hands. "For work as it is completed!" she sputtered. "Not for..."

"What?"

She regarded him with silent derision. "That's what I'm wondering."

It took him a second to follow. "Surely you don't think I'm trying to buy my way into your bed?"

She shrugged and kept her gaze locked with his. "You said it. Maybe you think that's a way to speed up what you'd clearly like to happen between us."

Matt hadn't been the only one who enjoyed their make-out session. He studied her brooding expression. "This isn't about the money," he asserted, stepping closer. He angled a thumb at his chest. "It's because I did what had to be done, without calling you every step of the way and asking your opinion."

Something in his words must have clicked, because he saw a flicker of acknowledgment in Jen's eyes. "Calling me would have been nice."

Matt had never been one to shift the blame for his mistakes, but in this instance, he knew he wasn't at fault. Stupidly naive, maybe, to think his gallantry would be received in the spirit it was given. He pushed on. "It would have been a waste of time. Yours and mine. Because the end result would have been the same. You would have ordered the repairs and had them done here, by the person we told you was the best." Matt sauntered closer and saw her eyes widen in sensual awareness. "And you know why?" he murmured.

Her lower lip thrust out petulantly. "Because I had no choice?"

He shook his head, his heart going out to her, because he knew what it felt like to want things to go one way, and have them constantly go another. "Because you love that van as much as I love my pickup."

"I didn't tell you that so you could use it against me," she retorted, looking distraught.

Matt put his hands on her shoulders and held her there when she would have run away from what was happening between them. "Say that again?"

Turbulent emotion tautened her pretty features. "I don't want you taking charge of my life."

He watched her, unsure how to help. "That isn't what I was doing."

Her mouth curved resentfully as she accused in a low, trembling tone, "That is exactly what you were doing, Matt." She tapped an emphatic rhythm against the center of his chest. "And. I. Don't. Like. It."

He caught her hand and held it over his heart, aware they were finally beginning to get somewhere.

Wanting her to open up even more, he asked, "What's really going on here? Are we talking about me now?" Certain he had her full attention, he waited another beat. "Or someone else?"

Matt's assumption was so on target, Jen couldn't help it, she swore in frustration and anger and confusion.

He grinned, pleased his needling was affecting her. He cupped her chin in his hand and urged, "Use your words. The ones not affiliated with your opinion of me."

Jen felt as if the situation had knocked the wind out of her. For the sake of her pride, she pretended that she wasn't glad to see Matt. Wasn't glad to have him trying to help her, even if everything he was doing and saying was wrong.

Her hands flattened against the front of his shirt. "What I am trying to tell you," she said, "is that I have been down this road before."

"With another take-charge guy. Your ex-husband, maybe?"

"Yes." Feeling as if her knees could no longer support her, she moved toward the only available seating—his bed—and sank down on the edge of it. "When it started out, I thought he was just being thoughtful and considerate. I didn't have any money. Dex did. He wanted life to be nice for me."

Matt sat down facing her. "What's wrong with that?"

Everything, as it happened.

Jen looked deep in his eyes and tried not to think about how he would look at her once he knew the whole truth. "By the time Dex and I divorced, I wasn't making any decisions for myself," she admitted miserably. "Everything was decided for me."

Matt furrowed his brow. "He wanted you to conform to what he thought was appropriate? For the woman who was his wife?"

Jen wished it had been that simple. Or that she had been strong enough to stand up for herself and fight for what she wanted.

But she hadn't been able to do it then. She'd been stuck in people-pleasing mode.

Embarrassed, she had to force herself to go on. "Dex wanted me to do whatever he thought was going to tick his parents off the most." Restless, she stood again and began to pace. "See, they were really controlling. They put all kinds of pressure on him, and he rebelled by marrying me. An artist who was more concerned about the quality of clay I was buying than the other details of my life."

Matt's expression gentled as he began to understand.

"They liked a woman's hair to be salon perfect at all times, so Dex insisted that I not do anything to it that wasn't completely natural." Jen paused next to the window and looked out at the rolling acreage of the ranch.

Bracing a shoulder against the frame, she turned back to Matt. "They ate haute cuisine, so he had us bring in food from the most lowbrow restaurants around for our dinner."

Matt came to stand next to her. "You lived with them?"

Remembering, she felt her heart constrict. "Oh, yes. That was part of the plan. He kept saying he wanted to build a place for us."

"And they were all for that?"

"No." Jen massaged the tense muscles in her neck. "His folks liked having him under their thumb. They just wanted to get rid of me, and have him marry someone more suitable. Someone of their social standing and all that."

Matt searched her face. "So what finally happened?"

Memories came as fast and devastating as the actual event. "They gave Dex what he wanted. Early access to his half-million-dollar trust fund. On one condition."

"He divorce you."

Jen nodded, stunned to this day by the cruelty of the event. "Yep."

"And you were hurt."

She raked a hand through her hair. "Relieved." She looked into Matt's eyes, swallowed, and forged on, "I knew by then that the marriage was going to end. I knew it had to end." She shook her head in regret, wishing she had been stronger. Less needy. "But I didn't want it to."

"Because you loved him. Or thought you did."

"Because I wanted it to be the opposite of my childhood," she said emotionally. How naive she'd been! "I wanted it all to work out in the end. And in the meantime, I had a roof over my head, food to eat and a place to work on my sculpting. So I just kept going, kept trying, kept thinking that if only I was the perfect wife and the perfect daughter-in-law and the perfect rising artist, everything would work out. That his parents would come to accept me one day." Jen drew a breath. "And in the meantime, I had Dex, who told me he loved me and that we would be happy when we were both able to make all our dreams come true. Mine was to make a living selling my art. And his was to start his own venture capital business."

"Did he?"

"Yes. He's very good at it. And he's now very rich. His parents are very proud of him. I'm successful now, too. So everyone lived happily ever after."

"Not quite."

She raised her eyebrows.

"Because you haven't moved on—emotionally—from the mistake, any more than I've moved on from my elopement."

A laugh bubbled up inside her. "And what would you have us do, Matt?"

"Jump back in."

Jen shivered, and not from air-conditioning vent above her head. "That's the best line I've ever heard."

And also the most seductive.

He grinned. "It's not a line."

Pulse thudding, she absorbed the sight of him, jaw unshaved, hair tousled, body hard and sweaty beneath the half-open shirt. Her fingers itched to discover the texture of all that sleek, tanned, hair-roughened skin.

And he wanted her, too.

She could see it. Feel it. Completely identify with it.

"Matt..." Jen whispered. Why was he doing this? Making her realize how badly she still needed to belong.

And the way he looked at her whenever they were alone made her think she belonged with him.

He knew it, too....

His eyes were two dark pools. "Take a shower with me."

Desire washed over her with an intensity she had never felt before.

He brushed a soft kiss to her temple before trailing more kisses across her cheek, her jaw. "Take a risk." He settled a hand on her hip, dragged his fingers up her spine. "See where this can go."

Goose bumps erupted on her skin. There was tenderness in his eyes and a smile that promised all sorts of wicked and wonderful things, if only she said the word.

Jen wanted passion in her life. She wanted—needed—to be loved.

What she didn't want was to be disappointed and have her heart broken again.

And Matt Briscoe had the power to do that.

More than he knew.

She shook her head but couldn't seem to make herself move away. So instead, she flattened her palms on his chest and closed her eyes. And felt the soft press of his lips on her forehead.

"We're so different, you and I." She gazed into his eyes. "I stopped trying to control everything a very long time ago."

Matt met her gaze in challenge. "And now you try to control nothing."

"Life is what it is." She had work, friends, a home. It was enough. More than enough. "I accept that."

"Then..." tugging her close, Matt held her against him and bent his head to hers "...accept this."

Chapter Seven

Jen meant to resist, she really did. But she was his for the taking the moment Matt tilted her head and covered her lips with his.

It didn't matter that she shouldn't be here, in his bedroom. Inhaling his scent. Feeling his heat. It didn't matter that she was a sensible woman whose heart was locked up, out of reach. He made a sound of pleasure that went straight through her, and their kiss deepened into an intense, satisfying tangle of lips and tongues. And Jen felt alive in a way she hadn't in years. She felt on the edge of a kind of contentment she'd never had. And she knew this was a once-in-a-lifetime experience. The kind that likely would not come again.

Matt thrust a thigh between hers. His hand slid down to the small of her back, riveting her in place, and turning the kiss into a full-body experience of raw, sexual power. And darned if she didn't want to give as good as she was getting.

She let Matt dance her backward toward the bathroom in his suite, kissing her all the while. And once there, she used the heel of her boot to shut the door with a thud.

Matt laughed and drew back to look at her.

"We're really going to do this."

"We're really going to do this," she whispered, already toeing off her boots.

He pulled his shirt over his head, his smile slow and sure, and so hot it singed every nerve ending in her body.

Her jeans went next.

Then his.

The mutual striptease gave her a thrill that turned her blood to liquid fire. Lower still, a quiver racked her.

He helped her remove her tank top, then her bra and panties. Her nipples tightened. "Beautiful," he murmured, touching and caressing her, then looking at her with a heavy-lidded gaze that had her wanting to fall into bed with him and never emerge.

She quivered once more, and then was kissing him again. And when kissing wasn't enough, she worked her fingers beneath the elastic of his sexy black briefs and helped dispense with them. Her eyes followed her hands. Lord, he was big and hard, Jen thought. Every inch of him was buff and hard and male. His eyes were burning with desire.

Lust consumed her, too.

He kissed her throat, her shoulder, moving lower to her breast. She had never felt as beautiful, as wanted as she did at that moment.

A liquid warmth filled her as he sucked her nipple into his mouth, rolling it with his tongue. Writhing against him, she sifted her fingers through his hair, kissed the top of his head. Gasping, she arched her back, surrendering to him.

When he rose again, smiling, the kiss turned maddeningly slow and sensual. She let her fingers play, too, until he groaned, turned the dial and guided her inside the glass-walled shower. Then he drew them both beneath the generous spray, cupped her head in his hand and kissed her again, the delicious heat of him countering the slowly warming water sluicing over them. Again and again he kissed her, until she gave herself over to his demand, and their bodies were plastered together.

When she could stand it no longer, he caressed her tenderly and groaned. "You've got me so off task."

It felt *very* on task to her.

He leaned over and kissed her again. "I intended to get cleaned up for you first."

His eyes met hers. Another thrill slid through her. Another whisper of arousal...

Matt reached for the soap, grabbed a washcloth from the hook. Aware this was her every fantasy come true, she watched as he rubbed the bar into a nice thick lather, then set it back on the shelf and began running the cloth over his body with the same steady expertise he did everything else.

Shoulders. Chest. Thighs...

Feeling left out of what looked like an awful lot of fun, Jen caught his hand, extricated the cloth. "Allow me."

He chuckled, his eyes darkening. Acquiescing, he leaned against the shower wall.

"I'm an artist," she whispered, grabbing the sprayer, too. "I learn best through touch." And what she wanted to learn most, Jen discovered breathlessly, was him.

Every dip and nook and cranny, every hard plane and rigid muscle, was washed and rinsed, touched and loved.

Turning her on.

Turning him on.

Suddenly the soapy cloth dropped and the kissing

commenced. The next thing Jen knew, he'd grasped her wrist, shut off the water, and was heading for bed.

His bed.

Which was, she soon discovered, infinitely comfortable. Especially with Matt stretched out beside her.

Pausing only long enough to roll on a condom, he steadied her, hands on her hips. "Still time to turn back," he said, his voice rough with desire.

Her own passion ready to explode, Jen shook her head. She would die if he didn't fill her soon. "No way."

"Then let's get you good to go." He slid down to the apex of her thighs, held her open, kissing and ravishing, until she was shuddering and gasping for air.

Jen clutched at him. "Now, Matt. Now…"

She felt his smile against her thigh. He moved upward. "My pleasure."

Being filled by him was like nothing she'd ever felt before. Jen opened herself up to him as he began to move in exactly the right rhythm to send her soaring. Emboldened by her pleasure, he thrust hard again, finding his own shattering release.

He kissed her through the climax, through the aftermath, and even after that. Jen had never had anyone want her once the passion had faded. It was a delicious sensation, sweet and satisfying, the tenderness between them a palpable thing. Which was why, she knew, she had to get out of there.

Fast.

MATT KNEW IT WAS TOO MUCH, too soon. He'd hooked up with Jen, anyway. And not for the strictly physical reasons she might suspect. He hadn't led her down here to seduce her into bed. He had come back down here to get away from her, from the closeness that threatened every time they were alone together.

And even when they weren't.

She had a way of looking at him, of understanding what was going on with him even when he didn't say a word.

He wasn't used to feeling understood—by anyone.

Up until now, it hadn't bothered him. Life was just easier that way. When he could keep everyone at arm's length.

The last place he wanted Jen was at arm's length.

Yet there she was, just minutes after they had both climaxed—out of his arms, out of his bed. Sheet draped modestly around her, she was gathering up her clothes, one by one. As if he hadn't already committed every inch of her sweet, luscious body to memory. And, he was willing to bet, she was equally familiar with his. Not that there wasn't room for improvement. They still had much to explore in the lovemaking department. In fact, he was already getting hard. "You really don't have to rush out. No one else is here, nor likely to be."

Jen managed to wiggle into her rose-colored bikini panties without dropping the sheet.

Unable to do the same with her bra, she dropped the sheet, turned her back to him and sat down on the bench at the foot of his bed. Head bent, she fastened the clasp of her bra in front of her, then twisted the lacy white fabric around and pulled it up over the globes of her breasts. Over her slender shoulders.

The straps fell into place with a snap.

Jen's chest rose and fell as she drew in a bolstering breath. "That's not really the point, Matt."

She turned to face him yet again, her nipples poking through the lace, belying the casual disregard of her words, whether she wanted them to or not.

Aware that his nipples were still erect, too, Matt folded his arms behind his head and lay back against the pillows, watching her. Wanting her.

Wondering if she had any idea how completely desirable he found her. Or how much he wanted to repeat their mind-blowing sex.

"Then what is the point?" he asked softly, irritated that she felt it necessary to lie to him about what she was really feeling.

Color flooding her cheeks, she pulled her tank top over her head.

She looked even sexier clad in just panties, bra and tank, her long silky legs and dainty feet planted defiantly apart.

Jen snatched her jeans off the floor and tugged them up over her knees.

The stone-colored fabric, worn and soft, pulled taut across her flat tummy. The waistband rested just above the line of her panties, revealing her sexy belly button. And cupping her sleek thighs and delectably round butt in a way that drove him crazy.

He sighed in disappointment as she tugged the hem of her tank down over her hips, cutting off his view of bare, silky skin.

A mixture of exasperation and defiance gleamed in her eyes. "You want honesty?"

Matt lifted a shoulder in a shrug. "Nothing but." He was certain, one wrong word from him and he'd never have the chance to lure her into his bed again.

Jen came close enough to perch on the foot of the mattress. Still safely out of reach, she gave him a level look. "I meant what I said to you earlier. I accept that

I'm done with roller-coaster romance and dreams of happily ever after. I know it's never going to happen to me. I don't expect it…and I don't want it."

"Then what do you want?"

She bent over to tug on her socks and boots. "To just take life as it comes. One day at a time. I don't want this…hookup…to have any repercussions."

"It won't."

Jen shot him a skeptical look. "I don't want to think about it or talk about it or expect that it will happen again. Because…" she leaned against the wall, arms folded decisively in front of her "…it's not going to, Matt."

He couldn't say he was surprised she was backing off, since she was no more inclined to let someone in than he was.

That didn't mean they couldn't react differently now. Especially when the chemistry was this good. "Why not?" He rose from the bed and began to dress, too. She caught his eye and went still.

He tracked the lift of her breasts as she held her breath. "It was good. "

"Very good," she confirmed, jerking her gaze away. "And that's where I want to leave it."

"DID YOU GET EVERYTHING you needed?" Celia asked, via phone, later in the day.

Jen looked around the studio with satisfaction. Flexible wire, sculpting tools and measuring tape were laid out next to containers of clay. She had scanned into her laptop the pictures she was going to use as her models. Special software had converted those images into three dimensional models, complete with precise measurements, that she could translate to whatever scale she wanted. Jen still wanted to blow up those same photos to poster size so she could have them set up all around her, for further inspiration while she worked. But that, she figured, could wait until the following day.

Right now, she wanted to keep working on the sketches of the first proposed sculpture.

"Yes. I unpacked and set up this afternoon." Jen sighed. *After my colossal mistake.*

"How are things with Matt Briscoe?"

Jen kept her tone noncommittal. "About as you'd expect." Sexy. Difficult. Too fun. And way too confusing!

Celia chuckled. "Hmm. I thought I glimpsed a little attraction there, beneath all the guff."

Good thing you can't see us now, then, Jen thought, her body still thrilling at the reckless way they'd made love that afternoon.

What had gotten into her, anyway?

Why was Matt Briscoe able to get past her defenses so easily?

And when had she lost all common sense? Hadn't she learned the last time not to fall for a rich guy?

If she wanted to know how far apart she and Matt were on that score, all she had to do was think about his casual attitude regarding the cost of her van repairs.

A sum that was ridiculously expensive to her meant nothing to him.

Lovemaking that—if she was honest—meant everything to her probably meant very little to him, as well.

And though Jen had acted as if she could have sex for the pure physical pleasure of it, she knew deep down that just wasn't true. With her, feelings were always involved.

Her heart had already been crushed once, by someone out of her league financially. She didn't need to have it trampled again.

So it was best to do what she had told Matt this afternoon, and just leave things as they were. Over. Done. Kaput.

"Jen?" Celia asked. "Are you still there?"

"Mmm-hmm." She shook off all romantic notions and once again focused on her friend from childhood. "How are things with you and Cy?"

Celia groaned. "That's what I wanted to talk to you about. I saw my OB today. I'm three centimeters dilated. The doc said the baby can come any time now. She wants me to keep my bag packed."

Jen smiled and tried not to feel a little pang of envy, since she'd likely never have a baby of her own. "That's great, Celia. Cy must be so excited."

"Oh, he is!"

They talked a little more about the upcoming birth and delivery, before getting down to gallery business, and then promised to talk again the next day.

Happy about the two sales that had transpired in her absence—and what that meant for the gallery books—Jen hung up.

Hearing the heavy thud of footsteps, she turned toward the door.

Emmett Briscoe appeared there. "Am I interrupting?"

Jen put her cell phone aside and rose to greet him, immediately concerned by how he looked. "Come in," she urged gently.

Emmett shuffled toward her, clearly favoring one leg. He appeared tired and wan. Perspiration dotted his forehead.

"Are you all right? Did you fall?"

He shook his head and drew a handkerchief from his pocket to mop his face. "I think I got a little overheated when I was coming inside just now."

It looked like a heck of a lot more than that. Jen slipped a hand beneath his elbow and guided him to a chair. "Forgive me for saying so," she said carefully, "but you look ill. We should get you to a doctor."

Grimly, Emmett shook his head again.

"At least call Matt."

"Absolutely not," he thundered, mopping his forehead once again. "Matt is the last person you should tell."

Well, something wasn't right. Emmett's left leg was trembling, while his right seemed perfectly fine. As were his hands. Which, Jen recalled, was the opposite of what had been going on this morning. Then, one of his hands had been trembling, and his legs had been fine.

She pulled up a chair and sat facing him, clasping his hands. "You want to tell me what's going on?" She waited for him to look her in the eye. "And don't give me the hangover business again, because I know one when I see one and this is not it."

His shoulders slumped in defeat. "You're right. It isn't."

The raw emotion in his voice frightened her. Jen gripped his hands more tightly. "Then what is it?" she asked, trying not to sound upset.

Emmett swallowed. Moisture glistened in his faded blue eyes. "Parkinson's, most likely."

What did he mean, *most likely?* "Have you seen a doctor?" Jen asked quietly.

"No." He mopped his forehead again, then he stared at her with steely determination. "And I'm not going to, either. Matt and I spent years watching his mother deteriorate, bit by bit. I'm not about to make the rest of my son's life about being my nursemaid. And that's what it would turn into. We both know that."

Jen couldn't argue. Matt was very protective of his dad.

But what if it wasn't Parkinson's disease? What if it was something else? What if early treatment might make all the difference in the prognosis?

"Matt's going to notice your symptoms," Jen warned.

"No. He's not. And you know why? Because he doesn't want to see them." The rancher sighed. "I understand that. I didn't see Margarite's infirmities, either, when she first got sick, because I couldn't bear the thought of anything really being wrong with her. So I convinced myself that she was just tired, or coming down with a cold, or getting over a virus. Anything and everything but what was really happening."

Jen knew what he meant. "I did the same thing when my dad was in the last stages of liver failure." Her voice cracked. "I—I couldn't admit to myself that he was..."

"Dying?"

She nodded, then fell silent. Memories overwhelmed her and tears pricked her eyes.

Emmett reached out and patted her arm. For a moment the two of them sat in silence, comforting each other.

"Besides," he said eventually, "I take great pains to avoid Matt on those days that are really bad."

She bit her lip. "You don't think he'll get suspicious?"

Emmett shrugged, still confiding in her as naturally as if she were family. "For a while, he thought I was seeing a woman."

Matt had thought it might be Jen. At least that first day when he'd come to see her in her Austin studio...

"I've shared this with you in the strictest confidence," Emmett continued sincerely. "You are not to tell Matt any of it. And I need you to swear on all you hold dear that you will keep quiet."

Jen knew what an important first step this was. The big, brash, larger-than-life Texas rancher had admitted to her he was ill. He was trusting her to help him. And she would.

"Yes. I promise," she said quietly, meaning it with all her heart.

Emmett's leg trembled harder. Jen put her hand on his knee to stop the involuntary shaking. "I won't tell anyone," she reiterated, applying gentle pressure. "Not until you—"

She was about to say "change your mind and give me the okay," when Emmett's head jerked up.

The rancher looked past her, flushed guiltily and pushed her hand off his leg.

The hair on the back of her neck prickling, Jen turned in the direction of his gaze and encountered the person she least wanted to see.

Standing in the doorway, looking angry as hell, was the man she had made wild, passionate love with just a few hours before.

Matt Briscoe stomped in.

"Won't tell anyone what?" he demanded.

Chapter Eight

Matt knew when two people had been caught red-handed. His dad and Jen were definitely up to something. What, Matt didn't know. Despite the fact that she'd had her hand on his father's knee, whatever was going on didn't seem romantic or sexual. And yet there was an undeniable air of intimacy in the room.

Flushing, Jen stood up and, with more grace than Matt would have expected, under the circumstances, moved toward the drafting table. "Your father was a little overcome by the sketches I just showed him."

She walked over to Matt, drawings in hand.

Matt noted that his father wasn't looking at him. Rather, he was sitting with his palm planted firmly on the knee Jen had just been touching. Emmett also seemed curiously transfixed on Jen. It was almost as if he wasn't sure what was going on, either.

Which was strange, Matt thought. If Jen was telling the truth.

He'd bet his bottom dollar she wasn't.

"Your dad doesn't want me talking about the actual possibilities for the sculpture until a decision is made. Which is fine with me. I actually prefer to keep any work in progress completely under wraps to all but the subjects, or patron commissioning the work."

Wordlessly, she handed Matt a few rough sketches. The other three she passed to Emmett.

His resentment building, Matt glanced down.

The proposed sculptures were beautiful.

And incredible, in how they captured the essence of his parents, and the deep, abiding love they'd had for each other.

Feeling a little choked up himself, Matt handed the sketches to his dad.

Emmett, who never cried, had tears in his eyes as he scanned the drawings once again.

Dabbing at his cheek with a handkerchief, he rose abruptly. "Excuse me." He left the studio without a backward glance, and somewhat awkwardly, from the sound of it, made his way down the hall.

Matt realized his dad must have been overcome with emotion.

The ache in his own throat grew.

Jen's eyes glistened, as she moved away. Without looking at him, she said, "Posthumous works can be tough to do. Especially in the beginning."

No kidding.

Matt felt as if he was about to start bawling, and he never cried.

At least he hadn't since his mom had died.

He walked over to the drafting table, where Jen stood. Her glance still averted, she made a big production of tidying up her pencils.

He thrust the sketches at her.

She spread them out carefully on the table.

"But when the work is finished, the bronze is usually very comforting because so much has gone into it. It's such a special memorial."

Jen paused to look down with a critical eye at the

photographs she'd used as a reference, and the sketches she'd made. "If you'd like to weigh in—tell me what you think about what I've done so far, what needs work, or what I might be missing…"

Matt shook his head, no more equipped to do that than his dad had been.

How was it possible that his mother could have been gone for ten years now, and the grief was still so raw?

He thought he'd gotten past this. Accepted fate. Moved on.

The truth was he was still as rocked by it as his father was. No wonder Jen had been reaching out, trying to comfort Emmett. She probably felt sorry for him and wanted to protect his macho image.

Matt didn't need her doing that for him, too.

"I don't think so," he said gruffly, ready to run from the scene like an emotional coward, just as his dad had.

He turned away from Jen and headed toward the door.

First, he'd had to dig his mom's paintings out of storage and carry some up; he had no idea which ones, since they still weren't unwrapped.

And now this… His dad all weepy over sketches and photos of his deceased wife, and Matt feeling the same.

Still, he had a duty to at least be civil to Jen. She probably knew what she was stirring up, but had to do it anyway, as part of her work here.

Swallowing, he paused in the doorway and glanced back, meeting her gaze. Somehow making his voice sound almost normal, he announced, "I came up to tell you that Scully has food over in the bunkhouse if you want to join him and the hands for dinner. That's what Dad and I usually do when Luz is off. But if not," Matt continued, with the requisite politeness shown to guests on the Triple B, "you're welcome to either have some chow sent over, or cook here. Naturally, you can help yourself to whatever is in the kitchen."

Jen held his eyes, looking as if she wanted to say something important, but didn't dare.

She swallowed, too, then nodded with the same careful politeness he'd shown her. "Thanks for the information and the invitation, but I'm not really hungry. I think I'll grab something later."

Matt couldn't say he was surprised. Sometimes solitude was the best medicine. And right now, he needed even more time on the range.

"Suit yourself." He tipped his head at her, then walked off.

JEN ENDED UP WORKING until almost ten. By the time she hit the kitchen, the rest of the house was silent. An indication that Emmett had either gone out or gone to bed. The same with Matt.

Trying not to feel disappointed about the lack of company, she opened the stainless-steel fridge. It was filled with all sorts of goodies, and she was still trying to decide what to eat when footsteps sounded behind her.

Matt walked in, a disgruntled look on his face. He was wearing a clean pair of jeans and a plain white T-shirt. His hair was damp and he smelled of soap and shampoo. Which reminded her of their lovemaking that afternoon.

Had it only been eight hours or so since they'd been together? she wondered wistfully.

It felt like a lifetime ago.

More than a lifetime.

She studied Matt's surly, withdrawn expression,

and couldn't help but wonder if Emmett was still feeling poorly. Or whether Matt had noticed. Even if he wouldn't yet admit to himself that his dad was ailing.

A feeling of unease sifted through her. She had to tread carefully here so as not to let anyone down. "Everything okay?"

Matt shoved a hand through his curly black hair. "Depends on what you mean by okay."

She drew a conciliatory breath and lifted her shoulders in a shrug. "Okay…"

Her pun did not elicit the smile she had hoped to see.

Which likely meant he was still wrangling with his residual grief.

All too aware that this was his domain, not hers, and she was simply a guest here—and at the moment, an inconvenient one—Jen shut the fridge.

Ignoring the hunger pangs in her tummy, she leveled an honest glance at Matt. "If you want me to clear out while you do whatever it is you came in here to do, I'll return later."

It was the least she could do, after thrusting Emmett and Matt back into the throes of grief, at least temporarily.

He rocked back on his heels. "You haven't eaten dinner yet?"

Her stomach growled. Hoping he hadn't heard that, she waved away his concern. "I got caught up in what I was doing." *I was also hoping to avoid running into you until I felt better able to honor Emmett's request to keep his health issues secret.*

Jen peered at Matt, noting he had shaved.

And though the clean-cut look wouldn't last on him more than a few hours, it was nice at the moment. Made it easy to see how ruggedly handsome he was, even without the masculine stubble. Worse, it reminded her how much she still wanted to throw caution to the wind and make love with him again.

But adding to the emotional confusion simmering between them would be foolish. Jen had stopped being foolish years ago, because she knew no good ever came of it.

Aware that Matt was still studying her, an implacable expression in his intent, sky-blue eyes, she swallowed. "Surely you ate."

He leaned against the kitchen counter, arms folded in front of him. "The storm the other night knocked down some fence. A hundred or so cattle wandered out, so they had to be rounded up and moved to another pasture until the fence could be repaired."

So he hadn't just been avoiding her.

"Sounds...challenging," Jen remarked.

His expression didn't change. "All in a day's work."

Was making love with her all in a day's work, too? she wondered, then pushed the thought away. She had to stop thinking about Matt in romantic terms. Otherwise, she'd never get over their "fling."

Never be able to finish her work here.

Keep Emmett's secret.

Advance her career.

Keep her heart intact.

Matt might be able to handle a casual affair, but she couldn't.

Not without losing a part of herself along the way.

Some of the tension eased. Matt moved past her, brought out a casserole of leftover chicken enchiladas, and containers of rice and refried beans. Set it all on the counter. He gestured at the fridge, which was loaded with other choices—all prepared by Luz, for weekend consumption. "Help yourself."

"You sure?" Jen eyed what Matt had chosen. It looked awfully good, even cold. There was plenty.

"I think we can share a meal, even if we don't 'share' anything else," he said wryly.

Such as another kiss?

Or climaxes that were sweet, sensual and satisfying enough to rock her entire world.

Jen successfully fought back a flush. She'd been wondering how long before he brought that up. "Matt…"

"It's okay," he said softly, looking at her as if he needed comfort only she could give. "I understand." He tucked her hair behind her ear, let his gaze rove seductively over her face. "Just so you know, you can change your mind anytime. All you have to do is—"

Footsteps sounded in the hall.

Matt dropped his hand, stepped back, but Jen's heart continued to pound.

Emmett walked into the kitchen, clad in a robe, pajamas and sheepskin-lined slippers. He smiled when he saw her. With relief, she noted he seemed to have recovered fully from what had ailed him earlier.

"I'm glad you're still up, Jen," he said with a smile. "I want to talk to you about the West Texas Ranchers Association annual summer gala in Fort Worth. It's a week from Friday. I'd like you to go with Matt and me."

Jen noted that Matt looked as surprised by the invitation as she felt. "The three of us?" she asked.

"Sure." Emmett shrugged in bemusement. "Why not?"

Matt lifted a brow, his expression inscrutable once again. Nervously, Jen turned back to his dad. "Won't that look a little odd?" She knew it would feel so, given all she was suddenly hiding. Her secret tryst with Matt, for starters. Then there was Emmett's supposed illness, which he insisted she keep from Matt. She hated being put in the middle, and worried that the emotional fallout could cause a permanent rift between father and son.

Not to mention what it would mean for her and Matt...

Heavens, how had this turned into such a mess?

Oblivious to the unsettling nature of her thoughts, he shrugged again. "We're all friends. Unless you'd rather take a date, which would be fine, too." He flashed a generous smile. "Whatever you decide on that score, I still think you should go. A lot of very influential people will be there. Potential patrons. I want to introduce you around. Let everybody know what you're doing for us."

Dex's parents had often said the same thing to her, only their purpose had been garnering sympathy from their friends, and wanting everyone to know what they were doing for poor little underprivileged Jen. Who never should have had the greed to marry their son.

And that painful past experience, Jen thought miserably, was exactly why she shouldn't go.

Showing art in her gallery was one thing. She was in her comfort zone. Social gatherings like the ball would only remind her of her failed marriage, and the humiliation she had suffered at her in-laws' hands.

"Of course, you're going to need formal attire." Emmett continued as if Jen had already accepted his invitation. "So I called Jenna Lockhart Remington this evening and filled her in."

The world-renowned haute couture designer who designed all the Oscar dresses? Jen's flush of embarrassment deepened. "I appreciate it, Emmett, but the Lockhart salon is *way* out of my league, pricewise."

Even if the company's flagship boutique was located in Laramie, Texas—home to all the Lockhart sisters and their wildly successful offspring.

Emmett took some juice from the fridge and poured a glass. "You don't need to worry about that, honey. I'm paying for it."

Matt looked at Jen again, with that same steady patience in his eyes.

Forcing herself to breathe, she shook her head. "Thank you so much, Emmett. I appreciate the gesture, but I can't let you do that. That really would not look right." People would talk. Matt would...

Well, who cared what Matt would think?

She would, that's who!

Emmett smiled, waving off her protest. "It wouldn't look right for you *not* to show up in an expensive gown, since all the dresses the ladies are wearing this year are going to be donated to an auction that will benefit Children's Hospital."

"Oh," she said, ignoring Matt's glance.

"Anyway..." Emmett drank his juice and left the glass in the sink "...any time you want to show up tomorrow, they'll let you pick out a gown, and do a fitting."

Appreciating the chance to help Children's Hospital, in a way she couldn't afford to otherwise, Jen smiled at him. "Thank you."

"No problem," he boomed. "Well, I'm headed on to bed. Night, y'all."

"Good night," Jen and Matt echoed in unison.

Emmett strode off, seeming, to Jen's relief, to be in fine form once again. Had she been wrong to worry? All she knew for certain was that she wouldn't feel good about the situation until he had seen a doctor and been thoroughly checked out.

But that was going to take some persuading...

An awkward silence fell.

Matt continued to study her another long minute, then went back to plating his dinner.

"Well, aren't you going to say it?" Jen said. She knew what he was thinking.

He covered his food with a sheet of waxed paper, slid it into the microwave and hit the reheat button. "Say what?"

Jen served herself some food, as well. "That your father has a way of getting people to do what he wants them to."

Matt reached into the refrigerator and got out two Bohemia beers. He uncapped both, handed her one. "It's not like you could refuse."

Jen found a lime, quartered it and squeezed a section into her bottle. "You, either." She paused to savor the combination of fresh lime and Mexican beer. "Are you going to take a date?"

Still waiting on his dinner, Matt eyed her above the rim of his bottle. "Depends." He let his gaze drift over her. "Will you come as my date?"

Tingling everywhere he'd looked—and especially where he hadn't—Jen shrugged. It wasn't that cool in the kitchen, but her nipples were contracting beneath her tank top. "I can't do that."

His gaze drifted there, arousing another flood of sensations, before returning to her eyes. "Why not?" He turned to get his plate, set hers in the microwave and pushed the button again. "I don't care who knows I'm interested in you."

Jen busied herself getting out the silverware and napkins. "Well, I care," she told him stiffly. "Besides, we agreed—"

Matt caught her around the waist and shifted her against him. He felt warm and solid. And safe.

"*We* didn't agree to anything," he murmured, kissing her temple, then her cheek. "*You* said it couldn't happen again."

Yes, she had. Jen closed her eyes. Why, oh why, had she been such a fool? Passion this strong was a once-in-a-lifetime thing.

She could enjoy it without getting her heart broken, couldn't she? If she was smart.

Jen kept her eyes closed as he kissed his way down her neck. She jerked in a breath. "You didn't argue."

Matt cupped her chin in his hand.

Jen opened her eyes.

Looked into his.

His gaze was tender. And filled with a yearning as strong and sensual as her own. He ran a strand of her hair through his fingers, admitting softly, "Only because I didn't figure pushing you would get me where I wanted to go."

Actually, Jen thought, it kind of was. He was just kissing her lightly and she was already fantasizing about taking him into the shower again and soaping him down, then moving right back to his bed.

Matt continued, in all seriousness, "I promised myself this afternoon—and now I'm promising you—that I'll slow down." He paused to let his words sink in. "Give us time to get to know each other."

That was quite a promise. And one she hadn't expected. Jen inhaled a shaky breath, aware that she was closer than ever to falling for him. Completely.

Unfortunately, love and reason did not often go hand in hand.

Feeling she owed it to him to be honest about this much, she predicted, "It's not going to change anything in the long run." Although it was already changing something now, because if he kept this up, she wasn't going to be able to resist him for long.

Matt smiled and kissed her lightly on the lips. He took her hand and led her to the table, then returned to the dinging microwave to get her dinner. "You keep telling yourself that. I'm going to tell myself something else entirely."

JEN WAS STILL THINKING about what Matt had said the night before, when she accepted Emmett's offer to lend her a car, and drove to town early the next afternoon.

She knew Matt was a decent guy. He loved his dad, still grieved the loss of his mother—although he tried to hide that—and meant well in general. The problem was, he assumed Jen and he could keep it casual, keep it private, and continue sleeping together without their emotions getting in the way.

And while that might be true for him, it wasn't for her.

She already had developed a huge fascination for him, which prompted her to do foolish things she had never considered before. Such as allow herself to be distracted from work. Mix business with pleasure. And make herself vulnerable to a man who was so far socially and financially out of her league it wasn't funny.

She had learned the hard way that men with Matt's background did not trust the intentions of someone from a background like hers.

They might say they did, in the beginning, but money always got in the way in the end.

Jen didn't want to see that happen to her and Matt.

She wanted at the very least for them to get to know each other and form a solid friendship.

And she knew Matt wanted that, too.

Whether they would be lasting friends remained to be seen.

Aside from each losing a parent, they might find out they had little in common save sexual chemistry. And if that was the case, well, their fascination with each other would probably fade.

In the meantime, what she needed to do was spend as much time working and as little time alone with Matt as possible.

The first order of business was the photo printing shop in town.

She'd already scanned the pictures on to her computer, so it was a simple matter to get them printed the way she wanted. From there, she went to the Lockhart Boutique on Main Street.

The dress salon was busy. A young actress was getting fitted for an awards show scheduled for later in the summer. A bride and her attendants were trying to select bridesmaid dresses—not easy, when there were so many gorgeous gowns and styles to choose from. Another young woman was trying to pick out a gown for the West Texas Ranchers Association summer gala.

Learning Jen was there for the same reason, the striking brunette introduced herself. "So you're the artist Matt has been talking about."

Jen made a face. "Good or bad?"

She laughed, as if that was a silly question. "All good, of course." She extended her hand. "I'm Emily

McCabe-Reeves, owner of the Daybreak Café across the street."

Jen had heard of her, too. She turned around, checking out in the three-way mirror the turquoise gown she was trying on. "Luz told me that's the one place in town I've got to be sure to visit."

Emily stepped up to have a look at the grass-green gown she had on. "You should visit us, too. My husband, Dylan, and I have a ranch not too far from the Triple B. The Last Chance Ranch for troubled horses."

Jen had driven past it on the way into town. It was a very beautiful ranch. Together, they each selected another gown off the rack of possibilities hanging outside their dressing rooms. "A lot of kids and horses out there today," she observed.

"Ah, well, yes," Emily admitted proudly, reaching for a sequined number. "Dylan's a horse whisperer."

"And lady whisperer, as well," the saleswoman teased, coming in with another armload of dresses for them to try on. "Given the way he tamed our Emily!"

Emily grinned, making no effort to deny it. "He also supervises community service, and teaches kids how to rope and ride. Matt is there this morning, volunteering."

So Matt had a philanthropic side, as well, Jen mused. "I didn't know that."

Emily stepped into her changing room and kept talking through the wall. "Yeah, well, it's not the kind of thing those guys brag about. But the men around here have big hearts, let me tell you."

Jen was beginning to see that.

If Matt didn't possess a big heart, he wouldn't be such a good listener and so kind to those around him.

Jen stepped back out to the mirror to look at the gown she had just put on.

"I know that's only the third dress you've tried on," Emily exclaimed, appearing in a midnight-blue silk, "but it is dazzling."

Jen looked in the mirror, stunned.

The silver silk-chiffon gown covered one arm and shoulder, leaving the other bare, in a way that was outrageously sexy. The skirt fell fluidly to her ankles in tiny knife pleats that swirled delicately and simultaneously clung to her curves. Thick silver lace, studded with elaborate beading, edged the neckline, sleeve and hem. It was, in a word, absolutely movie-star gorgeous, and just standing there, she felt like Cinderella on her way to the ball.

Emily turned to the saleswoman assisting them. "I'll take this one." She motioned to her gown, which was also incredibly beautiful and flattering in a way that only a Lockhart creation was.

"No problem. I'll get our seamstress to check the fit and mark any small alterations necessary, then ring it up for you."

"And I'm going to take this one," Jen said, telling herself it was okay for her to be doing so, since the gown and the proceeds would ultimately be going to help Children's Hospital.

Her dress was also pinned. Shoes and jewelry that matched were added to their orders. Emily would pay for hers. Jen's would be rung up on Emmett's bill.

Silently reiterating to herself that she had no reason to feel ill at ease just because she couldn't pay for her clothing on her own, Jen slipped back into the dressing room to change.

Yet something—some latent feeling of despair—existed.

She had felt bought and paid for once, by Dex's family.

She didn't want to feel bought and paid for by the Briscoes, even if this was all going to charity immediately after the event. So she would have to figure out a way to make it up, add to the general goodwill in the universe on her own. Meantime, she'd suck it up and think about the good deed eventually going to be done, because Children's Hospital was a very worthy cause.

When Jen and Emily were dressed in street clothes once again, they met outside the dressing suite. "So, I know we just met, but want to grab a cup of coffee… maybe a piece of pie?" Emily asked.

Jen could use a friend in the area. And she loved Emily McCabe-Reeves's cheery nature. "I'd love to, thanks!"

TEN MINUTES LATER they were walking across Main Street toward the Daybreak Café. Although it was only three o'clock, there was a Closed sign on the door of the charming establishment.

"I only serve breakfast and lunch," Emily explained, unlocking the door and leading the way in. "That means I'm home for dinner with my husband just about every night."

Jen looked around the charming Southern diner with its leather booths, fresh flowers and long, old-fashioned counter. "Sounds ideal."

"There's a lot to like about Laramie County." Emily shut the door behind them, with a jingle, then paused and cocked her head.

A murmur of male voices sounded in the kitchen and Emily's eyes lit up. "Hmm." Looking happier than ever, she put down her handbag and headed that way, motioning for Jen to follow. "I think I know that voice!"

As they neared, Jen realized she knew one of the

voices, too. Entering the kitchen, she saw the two men standing there and watched her plans to stay as far away from Matt Briscoe as possible evaporate.

"The problem is," the tall cowboy with the golden-brown hair and eyes was saying as he cut large slices of berry pie, "we need more donors if we're going to have a successful auction…."

"Maybe Jen can help!" Emily said. She kissed him, then turned to introduce her husband, Dylan Reeves, adding, "Jen is the bronze artist Matt's dad hired."

Dylan extended his palm, as warm and welcoming as his wife. "Nice to meet you, Jen."

She shook his hand. "And you." Although obviously financially well-off, Emily and Dylan were completely accepting of her in a way her ex-in-laws had never been.

Actually, Jen thought, pretty much everyone she'd met in Laramie County was nice. Although she was sure there must be a few sour apples. There always were.

Dylan offered Jen her choice of pie. They all looked absolutely delicious, but after a short and difficult deliberation she chose the chocolate cream. "I'd like to say I'm not going to put you on the spot, but it's for such a good cause," Dylan said, handing her a plate. "We're trying to raise money for a boy's ranch here in Laramie County, on a par with the one we already support in Libertyville."

Emily put on a fresh pot of coffee. "Where Dylan spent time as a kid." She accepted the pecan pie her husband handed her and added a dollop of vanilla ice cream.

All four of them pulled up stools at the stainless-steel worktable in the center of the kitchen. "I can honestly say my time there saved me," Dylan confessed.

Matt settled in next to Jen. Dylan and Emily sat side

by side, too, a fact that almost made it feel as if they were on a double date.

"Anyway," Dylan continued, "to start a satellite program here is an expensive proposition. We need donors of goods we can sell, to pay for the construction of a bunkhouse and half a dozen more therapy horses, plus a resident counselor or two. Emily and I have already donated the land, so it's going to be adjacent to our property."

The project sounded really good. Jen knew from her own difficult childhood how important safe havens were.

Already on board, she asked, "What can I do to help?"

Emily smiled with the legendary McCabe generosity. "Whatever you want. You could donate a copy of an existing sculpture...."

"Something original would probably be better," Jen suggested.

Matt's shoulder brushed hers as he turned to her. "The Last Chance Ranch is known for the wild mustangs it rescues and turns into therapy horses."

Jen mulled over options while she savored a bite of pie. "I could sculpt a mustang, maybe emblazon it with the Last Chance logo, and then, of course, have it bronzed. You could auction the original for as much money as you could get, and then sell copies at a lesser price thereafter."

"That's an incredible idea!" Emily beamed.

Dylan nodded. "You'd be doing a lot of good."

"Why don't you come out to the ranch now?" Emily gathered up the plates and slid them into the dishwasher. "Have dinner with us." She began pouring coffee in take-out cups. "We can show you around and talk about it some more." Emily slapped Matt on the back, her enthusiasm unabated. "We need your input, so you come, too, Matt!"

Suddenly, the unexpected meeting felt like even more of a double date.

Chapter Nine

"If I didn't know better, I'd think something very special was going on between the two of you," Emily teased Matt and Jen several hours later, as the four of them got up to do the dishes.

Jen flushed. She'd been trying not to give away her own interest, by avoiding touching, talking to or looking directly at Matt at every turn. He had shown no such compunction.

In fact, he couldn't seem to stop gazing at her.

He'd sat next to her at dinner, the same way he had at the Daybreak Café in town. When she spoke, he listened as if she were delivering a keynote address at a conference he really, really wanted to attend. Despite her efforts to play it cool, Jen had soaked up everything Matt had said and done, too. Even his smallest gesture was now committed to memory.

Just as their lovemaking was.

"Pay no attention to her." Dylan swatted his wife playfully with a dish towel and swaggered over to assist her. "Emily sees romance everywhere since we hooked up."

She stopped loading the dishwasher and aimed a look at her husband. "You notice it, too. I know you do. So what's up?" She turned to Matt, since Jen hadn't responded. "Is there more to this story? Have you two been secretly dating or what?"

"Not dating," Jen rushed to answer. Secretly kissing and making love, on the other hand...

She stifled a groan. She had to stop thinking like this. Stop *fantasizing*.

Matt slid her a long look and an even slower, sexier smile. "I want to date her, but she won't say yes."

A grinning Emily turned toward Jen. "Why not?"

"Probably had in mind lassoing herself someone much more handsome," Dylan quipped.

Any more handsome, Jen thought, slanting Matt a look from beneath her lashes, and she'd perish from the sheer pleasure of it.

She cleared her throat and played along with Dylan's attempt to get her off the hook. "Actually, I go for the short, stocky, in-touch-with-their-feminine-side type."

Which they all knew was definitely not Matt.

"Hey, I know a thing or two about the softer side," he declared, chuckling.

Emily cut in. "Knowing how to seduce a woman is not the same as understanding her."

Matt had the first part down, all right. Jen was still reeling from their first and only bout of lovemaking.

What he didn't seem to want to learn about was falling in love. And who knew if that would ever happen....

"So does he or doesn't he know about the softer side?" Emily continued, still trying to figure out what, if anything, was going on.

Jen realized everyone was looking at her, waiting for her to comment. She kept her expression noncommittal, reminding herself she was just trying to get through the day. "I really couldn't say."

"A LITTLE HARSH ON ME, weren't you?" Matt drawled after the two of them had said good-night and walked out to the driveway, where their vehicles were parked side by side.

Had he really expected her to admit to everyone she had a crush on him—a bad one? As he had.

And if that didn't say everything about the differences between them...

Jen figured they might as well discuss this now, in a semipublic place, instead of the privacy of the ranch, where he could without too much difficulty convince her to let him have his way with her. She stopped mid-step and pivoted to face him. "And why do you think that was?"

With a hand at her waist, he guided her away from the heat still emanating from the concrete driveway, and into the shade of a nearby tree.

Having gotten her where he wanted her, he let her go, then rested his palm on a leafy branch just above her head. "I don't know."

As always, when she was this close to him and he was looking at her that way, her knees felt a little wobbly.

Jen backed up until her spine rested against the trunk. The bark was rough, so she folded her hands behind her to wedge a little distance between the abrasive surface and the skin bared by her tank top. "Live dangerously, cowboy. Take a wild guess."

"Hmm..." Matt rubbed his jaw and let his gaze drift over her above-the-knee floral cotton skirt, bare legs and bejeweled sandals, then move back to her lips. He offered another slow, sexy smile. "Maybe because I mentioned the thing about you refusing to date me?"

There he went again, getting her to say exactly what

was on her mind. "And kept looking at me all through dinner."

He shrugged, unapologetic. Still enjoying the view. "You were seated across from me."

She stared at him, holding his gaze and trying to outlast him. "You gave us away."

Which kept her from being as in charge of the situation, and especially her feelings, as she would have liked.

His brows lowered in annoyance. "So what?" Apparently, he wanted to shout it to the rooftops. Which was a typical male response. The hunter always wanted to show off his prize.

"So," she retorted, aware that he was making her feel all hot and bothered again, without half trying. Jen swallowed around the growing tightness in her throat. "I thought we agreed that no one was going to know about...you know..." She shifted restlessly against the trunk of the live oak.

Matt dropped his hand from the branch and came closer. "The fact I'm hot for you and you're hot for me?" he queried in a low, gruff voice that was so sexy her knees wobbled all the more.

At the confident way he was stalking her, it was all she could do not to groan out loud. "Matt..."

"Jen..."

Suddenly, the distance between them was way too small. "I know you don't care what people say about you."

"So?" He shifted even closer, planting a palm on either side of her.

"Well, I do." How was it she was actually enjoying the sensation of being trapped between him and the tree? Could it have anything to do with his incredibly hard, strong, masculine body? Or just that she liked having the responsibility for what happened taken away from her, just for a little while.

She regarded him speculatively. "I was labeled a gold digger once." Keeping her gaze firmly locked on his eyes, and away from his talented lips, she paused to let her words sink in. "It wasn't a fun experience." Fun was slipping into a shower and sudsing Matt down. Fun was tumbling into bed with Matt.

Something flickered in his eyes. Something hard. But when he reached out to touch her face reassuringly, and spoke again, his voice was calm and gentle. "No one is going to say that about you."

The arrogance of his assumption brought her out of fantasyland and right back into the not-so-pleasant present. "Maybe not in front of you…"

"Not at all," he stated vehemently.

Jen let her gaze fall to his throat. She only wished life was that simple, that it didn't matter what circumstances a person was born and raised in. "They said it about your father's second, third and fourth wives, didn't they?"

Matt shrugged, completely accepting of that. "It was true in those three cases."

She planted a hand on his chest and pushed him out of her way. "Well, people are likely to think it's true about me, too."

He caught her arm before she could rush past, and swung her around so she was facing him and his back was to the tree. "You're not exactly demanding a big diamond and rushing me into marriage." He let his hand slide from her biceps to her waist.

Jen could have easily thrust it away. Instead, for reasons she really did not want to examine, she let his palm stay where it was. Maybe now was the time to reassure him.

"Nor will I."

"I know you think you hide your emotions. You don't. Whatever you're thinking and feeling is clearly visible on your face."

She went still as her heart squeezed. "What is my expression telling you now?"

He eyed her closely. "That you want me to kiss you."

Jen drew a deep, bolstering breath, and then looked him in the face. "No, I don't," she fibbed.

He went still for one telling beat, then drew her all the way into his arms, fitting her torso to his. "Say that again in a minute," he murmured huskily, still leaning against the tree. The corners of his mouth lifted. "And I'll believe you."

MATT KNEW HE WASN'T playing fair as he threaded his fingers through Jen's silky hair, lowered his mouth to hers and kissed her long and deep. Trouble was, if he let her put them in the just-friends category, he sensed they'd never get out of it. And theirs was not an attraction he could let go unexplored, without regretting it for the rest of his life. Not when just looking at her turned his heart upside down. Not when holding her against him felt this right.

He'd never before wanted anyone the way he wanted Jen. Never wanted to feel this close. Not when she was making that soft, low sound in the back of her throat, the one that signaled approval and want and need, and conjured up an answering yearning deep inside him.

He slid one hand low on her spine, to the delectable small of her back, and the other to her neck. Her hands moved to his shoulders, gripping him hard and bringing him closer yet.

He liked the way she held him, liked the way she kissed. It didn't matter that they were nowhere near a bed and had nothing even close to privacy; he kept right on kissing her. Heady with desire, he took everything she had to give, giving her everything he had in return, until she was straining against him…and they were quite literally rocking each other's world.

Unfortunately, they were still standing in the Last Chance driveway.

In plain view of anyone who cared to look their way.

Reluctantly, Matt ended the kiss, lifted his head. Saw the sleepy look of desire and acquiescence in Jen's gorgeous eyes. Noticed she still didn't move far, just a fraction of an inch, and that her breathing was as fast and uneven as his own.

Satisfied—yet not—he continued to hold her gaze. Saw her wonder, contentment…and then confusion.

"The night's still young," he said, hoping to make things right, and have a chance to woo her. "We've still got time for a date." A movie. Line dancing. Even coffee or an ice cream?

Jen shook her head, the barriers around her heart snapping right back into place. "I have work to do, Matt. A ton of it, as a matter of fact."

Somehow, he wasn't surprised to see her reach for the familiar and probably oft-used excuse. "That can't wait till tomorrow?"

"Sorry, no."

And she meant it, Matt realized, just as her phone rang. Saved by the bell?

Whereas he was drowning in disappointment. Wondering what tact to try next. Because one way or another, he wanted her to admit what he already felt—that they had something here, something real, something worth pursuing. All he had to do was get her to coop-erate. Which she currently wasn't even close to doing. Yes, she'd kiss him. She'd even let him make love to her. But she wouldn't let him close.

Not in the way it counted.

Showing none of the frustration he felt, Jen averted her head, fumbled through her purse, for her smart phone, and answered the call.

"Cy, hi!" She listened intently, then tears sprang to her eyes. "Congratulations!" she said thickly. "I'm so glad everything went well...the baby's healthy... Yes, yes! I'd love to talk to Celia!" Walking off, Jen headed for the car she'd borrowed, phone to her ear.

Leaving Matt to head for his pickup truck.

They drove back to the ranch the same way they'd left it. Alone.

"YOU DON'T HAVE TO WORK seven days a week," Emmett told Jen the following morning. "You're entitled to take the weekend off."

She realized that.

She also knew that allowing herself time to think about anything but her work was not a viable option.

Not when she was as obsessed with Matt as she was. Wanting...the impossible. Wanting to be able to fall in love with him. For him to fall in love with her.

Wanting all the things Cy and Celia had—marriage, children, a life together—to be possible for her, too.

And not just with anyone.

With Matt.

Even when she knew, realistically, how unlikely any of that was, she still wanted it.

Which was why she should stop thinking so far ahead, and stick to what worked for her. Taking life day by day. Worrying about herself and how she reacted to things. And not what everyone else—Matt and Emmett included—did or did not do.

"I usually work Saturdays. Sometimes Sunday, too, when I'm feeling inspired."

Emmett looked at the paintings hanging on the wall next to the enlarged photos of Margarite and himself. He gestured broadly. "And all this inspires you."

Jen nodded. "When I look at Margarite's paintings, along with the photos of the two of you together, I get a sense of who she was. What a fairy-tale romance you had, and how much you and she loved each other."

And I am so envious.

Emmett grinned fondly, recollecting. "It's that apparent?"

"Oh, yes." Jen rose and led him to the inspiration wall she'd set up.

She went through each photo, explaining the body language, pointing out he and his late wife always seemed to be touching each other, or standing with mirrored postures, or smiling and looking into each other's eyes.

Belatedly, Jen realized the same could be said of her and Matt, whenever they were near each other. Lest Emmett realize the same thing, she changed the subject back to Margarite's beautiful landscapes. "Did she ever show her paintings? Even informally?"

"No. She was never ready for that."

"That's such a shame. They're so beautiful."

"I think so, too," Emmett said proudly.

"Have you ever considered loaning her work to a

museum—the Amon Carter or the Sid Richardson, perhaps—that specializes in Western art?"

Emmett hesitated, a peculiar look on his face.

Jen sensed he was about to say something, but then footsteps sounded in the hall, and Matt walked in.

She hadn't seen or talked to him since they had kissed last night, and for a moment Jen was captivated. He was dressed in the usual twill work shirt and faded jeans, a straw cowboy hat perfect for the summer heat slanted over his brow. His handsome face was flushed and his blue eyes alert. He hadn't shaved, and the stubble on his jaw gave him a rakish look.

He seemed equally mesmerized by the sight of her.

Too late, Jen realized Emmett was standing there, taking it all in.

"Body language, hmm?" he murmured.

Matt shot him a puzzled glance. Before he could comment, he noticed the paintings and photographs displayed on the new inspiration wall.

Surprise turned to shock. Obviously taken aback by the emotional impact, he turned his face away.

Jen felt a momentary flash of guilt.

She probably should have warned both men, so they would have had a chance to be prepared.

Although Emmett seemed to be taking it a little better, for once.

Nodding a wordless acknowledgment to Jen, Matt turned to his father and continued in a brisk, businesslike tone. "I just got word that a ranch on the Texas-Oklahoma border is putting three hundred head of black Angus up for sale. I put in a bid. They're ours if we want them. But I want to look them over personally before I finalize the deal."

Jen wasn't surprised by that, given that Matt needed to personally control everything in his orbit.

Emmett nodded. "When will you be back?"

He shrugged. "A couple days. Maybe longer."

Jen tried not to be disappointed. Even though she'd done her darnedest to avoid him since they had last kissed…

"Depends on what I find." Matt continued conversing with his dad as if she wasn't even in the room.

Which was good, she thought, sitting down at the drafting table, resuming her sketching. Since she didn't need to be part of what was clearly a ranch—and family—discussion. And she was not—and would never be—part of the Briscoe clan.

"SORRY ABOUT THAT," Emmett said, after Matt had left. He strolled toward Jen, his gait slightly off balance. One of his hands was trembling, too.

The troubling symptoms were back. Jen could not ignore them. "Are you sure you don't want to see a doctor?" she asked quietly.

Stubborn as ever, Emmett sank into a chair and clasped his hands together, momentarily quelling the involuntary movement. "What I want is to get the first sculpture commemorating my love for Margarite done as soon as possible."

And then what? Jen wondered, torn between dueling loyalties. What would happen if Matt found out she had known about his father's infirmity and said nothing to warn him? When Matt, she was sure, was probably the only person who could talk sense into his dad. Would she and Matt even remain friends if that happened?

"And," Emmett added in a low, warning tone, "for you to keep this confidence."

Jen sighed. "You've put me in a difficult place."

He frowned. "Then I apologize. It does not, however, change my decision. There is no way I am putting Matt through a repeat of what he has already been through with his mother."

Jen bit her lip. "Even if it is Parkinson's disease, there are medicines that can help."

Emmett waved off the suggestion. "All they do is delay the inevitable. And sometimes they don't even do that. I don't want to be trapped in a body that no longer works. I don't want to be remembered as an invalid. When people remember me, I want them to think about this." He pointed to a photo of himself in his younger days. "I want their memories of me to be happy. Not tainted by illness, decline and despair."

That ego again.

Jen let out another breath.

Emmett stood, continuing his emotional declaration. "And I don't care if anybody understands that or approves or not. It's what I want. And what I intend to have. Because I've earned it."

Jen supposed he had. She rose to her feet, too. Gently touched his arm. "At least promise me you won't let this go unchecked."

Emmett leaned toward her as he headed for the door, allowing her to assist him. "I'll think about it. In the meantime, I'm leaving the ranch for a few days, too."

To get medical help on the sly, Jen could only hope.

"Neither Luz nor Scully work on the weekends, so you'll be on your own as far as meals and anything else goes."

Jen smiled. "Not to worry. I can handle being on my own." In fact, she kind of preferred it that way.

It was Matt—and her growing feelings for him—that she couldn't handle.

SEVEN HOURS LATER, Matt and the ranch crew boss faced off. "You don't need to be here for the roundup, loading and transfer back to the Triple B," Punchy said with the unstinting directness for which the veteran cowpuncher was famed.

Matt hesitated. He'd never slacked off before, but his mind wasn't on his work. He had a feeling the crew boss and all the hands knew it.

"I realize you and your dad have a guest back at the ranch. It's okay if you want to be there," Punchy continued.

Except his dad had gone to Fort Worth, on unspecified business. Again. Matt grimaced.

"The boys and I can handle the chore just fine on our own," Punchy continued with a provoking grin. "Heck, who knows? It might even go faster without you. You being so unusually distracted and all."

Matt chuckled, not at all surprised by the facetiously delivered advice. Punchy never danced around the edges of any subject for fear of how his words would be received. "Trying to get rid of me?" Matt asked wryly.

Punchy wiped the sweat from his brow, then sobered and said, more seriously, "I'm trying to get you to cut yourself a break. You've done what needed to be done here. You closed the deal. Maybe it's time you turned your attention to the home front."

Maybe so. Matt knew the cowboys would likely be gone another day. Maybe even two or three. That was a long time for everyone to be away from the ranch,

save the hired hand he'd left at the Triple B. "All right."
Matt reluctantly relinquished control of the situation.
"But you call me if anything comes up," he stipulated
firmly, "and I'll head right back."

Punchy nodded. "Sure thing, boss."

Only problem was, Matt noted in chagrin when he
finally got back to the Triple B close to midnight on
Saturday, the BMW Jen had been driving was not in
the driveway. The house was dark.

Telling himself he wasn't all that disappointed, or
worried, either, he walked through the air-conditioned
house, switching on a light here and there as he went.
Because he needed to figure out what was going on, he
checked the obvious places—the front hall, his dad's
desk, his own, and finally, the kitchen—for some sort
of note as to where she'd gone.

Nothing.

Wondering if she had decided to go back to Houston, to see Cy and Celia's new baby, he headed upstairs
for his bedroom, then decided to check the studio first.
Might be a clue there.

Unfortunately, it was as dark and quiet as the rest of
the house. He walked in, hit the lights and stopped short.

Jen had been busy.

An easel was set up, as well as a workstation for the
actual sculpting. But it was the artwork on the walls he
had avoided earlier that really captured his attention.

Glad for the solitude, and the time and privacy to
reflect, he moved closer.

"YOU'RE BACK," JEN murmured, half an hour later.

Matt turned to face her. He still hadn't shaved. His
curly black hair was as rumpled, his face as tired look-

ing as the rest of him. And yet she was so very glad to see him.

"Surprised, hmm?" he asked.

About a lot of things, Jen realized. Including the way she felt when she'd seen his pickup parked in front of the ranch house. Like maybe tonight wasn't going to be as lonely and depressing as she had expected, after all.

She moved closer, hands in the pockets of her khaki shorts. "Were you looking for me?"

Matt continued studying the life-size photographs displayed on the walls. Wordlessly, he nodded, but offered nothing more that would allow her to read his mind.

Jen sauntered closer, breathing in the masculine scent of him. "Is having all the photos and paintings in here hard for you?"

He gave an offhand shrug. "It's your studio."

"It's your home." Jen paused, not sure what was going on with him. She could see that he was feeling something he wasn't necessarily inclined to share. "I'm not saying I don't need them up to do the sculpture, because I do. I have to look at them constantly while I work. But I can do that back at my studio in Austin."

Matt's eyes darkened. "That's not what my dad wants."

This once, what Emmett preferred would have to take a backseat to the needs of his only son. "He wanted to be in on the work in progress," Jen corrected. "And he thought it would be easier if I was here on the ranch. Only now *he's* not here."

"And instead, I am."

Jen paused, trying not to read too much into Matt's sudden appearance. She turned her attention to the photograph of him and his mother, the one he had been studying so reverently when she'd walked in. "You really like that picture, don't you?" It captured the two of them riding horses with Matt about twelve years old.

A wry smile curved his lips. "It brings back a lot of memories."

Jen moved on to the next photo—of a slightly older Matt, again on horseback with his mom. "Did you two go riding a lot?"

A shadow crossed his face. "Not as much as I would have if anyone had told me the truth about what was going on with her." He shook his head, adding sadly, "She'd been diagnosed for about a year when this photo was taken."

"And you had no idea."

"None." Bitterness edged his tone. "And that really sucks, because had I known that our time to do things like that was limited, I would never have turned down her requests."

Jen understood the mixture of grief and guilt. She had struggled with the same. "How often was that?" she prodded, sensing Matt needed to unburden himself to someone.

He grimaced and shoved a hand through his hair. "It's hard to remember clearly. At the time I didn't keep track, but I'm pretty certain I turned her down at least once for every time she asked me to go with her. Maybe more."

This, Jen sensed, wasn't all Matt's fault. "Your mom knew she was sick, Matt. She could have forced the issue."

"She wasn't like that," he replied, still brooding over the loss. "All she wanted was for me to be happy. And sometimes, as much as she hated it, that meant me playing a video game, or watching something on TV or going somewhere with my friends, instead of hanging out with her."

Jen reached out and touched Matt's hand. "Even so… you were a kid. I'm sure she understood."

Matt curled his fingers around hers. "I should have been told the truth," he insisted with remorse.

Just as he should be told the truth about his dad, now. Jen pushed her guilt away. It wasn't her job to tell him what was going on with Emmett, or get in the middle of this.

She needed to stay out of it, while still doing everything she could to be the understanding friend Matt needed right now.

"I'm sorry," Jen said. She turned and looked into his eyes. "Sorry this brought it all back." She squeezed his hand, comforting him as best she knew how. "I wish there was something I could do."

Matt thought a moment. "Actually, Jen, there is."

Chapter Ten

"What do you think?" Matt asked Jen several hours later.

She admired the Texas landscape now hanging in the foyer of the ranch house. It depicted the end of a beautiful spring day, with the sun setting in a pink-streaked sky. Rough-and-tumble cowboys of all ages were gathered around a chuck wagon and a nearby campfire. In the distance fields of bluebonnets, cattle and horses stretched as far as the eye could see. "I think it's perfect." She turned to Matt. "Looking at it reminds me of everything I love about Texas in general and this ranch in particular." *And being here with you.*

Something about this ranch—something about spending time with Matt—made her feel that all things were possible. Jen didn't want that feeling to disappear.

He put the hammer back in the toolbox and shut the lid. Folded the soft cotton quilt that had protected his mother's painting, and set it on top. "I don't know why Dad and I ever decided to put these away in the first place," he admitted quietly.

Jen thought she knew. "It might have had something to do with wife number two or three or four."

Matt reflected in silence. "That's true. It was when Dad started dating again, almost immediately after

Mom died, that her belongings were packed up and put away."

Jen stroked Matt's hand. "Well, they're back now."

He grinned and clasped her fingers in his. "Thanks to you." He lifted her hand to his lips and kissed her knuckles.

A thrill slid through her, and she swallowed. "What do you think your dad is going to say?"

Matt shrugged and let her go. "Given how much he's been missing my mom lately, I imagine he'll be as happy as I am to see them."

Matt carried the toolbox to the mudroom and set it on the shelf. Returning to the kitchen, he glanced at the clock on the microwave. "Three in the morning!"

Jen couldn't believe it, either. She should be exhausted, but wasn't. "I guess time got away from us."

He brushed a strand of hair from her cheek. "I didn't mean to keep you up half the night."

"I enjoyed it."

Matt cocked his head, studying her for a long moment. Suddenly, Jen felt as if they were at the end of a date, instead of just an evening spent together accidentally. If they didn't part company now, she knew there would be consequences. The kind that could break her heart.

"Well…" She pushed aside her awkwardness, stood on tiptoe and brushed his cheek with a casual, but dismissive kiss. "Good night."

Matt flashed her a slow, sexy smile. He stepped into her and looked at her with those brilliant blue eyes. Rooted to the spot, she released a shuddering breath.

"Let's try that again." He fitted her against him.

"Matt…" Jen warned softly, aware how close she

was to forgetting to be rational, and falling head over heels in love with him.

"Jen…" he said just as quietly, kissing one side of her mouth, then the other.

She drew another halting breath. *I want you so much.*

Matt cupped her face in his hands and then kissed her with all the pent-up emotion of the evening. Sweetly and evocatively, again and again, the tender intensity of the embrace breaking down her resistance and speaking to the woman inside her.

She knew they were going to make love. If not tonight, then sometime. Because once had not been enough.

Would never be enough.

And if that was the case, there was only one way to keep from getting hurt. Accept the inevitable, but *on her terms.*

Jen broke off the kiss and buried her face in the warm, solid curve of his neck. Beneath her cheek, she felt the swift throb of his pulse, the scruffiness of his jaw, the warmth of his skin. Lower still, heat…and hardness.

He stroked a hand through her hair, the sheer patience and understanding of the move sending another thrill shooting through her.

Knowing he thought this was over, she lifted her head, gazed into his eyes, and suggested in a husky voice, "How about my bed this time?"

MATT DID NOT HAVE TO BE asked twice.

And although this was not what he had planned, he grinned in pleasure and cupped his hands beneath her hips, lifting her against him so her legs were straddling his waist. Laughing, she kissed his cheek and clasped his shoulders. Exhilarated, he carried her up the stairs, not stopping until they had reached her bed.

Ever so gently, he set her down in the moonlight pouring in through the windows, switched on the bedside lamp and immediately felt a change. From merely wanting her to something more. Something life changing for both of them.

Aware that he needed her more than he had ever needed a woman in his life, Matt gazed into her eyes and pulled her against him. Felt her immediately sink into their shared kiss with a soft sigh. Determined not to let it get out of control or go by too fast, the way it had the first time they'd made love, he slid his hands down her sides, past her breasts, to her waist. He dropped openmouthed kisses on her throat, the sensitive place behind her ear. Satisfaction roared through him when he felt her quiver in response. "You feel so good."

Jen kissed his jaw, sounding a little strangled as she dug her fingers into his pecs. "Just. Don't. Stop."

He chuckled, taking that as a very good sign. Still kissing her, determined to give her all the pleasure she deserved, he backed her playfully to the wall. With a soft sigh of acquiescence, she wrapped her arms around him, tugged his shirt free of his jeans and ran her palms up his back. Desire shot through him. The look in her eyes mirrored exactly what he felt.

Loving the way she responded to him, the way she gave back, he pushed her tank top above her breasts, reached around her to unfasten her bra, and then divested her of both. Her eyes widened in excitement and she gasped as he palmed the soft globes. Her nipples pebbled and her body reacted with tremors, she was so sensitive to his touch.

Taking that, too, as an excellent sign, he moved his

mouth to her breasts, nibbling and suckling, making sure there was nothing he missed. She arched up, pulling him to her.

"Now, Matt," she whispered.

Obliging, he shifted upward to kiss her again, reveling in the womanly feel of her. She rocked against him, her hands sliding over his back, his waist, reaching for his belt, and farther south.

"So impatient," he murmured.

She wriggled her fingers beneath his shorts to cup him, while shooting him a saucy look. "You have no idea...."

Her cheeks were bright with color. Loving seeing her like this, so reckless and open to everything, Matt let her undress him. Then, needing her naked, too, he tugged off her jeans and panties, and spread her legs wide, making room for his hard sex. Her breath caught when he stroked her, finding her center and the velvety wet heat. She moaned and melted into his body, her tongue tangling with his until he was as lost in the kiss as she was. Then desire drove him to his knees. Jen made another sound that was soft and womanly and...hungry. As ravenous as he. Touching and stroking, kissing and caressing, he figured out the when and the where and the how, building her orgasm, making her his, until she shattered in his arms.

Her legs collapsed. He rose, pulling her against his chest, his own body demanding release.

JEN HAD LET MATT MAKE the first moves.

Now it was her turn.

She burrowed in, pressing her face against his neck. "My turn to be in charge...." she teased.

Her body still quivering with reaction, she took his

hand and led him toward the bed. Accepting the condom he pulled from the pocket of his jeans, she set it
aside for the moment.

"We'll get there," she promised, loving the testosterone oozing from his pores.

Right now she wanted the same free rein he had
just enjoyed, and Matt, bless his heart, willingly gave
it to her.

Which was good, because his body was hard and
hot all over, and she wanted him. Wanted to take him
to heaven as surely as he had taken her.

Loving the unsteady way he was breathing, and the
hot, dangerously aroused look in his eyes, Jen palmed
his pecs and flat, sexy abs.

Leaning in to tease him with her tongue, she followed the arrow of hair all the way down the goody
trail, laughing softly as he groaned. His muscles flexed.
Pleased, she instigated another soft, sensual kiss and
another dozen caresses. Enjoying the mouthwatering
view of him, she thoroughly explored every impres-
sive male inch.

Until at last he could stand it no more, and caught
her by the arms, drawing her upward. Ripping open
the condom packet, and watching as she rolled it on.

He paused a moment to look his fill. The next instant he was sitting against the headboard and she was
astride him. With one hand moving delectably between
them, the other gripping her bottom, he kissed her pas-
sionately and pushed inside her.

The simultaneous possession of mouth and body sent
her rocketing right off the edge. Jen exploded in white
heat. Matt was right behind her, his kiss hard and fierce.
He made a low, rough, guttural sound, his body pulsing and thrusting within her, again and again, until she

didn't know where she ended and he began. Only that she needed this. Needed him. Needed more.

"Matt," she whispered, still shuddering with the impact of her climax. "Oh, Matt. You make me feel so good."

So good, I want you again. So good, in fact, I think I could be falling in love.

MATT HAD NEVER BEEN a slouch. He was, in fact, pretty damn good at anything he set his mind to doing.

So Jen's compliment came as no surprise. What was a shock was how much more he wanted from her than a heartfelt acclaim of his physical prowess.

It wasn't as if they were looking for anything complicated, permanent or even temporary.

Jen was the kind of woman who took everything at face value and lived one day at a time, accepting whatever limitations life handed her with grace and goodwill. For her, nothing was personal. It just was what it was. End of story.

Matt sighed.

Whereas he couldn't seem to live any way but long term.

And that was a problem. A big one.

He wanted to be able to control the situation. Contain his feelings for her. Manage her feelings for him.

That wasn't going to be possible. Which meant one of them could end up getting hurt. Maybe both of them.

Matt didn't want that, either.

Jen drew back and rested her palms on his shoulders. "You regret this," she surmised quietly, still searching his face.

"No." Matt shook his head. What he regretted was

not setting boundaries. He drew her close once again. "I'll never regret making love with you, Jen."

And to show her how much he wanted her—and always would—he shifted, drew her beneath him and made love to her all over again.

Jen didn't intend to spend the night wrapped in Matt's arms any more than she intended to go upstairs to his bedroom with him, get more condoms…and make love with him over and over again.

First in his shower and later in his bed.

But she did. After that, it was all too easy to stay cuddled against him for just a few more minutes. Even easier to wake in his embrace—to what sounded like a convoy of big trucks rumbling up the driveway.

"What the…" Matt lifted his head. Rubbing the sleep from his eyes, he leaped from the bed, looked out the window and swore.

Jen struggled to untangle herself from the bedcovers. "What's going on?"

Grim-faced, he reached for his jeans. "I'm about to find out." Looking angrier than she had ever seen him, he bolted from the bedroom, shirt and boots in hand.

Feeling less than calm herself, she ran a brush through her hair and dressed, too.

By the time she got outside, the argument between Matt and the foreman from Dallas Limestone & Granite—a big burly guy, the same height as Matt—was in full force.

"The contract is iron-clad."

Legs braced apart, hands on his waist, Matt stood his ground. "Yeah, well, I don't know anything about it."

The man grimaced. "Then talk to your father. He's the one who negotiated the deal and signed it."

Emmett had done this?

Jen could only wonder why.

"I plan on talking to him," Matt returned tightly. "But until then, get your trucks and all this equipment off Triple B Ranch."

"Where are we supposed to park it?" the foreman asked.

Matt glared, his expression more deadly than any shotgun. "Not. My. Problem."

Looking as if he wanted to punch something, too, the man threatened darkly, "You're going to hear from my boss about this."

Matt inclined his head. "I expect I will," he drawled.

Reluctantly, the foreman waved the trucks toward the highway.

Slowly, they began backing up.

Matt stood on the porch, satisfied that a calamity had been averted—at least temporarily—but still fuming.

It was a warm morning. Nevertheless, the stress had Jen shivering. "Anything you want me to do?" she asked, pacing nervously at his side.

"Yeah." Matt continued watching the departure. "Get on the phone. See if you can locate my dad."

Glad that he trusted her to be more than just a by-stander, Jen slipped inside the ranch house. Dutifully, she tried every number for Emmett she had—cell, office, Fort Worth hotel. Nothing.

Defeated, she returned to Matt's side.

He was still standing where she'd left him, jaw set, hands braced on his hips, watching stoically as the last of the trucks bearing heavy equipment backed onto the highway.

"Matt?"

He turned and stared at her for a long moment, his emotions in turmoil, his expression haunted.

Not sure what to do to comfort him, she stayed right where she was and softly brought him up to speed. "I couldn't find your dad, but I left messages everywhere. I stated what happened and asked him to call you immediately."

His broad shoulders tensing all the more, Matt exhaled roughly. A string of swearwords followed as he shoved his fingers through his hair. "I cannot believe my dad is doing this again!"

"Doing what?" Jen asked, wishing something would make sense. All she knew for certain was that if Matt was upset, she was upset.

Eyes dark, he took her elbow and strode toward his pickup. "Come with me," he said gruffly. "And I'll show you."

Chapter Eleven

Ten minutes later, Jen got out of the truck and simply stared, unable to believe her eyes. Some twenty feet away from the pasture fence was what looked like an enormous pit, as big as a college football stadium. "How deep is it?" she asked Matt in shock.

He opened the gate and allowed her to walk through. "Approximately eighty feet—so far."

She shook her head, sympathizing with his dismay. "I had no idea this was here."

The corners of his lips inched downward. His sunglasses hid his eyes. "Most outsiders don't. You can see it from the air, of course, but the pit itself is well hidden in the Triple B's fifty thousand acres."

They walked through tall grass toward the edge of the crater. It was even more imposing up close.

"The entire ranch is sitting on limestone."

Jen turned to look at Matt, and he wrapped his arm about her waist.

"My great-grandfather discovered it, and he harvested it to build the original ranch house, which is now the bunkhouse. My dad continued the tradition when he built the house we live in now for my mother."

Jen leaned into Matt's strong, virile embrace, luxuriating in the welcome heat of him and the hard muscles of his body. Beneath her hand, the beat of his heart was as strong and steady as the rest of him. "When did you start selling it?"

He let out a breath. "My dad used it to pay for his divorces." Matt was quiet for a moment. "It made sense at the time. Dad's an extremely chivalrous man at heart, and he felt responsible for the marriages not working."

Jen understood that. Matt was just like his father in that respect.

"Try as he might, there was just no way Dad was going to love any other woman the way he loved my mom. Although he thought differently each time he married." Matt's mouth tightened. "Anyway, he offered each wife a respectable settlement, and harvesting the limestone paid for all three divorces."

Jen knew how hard it was when the family you loved let you down. Searching for a way to comfort Matt, she murmured, "Well, at least he didn't let any property go."

Deliberately, Matt took off his sunglasses and hooked them in the open collar of his shirt. He paused, his expression calm, but just behind it she could sense his anger. "We have a huge pit in the middle of the ranch."

"Yeah, well," Jen really didn't know what to say about that. The bright rays of the sun slanted over them, bathing them in the shimmering brilliance of the Texas summer. "Kind of your own little Grand Canyon?" she joked.

Her attempt at humor failed.

Matt paced the perimeter. His handsome face was lined with the growth of two days' beard. Exhaustion rimmed his eyes. Thanks to the lovemaking they'd indulged in, neither of them had had enough sleep.

He shook his head, his worry evident. "Dad told me he was done with this."

She shoved her hands into the pockets of her jeans and rocked back on the heels of her boots. "Maybe he is."

Matt shook his head. "Those trucks and crews this morning said otherwise."

"You really think he signed a contract with Dallas Limestone & Granite?"

"I do." Matt paused and swallowed hard. "I just don't know why." Pushing back the brim of his hat, he turned to look at her. "We don't need the money—not even for the work he's commissioned from you. He carries a healthy balance in his checking account, and the ranch is firmly in the black." Matt paced some more. "There must be a reason."

"I'm sure he'll tell you what it is when you talk with him," she stated, doing her best to keep her tone light and reassuring.

Matt slid her an inscrutable glance. "He didn't tell me about the crews."

A hot, dry breeze wafted over them. "Maybe he didn't have time."

Matt let out a rough, ragged breath, took off his hat and swept his fingers through his hair. "Or maybe he was just avoiding it because he knew I wouldn't approve."

Or because if Emmett told you, you might figure out that something else was going on—like the fact that he was sick—and interfere with his plans to run off when the time came.

Jen swallowed. "That, too."

Another silence fell. Unable to bear his constant scrutiny, she moved away.

Why had Emmett put her in such an untenable situation?

Why couldn't she figure out what to do that wouldn't betray either Matt or Emmett?

And most of all, why was she thinking that any of this was her problem, anyway?

When she had nothing to do with any of it, and certainly no control over anything either man did. Nor did she want control.

It was enough just trying to live her own life, on her own terms.

Matt looked at her and asked in a quiet tone, "I know you haven't known my dad all that long, but…does he seem okay to you?"

Guilt flooded her. "What do you mean?" she asked nervously.

Matt shrugged, his own worry evident. "In the conversations you've had with him, is he making sense?"

Well, that was a matter of opinion, Jen thought, recalling Emmett's decision not to go see a doctor about the mysterious neurological symptoms he had been having. But that wasn't what Matt was asking. Trying to answer him as honestly as possible, she said, "He seems very much in command of his faculties."

Matt muttered, "If he were in command of his senses, he wouldn't be doing this. Not without a damn good reason, anyway!" His phone chimed. He pulled it out of his pocket and looked at it.

The scowl was back on Matt's ruggedly handsome face. "That was a text from Dad. He's back at the ranch house." He extended a hand to Jen, making them a team once again. "Let's go."

MATT WASN'T SURPRISED to see his dad braced as if for battle the moment he and Jen walked in the door.

His movements stiff, Emmett turned away from the

fireplace mantel and the picture of Margarite he had been studying. His back to the hearth, he snapped, "You should not have turned the crews away."

Matt strode closer, fighting to control his own temper. His dad had been acting peculiarly for months now, shutting him out more than letting him in, and now this?

Aware Jen was busy shrinking into the background, Matt searched his dad's eyes and found nothing except more evasion. "So it's true?" He resisted the urge to punch something. Anything. "You're really going to do this? Again?"

Emmett's expression hardened. "Demand for quality limestone is up."

As if that justified it! "There's a crater the size of a football field in the middle of the ranch, Dad."

Out of the corner of his eye, Matt saw Jen start to slip away. He caught her wrist and drew her back—not sure why he needed her there, just knowing that he did.

"When they finish this time, we'll fill it with water and stock it with fish," Emmett promised.

Would that change anything? "If we want to go boating or fishing, we can go to Lake Laramie," Matt countered.

But Emmett didn't want to do that, any more than he wanted to tell anyone what was going on with him. "I know you don't agree with what I've done," he said with a weariness that seemed soul deep.

Matt scoffed. "You're damn right, I don't!"

"But the decision has been made, the contracts signed, and there's no reversing it."

The question was why. If not a woman, then what? "Is there something you're not telling me?" Matt asked.

Emmett ignored the question. "It's my money. My land. I can do what I want with it. When you inherit it, son, you can do that in turn. Now, if you two will excuse me, I've got to call the limestone company and see what I can do to smooth things over." His expression grim, he strode off.

Matt turned to Jen. She looked pale and uncomfortable, and he could hardly blame her. "I'm sorry you had to hear that," he said.

She shrugged. Now that the quarreling had stopped, she seemed a lot more tolerant of Emmett's bullheadedness. "It's not that bad. It's just a quarry, Matt. You still have plenty of land. Maybe it's a good thing your dad is building up some cash reserves."

Her attempt to reassure him made Matt wonder. "Has my dad been talking to you about any of this?" He knew Emmett and Jen had spent a fair amount of time together and seemed to be able to talk rather intimately.

Jen looked taken aback by the question. She turned and headed through the hall toward the kitchen. "I was as surprised as you were this morning when the trucks drove up."

Matt knew that was true.

Yet...

He followed her, studying her closely. "If you thought there was something I needed to know, you would tell me, wouldn't you?"

Jen went completely still and for a moment, he thought she wasn't going to answer. Then she opened the fridge and got out a carton of eggs and a package of bacon. She set both on the counter, then added butter, jam and bread. "You know my father was a binge drinker."

Matt nodded, not sure what that had to do with this.

Jen layered bacon in a skillet and set it on the stove. "Alcoholism is a family disease." She turned the flame to medium, then went back to the fridge to get out the orange juice. "It doesn't just affect the drinker, it affects everyone."

Matt leaned against the counter, listening intently.

"And when I was younger, I did what most families in that situation do. I tried to protect my dad by looking the other way, when I could tell trouble was brewing that would lead to a binge. Or I'd cover for him and try to protect him that way."

Figuring he should help, too, Matt began making coffee. "When all you were doing was enabling."

"Right." With the ease of someone who had been cooking a long time, Jen set four slices of bread in the toaster, and went back to turn the bacon.

"Later, I realized keeping my dad's secrets was not a good thing for me to be doing."

Matt could see that.

"And ever since, I've tried to live my own life...and worry about me. I made the conscious decision to let other people make their own decisions and live with the consequences of those decisions, without me getting involved or trying to somehow control the outcome."

Hence her one day at a time attitude.

Her refusal to try and control anything was, in essence, her way of trying to save herself.

The aroma of brewing coffee mingled with that of the cooking bacon. "You think when it comes to my dad and his financial decisions that I'm interfering where I have no business doing so?"

Jen poured two glasses of juice, handed one to Matt. "I think you're worried. I think you've communicated that to your dad, and he understands it."

"But it's not going to change anything."

Jen tilted her head. "It doesn't look like it." Sighing, she sipped her drink.

Disappointment washed over Matt. "So you think I should just stand by and let my dad do what he's going to do? And not even try to talk sense into him?" he asked skeptically.

"Truthfully?" Turning, Jen removed the bacon and broke four eggs into the pan. "I don't think there is anything else you *can* do."

"I THOUGHT I'D FIND you here."

Jen looked up from her worktable to see Matt's father walking in. Emmett seemed to have recovered from the scene that morning, whereas she was still struggling with her dual loyalties.

More than anything, she wanted to be able to confide in Matt. Not telling him everything she knew had wedged a distance between the two of them that she didn't want.

Yet what choice did she have? Emmett was her client and she his trusted confidante. Matt was her lover and her friend.

Both needed and wanted to keep her in those particular roles.

And much as she hated the difficult spot she found herself in, Jen did not want to lose the closeness she had found with either man. Emmett filled a paternal role that had been empty a long time. Matt meant something to her, too. Maybe, under the circumstances, too much.

Not that it mattered. She would stay neutral. Retain good, amenable and hopefully fulfilling relationships with both.

She smiled at Emmett. "It's definitely my favorite place on the ranch. The light here is spectacular."

"You're already sculpting."

Jen showed him the wire armatures for the two horses, the riders depicting Emmett and Margarite, as well as the base the sculpture would eventually be mounted on. She explained how each would take shape. "Once the armatures, or frames, are set, I frost the forms with wet clay, to further define the basic shapes. When that's completed I use sculpting tools and gradually add the detail of the faces and bodies and so on." She demonstrated as she worked.

Emmett shook his head in admiration. "It's going more quickly than I had imagined."

Jen sighed, a little overwhelmed by the enormity of the task she had signed on for. She wasn't used to promising so much of her future to any one client or exhibit. But there was no doubt it would be good for her career. "There's still so much to do. Molds to be made and taken to the foundry."

Emmett eased into a chair. Today, Jen noted, was a good day. Although still moving a little stiffly at times, he didn't seem to be trembling.

"The point is, I like what I've seen so far," Emmett continued. "And I like having Margarite's paintings all over the house, too." He glanced at Jen fondly. "I don't know how you talked my son into that."

"Actually, it was Matt's idea." Jen continued carefully adding clay to the armatures. "I just helped."

"Well, it's nice, seeing them all out again." Emmett winced, rubbing his knee, which had started to tremble ever so slightly.

Jen swore silently. *He's in pain.*

Pretending he wasn't, he said, "Speaking of my son, do you happen to know where he is?" Emmett rose and moved about the sunlit studio.

Jen nodded. Matt had taken off right after she had cooked him breakfast. Matter-of-factly, she reported, "He borrowed a few cowboys from Jeb McCabe—since the Triple B hired hands are all up near the Oklahoma border, rounding up that new herd y'all just bought."

"That's right," Emmett murmured.

"Matt, Jeb and the others are out in the pasture near the limestone pit, making changes to the fence, so the trucks and heavy equipment can get through."

Emmett walked over to the window, whatever discomfort he felt hidden now. He turned so his leg was away from Jen. "I'm guessing Matt is still upset."

I have to stop constantly monitoring Emmett's health. It's no different than measuring the whiskey, and it's going to drive me crazy.

Jen shrugged. "You should ask him."

Emmett walked around the studio, examining the enlarged photographs of him and his late wife that Jen had on display.

"Our arguing used to make Margarite unhappy, too," Emmett murmured thoughtfully, pausing to look at a picture of a ten-year-old Matt and his still-healthy mother.

The photos all packed a powerful emotional punch. Jen was not immune to the poignancy. "Then maybe you shouldn't do it," she said thickly, thinking how much loss the Briscoes had suffered, and all they still had. If only they weren't too stubborn to recognize it!

Emmett went to look at one of his wife's paintings. "Fathers and sons were born to disagree."

Talk about a lame excuse! "I wouldn't know about that."

Unable to keep herself from butting in, just a little,

Jen added pointedly, "What I do know is that Matt is really upset about everything that's going on right now."

Emmett lifted a brow. "And you think I should do something about it?"

Her own back aching from the tension, Jen stood. "It doesn't matter what I think." She walked over to Emmett and looked him in the eye. "It matters what the two of you think."

His craggy face gentled. "You care about Matt, don't you?"

She struggled to answer honestly while still maintaining her privacy. "We're becoming pretty close friends," she said finally, knowing that wasn't the half of it.

Emmett nodded in approval. "He needs a woman like you in his life."

Maybe he did and maybe he didn't, but unless Matt realized that... Jen swallowed. "He needs peace of mind. He won't get that if you try to matchmake."

Emmett flushed. Guilty as charged. "That's not what I'm doing."

It was her turn to lift a brow.

"I'm just observing," he protested. "I see the way he looks at you. And I see the way you look at him. Whether you want to admit it or not, there are sparks."

JEN KNEW THERE WERE sparks. She and Matt had practically combusted every time they'd made love.

But chemistry was not enough to guarantee a connection would go anywhere but the bedroom.

And as time went on, and she saw others finding their one true love, Jen was beginning to realize that she wanted permanence, too.

Maybe even marriage, if it could be the kind Cy and Celia had, or Emmett and Margarite had once enjoyed.

Unfortunately, there was no crystal ball that would give her a glimpse into the future. All she could do was wait and see what evolved with her and Matt and the incredibly intense chemistry they had.

Well, that, and work. And work some more.

So that was what Jen did. She coated the armatures of both horses, as well as the figures of Margarite and Emmett, with wet clay, stopping only when the light faded and her hands were too tired to continue.

She relaxed in a bath, then met Matt and Emmett in the dining room at eight, for dinner.

Conversation was cordial, but the underlying mood in the room was tense and unhappy.

Jen begged off early and went to her room.

She Skyped briefly with Celia, Cy and their adorable new baby girl, Cassandra, answered her email, then turned off the computer, and eventually, her bedside lamp.

That was when she heard a soft knock at the door.

MATT KNEW IT WAS LATE. Jen might even already be asleep.

He'd been in such a foul mood today that she had every right to want to avoid him. But luck was with him. She opened the door a crack.

She was clad in a tank top and loose-fitting sleep shorts that fell to mid-thigh. Barefoot. Face scrubbed. With her soft chestnut hair tousled and sexy, she was pure woman.

His body responded. Holding one hand behind his back, wishing he didn't feel quite so rough around the edges, he asked, "Can I come in?"

She looked at him the way he had initially looked at her when she had first accepted the commission—with wary caution. Her gaze swept over his untucked shirt and jeans and sock-clad feet before returning ever so slowly to his eyes.

Desire simmered between them, more powerful than ever.

Jen kept her guard up. "Your dad…"

Matt wasn't going to pretend he didn't want or need Jen. "Went to sleep right after dinner."

Some emotion crossed her face at that, but Jen recovered quickly and narrowed her eyes. She remained where she was, her body wedged in the slight opening between door and frame. "I'm not sure this is a good idea," she told him flatly.

Matt knew it wasn't—if they wanted to keep their hearts intact. But he wasn't sure he still did. He faced his quarry. "You haven't heard my proposal yet."

Her nose wrinkled as she repeated softly, "A proposal."

"Mmm-hmm."

She looked him over speculatively and he wished he knew what she was thinking. Wished life were simpler. That he'd found her first, instead of his dad, and was free to pursue her with no strings attached.

Finally, she propped one hand on her hip, clung to the edge of the door with the other and said, "What kind?"

He took in the pink of her cheeks, and the mixture of vulnerability and vibrancy in her eyes. "Let me in and I'll tell you."

Jen took her time considering. Finally, she swung the door open and stepped back, but only two paces. Crossing her arms, she said, "I'm waiting."

Matt showed her what he had been hiding. A plastic grocery sack.

"Wow. Now I'm really impressed."

"Don't get too excited," he teased.

She wrinkled her nose. "Don't you wish."

"That is, until you look." He opened the bag. Inside were two cartons of premium ice cream, two bottles of her favorite brand of sparkling water and two spoons he had pilfered from the silverware drawer in the kitchen. "It's a hot night." And what was better in the heat of a Texas summer than cold ice cream and a gorgeous woman who was as hot for him as he was for her?

Jen groaned, whether in anticipation or dismay, he couldn't tell. "You really like to live dangerously, don't you?"

With you, I do. Not sure where that had come from, Matt ignored the demands of his body and turned his attention back to the ice cream cartons. "Ladies first."

Jen tapped her lip in a parody of indecision. "Chocolate almond coconut and chocolate cherry vanilla." Her smile lit up her face. "How did you know my two favorites?"

"Cy and Celia."

Finally, he had really surprised—heck, maybe even impressed—her. Hot damn.

Jen blinked and asked in mild shock, "You called them?"

"Email," Matt confirmed, glad to at least be invited into Jen's lair. He shut the bedroom door behind him. "They were only too happy to supply the data."

She groaned again, this time in dismay. She set the ice cream down and drew up the covers on the bed, then sat cross-legged on top of the comforter. "My friends are going to draw all sorts of conclusions from that, you know." She handed him his share of the loot.

"Good." Matt sat facing her, giving her plenty of room. "I'd like it if people thought we were both off the market."

Jen went still.

Valiantly, he pushed on. "I'm asking you if you want to be exclusive."

Another silence. This one was less shocked, more thoughtful.

She worked the top off the ice cream container. Stuck the spoon in. Waited. "We haven't had a single date yet."

Matt wondered if she had ever looked more beautiful. Or out of his league. "This doesn't count?" His voice had a telltale rasp.

She shook her head. "Nope."

He was prepared to work harder, especially when he wanted something as badly as he wanted Jen. "Well, then," he drawled, with a teasing smile and a playful wink meant to put her at ease, "we better rectify that." He took another risk. "How about you go to the West Texas Ranchers Association gala as my date?"

Jen hesitated a beat too long. "How about if we do it after that?" she said finally.

Disappointment sifted through him. Not just because she had turned him down, but because of what her turning him down might mean.

"How come?" he asked casually, still holding her gaze.

Jen bit her lip. "Because I already promised your father that I'd let him introduce me to some prominent collectors who might want to commission some works from me. And when I do go out with you, on our first official date, I'd like it to be just you and me...and no one else."

Matt watched her take a bite of ice cream, then took a bite in turn.

"All right. I can understand that." He thought a moment. "How about this, then? The gala is on Friday night, so instead of coming back on Saturday, we'll spend the weekend in Fort Worth. And have several dates there, just the two of us." Where he could really wine and dine her, without interference.

This time Jen smiled. "Wow. Sounds like you really want to please me."

"I do." Matt took her hand and kissed the back of it. "And I will."

Chapter Twelve

The morning started out great. Jen was definitely feeling the afterglow of an evening spent flirting and hanging out with Matt. Her van was finally ready to be picked up, and Luz, who was on her way into town to do her weekly grocery shopping, offered to drop Jen off at the auto shop en route.

That happiness faded as soon as she was presented with the repaired vehicle. Jen stared at the gleaming white van with the buffed interior and fancy hubcaps. "That's not...that can't be mine."

Holly, the service manager, beamed with pride. "Matt said you would be surprised."

Jen pressed her fingertips to her eyes. "Surprised isn't the word for it," she muttered under her breath. She walked around the vehicle, examining the relic that now looked brand-new. If you could account for the twenty-year-old design, that is.

Trying not to consider the implications of Matt's actions, Jen walked the perimeter and let out a breath. "Did someone paint this?"

"Yep." Holly rocked back on her heels. "Nice job, huh?"

Imagining how much it was all going to cost, Jen

felt on the verge of a panic attack. "And the wheels and the hubcaps…"

"Are all brand-new," she affirmed, consulting the clipboard in her hands. She scanned one page, then two others. "As well as the transmission, the radiator, all the belts and hoses, windshield wipers."

Trying not to faint, Jen wrung her hands together. "How much is all this going to cost?"

"Nothing. Matt Briscoe paid for it, when he arranged for service."

Jen's temper soared. She offered a tight smile. "I still need to see the damage."

Holly cocked her head and studied Jen for a long minute. "Sure? 'Cause there's really no need."

"I want to see it."

With a sigh, she capitulated and handed over the clipboard.

As Jen had feared, the charges were enormous. She swallowed and handed back the pages of itemized charges.

Holly continued looking at her as if she thought Jen had lost her mind. Finally, she drawled, "If you don't mind me saying so, you don't look all that happy about this."

Jen bit down on an oath, knowing it wouldn't be fair to take her anger at Matt out on the service manager, even though the woman was butting in where she shouldn't be. "I'm not."

"Well, if you ask me, honey, you should be ecstatic!"

Jen leaned against her beloved van and lifted a brow, curious as to why.

Holly came nearer and her voice dropped to a confidential murmur. "Do you know how many women around here would give anything to be in your place?"

Given how sexy and charming and rich Matt was, Jen guessed quite a few.

"You've got yourself quite a catch!"

"I don't..." Jen swallowed, then tried again. "We're not..." What *were* they?

They hadn't even had a first date...

Yet here he was, making waves in Laramie County by purchasing thousands of dollars of van repairs for her. Publicly, no less!

What did that make him?

What did that make her?

What, Jen wondered, did any of it mean?

MATT WAS ELBOW DEEP in the ranch books when Jen stormed into the study. She looked loaded for bear. Which was not what he expected. He leaned back in his chair, enjoying the sight of her in a turquoise tank top, white denim skirt and flip-flops. Her hair was in sexy disarray, wisps slipping out of the fancy twist on the back of her head, but she didn't seem to notice as she drew a deep, bolstering breath. "Something wrong with your dress?" Matt asked, knowing something had in her a tizzy.

She stared at him for an interminable beat, then narrowed her eyes. "What?"

He put down his pen, still watching her closely. "For the gala. I thought you were picking it up this morning."

Jen pressed the heel of her hand to her forehead in frustration. "Darn it." She stamped her foot in frustration. "I was so upset I forgot!"

He rose from his chair and strode toward her. "Upset about what?"

"What do you think?" She held her chin high and

circled away from him, putting more distance between them. "My van!"

Matt took the hint and went back to the desk. He sat on the edge of it, legs stretched out, hands braced on either side of him.

Damn, but she was pretty, with pink color flooding her cheeks and the gleam of agitation in her eyes. Pretty enough to kiss…if she'd let him. Which she clearly would not.

Still trying to figure out what was going on with her, he observed, "I thought the auto shop did an excellent job."

"You saw it." The three words carried a wealth of accusation.

"Yeah. Well…" Restless, Matt stood once again. "It hadn't been entirely fixed. They were still waiting on a couple of the parts, but the paint job was done and the new tires and hubcaps were on."

Jen marched closer, looking sexier than ever. Her plump lower lip slid out. "I never asked for that."

Matt tried but could not quite keep the exasperation from his voice. "I thought you'd be happy!"

She propped her fists on her hips. "In what universe?" she practically shouted. "I mean, wasn't it enough that you took it upon yourself to order a new transmission and all the belts and hoses and stuff replaced?" Her voice, still accusing, dropped a notch. "Which, by the way, you didn't tell me about, either."

Suddenly as frustrated with her as she was with him, Matt replied, "I didn't figure that I had to tell you." Taking advantage of their proximity, he leaned down until they were nose to nose. "I assumed it would be a given, since it would be completely impractical to keep the worn-out belts and hoses when you're putting in a brand-new radiator and transmission." He straightened slowly and continued in a tone meant to annoy her, "Unless, of course, you like having car trouble?"

She folded her arms and glared at him contentiously. "That was *my* decision."

Ignoring the erratic intake of her breath and the clear definition of her breasts beneath the clinging cotton tank, he shrugged. "Then I stand corrected."

"Furthermore—" Jen's brows lowered over her long-lashed eyes "—the fact that you took charge of my repairs and paid for all of it has tongues wagging all over town."

He regarded her with silent derision, still not seeing what the big deal was. He was proud of what they felt for each other. "So people know that I...that we're..."

Undeterred, she interrupted sharply. "Can't put a label on it, can you, Matt?"

"Do you want us to put a label on it?" he countered, in a tone that was just as challenging.

Shock turned to wariness. Jen swallowed. Stepped back. "Heavens, no!"

Matt blinked. "Then?"

Another silence fell, this one more palpable.

Matt struggled to get to the source of the problem. "Is this because I got you car repairs instead of a diamond necklace?" Some women wanted only highly romantic gifts, he knew. He hadn't figured Jen was one of them. Had he been wrong?

She aimed a lethal look his way. "I don't want a diamond necklace from you!"

Okay, that was insulting. Matt scrubbed a hand over his face. "Why not?"

Wasn't he good enough? Was she not serious enough about him to accept such a gift, even though he was

damn serious about her? He'd thought just the fact that
they were making love demonstrated some level of commitment. At least it had on his part. That she hadn't
wanted to spell it out was okay with him; he didn't
particularly want to jinx things by talking it to death,
especially this early in the game. Nor had he minded
her wanting to take things day by day. He knew it was
how she operated. Matt, on the other hand, was always
thinking long term even when he wasn't talking that
way.

Jen threw up her hands, still struggling to make him
understand the root of her feminine fury. "Because it's
impractical! And I'm not a diamond necklace kind of
woman."

He got that. She didn't seem to be much for designer
anything. And that was okay with him, too. He liked
a woman who valued what was truly important. Like
transportation. "So, when you get a gift, you prefer
something less…decorative."

"Yes."

"Then I was right," he theorized bluntly. "Car repairs are a good gift."

Jen clasped her hands on top of her head and groaned
dramatically.

He grinned, amused despite himself. When this was
all over, and hopefully, it would be soon, he was going
to kiss her until they both couldn't think of anything
but making love again.

She made a face. "Matt, you're missing the point."

It was his turn to groan out loud. They were so far
from kissing again it wasn't funny. "Then what is the
point?" he asked with building frustration.

She came closer. Drew a deep breath and forced herself to calm down. "You don't need to be giving me a gift at all."

Oh, really. Well, he could be stubborn, too. And in this, he did not like to be told what he could or could not do. Especially by the woman he was completely fascinated with. "Suppose I *want* to give you a gift?" *Suppose I want to show you how I feel?* He lifted his eyebrows, daring her. "Then what?"

Jen scoffed. "Then nothing, because I don't want one. So—don't."

She stared at him.

He stared back.

"Look." Matt tried one more time to reason with her. "You can't be driving back and forth from Austin in a vehicle that could break down at any time and leave you stranded out in the middle of nowhere, possibly with no cell phone reception. You tried that already, remember? The night it stormed? It wasn't exactly fun, was it?"

She huffed. "You can't control everything, Matt. You can't control this, and you can't control me."

He damn well could keep her safe! "Want to bet?"

Jen looked as if she wanted to deck him. "You're not helping your case."

Neither was she, Matt thought, aware that this was their first real argument as a couple.

Emmett walked in, disapproval etched on his face. "What the devil is going on here? I can hear you bickering all the way down the hall."

Briefly, Jen explained, making it sound as if Matt had been purposefully trying to undermine her.

Emmett frowned at him. "Obviously, you made a mistake, son."

"Ha!" Jen said, perking up immediately.

Emmett eased into a wing chair and sat with one hand tucked beneath his hat, the other worrying the brim. "You don't paint a woman's vehicle without asking her what color she wants it to be painted. Plus, if you did that, you probably should have replaced the interior carpeting and seat covers and so on as well, instead of just having what was there detailed."

Jen groaned and clapped her hands over her ears. "Seriously? That's what you understand the problem to be?" She whirled on Emmett in turn.

So it's not just me who is clueless here, Matt thought, happy to have his father thinking along the same chivalrous lines.

Emmett shrugged. "Well, unless..." He peered at Jen, considering. "You wanted a diamond necklace?"

She muttered something about "idiots" and "too much money" and "the real world" that Matt was glad neither he nor his father could completely decipher.

Frowning at Jen this time, Emmett suggested in fatherly concern, "Whether it was the gift you wanted or not, maybe you should just appreciate it."

Her eyes widened and she made a low, disgruntled sound.

Matt groaned. "Dad, stop helping me."

Emmett persisted anyway, lecturing Jen the same way he usually lectured Matt. "It's not polite to look a gift horse in the mouth, Jen."

She lifted an autocratic brow. "You're absolute right—it isn't. You know what else isn't polite?" Jen fumed. "Overstepping your bounds! Meddling in someone else's life!" Eyes glittering, she turned on her heel and stormed out of the room.

Matt blew out a gusty breath and sank down in a

chair opposite his father. So much for thinking he understood Jen, even a little bit.

JEN WAS STILL FURIOUS hours later when she drove over to the Last Chance Ranch. "Thanks so much for picking up my gown," she told Emily. "You saved me a trip back to town." That had been another hour or more that she'd been able to sculpt. Not that she'd concentrated all that well. She'd been thinking about Matt and his presumptuousness, and what that likely meant in their future dealings with each other.

"No problem." Emily carried the carefully wrapped ball gown out to Jen's van. Together, they laid it in the back, so the delicate chiffon and lace wouldn't get mussed. "I had to pick up mine, too...and besides, I knew you were coming out here to photograph the mustangs."

Jen smiled. "It's a perfect day for it."

Emily waited for her to get her camera out. "You excited about the West Texas Ranchers Association gala? Or dreading it?"

Jen looped her Nikon around her neck. Together, they walked toward the pasture. "I have mixed emotions. Black-tie balls are not really my thing."

"I used to feel the same way—it's a bummer, having to go to a dance if you're unattached." Emily grinned, a small smile on her face. "Now, of course, it's different. I love having the chance to get all dressed up, dance with my husband and spend the night with him in a four-star hotel."

There was no doubt Emily and Dylan were deeply in love. "That does sound nice," Jen murmured.

Immediately, she thought about Matt. He would look

so handsome in a tux. The epitome of masculine gallantry.

Jen had been fantasizing about the ball—and their first "real" date, which was supposed to follow.

Now, of course, given how they had argued...

Emily studied Jen. "You seem a little down."

She aimed her camera at the three mustangs currently in the corral—a big paint, smaller gray and a beautiful black horse. All were sleek and strong and would serve as great models for the sculpture she was going to donate to the fundraiser for the boys ranch.

"Is everything okay?" Emily pressed, looking concerned.

Jen shrugged. "It's been quite a week. My two best friends just had a baby."

Emily stepped back to give Jen room to work. "That's always hard if it's what you want and you're nowhere close to getting it."

Unfortunately, it was what Jen wanted, and worse, she wished she could have Matt as her baby daddy. How premature and foolishly romantic was that?

Sighing, she moved along the fence to shoot the horses from another angle. "Don't get me wrong. I'm really happy for Cy and Celia." Baby Cassandra was gorgeous and healthy, the culmination of their dreams.

"Just sad for yourself, and that's okay. You're entitled to the whole range of feelings."

Jen's range of feelings regarding Matt were what kept getting her in trouble.

"What else is happening?" Emily persisted. "How's your love life going?"

Jen grimaced. "Badly."

"Really? That's not the impression I got the last time I saw you and Matt together."

Figuring she had enough photos, at least for now, Jen put the lens cover back on her camera and explained what had happened with the van.

"Yeah, I heard about that," Emily said wryly. "Everyone in town has. Probably going county wide as we speak, given how 'eligible' a bachelor Matt is. And how wealthy and handsome and nice and so on."

Jen walked with her back toward the ranch house. "I already got one sermon today, on how lucky I am to have Matt interfering in my life."

Emily chuckled. "And you're pissed."

Jen followed her inside the ranch house. "Wouldn't you be?"

"Absolutely." She took a couple bottles of sparkling water out of the fridge and handed one to Jen. "What is it about men—my dad and brothers included—that makes them think we need them to rescue us? It must be in their DNA."

Jen uncapped her bottle and took a long drink. She wiped her lips with the back of her hand. "Rich men are worse. No offense."

Emily grinned. "None taken."

"But?" Jen prodded, seeing something else in her friend's eyes.

Emily pulled out a chair. "Sure you're not overreacting?" she asked as she sat down at the kitchen table, clearly ready for a heart-to-heart. "I mean, I know it's a lot of money to you and me, but to someone of Matt Briscoe's wealth, what he spent on your van is penny ante change."

As Emmett had pointed out.

Jen sighed and took the chair opposite. "My feelings should still matter."

Emily rested her chin on her fist. "Just as the Briscoes' feelings should matter to you. I know you two come from different walks of life, but consider giving them the benefit of the doubt, and try meeting them halfway."

As much as Jen was loath to admit it, she knew Emily was right. This wasn't all about the van, much as she wanted to pretend that it was. It was about her past, her issues. And the sooner she leveled with Matt about that, the better off they would be.

"Got a minute?"

Matt looked up from the spreadsheets covering his desk.

Jen was standing in the doorway. Looking more beautiful—and hesitant—than ever.

A protectiveness he wasn't used to feeling welled up within him. Being thrust into the middle of the constant tension between him and his dad hadn't been easy for her, but she was handling it.

And what had he done in return?

Trampled—albeit unwittingly—over her boundaries.

He stood and welcomed her into the room. "For the record, I understand I crossed the line." It was way too early in their relationship—especially with a woman like Jen—for him to be giving expensive presents. A fact that, when he'd taken the time to consider it, made him admire her all the more.

Reluctantly, he offered, "So if you want to put together some sort of repayment plan…" *Even though I'd still rather pay for it and consider it my first step in watching out for you….*

Relief softened her slender frame. "I do. Thanks, Matt."

He wasn't surprised by her decision but he was a

little disappointed. He had hoped that if he met her halfway, the barriers would start to come down, and she would meet him halfway, too. Allow him to assist her financially, or in whatever way she needed, a little more. Instead, she was clinging to her independence as fiercely now as when she had met him.

Still, they *had* slept together…and were still spending time with each other.

She had confided in him and let him be close to her in other ways, too. That was something. And for now, that would have to do.

Slowly, he closed the distance between them and took her into his arms. "So we're okay?" he asked, brushing the hair from her face.

She didn't pull away.

The corners of her sexy lips curved slightly and a warm look entered her eyes. "I'm not ticked off anymore."

He luxuriated in the feminine softness of her slender body resting lightly against his. The silky texture of the tousled chestnut hair brushing her bare shoulders. "That's nice to hear." Almost as nice as it was to see her here again, on the ranch.

She hadn't been gone all that long, but it was too quiet—and way too lonely—without her.

Jen splayed her hands across his chest. "And I want to apologize, too." She played with the buttons on his shirt, then looked up at him sincerely. "For flying off the handle the way I did." She shook her head, lips twisting in regret as she searched his face. "I could have told you how I felt without losing my temper."

There she went, using politeness as a shield again.

"It's okay to lose your temper, Jen." Okay to not be perfectly cordial and emotionally contained.

She took a breath, stepped back. "I don't want to." She walked across the room, on the pretext of looking at a picture of him and his father. "I want my life to run smoothly, to always be on an even keel."

Needing to understand, Matt settled on the edge of his desk. "And yet something about what I did triggered a reaction from you that you couldn't control." He reached for her, pulled her close.

This time Jen didn't fight it.

She nodded in acknowledgment and with a sigh, wreathed her arms around his neck. "The van hasn't always been just a source of comfort and continuity to me." She grimaced. "It's also been a source of contention."

Matt massaged the tense muscles of her shoulders. "How so?"

She compressed her lips. "My previous in-laws hated it. I mean, really hated it. They wouldn't even let me park it in front of their house."

"That was pretty snotty."

Jen let out a shudder. "If it was on the property at all, it had to be hidden in the garage, with the door shut, and they didn't even like that."

The hurt in her voice killed him. "So me having it painted…" Matt said slowly.

Jen flushed and averted her glance self-consciously. "Made me wonder if you weren't a little put off by its age and general condition, too." She lifted a hand before he could defend his actions.

Her expression serious, she continued, "I know you drive your old pickup, the one you got for your sixteenth birthday, but that's different."

He wrapped his arms around her and brought her in closer. "How?"

She ran her fingers thoughtfully over his chest. "It's a classic. And it's perfectly maintained and painted. The interior is still really nice." She sighed almost wistfully as her hand finally stilled. "Plus you're a cowboy, so you're sort of expected to be attached to your horse and your truck and your ranch."

She made it sound so romantic. And Matt sensed, in a way, it was.

Aware that females didn't usually get attached to old vehicles the way a lot of guys did, Matt ran a hand down her arm. "I don't mind that you drive a van," he said, luxuriating in the drift of lilac perfume. "I just wanted you to be comfortable."

"And safe." Jen twisted her lips. "I know."

He studied her, sifting his hand through her hair. "But there's more to it than that, isn't there?"

Her elegant eyebrows knitted together. "It just brought home to me how different our lives have been... and are likely to continue to be."

Matt could understand her caution. He still hated to see her sell herself short. "I don't know about that. The cost of your sculptures is really going up. Soon, you'll be able to splurge on any luxury you want and buy whatever type of automobile you choose. Heck, you can be like my dad, and have one for every occasion," he joked.

To Matt's dismay, Jen remained uneasy, as if she didn't think that would ever be the case.

She released a soft, fatigued sigh. "Speaking of your dad, where is he? I'd like to apologize to him, too."

"If you want to do it in person, it will have to wait until tomorrow. He went on to Fort Worth."

Jen stepped away and began pacing the room. "I thought we were all going together."

So did I. "He said he had some things to do before the gala. Which makes me wonder if maybe there isn't a woman in this situation somewhere for him, too."

Tensing, Jen swung back around.

Matt continued his guesswork. "There has to be something going on that is causing Dad to tear up the ranch and sell off the limestone again."

She cocked her head.

"I've looked through everything in the ranch books, checked and double-checked every fact and figure against my own records, and those of our accountants and lawyers..."

Her eyes met his. "And...?"

"Nothing," Matt grumbled, balling his hands into fists. "The ranch is solidly in the black. There is no debt. Yet my dad just found it necessary to quickly raise several million dollars. And the only time he has ever done that was when there was a woman involved."

Jen appeared uncomfortable again, and that in turn made Matt uneasy. He needed to be able to talk about this with someone. Hell, he wanted to be able to talk about it with her.

"What are you going to do?" she asked quietly, after a moment.

Aware that her walls were going up again, the way they always did when the talk between them turned too intimate, Matt vowed, "I'm going to find out what is going on 'cause something—or someone—is pushing my dad to make these moves."

Without warning, Jen's eyes filled with turbulent

emotion. "And then what?" she asked, even more quietly, as if fearful of his response.

And she had reason to be—given how he felt about anyone harming his family. "Then whoever is behind this is going to have to deal with me," Matt predicted grimly.

Chapter Thirteen

"Oh, no. Don't tell me he's here," Emily McCabe-Reeve murmured in Jen's ear shortly after the two of them entered the hotel ballroom the next evening.

Jen followed her new friend's gaze to the tall, blond, incredibly handsome man standing next to the orchestra hired for the black-tie event. "Who is he?"

"Vince Owens. He owned property in Laramie County for a while."

Jen continued regarding the tuxedo-clad cowboy. Charm radiated from him as he greeted one partygoer after another—clapping shoulders, kissing cheeks and shaking hands.

A few guests were obviously happy to see him.

Most merely tolerated him.

Not a good sign, Jen thought.

Plus, he kept surreptitiously looking their way as he made the rounds of the crowded ballroom. "He doesn't appear to like you, if the way he's glaring is any indication."

Emily's frown deepened. "That's because my last name is McCabe. Although," she added with typical devil-may-care cheer, "I'm sure he is not too fond of any of the prominent families in our parts."

Nor they him, Jen noted, as Vince Owens got closer.

Emily laced an arm around Jen's waist and drew her in the opposite direction. "Just stay away from him. You'll be fine."

Matt and Dylan returned with glasses of champagne for all. "Any sign of Emmett?" Emily asked.

Matt exhaled in obvious frustration. "Just a text, about ten minutes ago. He said he was 'unavoidably delayed' and might have to skip the evening."

Disappointment spread through their little group. "Oh, I hope that's not the case," Emily lamented.

"Me, too," Jen murmured. Because if Emmett was a no-show, it could mean that he was having more symptoms—and that would not be good.

"Don't worry," Matt said, leaning in to slip his arm around her waist. Misreading the reason behind her concern, he murmured, "I texted Dad that I would introduce you around. He gave me a heads-up on who the big-time collectors of Western art were."

Embarrassed that Matt could think her that crass, she said, "You don't really have to do that."

Sensing tension, Emily interjected, "I think this is our cue to slip away." Waving, she and Dylan set down their glasses and headed for the dance floor.

Alone with Matt again, Jen guided him to the edge of the ballroom, where they could talk more privately. "It was really sweet of your dad to want to promote my career that way." She sipped her champagne and continued talking sense to Matt. "But—"

"No buts." He discreetly squeezed her forearm. "Dad may have let you down. Heck, let us both down, with all his mysterious behavior lately, but it doesn't mean I will. So hitch up your big-girl pants—" Matt gave her a humorous, yet heat-filled gaze "—and let's get a move on."

Jen grinned, emotion bubbling up inside her. "Okay. But only for a little bit. Then I want us to enjoy the party."

She wanted this to be a great prelude to their first real date, the following day.

As it happened, the introductions that followed went a lot easier than she'd expected, maybe because Matt was clearly so happy to be with her, and proud of what she did. And maybe because the people in the West Texas Ranchers Association were among the friendliest and kindest people she had ever met. Whatever the reason, Jen had a seriously good time meeting everyone Matt introduced her to. The only problem was Vince Owens.

He kept watching her, and something in the way he looked at Emily reminded Jen of the way her ex-husband's parents and their friends had viewed her, too.

It wasn't until Matt excused himself to get more food from the buffet that Vince Owens came closer and slid into a chair next to Jen.

"So," the tall blond interloper said, a smirk on his handsome face, "where do I sign on?"

Cruel experience told her where this was headed. Jen worked to keep her emotions in check. "Sign on for what?"

"I heard rumors about the arrangement you made that landed you a bedroom on the Triple B. Although..." Vince smiled suggestively "...I heard it was with Emmett Briscoe, not his son."

Just how obnoxious was this man? Out of the corner of her eye, Jen could see Matt, waylaid next to the buffet table, talking to Emily's dad, Shane McCabe. Thankful that he wasn't around to witness her humiliation, she pretended she hadn't registered the innuendo and explained matter-of-factly, "My commission is with Emmett."

"Hmm...so where does the son come into it?" Vince leaned toward her, his bourbon-scented breath brushing her face. "Are you sculpting him, too?"

Oh, God. And she thought she'd left this sort of treatment behind when she got divorced! Jen's anger flared. "No."

"I don't know why not." Vince shrugged, his eyes gleaming suggestively. "He probably looks pretty good in the buff. Not as fine as me, of course. But the only way to tell that is to see for yourself. And...compare."

This had gone far enough. Jen no longer cared if she made a scene. Making no effort to hide her revulsion, she stood. "Whatever you think, you're mistaken."

Ignoring her icy warning, Vince reached out and gripped her wrist. When she tried to pull away, he held her harder. "All I'm asking for, honey, is the same deal," he said smugly. "Or, hell, I'll even go you one better. I'll pay you five percent more than they are, if that's the holdup."

"Let her go."

Jen froze at the sound of Matt's voice behind her. Dimly, she became aware that all conversation around them had stopped.

She was so embarrassed she wanted to die.

Vince rolled unsteadily to his feet. "Mind your own business, Junior."

Matt stepped in, fury emanating from every pore. "She is my business."

"Really?" Vince taunted. He turned to leer at Jen in a way that caused the room to go even more silent. "'Cause she just intimated that she's not."

Jen tried to subtly get her wrist free without making a scene. To no avail.

Jaw clenched, Matt stepped closer. "I'm going to tell you one more time, Vince—"

"That's Mr. Owens to you, pipsqueak."

Jen reached out to grasp Matt with her free hand. "Don't. Please." *Please don't make a scene. Not on my behalf.*

Matt ignored her. Determined to take control of this situation, which was getting uglier and more public by the second, he continued to regard Vince with a death glare. "Let. The Lady. Go."

Vince chuckled. "Not until I work the same deal that you and your proud papa have—commissioning art in exchange for this pretty filly's time and attention."

Oh, Lord, you shouldn't have said that.

Aware she had just been made to sound like a hooker, Jen winced.

Matt took a swing at the other man. Knocked off balance, Vince crashed into the table, then hit the floor. Only to spring back up like a jack-in-the-box gone rabid, grab Matt's shirtfront and pull him down with him.

Matt took an uppercut to the jaw, then delivered another punch to the gut. Ladies screamed. Men put their arms out and stepped back to clear the space. And a fistfight, the likes of which the West Texas Ranchers Association hadn't seen in years, ensued.

To Matt's frustration, Jen took little comfort in the fact that he won his chivalrous battle on her behalf. "You did not have to hit him," she scolded, as soon as they retired to the privacy of Matt's hotel room.

Unable to help but note how gorgeous she looked in the silvery evening gown that draped one arm and shoulder and left the other bare, he shrugged. Eyes still on her, and the way the dress swirled around her long, luscious legs, he tossed off his tuxedo jacket, undid his bow tie and collapsed in a chair. "Sure I did."

The sting of her public humiliation still heating her cheeks, Jen added water to the ice in the bucket. Clearly still working through her adrenaline rush, she responded indignantly, "I was handling the situation."

Matt undid the first few buttons of his shirt as Jen pulled up another chair and sat kitty-corner to him, her chiffon-covered knees pressed against his thigh. He winced as she removed the bloodied towel from his scraped knuckles, and reminded her, "You couldn't even get your wrist free."

She clenched her teeth as she plunged Matt's hand in the icy water. "I would have stomped on Vince's foot with my stiletto eventually."

"What kept you?"

She scowled. "I was trying not to make a scene in the middle of the ballroom!" She jumped up and went into the bathroom.

Matt heard the sound of water running.

Jen returned, damp washcloth in hand. Frowning, she sat down again, leaned over and pressed the cloth to left side of his jaw, then his cheekbone. "Now all that people will remember about me was that I'm the up-and-coming sculptor who was the subject of a fistfight between you and Vince Owens."

Matt grunted and pulled away. That side of his face stung, which probably meant it was scraped up, too.

"I'm not going to apologize for coming to your aid. Vince Owens had it coming!" And Matt knew that if he hadn't stepped in when he had, some other guy would have.

Jen refolded the cloth, so the surface was clean. Cupping his chin, she leaned in again to continue the first aid. "That's not the point."

His blood pressure rose. "Then what is the point?" he demanded.

Glancing at him, she sat back. "Because of my background—because I grew up poor and you grew up rich—this kind of stuff is going to keep happening, Matt."

He sensed she wanted him to put up a fight, so she could list all the reasons they were wrong for each other. "No," he said softly. "It won't."

Appearing overwhelmed by the events of the evening, she challenged, "Have you ever dated anyone who grew up below poverty level before?"

Tensing, Matt leaned forward and took her hands in his. "The fact that you came from nothing and made yourself something makes you all the more attractive to me."

"I know that." Jen stood and walked away.

"And?"

She paced, her teeth worrying her lower lip. Finally, she turned and looked at him with barely suppressed anxiety and a weariness that seemed to come straight from her soul. "I'm not sure I can go back to that kind of life, where everyone wonders if I am a gold digger and my every move is suspect." She shook her head, her beautiful eyes glistening. "It's a miserable way to live, Matt."

He closed the distance between them. Fearful of losing her, he took her in his arms. "Even more miserable would be me living without you."

Figuring the only way he could convince her of that was to show her, Matt lowered his mouth to hers. He stroked the side of her neck with his thumb. And she opened her lips to his. Her breasts pressed against his chest, the warmth of her seeping through the starched fabric of his shirt. Her mouth pliant beneath his, she wreathed her arms about his neck and arched against him.

He kissed her the way he had wanted to all evening. With no restraint. She was so beautiful, so soft and feminine. And so responsive.

Determined this would be their most satisfying love-making yet, he cupped her breast through her gown, felt her nipple pebble against his palm.

"Matt! The dress."

He lifted his head, not sure he understood.

"We have to be careful. It's going to be donated to charity, remember?"

He chuckled at the reason for her concern. "Then there's only one thing to do," he declared.

"Get it off me," Jen guessed.

"I can help with that." Gently, he eased her out of her gown. Blood rushed to his groin as he took in her silk-and-lace bustier and thong. He looked his fill, then swept her up and carried her across the room. "Damn, you are gorgeous."

She flushed with pleasure, gestured winsomely. "The bed…"

"We'll get there," he promised, the passion in her eyes urging him on, compelling her to surrender. "In due time…"

For such a long time, Jen hadn't allowed herself to dare think about falling in love, or being loved in return.

Matt changed all that.

The intensity of his kiss drew forth a well of emotions she wanted to pretend didn't exist, but couldn't.

She loved him. She was in love with him. And even though he hadn't said the words, hadn't even come close, he acted as if she meant everything to him, too.

He lifted her so she was sitting on the bureau, arms wrapped around his neck, his strong hard body ensconced in the open V of her legs. "It's not fair," she whispered. "You're still dressed."

"We'll get there, too." He kissed the side of her neck. Still driving her mad with sensation, he unsnapped the hooks of her bustier. She trembled as his palms molded her breasts, his thumbs rubbing over the tender crests.

Wanting, needing more, Jen tangled her fingers in his hair, wrapped her legs around his waist and brought his mouth back to hers. Their lips fused. Tongues tangled. Overwhelmed by the explosion of heat and yearning, she returned his caresses with everything she had, wanting the bliss—and the intimacy—only Matt could bring.

One by one, she undid the buttons on his shirt, then parted the fabric. She ran her hands across hard muscle and smooth skin, unable to take her eyes from his broad shoulders, nicely sculpted chest, well-defined pecs and flat abs.

And lower still...

As Jen opened his fly and eased the zipper down she smiled with appreciation.

Moments later, Matt stepped out of his clothes.

Then her bustier fell to the floor.

The only thing left was her thong.

Seeming in no hurry to get that off, he eased his fingers beneath the elastic, then lingered, the possessiveness in his touch making her feel deliciously ravished.

"Matt..." Jen murmured, as he kissed her shoulder, the underside of her breast.

Hands on her hips, holding her captive, he pulled her toward the edge of the bureau.

"Do you like this?" He sank down on his knees and pressed a kiss to the already damp silk.

Her body ignited, and she was so consumed with wanting him deep inside her that she could barely breathe.

"You know I do." Urgency swept through her. She made soft, breathless sounds of pleasure.

He kissed her inner thighs. "And this?"

She clasped his head in her hands. "Yes."

His gaze traveled over her, the desire in his eyes unmistakable as he found her with his hands, and then, eventually, with his lips. Making her blossom. Letting her know he was the one in charge.

But control, Jen thought, was a two-way street.

Trembling with need, near the brink, she gasped, "No, Matt. Not without you. Not this time."

The thong came off.

Matt possessed her with one smooth, sure stroke. Jen wrapped her legs tighter, arching against him, welcoming him in. Easing his hands beneath her, he lifted her, holding her close, going deeper.

Their bodies blended.

Her spirit soaring, heart brimming with unexpected, undeniable love, Jen kissed him again. She reveled in the hard, hot demand of his passion, and then there was no more thinking, no more delaying, only this sweet, melting bliss. And an afterward that was so tender and emotionally satisfying, it was unlike anything she had ever known.

Chapter Fourteen

Jen heard the steady, insistent knocking on the door, and groaned.

Feeling disoriented, she lifted her head and looked around, to find herself in bed, cuddled up next to Matt, her head on his chest. Her arms were around his shoulders, one of her legs was nestled between his. He had his arms wrapped around her, too. She felt warm and safe, and darn annoyed at the continued rapping on their hotel room door.

Where was the Do Not Disturb sign when you needed it?

Finally, Matt roused slightly, too. He turned his head to peer at the bedside clock. "Seven in the morning." He dropped his head back on the pillow and pulled her closer. "Maybe they'll go away."

"And maybe," Jen said, sitting up abruptly, embarrassed to be caught in flagrante, given that everyone they knew at the ball last night was staying on the top three floors of the downtown hotel, "they won't."

Matt ran a hand down her spine, looking playful and intent on making love with her. He rolled her beneath him and pinned her to the mattress once again. "It's probably just the maid…"

Jen wished. "This early?" she gasped, body tingling.

"Which is exactly why she won't come in," Matt theorized confidently as he kissed the slope of Jen's collarbone. "It's too early to just—"

"Matt?" a familiar voice commanded from the other side of the door. "It's important, son. If you're in there, open up."

He swore and jerked to a sitting position. As did she.

"I can't locate Jen," Emmett continued, in obvious concern.

Mortified, she bolted from the bed, grabbing her dress, bustier and thong as she dashed into the marble bathroom.

Her face burning, she shut the door—ever so quietly. Immediately grabbed a robe and shrugged it on.

Jen heard the door to the hotel room open and then close.

Oh, God, where were her shoes? Were they alone enough to indict her?

"You could have called," Matt told his father, sounding really annoyed.

"I tried. Repeatedly. You had the privacy setting on the room, and your cell was going straight to voice mail."

Vaguely, Jen recalled shutting off both their cell phones after the first time she and Matt had made love. Quietly, she picked up a brush and ran it through her hair, but there was nothing she could do about the chapped state of her lips, or the whisker burns on her cheek. Or the fact that she looked like she had just spent a wild, reckless night making love to the man who had fought for her honor. And won...

On the other side of the door, Matt was saying grumpily, "That's because we kept getting a wrong number in the middle of the night."

Someone, Jen recalled dimly, had partied too hard and been a little too "happy" to dial correctly.

"We?" Emmett rumbled, immediately picking up on Matt's slip of the tongue.

A long pause followed.

Jen winced, knowing the jig was up.

"Was Jen in here with you?" Emmett demanded, clearly shocked by their recklessness. "Is she *still* in here with you?"

"Dad…" Matt's voice had a warning tone.

Not about to let him face his father alone, when she was just as responsible for this, Jen opened the door.

Emmett, who had been pleased about the idea of a romance between the two of them, was not pleased to find that she had spent the night with Matt in a hotel room, when she had her own private quarters just down the hall.

"So it's true?" Emmett looked at Matt's bruised fist with a critical eye. "You were in a brawl last night, too?" His voice dripped with disgust.

Trying not to think about another father who had been similarly upset over his son's involvement with her, Jen swallowed. This wasn't like her marriage. It wasn't the same at all.

And yet the end result was exactly the same.

"A couple of punches isn't exactly a brawl," Matt argued.

Emmett scowled. "It's the only thing people are talking about after the gala last night. I had several emails and texts before I even went down to breakfast."

Jen wasn't surprised about that.

It had been the only hint of real drama in an otherwise cordial but serene evening. Most had also felt—as Matt had—that Vince had had it coming to him, and

had applauded Matt for having the guts to finally set
the obnoxious rancher back on his heels.

"I have to say," Emmett continued sternly, "I'm disappointed."

No kidding, Jen thought, picking up on the slight
tremor in Emmett's left hand. She hadn't seen him look
this upset with his son...well, ever.

Worse, she knew the fight would not have happened
if Vince hadn't been coming on to her. Or if she had
managed to extricate herself from the ugly situation
sooner.

Instead, worried about causing a scene and embarrassing everyone, she'd tried to wait him out, in the vain
hope that Vince would desist and go away on his own.

Emmett slipped his hand in his back pocket and
stared at Matt. "Your mother and I raised you to be a
gentleman." Mouth tightening, Emmett gestured at the
hotel room and the very rumpled covers on the king-
size bed. "Obviously, you've given no thought to Jen's
reputation...."

My reputation, Jen thought cynically, *is the least
of it.* What she was really worried about was being
the wedge that drove Matt and his dad even further
apart. And then there was the stress of it all, and what it
might do to Emmett's already admittedly fragile physical state.

Was one of his knees trembling slightly, too?

"If you had," Emmett continued, "you'd be focused
on giving her a proper courtship, getting her to marry
you...instead of diminishing her and yourself with an
illicit tryst...."

Was that all it had been? Jen wondered. Was she
the only one here who had found the entire encounter
with Matt highly romantic and emotionally satisfying?

"Yeah, well…" He remained focused on his father's face. "I'm not like you, Dad," he retorted bitterly, clearly stinging from the irate dressing-down. "I don't hold on to romantic ideals that stopped being relevant years ago."

"Meaning?" Now Emmett looked like he wanted to punch somebody out, Jen thought.

"Meaning," Matt growled, "I don't have to be married to have sex with someone. Or, like you, foolishly marry and then divorce every woman I want to have sex with!"

"Maybe you should. At least then you wouldn't be damaging a woman's reputation."

"I *really* should not be here," Jen said, meaning it with all her heart. It was awful, being caught between the two quarreling Briscoe men.

Her intended departure brought them up short. Matt and his dad flushed guiltily.

"No. I'm the one who should have been more circumspect.… I know my son. I know how he thinks."

Emmett had known, Jen thought, that Matt was interested in her and would go after her.

"I'm sorry for intruding," the other man said stiffly.

Jen held up a hand. The hallmark of any strong family was the ability to say you were sorry—and mean it—and then move on together, determined to do better in the future.

Like it or not, agree or not, this had been a huge misstep on all their parts.

"I'm sorry there was something for you to intrude on, Emmett. It was never my intention to do anything to embarrass you," Jen said quietly. The senior Briscoe had been nothing but kind to her. And he was giving her a huge opportunity, artistically. There was no way she could bear a grudge. Especially when she knew all Emmett had been trying to do was protect her.

"I owe you more than that," she added.

Emmett's expression gentled, then turned serious once again. "How about I go down to the lobby and wait for you there? As soon as you're ready, I have something very important to show you both."

Hoping there would be at least one mystery solved, Jen asked, "Is this what you've been spending all your time on?" What kept taking him away from the ranch— and his son?

Emmett nodded. "It's essential you see this today," he declared.

But typically, Jen noted, he offered nothing more.

Matt and his father exchanged terse glances. Truce called—albeit reluctantly—Emmett stated, "I'll be waiting for you," and left the room.

Matt turned to Jen, his own frustration unabated. She knew how he felt. If she could only erase the last half hour of their lives, and all the humiliation and up-heaval that had gone with it... The new uncertainty it had caused...

Because now, like it or not, she was reevaluating her relationship with Matt.

She'd thought no one would get hurt.

Clearly that was wrong.

Emmett was hurt.

Matt was upset.

And she was thrown completely off-kilter, too. To the point that neither she nor Matt knew what to say to each other.

He scrubbed a hand over his face, and grimaced when he touched his sullen jaw. "I'm sorry, Jen. So sorry. That whole thing—"

Had ruined their wonderful, romantic, passionate interlude.

She held up a hand, wanting only for the unease between them to end. "You don't need to apologize to me, Matt."

She sympathized. She knew how awful it was to be humiliated by a parent. Being treated like an errant teen who had no idea of the consequences was even worse. "What happened just now was embarrassing for all of us."

Matt studied her. "You don't seem mad at my dad."

How could she be, Jen wondered, when all Emmett had really been trying to do was keep her from getting hurt?

What he hadn't understood was how enthusiastically she had signed on for this affair. Even knowing she and Matt weren't suited for each other, long term, and that the relationship was destined to end.

Jen struggled to keep her own attitude matter-of-fact. "Your dad reacted emotionally, Matt. It happens." She shrugged. "He wants to move on from that, and I think we should, too."

But Matt couldn't let it go. Regarding her carefully, he stepped closer. "Still, what I said about Dad's old-fashioned attitude toward marriage—"

Jen knew what a sore point that was between the two men.

Not ready to be touched, not yet, Jen slipped by Matt and moved back toward the bathroom. Standing just out of sight, she slipped on her undies and then her dress. Walking back out, she turned and lifted her hair so he could help her with the zipper. "I know what point you were making to your dad, and it's a valid one. I understand what upheaval that attitude has brought to your lives." Jen tried not to quiver as Matt's hands brushed her bare skin as he zipped her gown. "Divorce is awful under the best of circumstances. Your dad has been through three, since your mother's death, and by extension, so have you. It makes sense you'd be wary of it." Jen found her purse and rummaged through it for her hotel room entry card. "Heck, I'm wary of it," she joked weakly, "and I've only been divorced once!"

His expression sober, Matt walked her as far as the door. He paused, hand on the portal just beside her head, and looked determined to have his say before she left. "It still came out sounding all wrong."

Jen tilted her head back and pushed away the tantalizing image of Matt making love to her. Of her worshipping him in return. Keeping track of the conversation with effort, she murmured, "You don't have to marry me to sleep with me." *Although it would be nice if you loved me...just a little bit.*

Matt lifted her hand and kissed the back of it. "It sounded like I was using you."

And if I was honest, I would admit I was using you, too—because it felt good to be close to someone, to be wanted and needed, even if only in bed.

"We had an agreement, Matt," Jen reminded him, tightening her fingers in his. "To take things one day at a time."

He nodded, not taking his eyes off her, then leaned down to kiss her temple. "And we need to discuss that. Soon," he promised firmly.

Jen pushed away the little tendril of hope that Matt might secretly want more than they'd agreed upon, just as she did. "But not while your father is downstairs in the lobby, waiting on us," she said.

A discussion like that would take time. And time was something they did not have.

"DAD, YOU CAN'T PARK HERE," Matt said half an hour later, still looking as on edge as Jen felt. "It's a no-parking zone," he continued as Emmett angled his luxurious SUV against the curb in front of a very elegant, white Southern mansion several blocks north of Sundance Square.

Emmett shrugged off the advice with his typical ego. "No one is going to tow my Escalade." He got out a little stiffly and walked around the front of the vehicle.

With relief, Jen noted the hand that had been trembling this morning was perfectly still now. She didn't want Emmett to be ill.

"Besides," he continued expansively, "we aren't going to be here that long."

Jen hurried to keep up with the two tall men's long strides. After a quick shower and a change of clothes, she felt so much better. "Why *are* we here?" she asked.

Emmett beamed proudly. "I want to show you the home of my new museum."

Matt and Jen blinked in tandem. "Your what?" Matt asked.

Emmett adjusted the brim of his Stetson. "I finalized the sale yesterday. That's why I wasn't at the gala. I was busy negotiating terms and signing papers."

"Museum," Matt repeated, scrubbing a hand over his face.

Emmett paused to unlock the mansion door. "I'm going to renovate it and establish an art museum here, in my own name, similar to the Amon Carter and Sid Richardson museums." He pushed open the door to the empty residence and ushered them inside.

The wood floors were in terrible shape, as were the elaborate woodwork and walls. But the neglect was all cosmetic and could be fixed.

Emmett escorted them through the big, airy rooms with their twelve-foot ceilings, then paused to lean against the carved oak banister of the broad staircase.

He suddenly seemed a little winded, but that could be due to the excitement he was feeling and the swiftness with which he had conducted the tour, Jen thought.

Still beaming, Emmett stated, "I'm going to showcase all of Margarite's work, as well as Jen's sculptures commemorating my life. Not to mention up-and-coming Texas artists who also specialize in Western art."

Jen was stunned. So was Matt.

This was more than she ever could have expected. Or even knew what to do with.

"Eventually, the museum will be self-supporting, with gift shop sales, but..." Emmett paused as a flashing light on the street caught their attention.

Matt said a few choice words at the sight of a Fort Worth police car next to the Escalade, a tow truck pulling up right beside it. Muttering a salty equivalent of I told you this would happen, he rushed outside, calling, "I'm going to try to talk you out of a ticket."

As soon as the door closed, Jen looked at Emmett, who had taken off his hat and was hiding a trembling left hand beneath the brim. "Your symptoms are worse."

For once, he didn't try to downplay it. He sat down heavily on the stairs and tried to hide the twitching in his right hand, too. "Which is why I'll soon be leaving, and finishing this museum will be up to you," he told Jen.

She couldn't believe he was serious! "You can't do this. You can't go off and leave your son."

Emmett dug in stubbornly, as his hand twitched all the more. "I told you, I am not going to saddle Matt with the ordeal of nursing another parent through a long and horrible illness. He deserves a happy life, free of that kind of heartache." The older man lumbered unsteadily to his feet to make his point. "He loves you. And you love him…I see that now." Emmett paused, his eyes glistening moistly. "You'll make him happy, Jen." His voice dropped to a husky rasp. "The alternative won't."

Behind them, the front door opened and Matt walked in. "What alternative?" he asked with a frown, immediately picking up on the fact that he had missed something important.

And once again Jen was faced with the prospect of either shutting him out, or finally spilling the truth.

MATT STARED AT JEN. He saw dread flicker in her eyes once again, and any doubts he had about her innocence fled. "You know something about all this, don't you?" About whatever it was his father was keeping from him. "Something more than what Dad just told us."

Jen went very still. "I just found out about the museum."

Matt knew evasion when he heard it. So it hadn't been his imagination! The two of them were keeping secrets, deliberately shutting him out. "Was this museum all your idea?" Was she in it for the money? The fame? The power to help other new and struggling artists?

None of this squared with what he knew—what he *thought* he knew—to be true about Jen.

Visibly shocked and hurt, she laid a hand over her heart. "No. Of course not."

Matt studied the flush of pink in her cheeks, the difficulty she still had meeting his gaze, and knew she was guilty of something. "Then what's going on? And don't try and tell me nothing, because I can tell that something is!"

Jen's shoulders stiffened defensively and she fell silent. And most damning of all, his own father wouldn't look him in the eye, either!

Instead, Emmett gazed out the window to where the policeman stood, still tapping his foot, the tow truck hovering nearby. "I'm going to collect my SUV and head on home," he announced hurriedly. "You two stay and enjoy yourselves for the rest of the weekend, as originally planned."

He slapped his hat on his head, grabbed his car keys from his pocket and rushed out the front door. Matt watched as his father paused to thank the policeman for not writing a ticket, then climbed into the Escalade and drove away.

Silence fell between them. Jen looked around, as eager to be out of there as Emmett had been.

But there were two problems, Matt and Jen realized simultaneously. "Great," he fumed. "Dad left us without transportation."

She reached for her cell phone. "And a key to the mansion so we could lock up."

Matt covered her hand with his. "Forget that. We have more important things to discuss."

Jen lifted a brow, wary and on edge once again.

He edged closer, stunned by the depth of his feelings for her. "I am tired of being shut out of this secret, whatever it is." Tired of being on the outside, looking in.

Jen lifted a palm, and a shadow of regret crossed her face. "You need to talk to your dad about this."

"I'm talking to you, Jen," Matt said, his resentment building.

She gave him a chiding look. "I told you before. I don't want to be in the middle of any disagreements between you and your dad."

Matt hated feeling so paranoid. "You already are."

Silence fell and distress glittered in her eyes.

Realizing his father was somehow to blame for her conflicted state, Matt clenched his jaw. "I'm tired of being left out in the cold, Jen. Tell me what's going on."

She flinched, looking guilty as all get-out once again, but folded her arms defiantly. "Or?" she prodded, lifting her chin.

Matt had no choice. "Our relationship is over."

JEN COULD SEE MATT MEANT what he said.

It didn't change her course of action.

There was only one person who could change Emmett's mind about leaving, and that was Matt. "You need to talk to your father before it's too late."

His eyes gleaming dangerously, Matt stared down at her. "Too late for what?"

Not about to let him make her feel in the wrong here, she grabbed his arm and commandeered him toward the door. "Just go after him."

Matt's eyes were utterly implacable, his lips grim. "If I didn't know better, I'd think by the way you're acting that this was a matter of life and death."

Just as it had been with his mother, when Emmett had neglected to tell Matt that Margarite was ill.

"Please, Matt," Jen said hoarsely, "just do as I ask, for all our sakes."

Confront your dad. Work it out with him. Then, and only then, come back to me. See if there's anything left to work out. And right now, Jen wasn't sure there was.

Matt still refused to budge.

Sadly, Jen could see this was no different from her marriage. Her ex had expected her to be loyal only to him, and then had blamed her for everything that went wrong with his relationship with his folks, too. There was no happiness down that path. None at all.

"You understand I can't be with a woman who keeps secrets from me," Matt warned, very very softly.

Knowing what was at stake here, Jen worked to control her growing disillusionment. "And you understand," she countered, mimicking his low, reproach-filled tone, "that in not respecting my commitments, you're not respecting me?"

Like it or not, she'd made a promise to Emmett. She could not break that vow. Not even for Matt. Not even when it was a condition for continuing their relationship.

An unhappy silence fell.

They stared at each other, neither giving ground. Neither willing to cede control.

Or say what they both now knew to be the truth— that they never should have become involved in the first place.

Because it was true.

They were just too different.

She would never be the woman Matt wanted or needed, not long term, anyway. She had the wrong background, the wrong priorities, and a heart that turned out to be way too vulnerable and open to loving him, after all.

It was ironic, Jen thought, that only now—when it was clearly too late for them to bridge the gap between expectation and reality—that she'd realize what she really felt for him.

Silently, with tears sliding down her face, Jen watched Matt walk out of the door…and out of her life.

Chapter Fifteen

"You weren't kidding when you said the Briscoes had fixed up your van." Celia engulfed Jen in a warm, welcoming hug. "It's even painted!"

Jen shifted her sunglasses higher on the bridge of her nose. August in Austin was hot—and humid, too. A fact that only added to the misery of her day.

She'd caught a ride back to Laramie County with Emily and Dylan, both of whom had pretended not to notice that she was way too quiet the entire ride and struggling not to cry.

Once at the Triple B, she'd been relieved to find that neither Matt nor Emmett were there, which made packing up her things in the van quick and easy.

Numb with remorse—for being naive enough to let the Triple B feel like home—she'd driven back to Austin, missing Matt already.

And now she just felt numb again. So numb. As if she'd never be happy again...

But there was still work to be done. And thanks to her multitude of recent mistakes, many new problems to be solved.

Pretending a nonchalance she couldn't begin to feel, Jen stretched the stiffness from her body. Glad her eyes were hidden by the dark lenses, she flashed a crooked smile and turned away from the probing glances of her friends. "Now all I have to do is figure out how to pay for the ten thousand dollars worth of repairs Matt ordered." She plucked her handbag from the passenger seat and looped it over her shoulder with unnecessary care.

Shrugging, Jen straightened and shut the van door. "Which isn't going to be easy, given the fact I'll no longer be doing a whole series of work for Emmett Briscoe."

Celia looped a comforting arm around Jen's shoulders. "You're not?"

She shook her head. "I'm just finishing the one I've started—in payment for the hospitality they showed me the last two weeks, putting me up, loaning me a car, paying for a trip to Fort Worth, and so on."

Cy moved to Jen's other side, looking ready to do battle on her behalf. "Things are really that bad?"

Meaning unsalvageable?

Jen hated to be the bearer of bad news to the happy parents, but since their financial futures were interlinked, she had no choice but to be honest.

She opened the back of the van and brought out the cooler containing the very carefully packed, half-completed clay sculpture. "They really are," she said softly. "At least with Matt and his dad." She squared her shoulders as Cy went on ahead to open the service door to the gallery. "The good news is I met a lot of collectors at this party I went to in Fort Worth last night. I've already gotten a couple of emails from prospective clients wanting to talk about commissioning a sculpture."

Celia beamed as Jen set the cooler down on her desk. "Well, that's great," she enthused.

Jen set her shoulder bag down, too, declaring with forced optimism, "There's always a silver lining somewhere if you look hard enough." And right now she was determined to forget she had ever been foolish enough to fall in love with Matt. Determined to pick herself up and get on with her life.

She tiptoed over to the bassinet tucked in a corner and for the first time laid eyes on the newest member of the gallery team. Dressed all in pink, the sweet-faced baby girl had long-lashed eyes and wisps of dark curly hair.

Jen placed her hand over her heart. "Oh, guys. She's absolutely gorgeous!" And the image of her parents.

Cy beamed. "We sure think so."

Celia lifted her out so Jen could hold her.

Jen cuddled the sleeping newborn against her chest. Cassandra was so soft and fragile, so perfect in every way.

Jen's throat tightened. Just yesterday, she had hoped that she and Matt would one day share the same kind of happiness.

But they weren't going to, so...

Once again she dragged her attention to the present, and the problems she *could* do something about. She frowned at Celia and carefully handed the infant back to her. "Aren't you supposed to be on maternity leave?"

Snuggling her baby close, her friend shrugged off the concern. "I just came in for a few hours to do the end of the month books, while Cy worked on molds for the latest crop of baby shoes and rattles we're bronzing."

She stepped nearer and rested her head on his shoulder. "This way, we could all be together."

They made such a happy family.

Another wave of longing swept through Jen, and she swallowed. "Be sure you take enough time off," she scolded affectionately. "Both of you. I want you to enjoy every minute with little Cassandra."

Because happiness, like everything else good in life, was fleeting....

Jen helped them pack up the baby and head out to their station wagon. "Maybe you should come home with us for dinner," Celia said, still looking concerned.

Before Jen could reply, a big Escalade drove up.

Emmett Briscoe got out.

Cy looked at Jen, protective as always. "Do you want us to stay?"

"No."

Cy looked at the aging rancher headed their way. "You sure about this?"

She nodded. "Emmett and I have a few things to talk about. Preferably alone."

"Okay, but you call us if you change your mind," Cy said.

Jen thanked them, then ushered Emmett into the gallery. She noted with a pang that both his hands and one knee were shaking.

Looking as if he felt a little weak, he sat down in a chair, opened his briefcase on his lap and then got right down to business. "I have the contracts for the Emmett Briscoe museum. They need to be signed immediately," he told her gruffly.

A couple weeks ago, Jen would have jumped at this opportunity. Now, because of all that had happened, it just created a boulder-size pit in the bottom of her stomach.

Oblivious to her dismay, Emmett continued briskly, "My attorney will let you know how to contact me, once I'm settled, because I want to be kept informed of how the museum is progressing."

"Will Matt know how to get in touch with you, too?"

Emmett handed over a thick file. "I'm still working on how I'm going to manage that."

Jen passed the file right back to him. "Then my answer is no."

Emmett held it as if it were nuclear waste. "I beg your pardon?"

Jen moved to the other side of her desk and sat down. Heartsick, but no less resolved, she rocked back in her chair and pressed her fingertips together. "I'm turning down your offer and—save the one sculpture I'm working on now and do plan to finish—ending our association."

For a long moment, Emmett just stared at her. Then he set the file on her desk and rose, a little unsteadily, which confirmed Jen's assessment that the rancher's symptoms were getting worse. "Is it money?" he asked, clearly upset. "Am I not paying you enough? Because if it is—"

Jen lifted her palms. "No. For heaven's sake, no—it's not the money!" she said emotionally. What was it with rich people, anyway? Why did they think it always came down to cold hard cash?

Shakily, he settled back in his chair and gripped the armrests. "Then what is it?" he demanded.

Knowing honesty was always the best policy, Jen told it like it was. "I can't do this, Emmett," she said brokenly. "I thought I could take the situation with you and Matt the way I take everything—one day at a time."

Emmett clasped his hands together hard, listening intently.

"I'd let you and Matt each handle your problems, and I would handle mine...and we'd all be accountable for our own actions."

Her visitor continued working to quell the trembling in his hands, with little success. "Sounds good to me."

Jen struggled to not get too involved. To not feel responsible for caring for this man who was unlike her father in so many ways—and so like him, too, in how he refused to let anyone get close, and refused to acknowledge his pain.

"It's not good, Emmett."

He stared at her in unhappy silence, begging her to change her mind.

Jen leaned across her desk, every bit as intent as he was. "You see...I know what's going on with you." She swallowed. "That you may be seriously ill and are refusing treatment, and worse...that you're keeping your son in the dark about all of it."

Emmett's façade began to crack.

She sucked in a deep breath. "I know you think what you're doing is in Matt's best interest. But the truth is, you're not behaving honorably at all."

"I promised myself I would always protect him."

"You're not sparing Matt pain," Jen countered. "You're inflicting it on him. And as much as I care about Matt, as much as I would like to be able to just go to him and tell him the truth about my suspicions, I can't do that."

Emmett leaned back in his chair, his whole body

suddenly, incredibly still. "Why not?" he challenged gruffly. "If you're so convinced I'm in the wrong?"

Jen stood, picked up the folder and his briefcase and handed them to him. "Because it's not my place, Emmett. It's yours." Aware that her heart was breaking for the second time that day, she helped him to his feet and ushered him to the door.

She hated to do this, especially when he had been so kind to her, but she knew it was best for all of them to make everyone, including her, toe the line. And that meant no more covering, no more enabling, no more trying to solve anyone else's problems for them.

"So...this is it?" Emmett muttered, looking shocked that she had said no to him.

She nodded, her own mood grim. "Until you decide to treat Matt like the loving, wonderful, compassionate and caring man he is..." a lump rose in her throat, and she had to swallow back a sob to go on "...until you take steps to relieve me of this terrible secret you have entrusted me with..." *a secret that has damn near ruined my life* "...I can't see or have any dealings with either of you."

"SHOULDN'T YOU BE OUT roping or riding or trying to figure out how best to woo Jen?" Emily asked.

Matt knew closing time had come and gone at the Daybreak Café.

The waitstaff had pretty much packed up and gone home. "Just thought I'd sit here and finish my coffee," he grumbled. Maybe find some sympathy and understanding. "But if you want me to leave..."

Emily put her hand on his shoulder, then slid into the booth opposite him. "I have three brothers. And a husband. I know a lovesick man when I see one. What's going on? Is Jen mad at you for punching out Vince Owens on her behalf the other night?" She sighed. "'Cause I have to tell you, as flattering as it can be to find yourself in the center of a manly brawl, it's also a little embarrassing."

Matt scrubbed a hand over his jaw. Jen had been gone three days. Three days that felt like three years. "I don't regret punching Vince." He would do it again in a heartbeat. "He had it coming for speaking to Jen that way."

Emily peered at him. "Then what do you regret?"

Matt's gut twisted. He still found the depth of Jen's betrayal hard to accept. He choked the words out. "She's been lying to me."

Emily scoffed. "I find that hard to believe."

He flattened his palms on the tabletop. It was true, much as he didn't want to believe it, either. "By omission."

"Okay." Emily listened compassionately. "I'm still not following, but...okay."

Knowing it was time he confided in someone, got a second opinion, Matt pushed on. "My dad has been acting crazy. Jen knows something about what's going on, but she won't tell me anything. She just says I should ask him, which I have, and it's done absolutely no good."

"And you think her first loyalty should be to you."

"Damn straight I do," he said in a sulky voice.

"And you're angrier at her than you are at your dad."

Matt thought about the way he'd let Jen into his life, into his heart. Thought about the sexy, incredibly satisfying way they'd made love. "Hell, yes, I'm mad."

"Why?"

"Because I thought we had something." The kind of something that would have induced Jen to stay in Laramie County long after the sculpting gig had ended. That would have kept her on his ranch, in his life, in his bed. That would have led to a happily ever after that hadn't been in the cards for him until she'd entered his life.

"Something special," Emily prodded gently, trying to get him to qualify it.

"Special" didn't even begin to cover how Jen had made him feel. But knowing there were no words to adequately describe the tenderness she'd brought forth in him, or the heat of their passion, or the way they shared the most intimate details of their lives with each other, he simply shrugged. "Yeah."

Emily studied him, like the sister he wished he'd had. "And now…?"

Matt grimaced as the hard facts of the situation brought him back to a reality he would rather not face. "How special can what we shared be if Jen sides with my father over me? If her first allegiance is to anyone *but* me?"

"Is that what's she doing? Or is she just respecting a confidence?"

"What's the difference?" He glowered across the table.

"Well, a lot." Emily got up and brought over two clean mugs and a pot of coffee. "If someone comes to you and tells you something he doesn't want anyone else to know, then you have to honor that." She cleared the old mug away and filled the two new ones.

"Even if that person is making a mistake? Or a lot of mistakes? Really big ones?"

Emily went back to the counter and returned with some freshly baked cookies. "I heard what your dad is doing, starting a museum. I think it's great. He's going to help a lot of new, young artists, including Jen."

Matt blew out a breath and tried to make sense of the latest bombshell his father had dropped on him. "Jen's not going to be a part of it."

"You're kidding."

He thought about how dejected his father had looked when he'd relayed the news. As if he couldn't believe what Jen had done, either. As if he felt kicked in the gut, as Matt did.

He gestured inanely. "Under the circumstances, she thought someone else should take over running of the museum."

Emily stirred cream in her coffee. "That's a pretty major sacrifice. Especially for someone who's just on the cusp of really making it as an artist." She sipped, then rested her chin on her fist. "I don't know if I could be that unselfish."

Matt knew where this was going. "You might as well say it," he ordered grumpily, quaffing his fresh coffee so quickly he burned his throat. "You think I'm being a horse's rear end."

"What I think is that you're unfairly holding Jen responsible for things that are out of her control. She never asked to be caught between you and your dad. Emmett put her in that situation, and then you made it worse."

Matt's gut roiled from too much acid and too little food. "If she had just told me what was going on with Dad…"

"Then your father would have been ticked off at her. So even if you were happy that she'd caved, Emmett wouldn't be, and you would all still end up miserable.

Face it, Matt," Emily chided. "There are only two people who can fix this. And Jen isn't one of them."

THREE DAYS LATER, Cy stopped by Jen's worktable on his way out. "How long are you planning to stay tonight?"

She glanced up from the clay images of Emmett and Margarite Briscoe. She was surrounded by pictures of them, to no avail. All looking at them did was remind her of Matt. How much she cared about him. How heartsick she felt.

Jen bit her lip. "I don't know." She shook her head, not bothering to hide her frustration with this and everything else in her life. "I can't get the expression on the faces right...."

Cy gave her a friendly pat on the head. "Just don't wear yourself out, okay? You've been burning the midnight oil for the past few days."

Jen knew it was the only way she could survive losing the man she loved. But unlike Emmett and Margarite, she and Matt would never have a marriage, a life together, or a child. They wouldn't, she thought sadly, even have a continuing affair.

Knowing if she talked about it, she'd cry, and that if she started to cry, she probably wouldn't stop, Jen inhaled sharply and winked at Cy. "Save your newfound parenting skills for little Cassandra," she teased.

He smiled back at her, with concern in his eyes.

"Seriously," Jen continued. "Better go on home. I know baby Cassandra and Celia are waiting for you."

Cy turned away dutifully. "All right. Let me know if you need anything."

Already absorbed in her work again, Jen nodded. "Sure thing."

Why wouldn't these figurines cooperate? Why were they—like happiness—so elusive?

Cy headed down the stairs to the gallery on the first floor. The door opened and closed. Then footsteps came her way again. Jen looked up, expecting that Cy had forgotten something.

Instead, Matt stood at the top of the stairs.

He looked good. Handsome. He was dressed in his usual jeans, boots and a navy blue shirt. She could tell he had shaved that morning, but the shadow of an evening beard rimmed his jaw, and another, wary shadow appeared in his eyes.

His lips formed a solemn smile. "Cy let me in."

Jen's heart leaped in her chest. She had the urge to drop her sculpting tools, jump up recklessly and propel herself into his arms. However, the defensive side of her—the one that remembered all too well how he had thrown down an ultimatum just five days before—kept her firmly in place.

Trying not to lose herself in his very serious gaze, she shrugged. "Obviously. The question is why." She jerked in a breath and feigned serenity. "Cy's usually pretty protective of me, you know." She wiped her hands on a towel and stood. "My unofficial big brother."

Matt offered a slow, steady smile and slowly came toward her. "As your unofficial big brother, Cy wants you to be happy."

Well, at least some things never changed, Jen noted, shaking her head at Matt's smug confidence. "And you're the key to that," she countered drily, wishing her legs would stop feeling so wobbly.

"Cy seems to think so." Matt lifted his hand and tucked a strand of hair behind her ear. "At least he said as much on the phone last night." He wrapped his other arm around her.

Jen stopped breathing as he pulled her close. "You talked to him?"

Matt slid a hand down her spine, fitting her against him. "And Celia. My dad. Luz. Sully. A few more of the McCabes. And, of course, Emily and Dylan."

Jen stared at him, aware their hearts were beating in the same quick cadence. "Anyone else?"

Matt tilted his head to one side. Obviously, he had to think about that. "Well, my horse."

Jen laughed. "You're really funny, you know that?"

His eyes darkened. "I'm trying."

So was she. To not fall back in lust with him, to not stay foolishly in love. To not put either of them in a position where they could be hurt. It had been hard enough losing Matt once. She couldn't bear it if it happened again. She swallowed. Took a big step back. "Seriously, Matt. We said everything we had to say the last time we saw each other. Maybe it's best we just leave it at that."

He guided her into a chair and pulled up another, so they were sitting, knee to knee. He clasped her hands firmly. "We didn't begin to say everything we needed to, which is why I'm here."

Something in her softened. "I'm listening."

"I talked to my dad. I know what he's been hiding."

Tears of relief stung Jen's eyes.

"He told me all about the symptoms he's been hiding from me. Jen..." Matt gripped her fingers tightly. "I know what a hell of a position he put you in, asking you to keep that secret."

She leaned into Matt's touch, so happy to at last be

able to confide in him. "That's the least of it. His refusal to get treatment—"

"Is in the past," Matt reassured her. "He's at the Mayo Clinic as we speak, being evaluated. And I owe that all to you. Your talk with him made all the difference."

Jen looked down at their intertwined hands. "I'm sure you had something to do with his seeking treatment, too."

"The point is…" Matt tightened his grip on her possessively "…we both owe you a lot. The way you stood up to us made us see how wrong we were to put you in the middle of this. And I'm here to promise you, on both of our parts, that it will never happen again."

Relief poured over Jen. She basked in the warmth and strength of him. "That is so good to hear."

"We also want you to finish the commissioned work for my father, and oversee the Briscoe museum, as planned. It's important work, Jen. We both want you to do it."

Suddenly, all her professional dreams were coming to fruition. Except… Jen extricated herself. Pushing back the chair, she moved a safe distance away. "I don't know that I can."

Matt came after her, his eyes quiet and assessing. "Because of me."

Honesty is always the best policy. Don't beat around the bush. Just tell him. Jen tilted her chin and looked him square in the eye. "Because I'm still in love with you. And that's going to complicate things unnecessarily."

The words seemed to echo in the silent studio. Matt's hands came up to cup her shoulders. "Say that again?"

He searched her face as if he couldn't quite believe what she'd said.

Jen could hardly believe it, either. She had guarded her heart so carefully, tried everything she knew to keep from falling for another rich man. But it was true. And he might as well realize it.

She shook her head helplessly. "I'm in love with you, Matt," she blurted out, taking a huge risk. "I know, I know." She splayed her hands across his hard chest. Felt his heartbeat drop into a slow, heavy beat. "We promised each other it would be a one-day-at-a-time, nice and easy, take-things-as-they-come arrangement, but—" she laughed, a little brokenly "—what can I say?"

Jen rubbed her eyes with the heel of her hand, brushing the moisture away. "I'm a fool. I fell in love with you. And not just in love, but head over heels, forever-and-ever love. So—" she blinked away a fresh flood of tears "—the thought of being in a position where I have to see you and your dad all the time, and be reminded of everything we had, plus everything we'll never have…" She gave a little hiccup, embarrassed to have so thoroughly laid bare her soul. "You can stop me anytime, you know?"

His lips twitched; his eyes warmed. "Why would I want to do that?" he asked softly. "When I'm finally finding out what is in your heart?"

"Well, now you know." Afraid to even look at him, Jen turned away.

Matt tugged her back. "Now I do." He held her in his arms as if he would never let her go. Rubbed a thumb across her lower lip. "And now it's time you found out what is in mine," he said sincerely, his voice dropping to a husky timbre. "I love you, too, Jen, with every fiber of my being. And I have since—well, I don't know when it started. All I can tell you is that it's never going to end. Because my love for you is the forever-and-ever kind, too. The kind that gives you a reason to get up in the morning and keeps you warm at night, the kind that is strong and all-encompassing, and wildly unpredictable."

He dragged in a breath. "And for me that was the problem. I don't know if you've noticed," he admitted, deadpan, "but I like having things under my control."

An understatement and a half! Jen chuckled. "Just a tad."

"I couldn't control this, Jen, any more than I could control you, and that frustrated the living daylights out of me."

She wreathed her arms about his neck and rested her head on his chest. "But now you're cool with me. With this love we've found?"

He threaded his fingers through her hair, pressed a kiss to her temple. "I will be," he promised in a shuddery breath. "As soon as you agree to give me the chance to make everything right."

Jen lifted her head and looked deep into his eyes. "It already is," she vowed softly, hugging him closer still, finally ready for the kind of soul-deep commitment that would bring them both the happiness they sought. "You're more than the love of my life, Matt, you're my future."

"And you," Matt promised, kissing her sweetly, evocatively, "are mine."

Epilogue

Twenty months later...

Matt took Jen's hand in his, bringing her close to his side. He proudly surveyed the collection of his mother's paintings of the Texas landscape, then locked gazes with her. "You were right about February 14 being the perfect time for the opening of the Briscoe Museum."

Jen had known there was no better way to introduce the featured exhibit, A Texas Love Remembered, than Valentine's Day. She squeezed his hand and returned his affectionate smile. "Thanks for ceding control of that decision to me."

Matt shook his head at her as they moved into the next gallery. "Even though our little one is expected literally anytime now..."

"Trust me." Jen patted her ever expanding stomach. "This baby is not going to appear during the evening's events."

Matt lifted Jen's hand to his lips. "You're sure about that."

Reveling in his tenderness, she nodded solemnly. "We've had some talks about it, and our baby understands the importance of art, as a commemorative venue."

Matt looked around at the twenty bronze statues handsomely displayed on white marble columns. "You certainly captured the love my mom and dad had for each other."

Emmett strolled up to join them, looking happy and robust. "I particularly like this statue." Matt's dad nodded at the depictment of himself, Matt, Jen and their new baby, gathered around one of Margarite's paintings. "It brings together the past and the future in a way she would have really liked."

Basking in the praise, Jen squinted at Emmett playfully. "You're not just saying that because you're my father-in-law—and chief patron—are you?" Although he was also underwriting the works of other young artists Jen had discovered, whose works were also on display.

Emmett grinned. "I'm saying it because it's true. Although we do owe you, Jen." He turned solemn. "If not for you and the push you gave me, I'd be off alone somewhere, thinking I had some terrible disease."

"When instead," Jen remembered, "it was only a re-action to the cholesterol medication you were taking." A swift change of prescriptions, and Emmett was fine.

He grinned. "I'm very happy you married my son, and I'm really happy you're blessing me with a grand-child. Although—" his silvery brow furrowed "—it sure would be nice if I knew whether the baby was going to be a boy or a girl."

"I told you, Dad," Matt interrupted cheerfully. "Jen and I decided we wanted to be surprised."

As it turned out, they didn't have long to wait.

No sooner had Jen and Matt returned to the high-rise apartment they were keeping in Fort Worth for the times they had to be in the city, and undressed and got ready for bed, then Jen got right up again.

Matt, who'd been all set to cuddle, switched on the bedside lamp. Immediately on full "daddy alert," he demanded, "What's wrong?"

She stared at the liquid pooling around her feet, aware she was feeling very peculiar. "Either it's raining in here or my water just broke."

Matt threw back the covers and vaulted to his feet. "Get your bag!" he commanded hurriedly. "I'll call the hospital!"

Aware she hadn't even had her first contraction yet, Jen chuckled. Sedately, she headed for the bathroom to get a towel. "They don't have my records, remember?" Thinking it might be a good idea to wash off the amniotic fluid, she turned on the shower. "I'm supposed to have the baby in Laramie."

"Well, that's not happening now," he said, frowning even more as she shucked her gown and stepped into the shower. "Lucky for us, Harris Methodist Hospital is just a few blocks away."

"Matt…" Finished, Jen stepped into the towel he held out. "We've got plenty of time…."

And, as it turned out, they did.

Eighteen hours and twenty-four minutes, to be exact.

But when Maggie Lynn Briscoe entered the world, she let out a lusty, healthy cry that Jen and Matt were certain could be heard several city blocks away.

Of course, both of them were crying, too. Happy, excited, bursting-with-love tears that commemorated their feelings for each other and their beautiful baby girl.

The nurse wrapped Maggie in a blanket and handed her over to the two of them to soothe.

As soon as their daughter heard their voices, she stopped, blinked and looked up at them in wonder.

Matt leaned over and kissed his wife and baby. "No

question," he told Jen, in a husky voice laced with wonder. "This is the best day of my life. Bar none."

Jen nodded as the happiness she felt grew to unimaginable heights. "Mine, too," she whispered emotionally, kissing Matt, and their baby, and then Matt again.

Trembling, she took her husband's hand in hers and squeezed tight. "But just so you know, we have plenty more of 'em to come," she promised.

And they did.

* * * * *

Watch for the next book in Cathy Gillen Thacker's
LEGENDS OF LARAMIE COUNTY *miniseries,*
THE TEXAS RANCHER'S MARRIAGE
coming November 2012, only from
Harlequin American Romance.

Found: One Baby

Chapter One

It wasn't the first time Michelle Anderson had noticed a "gift" left on Thad Garner's front porch. In the three months she had lived across the street from the sexy E.R. doc, a parade of hopeful single women had presented the most eligible bachelor in Summit, Texas, with everything from baked goods and homemade casseroles to gift baskets and balloons. But this was the first time she'd seen an infant car seat, diaper bag and a Moses basket left there.

Aware the latest offerings hadn't been there when she'd left the house for her early-morning run, Michelle wondered if the baby gear was supposed to be some sort of message.

If so, it was an interesting one, given that Thad Garner had the reputation of a player and the attention span of a gnat when it came to women.

The handsome thirty-three-year-old doc *said* he wanted a wife and kids. *Sooner,* rather than *later.*

But he rarely dated a woman more than two or three times before ducking out of her life as genially as he had eased in.

"The chemistry just isn't there—I'm hoping we can be friends" was what he reportedly said more often than not.

But that wasn't what the women of Summit wanted.

They wanted the passion Thad declared lacking from his side of the equation.

They also wanted, Michelle thought with a sigh, what she wanted—when the time and the man were finally right. Marriage, a fulfilling life together, kids. As well as a career. Realistically, she didn't know if it was ever going to happen for her.

Professionally and financially, everything was in place. She was thirty-two. Partner in a law practice. Had her own home. She was even considering adopting a baby on her own and—

Is that the sound of a baby crying?

It couldn't be, Michelle thought as the high-pitched sound sputtered, stopped and then resumed, now a frantic, all-out wail.

She scanned Thad's porch and yard, as well as the street. At seven on a Saturday morning, the area was usually quiet. Not today. Not with the unmistakable sound of a crying infant.

Heart pounding, Michelle jogged across the street and onto Thad's lawn. She hurried up the steps to the covered front porch of his Craftsman-style home.

Sure enough, an infant, red-faced and upset, lay in the elaborately decked-out Moses basket. He—Michelle assumed it was a boy because he was swaddled in blue—couldn't have been more than a few days old.

Heart going out to the tiny thing, Michelle knelt down on the porch. She removed the soft blanket covering the squalling child and lifted him out of the portable baby bed and into her arms.

And it was at that moment the front door jerked open.

Her too-sexy-for-his-own-good neighbor stared down at her.

And Michelle's heart took another giant leap.

THAD RUBBED HIS FACE with the palm of his hand and tried to blink himself all the way awake. "What's going on?" he demanded, sure now he had to be fantasizing. Otherwise, his gorgeous, ice princess of a neighbor would not be standing on his doorstep with a baby in her arms. "And why were you ringing the doorbell like there's a house on fire?" he asked gruffly. He'd thought he dreamed it, and had gone back to sleep—until he heard the infant crying.

Michelle Anderson's glance trailed over his bare chest and low-slung pajama pants before returning to his face. A warm flush—at odds with the cool mountain air   spread across her pretty cheeks. "I didn't ring the bell," she said.

Thad had no idea how long ago it had been when he heard the bell. Five minutes? Fifteen? It still felt like a dream. Except for the flesh-and-blood woman and tiny newborn in front of him. "You're sure standing here next to it," he observed wryly.

"Only because I wanted to ask you what was going on," she shot back.

Aware he probably should have grabbed a T-shirt before bounding outside, Thad studied Michelle and the newborn in her arms. He didn't know why, but she seemed to be accusing him of something nefarious. "You're the one with the baby," he pointed out.

Michelle patted the baby snuggled against her. The protective note in her sweetly feminine voice deepened. "True, but I'm not the one who left said baby on your front porch."

She sounded like a lawyer. "What are you talking about?"

She pointed to the infant paraphernalia next to her feet. "Someone left a baby on your doorstep."

Single women in Summit had done a lot of crazy things to get his attention, but this topped everything. "Someone should have told you it's way too late for an April Fools' joke," Thad scoffed.

"I'm well aware today is April sixth," Michelle replied coolly, "and if this *is* a ploy to get your attention, Dr. Garner, I assure you, it's not mine."

Thad looked into Michelle's face. He rubbed the last of the sleep from his eyes. "Why would anyone leave an infant with me?"

Michelle motioned at the piece of white paper wedged between the side of the baby bed and the mattress in the bottom of it. "Perhaps that envelope will tell you."

Thad knelt down to get it. His name was scrawled across the front, all right.

He tore into it and read.

Dear Thad,
Brice and Beatrix may have changed their minds about becoming parents—I haven't. It's up to your brother, Russell, to decide what to do about William, since William is his kid.

I'm sorry it didn't work out, but again, it's not my problem. I did what I signed on to do. And that's all I'm going to do.
Sincerely,
Candace
P.S. I hope you have better luck tracking down Russell than I did.

"What the...?" Thad muttered, scanning the letter once again.

Still trying to make sense of what it said, he held it out so Michelle could read it, too. "Who are Brice and Beatrix?" she asked with a frown.

Aware the baby looked blissfully happy snuggled against his neighbor's soft breasts, Thad said, "No clue."

Michelle pulled the blanket closer around the baby's tiny body. "Candace?"

Thad shrugged and studied the wisp of dark, curling hair escaping from beneath the crocheted blue-and-white knit cap. The baby's clothes looked expensive. "Also no idea."

"But Russell...?"

"Is most definitely my brother and my only living relation," Thad replied, taking in the baby's cherubic features and fair skin. Was that his imagination or did William have the Garner nose? And Garner eyebrows? And chin?

He knew his older brother prided himself on his vagabond lifestyle, but could Russell really have turned his back on his own son? Or did he not know about him? Had the mother of this obviously unwanted child decided Russell was a bad bet as a father and put their baby up for adoption without consulting Russell? Only to have the adoptive parents back out at the last moment?

Michelle stared down at the baby as if he were the most adorable infant ever to grace the earth. Thad knew how she felt—the kid was certainly cute enough to grace a baby-food ad.

Michelle looked up at Thad. "Do you think your brother even knows he's a father?"

Thad exhaled. "Hard to say."

Irritably he scooped up the diaper bag, infant car seat and Moses basket and set them in his foyer. "Please come in," he said gruffly.

Michelle did so, albeit hesitantly, warily.

Not that she had ever been particularly friendly with him, Thad thought.

Since moving to Summit some three months earlier to take over the law practice of a retiring local barrister, she'd barely had the time of day for him. He wasn't sure why she was so aloof, at least where he was concerned. He'd never been anything but cordial to the attractive attorney.

Of course they hadn't encountered each other all that often. She worked from nine to six Monday through Friday. His shifts were generally twelve hours and varied according to the demands of the Summit, Texas, emergency room.

Nevertheless, he'd had a hard time keeping his eyes off the willowy strawberry blonde.

Michelle Anderson carried herself with the self-confident grace of an accomplished career woman. On workdays she could usually be seen in sophisticated business suits and heels. On weekends and evenings, she was much more casual.

This morning, she was wearing a pair of navy running shorts that made the most of her long, shapely legs, a hot-pink-and-navy T-shirt that paid similar homage to her breasts. Her running shoes and socks were white. Her hair was caught up in a ponytail on the back of her head, and the few escaped tendrils were attractively mussed. Her peaches-and-cream complexion had a healthy glow, while her emerald-green eyes held the skepticism of a woman who had seen and heard way too much in the course of her profession.

But then, Thad thought, walking over to snag a navy blue T-shirt off the back of the sofa and pull it on, so had he…

"Well?" Michelle asked, bouncing slightly to comfort the now-squirming newborn, as Thad slid on a pair of moccasins and came back to stand beside her. "Does that letter make any sense at all to you?" she demanded.

Thad watched the baby root around as if looking for a nipple. "Unfortunately, yes," he admitted reluctantly, not proud of this part of his family heritage. Spying a baby bottle in the pocket of the infant seat, he plucked it out and unscrewed the lid.

The formula smelled fresh. He screwed the top back on and handed it to her. "My brother is as reckless and shortsighted as they come."

"Meaning?" Michelle offered the bottle to William and smiled when he latched on immediately.

Thad frowned. "It's possible Russell's gotten himself in a mess and left me to clean up." And that was all Thad was prepared to say until he had talked to his only sibling.

AT THAD'S INVITATION, Michelle sat down on the sofa and gave William his bottle while Thad went off to make some phone calls.

When he returned some thirty minutes later, he was dressed as if for work, his broad shoulders and impossibly masculine chest covered by a starched green shirt and tie, his trim waist, hips and long, sinewy legs draped in khaki dress slacks. His custom-made leather boots were buffed to a soft sheen.

He smelled…so good. Like the forest after a drenching spring rain. And he looked great, too—his square jaw newly shaven, his golden-brown eyes alert with

interest. "I left messages for Russell everywhere," he reported grimly.

Trying not to notice how the early-morning sunlight streaming in through the windows glimmered in his short, sandy-brown hair, Michelle shifted William to her shoulder to burp him. Up close, she couldn't help but notice—once again—how ruggedly handsome Thad was. No wonder all the women in town were wild about him. When she tore her gaze from his chiseled jaw and sensual lips, it was only to meet the warm intimacy of his amber eyes.

Finally she found her voice. "Any idea how long it will take for your brother to get back to you?" she asked, surprised at how casual and unaffected she sounded.

Thad looked unhappy. "No telling." He clipped a pager and cell phone to his belt, searched around for his keys. "Russell could be in any time zone. He's a photojournalist for a wire news service, always off on assignment somewhere, but he checks his messages every day, unless he's in a war zone. Then, of course, it can be harder to get in touch with him."

Michelle was rubbing William's back gently. "What are you going to do?"

Thad eyed her reluctantly. "That's what I wanted to talk to you about." He sat down next to her and smiled tenderly at the baby, who was looking back at him with sleepy blue eyes. "I'm due at the E.R. in twenty minutes. I'm trying to get someone to cover my shift for me. Meanwhile, I need someone to watch William." He offered his index finger to the baby and grinned when William instinctively wrapped his tiny fist around it and held on tight.

Anxiously, Thad looked back at Michelle. "You know any babysitters I could call on short notice?"

Michelle knew what he was really asking. "You can't take him with you to the hospital?"

Thad shook his head. "It'd be a bad idea. Too many germs in the E.R."

He had a point there. She looked down at her tiny charge. It didn't matter what she thought of Thad. This child needed tender loving care. "How old do you think he is?" she asked softly, smiling when William finally let out a healthy-sounding burp.

Thad chuckled, too. "A few days. Maybe."

And already abandoned. Michelle felt tears welling in her eyes. "That's what I thought, too," she murmured thickly. She wished she could simply take William to her place and give him the home he deserved. But life was never that simple. Wishes were never granted that easily. She would not get the baby she wanted in her life this way.

"So back to the babysitter dilemma," Thad persisted, oblivious to the yearning nature of her thoughts. "Any idea who I could call?"

"Besides any of your legion of female admirers?" she quipped, offering the last of the bottle to William.

"I'm serious."

So was she. Michelle tested the waters with an idea. "Violet Hunter knows a lot about kids."

"We dated a couple times, when I first came to town."

So Michelle had heard. The pretty single mom had been one of Thad's most persistent admirers.

"It was about six months after her husband died," Thad continued cryptically. "It didn't work out. From what I can tell, although it's been about two years now, she's still pretty vulnerable."

Michelle had met the twenty-nine-year-old nurse—

and her two little girls—at a charity fundraiser the previous summer. She was very nice. And very much in the market for another husband.

She looked at him, waiting.

"I don't want to give Violet the wrong idea," Thad said finally.

Michelle studied him. Close up, he didn't appear to be the kind of guy who enjoyed stringing women along. In fact, the opposite. Life had taught her that appearances could be deceptive. She did better relying on facts in her personal life, just as she did in her practice of the law.

"And the wrong idea would be?" she probed.

Thad regarded her with the patient cool of an expert witness. "That something might be possible when it's not." Regret turned down the corners of his mouth. "And if I call Violet—or someone else I've dated—and tell them I need help with the baby I suddenly have on my hands…"

"You'd probably be getting more than chicken enchilada casserole on your front porch," Michelle said wryly.

"Exactly."

"Whereas if you were to put me in charge…"

He suddenly seemed defensive. "It's pretty clear where you stand regarding dating me."

"But you've never asked me out, so I've never had the opportunity to turn you down."

"But you would," Thad countered.

True. If only because she didn't want to end up wasting her time again on something that was never going to happen. Only this time, given Thad's rep with the local ladies, she would know that going in. Deciding, since they were neighbors, it was best simply to be honest, she shrugged. "I don't date players."

His lips tightened. "I'm not a player."

Michelle kept her eyes off the sinewy lines of his shoulders and chest. She did not need to remember how he looked clad only in a low-slung cotton pajama bottom, or be thinking about the crisp, dark hair arrowing straight down the goody line. She closed her mind to any further licentious thoughts. "Right."

"I'm just honest about whether or not I see a future with a woman."

Doing her best to slow her racing pulse, she got a hold of her out-of-control fantasies and retorted, "And you usually don't."

"Usually isn't always," he replied cryptically.

Which meant what? Michelle wondered. He'd had his heart broken, too?

Disconcerted—because that would give them something in common—she returned her gaze to the newborn nestled in her arms.

If William were *her* baby...

But he wasn't, Michelle reminded herself firmly.

Still, the little guy was here now. He needed someone to watch over him until this mess could be sorted out. Someone who wouldn't leave him on Thad Garner's doorstep all by himself.

"Believe me," Thad said, sounding as protective toward this tiny baby as she was, "if I had any other job, I'd stay and take care of the little fella myself. But I can't leave the E.R. short-staffed. We've got the only trauma center in the entire county."

Lives depended on Thad.

Just as William, it seemed, was momentarily depending on her.

Before Michelle could stop herself, she was pushing

aside every self-protective instinct she had and volunteering. "Fine. I'll do it."

Thad's eyebrows lifted in amazement. "You sure?" he said finally, standing. "It's going to be twelve hours, unless I'm able to find someone to cover the rest of my shift for me."

Forcing herself to shove aside the memory of another child, another time, Michelle stood, too. There would be no such heartbreak this time because she wouldn't allow herself to get that involved with William or Thad.

Loving the way the now-sleeping William snuggled against her, she brushed off Thad's concern. "I didn't have much planned for today, anyway," she fibbed. Her flower beds could wait.

Thad breathed a sigh of relief. "Thanks. I really appreciate it."

Michelle had a few stipulations of her own. "I want to watch him at my house, though." The less she knew about Thad, the less time spent in his abode, the better.

"Of course." Thad gently brushed his fingertips across William's velvety cheek.

The air between the three of them reverberated with tenderness.

With apparent effort, Thad dropped his hand, stepped back and looked over at the baby gear in the foyer. "I hope everything you're going to need is here."

Michelle lowered her face to William and smelled… spit-up. Knowing that was something that could easily be taken care of, she said quietly, "If you'll carry the stuff across the street, I'll sort through it."

"No problem." He plucked up the items and followed her out the front door. "I owe you big-time for this," he told her solemnly, falling into step beside her.

"Yes," Michelle agreed. "You do."

WHERE TO START? Michelle wondered as soon as the door shut behind Thad, and she and William were alone. She supposed it best to change William's diaper.

She slung the diaper bag over her shoulder and carried him upstairs to her bedroom. His eyes were open again as she laid him gently down on the soft cotton quilt on her bed. "You know, we hear about things like this all the time," she told him as she pulled a diaper and a packet of wipes from the bag. "Babies being left in the strangest places. I just want you to know that you shouldn't take it personally. Candace was only doing what she thought best, taking you to your uncle Thad's house."

Although why Candace had simply left him in the Moses basket on the front porch was anyone's guess. "But I don't want you to worry," Michelle continued reassuringly. "Because we are going to find your parents and get this all straightened out."

One way or another, they would find a great home for William. Even if it meant calling the police and social services.

"In the meantime, I'm going to take care of you today, and then your uncle Thad is going to look after you. And before you know it, this little blip in your existence will be over. And it'll all be good."

All she had to do, Michelle thought as she went about getting everything she needed out of the diaper bag, was not get emotionally involved in a situation that was ultimately a win-lose proposition for her.

Winning, because she got to spend time with the most adorable baby she had ever seen.

And losing, because she was going to have to let him go.

Just as she'd had to let Jared and his son, Jimmy, go.

And that was as painful an event as ever, Michelle mused, unsnapping the legs of William's designer duds.

Before she could get the diaper off, her phone rang.

Seeing Thad Garner's name flash on the caller-ID screen, she grabbed the portable off the bedside table.

"How are things going?" he asked.

It was ridiculous how glad she was to hear his voice. She hit the speaker button on the receiver and set it on the bed. Doing her best to play it cool, she said, "You just left him five minutes ago!"

"More like seven." Thad paused. "It sounds quiet."

Talk about overprotective! "He seems happy enough," Michelle allowed.

"He's awake?"

"Yes. I'm in the process of changing his diaper."

"While we talk?"

"Believe it or not, I can multitask." She used a baby wipe on William.

"How does the diaper area look? Everything okay?"

William turned his head slightly toward the sound of Thad's voice.

Michelle smiled. "As far as I can tell. It looks like he had a circumcision."

"Did they leave any antibiotic ointment for the stitches?"

"Yes." Figuring he would know, she asked, "How often are you supposed to apply it?"

"A very thin layer three times a day."

Michelle made a note of that. "Since we don't know when it was done last, should I go ahead and do that now? Or wait till later?"

"Go ahead and put some on now just to be on the safe side."

Michelle did as directed.

Thad paused. "Is there a pharmacy label on the ointment?"

Once again, they were of one mind. Had there been a label, there would have been a patient last name and a prescribing physician and hospital or pharmacy name, as well. "No. It may have been on the box the ointment came in—but that's not with his belongings." She confirmed this with a second look through the bag.

"Too bad. It would have helped to have more to go on than first names."

Michelle agreed wholeheartedly. Right now, of the four people ostensibly involved in this fiasco, they only knew how to contact one, and he might be out of the country! "Did you hear from your brother?" she asked, hoping that might have been the real reason for the call.

"Not yet." Thad sighed his frustration.

As long as she had "the doctor" on the line, Michelle asked, "Would it be okay if I gave William a sponge bath? He smells a little like spit-up."

"How's his umbilical cord?"

She checked it out. "Kind of, um, brown. Still hanging on."

"Not infected?"

"No."

"I think a sponge bath would be okay," Thad said in that thoughtful voice doctors used when tending to patients. "Just make sure the water temperature is lukewarm. And don't get the cord wet—keep that area dry."

Michelle resnapped the Onesie and tucked the blanket in around William to keep him warm. "I'll go to Dr. Greene's website on the internet and read up on the proper procedure before I start, just to make sure I do everything correctly."

Another pause. "You know about that?"

Michelle tried not to take offense at the surprise in Thad's voice. "All my friends back in Dallas have babies. All of them use that website as their primary reference."

"No wonder you seem so at ease with a newborn," he said.

That wasn't why.

But Michelle didn't want to tell him about the year she had spent taking care of another infant, only to lose him—and his father—in the end.

"Anything else you need?" Thad asked helpfully.

Michelle studied the contents of the diaper bag. "As far as I can tell, there appear to be enough diapers, clothing and formula to last a couple of days." She wondered if Thad would even *have* the baby that long. She knew better than anyone that the situation could change in an instant, that Brice and Beatrix or Candace or even Russell could show up to claim the baby. Which again was why she needed not to become too attached or overly involved in this situation.

Oblivious to her concerns, Thad continued, "If you need anything else, let me know. I'll pick it up on the way back."

This was suddenly getting way too cozy for comfort.

Reminded of the last time she'd had her heart broken, Michelle picked up William and held him. "Aren't you supposed to be at work?" Michelle asked impatiently, beginning to see why women fell so hard for the notoriously sexy doctor.

"In two minutes." Thad paused. "I just wanted to check with you before I actually went into the hospital and let you know how to page me in case anything else comes up." Thad gave her the number. "Call me if you need me. Otherwise, I'll check in with you later," he promised before he hung up.

With a sigh, Michelle turned back to the fragile bundle in her arms. "Looks like it's just you and me, little guy," she said. She smiled, realizing he was already fast asleep. "At least until your uncle Thad returns."

Chapter Two

Thad expected to have half-a-dozen calls from Michelle Anderson during the day.

There were no phone calls.

And the two times he did call her, just to check in, she had sounded a little exasperated.

He guessed he couldn't blame her.

She probably thought he didn't trust her to take care of William in his absence. Nothing could have been further from the truth. Like animals, children knew instinctively whom they could trust and draw comfort from. William had recognized Michelle for the maternal soul she was from the moment she picked him up and cradled him gently in her arms.

Still, the moment his shift was up, Thad headed out the door and drove the short distance home. He parked in his driveway, then headed across the street.

As he approached the front porch of her Arts and Crafts–style home, he noticed the windows were open. Mounting the front steps, he heard Michelle singing softly. He glanced through the window. She was sitting in an old-fashioned rocking chair he hadn't seen earlier, William in her arms.

Thad couldn't tell if the baby was awake or asleep— he couldn't see William's face—but the moment was so tender and loving it stopped him in his tracks. This, he thought, was what parenthood should be about. This was the kind of life he and his brother should have had as kids, even after their mother died.

But they hadn't. And there was no going back. Only forward. To the family he wanted to create.

All he needed was a woman to love.

He rapped on the screen.

The lovely vocal rendition of "Brahms' Lullaby" stopped. Michelle rose slowly and walked over to open the door and let him in. She had changed into vintage jeans and a pale blue knit shirt that clung to her curves. Her apparently just-shampooed hair had dried in a tangle of soft, strawberry-blond curls. He had never seen her wear it that way, but he liked it as much as the sleek, straight style she usually wore.

"William looks...happy," Thad noted. And so did she.

A pretty pink blush lit Michelle's cheeks. "He's very happy," she said, meeting Thad's eyes, "as long as he's being held." She frowned in concern. "Every time I get him to sleep and put him down, he wakes up after about ten minutes and completely freaks out."

"Probably remembering..."

"Waking up alone on your front porch?" Michelle asked. "That's what I was thinking."

Thad shook his head. His brother was very much like their father had been while he was alive. Neither held much regard for familial responsibility or blood ties. Their lives were all about the latest career challenge.

Thad shoved his hands through his hair in frustration. "Damn Russell," he muttered.

Michelle exhaled softly. "Haven't heard from him, I take it?"

"No. And I've left several messages." Thad felt the vibration of his phone. He took it off his belt clip, looked at the caller ID. Speak of the devil. "Finally!" Scowling, Thad put the phone to his ear. "Where are you?" he barked.

"I'm on assignment in Thailand. What's the emergency?" Russell demanded, sounding equally irritated.

"A baby was left on my porch this morning." Briefly, Thad explained.

Russell swore like a sailor who'd just found out his shore leave was canceled. But typically, he offered no explanation or apology.

Thad pressed on. "Did you know you were having a baby with Candace when you left the country?"

"I assumed she was pregnant," Russell retorted, surprisingly matter-of-fact. "I didn't know for sure."

And obviously hadn't bothered to find out, Thad thought irritably. "Why didn't you mention it to me?" he demanded.

"Because her pregnancy wasn't relevant to my life," Russell grumbled.

Figuring he was going to need legal advice sooner rather than later, Thad activated the speaker on his phone and motioned Michelle closer, so she could listen in on the conversation.

"What do you mean Candace's pregnancy wasn't relevant to your life?" Thad asked.

Russell exhaled. "It was a surrogate arrangement. I donated sperm for a couple of friends."

Okay. That made slightly more sense. Thad withdrew the pen and notepad he habitually carried in his shirt pocket. He wrote "Help me out here" on a slip of paper and handed it to Michelle.

She edged closer, concern on her face. "According

to the note left with baby William, Brice and Beatrix changed their minds about becoming parents," Thad told his brother.

"You'll have to ask Candace Wright about that," Russell insisted.

Thad jotted down the last name of William's birth mother. "Do you have a phone number?"

Another disgruntled sigh. "She lives in Big Spring. That's all I know."

"What about Brice and Beatrix, the adoptive couple?"

"The Johnsons live in San Angelo. Listen, I can't do anything from here—you're going to have to straighten it all out."

"How?" Thad shot back, aggrieved his brother could be so cold. "I don't have paternity."

"Neither do I. I signed away all my rights at the fertility clinic before the surrogate was even impregnated."

"We're going to need a copy of those papers ASAP," Michelle told Thad, switching into lawyer mode.

"Who is that?" Russell demanded.

"Michelle Anderson," she introduced herself. "I'm a neighbor of your brother's—I found the baby."

"She's also an attorney," Thad interjected.

Michelle asked Russell, "Is there any way we can look at those papers you signed?"

Russell harrumphed. "They're in one of the boxes I left in Thad's attic. If you can find them, you can have 'em. Aside from that, I don't want anything to do with this. Like Candace Wright, I've done my part."

It wasn't that simple, Thad knew. "If what Candace said is true...if Brice and Beatrix have changed their minds about taking William into their family... Genetically, the child is half yours."

"Not to my way of thinking," Russell snapped.

"He's a Garner." And that, Thad thought, should mean something.

Russell scoffed. "What would I do with a kid? I don't have a home and I don't want one."

Every fiber of Thad's being told him it would be a mistake just to walk away. Anger rising, he said, "You can't just stand by and do nothing while this child you had a hand in creating is abandoned."

"Sure I can," Russell replied. "And you know why? Because it would be best. The kid doesn't need a father like the one we had. And that's what I am. However, if you think you can do better, if you want to jump in, Thad, be my guest. Just leave me out of it."

The connection ended with a decisive click.

Thad locked gazes with Michelle, not sure whether he was sorry or glad she had heard all that. He swore. "What a mess."

YES, MICHELLE THOUGHT. It was one heck of a mess.

Deciding it was time to try again, she carried the sleeping William over to the elaborately lined Moses basket, and set him down gently on his back. She tucked a blanket around him to keep him warm. Relieved he still appeared to be asleep, at least for the moment, she walked over to the window where Thad was standing. "I'm not sure I should be involved in this situation."

Thad looked surprised, then confused. "You're a lawyer."

Her pulse picked up as she pointed out, "I'm not *your* lawyer."

Thad tilted his head. "You could be."

She kept her expression impassive. "This is a family-law case."

He raised an eyebrow. "And you have a background in family law. A pretty good one, from what I've heard."

That was then, Michelle thought. This was now. And she knew better these days. She lifted her hands in a vague gesture of dissatisfaction and stepped away. "I did so much of it the first five years out of law school that I burned out on it. My current practice focuses on the needs of small business, wills and estate planning, real estate and consumer law. My law partner—Glenn York—docs all the divorce, custody and adoption cases for our firm."

"I know his reputation. He's very good." Thad paused. He glanced over at the sleeping William, then back to Michelle. "I'd still prefer you handle it."

His was not an uncommon reaction. People with legal trouble often latched on to the first person who appeared able to help them out of it, without bothering to verify credentials or search out expertise in that specific area of the law. "You don't even know me," she said.

"You've handled the situation well so far."

That wasn't the only reason, Michelle decided. "You're embarrassed by your brother's attitude, aren't you?"

A muscle worked in Thad's jaw. "Wouldn't you be?"

Michelle tried not to think how easy it was to be here with Thad like this. She shrugged. "I learned a long time ago not to judge people by the messes they get themselves into." She had always been trained to look at both sides of every issue. "Besides, it sounds as if your brother was trying to do a good deed for someone. It just didn't turn out the way he expected."

Thad sobered. "I hadn't thought about it that way."

Michelle called upon even more of her law-school

training. "Your brother may change his mind about the child."

Thad's mouth took on a downward slant. "No. He won't."

"How can you be so sure?"

"Because of the way we grew up." Thad's mood turned reflective. "Our mom was really great—loving and fun, smart and kind—but she died from an aneurysm when Russell and I were in elementary school. We barely knew our dad—he was a geologist for an oil company. I've no doubt he loved us in his way, but he wasn't interested in being a hands-on parent. Nevertheless, he left the project he was working on in South America and came back to Summit to take care of us." He exhaled. "For the next ten years or so, he worked assignments around the state. When we hit our teens and were old enough to stay alone, he went back to the more exciting gigs in South and Central America. From that point on, until he died five years ago, we rarely saw him because he was just never home."

Michelle touched Thad's arm gently. "That sounds lonely."

Thad glanced at her hand, then said, "Summit's a close-knit community. We had a lot of people looking out for us. Plenty to eat. And the house across the street to live in."

But, Michelle speculated, not what he had obviously wanted most—a loving, emotionally engaged and interested parent on the premises.

"What was your childhood like?" Thad asked, his rumbling drawl sending shivers over her skin.

She figured she might as well be honest, too. "I grew up in a well-to-do suburban enclave of Dallas. I was an only child of two very loving but ambitious people." She paused. "So let's just say, for me, failure in any venue was not an option."

Thad chuckled sympathetically. "You're giving me new appreciation for my laissez-faire teens."

Michelle sighed. The understanding look on his face soon had her confiding further in him. "Don't get me wrong. I had plenty of attention and everything I needed to succeed. Including special tutors and private coaches when necessary."

Thad seemed to know instinctively there was more. "But…?"

"There were times when I felt as if I had been born on a treadmill set at high speed with no way to get off." Times when she had felt she would never please her folks no matter how much she accomplished. Michelle forced herself to go on. "My parents were both tenured university professors and department chairs. When they weren't hovering over me, urging me to greater heights, they worked all the time."

William stirred and began to whimper again. She went over to pick him up before he began to wail in earnest. Soothing him with a cuddle and a kiss, Michelle walked back to Thad.

"That sounds rough," he said.

Michelle nodded and handed the baby to him. "Too much so for my folks," she admitted, watching with pleasure as William snuggled up to Thad every bit as easily as he had snuggled up to her. Then she frowned. "My mom and dad both died of stress-related illnesses a few years ago. Their health problems spurred me to reevaluate my own life. I decided I didn't want to continue to live in the big city, so I began saving money and looking around for a place to live a quieter life."

"I know what you mean. I went to medical school and

did my E.R. residency in Houston. By the time I'd finished, I'd had enough of rush-hour traffic and crowds. When there was an opening at the Summit hospital, I jumped at it."

William's lashes shut. His breathing grew deep and even once again.

"But we digress," Michelle said.

Thad cast a loving glance at the infant in his arms. "Yes," he said softly. "We do."

Forcing herself to pull back emotionally, before she got in way over her head, Michelle said, "You need to get this situation with William sorted out as soon as possible."

Before either of them fell even more in love with this abandoned little boy.

THE FIRST ORDER of business, they both decided, after they had resettled the sleeping William in his bed, was to get the addresses and phone numbers of the people involved. That turned out to be easy enough. An internet search quickly gave them contact information for Candace Wright, as well as Brice and Beatrix Johnson.

Aware he was so far out of his depth it wasn't funny, Thad asked, "Any advice on how I should handle this?"

Michelle glanced sideways at him, reminding him, "I'm not going to represent you."

Thad wondered if she had any idea how beautiful she looked in the soft light of her elegantly decorated living room, feet propped up on the coffee table, laptop computer settled on her jean-clad thighs. He propped up his feet on the coffee table, too, next to hers. "You could still advise me as a friend."

Her eyes remained on the screen as she studied the

information there. She typed in the print command. "Are we friends?"

Somewhere in the too-quiet depths of her house, he heard a laser printer start up. "I think we're getting there." As she put her laptop aside and moved to stand, he inhaled the orange-blossom fragrance of her shampoo.

He stood, too. "Why? Does that bother you?"

He followed her down the hall to the kitchen. A home-office space had been built into one wall, with floor-to-ceiling kitchen cabinets on either side. The printer was on the shelf above the desk. She plucked several pages out of the tray and gave him a look of lawyerly calm. "These are highly unusual circumstances."

No argument there. Thad shrugged, aware he hadn't been this affected by a woman in a long time. If ever. "What better way to get to know each other?"

Her lips curved cynically. "I hope you're not hitting on me."

Was he? "Wouldn't think of it." Thad matched her semiamused tone.

Silence fell between them. Knowing this would all go a lot easier if Michelle were there to help him and their tiny charge, Thad walked back to the living room with her. "Just help me get through the rest of the weekend," he proposed.

In his bed, William pushed out his lower lip in indignation and began to whimper once again.

"Then if I need to hire someone, I'll do it on Monday morning." He picked up William and cradled him in his arms. The little guy couldn't have weighed more than eight pounds and still had the faint redness of skin all newborns had. Yet he already had so much personality. "I don't want to screw this up. This little guy has already been through enough." Thad fought the unexpected tightness in his throat, continued in a voice that sounded rusty, even to him. "And since my brother is not acting responsibly…"

Michelle turned away, but not before Thad thought he saw a glint of empathetic tears in her green eyes. She cleared her throat. "Speaking of Russell, maybe you should try to find whatever it is he signed and make sure those papers state what he thinks they do."

"Good point." Legal jargon could be as confusing as medical terminology. "You want to come over with us, help me search?"

Surprise mingled briefly with disappointment in her eyes. "You're taking the baby tonight, then?"

"I figured I'd keep William at my place tonight since you had him all day." Thad gazed at Michelle. She looked like she'd just lost her best friend. "You can stay over, too." The invitation was out before he could think.

She took it completely the wrong way. The droll expression was back on her face. "Uh, thanks, but…no."

He held up one palm. "I'll be the perfect gentleman."

She rolled her eyes. "I'm sure you would be."

She fit the crocheted cap on William's head and helped Thad bundle him up in a blanket. When that was done, she picked up the diaper bag and Moses basket, while he held the door for both of them.

Together, they strolled down the front walk and across the street. Thad led the way up his front porch, wishing he'd thought to turn on the lights before he'd gone over to Michelle's home.

"So, my rep is that bad?" Thad shifted William to one arm while he unlocked the door and hit the lights.

"Or good." Michelle preceded Thad inside in another

drift of orange blossom. For the first time he realized how disorderly his home was.

"Excuse me?" he asked in confusion.

"It all depends on how you look at it," she explained.

Thad switched on more lamps, wishing he'd thought to vacuum or dust in the past month, instead of sitting around reading medical journals and working out at the hospital fitness center in his spare time.

"Please continue," he prodded her.

She looked him straight in the eye. "You've got a reputation for dating around, not sleeping around."

"Good to know," he said.

The sparkle was back in her eyes. "Isn't it?"

Thad figured it wouldn't hurt to flirt. Especially since she'd started it. "As long as we're on the subject, want to know what your rep in the community is?"

DID SHE WANT TO KNOW?

His goading look was all the provocation she needed. "Well, I guess now I have to know."

Thad put William over his shoulder and gently patted his back, then turned his attention back to her. "Ice princess."

Okay, that hurt. A little. Especially since she'd done nothing to deserve it.

She made her eyes go wide. "Really?"

"Mmm-hmm." Thad stepped closer, still patting William on the back. "Word is, you've been asked out by at least twenty guys—"

"I think that's a small exaggeration," she said.

"—and said no to every single one," Thad finished smugly, leaving no doubt that he'd been investigating the details of her romantic life, or lack thereof, too.

She shrugged, aware her pulse was racing, and defended herself. "Well, that's because I won't go out with someone if I don't see hope of anything…happening."

A smile tugging at the corners of his mouth, he leaned down so they were practically nose to nose. "How can you know if you don't go out with them?"

"I just do."

He let his gaze drift over her slowly, before returning to her eyes. "See, I don't buy that," he told her with lazy male confidence. "I don't think you can begin to know someone unless you spend one-on-one time together. You've got to take a risk—"

Michelle smirked. "Well, I hear you've done plenty of that."

"—to reap rewards." He sneaked a peek at the baby on his shoulder. He grinned when he realized that William was sound asleep again. He walked over to the Moses basket and gently laid the baby down, covering him with a blanket.

Trying not to notice how naturally Thad had taken to being a daddy figure to the abandoned little boy, Michelle rocked forward on her toes.

The thought of Thad reaping rewards with any other woman bothered her more than it should. Marshaling all her defenses, she asked sweetly, "How's that method working out for you so far?"

"I haven't hit pay dirt yet." His gaze slid past the delicate hollow of her throat, to her lips and then her eyes. "I will."

She took a deep breath, dropped her gaze. Then found herself remembering the way he'd looked, shirtless and just out of bed, that morning. Flushing, she tore her eyes from the masculine contours of his chest. "*Sure* you will."

"Make fun all you like," he said. He stepped closer. "You need to take more risks."

His words hit a chord. She'd heard the same from others, too. "Just see if you can find the papers," she instructed irritably, deciding Dr. Thad Garner was the last man she would ever get involved with.

Thad sighed. "Wish me luck. That attic is a mess."

"It's not there," Thad reported in frustration a short time later.

He'd only been up in the attic twenty minutes, Michelle thought. She removed the bottle she'd been heating from the bowl of warm water. "Are you sure?"

Thad looked at William, who was lying patiently in his Moses basket, eyes wide open, trying awkwardly to get his thumb to his mouth. "I checked through the most recent boxes."

Which meant Thad hadn't checked through everything belonging to his brother, Michelle deduced. "Maybe it's in an older box," she suggested, wiping the outside of the bottle dry. "Do you want me to go up and look?"

Thad glanced at her clothes. "It's kind of grimy up there," he warned.

Michelle tested the bottle on the inside of her wrist. "Not a problem. You'll have to feed William, though."

"He's ready to eat again?"

"Yes, he is." Michelle handed Thad the bottle of formula.

Thad smiled, as if he relished his first chance to give William a bottle.

"You know, we could probably just wait and ask Candace Wright."

"That's assuming we can find her and she'll talk to

us. She may not. In any case, it's best to be as prepared as you can be before you walk into a situation like this." She sighed. "So if Russell thinks the papers he signed are in the attic, I think we need to do everything possible to find them. Because if we can find them, then we will know what attorney he used to prepare them."

"What if they didn't use an attorney? What if they just went online and printed out some do-it-yourself forms and signed those?"

Michelle exhaled. "Then none of what they've done may be legal. But again, we're getting ahead of ourselves." She held up a staying hand. "How do I get to the attic?"

Thad picked up William and the bottle. "We'll walk you up there."

Thad motioned her up the stairs. Past the master bedroom, with its heavy mahogany furniture and big, comfortable-looking bed. There was a stack of books and what looked like medical journals on both nightstands. Baskets of what looked like clean, unfolded laundry, and an overflowing hamper. On down the hall, past another bath and bedroom, decorated in teenage-boy motif, with a big sign on the door that read Russell's Room—No One Else Allowed. Next to that was a study, with a desk and cozy leather armchair and ottoman. Along one wall was a stack of gift boxes, reminding Michelle of all the women in town who were chasing him. Before she could stop herself, she blurted, "What's this? The trophy room?"

"I'm planning to donate it all. I just can't do it anywhere in town. 'Cause someone will know and then I'll hurt somebody's feelings…and I don't want to do that."

She could see he was serious. "It must be hard to be you," she said drily.

He returned her droll look and opened a door leading to the third floor. "Up there."

Michelle hit the switch next to the door. Light flooded the third floor and spilled down the rough wooden stairs. "Thanks."

Thad wandered back in the direction they'd come. "William, let's go into the master bedroom and have ourselves a bottle, shall we?"

Shaking her head, Michelle headed up the stairs. Thad was right. It was a mess. And a pretty big one. Most of it seemed to be Russell's, judging by the name scrawled in black Magic Marker on the sides of boxes.

She began looking. And looking. And looking. Finally, thirty minutes later, she hit the jackpot. Or at least she hoped she had. She found a metal lockbox, the kind where people tended to store their important papers. Only problem was, she noted, it was locked.

Footsteps sounded on the stairs. Thad came up to stand beside her. "Any luck?"

She waved her find. "This could be it."

Thad towered over her, six feet two inches of attractive single male. "I didn't know he had that up here," he murmured in a low, sexy voice.

Once again, Michelle forced herself to set her attraction to the handsome doctor aside. She moved past him and headed briskly down the stairs. "Where's William?"

Thad followed laconically. "In his Moses basket, asleep."

Which meant she now had Thad's undivided attention, at least for the next ten minutes or so, until William awakened again. She ignored the tingling in her midriff and forced herself to stay focused on the task. "You don't happen to have a key for this?"

He shook his head.

"How about a paper clip?"

"In my study."

They peeked in the master bedroom, where William was sleeping, then ducked into the study, opened a desk drawer and rummaged around. Finally he produced a paper clip and handed it over.

She could feel him watching her as she sat on the edge of the desk and began to work on the lock.

She looked up. The intent, appreciative, all-male look in his eyes made her catch her breath. "What are you thinking?" she demanded.

Thad tucked a finger beneath her chin, moved in closer. "This."

Chapter Three

Michelle had plenty of time to duck her head and step away—if she wanted to avoid the kiss.

She didn't.

Maybe because kissing him was all she'd been thinking about since he'd answered the door that morning, fresh out of bed.

Actually, she reminded herself sagely, the zing of awareness had happened a lot sooner than that. He'd caught her attention as soon as she realized who was living across the street from her.

The parade of women making their way to his front door—plus his reputation as a love-'em-and-leave-'em type—had kept her from acting on that purely physical attraction.

But coming face-to-face with him this morning, being close enough to touch that powerful, masculine body, had forced her to see him in a new light.

Not just as a neighbor or a guy she was too wary of to befriend.

But as a man who conjured up the kind of romantic daydreams and pure, physical lust she didn't know she possessed. And seeing him with William, knowing how deeply he cared about family, even when it seemed that the only family he had left didn't care all that much about him, had added another dimension to the mystery that was Thad.

So when Thad angled his head and his face drifted slowly, inevitably closer to hers, Michelle gave in to the curiosity that had plagued her for months now and let it happen.

She opened her mouth slightly and let his warm, sensual lips make contact with hers. And then suddenly his arms were around her, dragging her closer, so that every inch of her was pressed against every inch of him. Hardness to softness, heat pressed to heat, she was wrapped in a cage of hard male muscle and passionate determination. Her heart beat wildly and she tilted her head back in open surrender. His tongue swept into her mouth, blazing a path that was as tender as it was fiery. She stroked her tongue against the potent pressure of his, knowing she hadn't made out like this…since… Had she *ever* made out like this? Had her insides ever sizzled from just a kiss?

Michelle didn't think so. Which was why, she realized abruptly, she couldn't let it continue. She'd be in *way* over her head.

She flattened her hands on the hard wall of his chest and tore her lips from his. "Stop!"

Just that swiftly, Thad did.

He drew back, loosening his hold on her, not letting go completely. "What's wrong?"

She lifted her brow. "You even have to ask?"

This time, he did release her.

He stepped back and settled on the edge of his desk. Long legs stretched out in front of him, hands braced casually on either side of him, he met her gaze. "I have to admit…I'm confused," he murmured, making no effort to hide his continuing desire, "since I thought we were getting along like a house on fire."

They had been. She hitched in a breath and qualified, "For all the wrong reasons."

His brow furrowed.

She held up her hands in a gesture that warded off further intimacy. "It's not you and me, Thad. It's the *situation*. Our emotions are heightened. Finding William this morning...well, it upset our whole world. So naturally we have a lot of extra adrenaline and emotional energy to burn off, and we did that by ending up in each other's arms."

The look he gave her was skeptical. One corner of his just-kissed mouth quirked up, reminding her of how great he tasted. "That all sounds very reasonable—except for one thing. I work in a hospital trauma center, Michelle. I'm used to a hell of a lot more upset and stress."

She flushed with an embarrassment she could not contain. Held his eyes with effort. "So maybe I'm the only one with an excess of adrenaline and emotion."

He sobered immediately. "Well, maybe—but we still haven't figured out how we're going to handle this situation with William."

Trying hard not to focus on the *we* in his approach, Michelle decided more physical distance between them was needed. She sat down on the leather reading chair in the corner and went back to working on the lock. "First of all, William was left in your care, so it's really your call how you want to proceed."

He settled more comfortably on the edge of his desk. "I want your professional advice."

Michelle slipped into the much more comfortable lawyer mode. "I suggest you speak to Candace Wright first—since she is the person who apparently left William in your care, and Beatrix and Brice Johnson next. Find out what went wrong with the surrogate arrangement and if the Johnsons really have changed their mind, or if this is all some sort of big misunderstanding."

Thad paused, looking none too happy about the possibility someone might want William back. "You think it's possible the surrogate and the Johnsons somehow got their signals crossed?"

Michelle had stepped into far worse adoption quagmires. She shrugged, admitting, "It happens."

Another pause. "Does Candace Wright have any legal rights to William?"

Good question, Michelle thought. "Only if she is the egg donor, as well, and that's not the case in ninety-eight percent of the surrogate arrangements these days." Thad gave her a quizzical look, prompting her to continue explaining. "When the surrogate is also the biological mother, it's literally her child, too, in a purely physical sense, and that mutual DNA complicates how she feels about giving the baby up at birth. So these days, a donor egg, as well as donor sperm, is generally used—the surrogate is simply a host. That makes it a lot easier for the surrogate to surrender the baby at birth."

Thad took that in. "So if that was the arrangement..." he said eventually.

"Then Candace Wright has no legal right or responsibility to the child. The egg donor would also have terminated her legal rights to the baby before implantation, just as your brother did. However, she could be in a position now to reverse that and make a claim on William if no one else wants him." Michelle sighed. "And right now we have no idea who the egg-donor-slash-

William's-biological-mother is. But either the Johnsons or Candace Wright will probably know that."

"How do you know so much about surrogate arrangements?"

"Two reasons." Michelle felt a give in the lock she was still trying to undo. "It's now an essential part of family law. And I handled a contract for a client."

Thad's eyes lit with renewed interest. "Did it turn out all right?"

Michelle nodded. "That one went without a hitch. But it was a different situation. The surrogate was the wife's sister. A medical condition prevented the wife from carrying a pregnancy to term, but they were able to use the egg and sperm of the husband and wife, so it was all pretty clear."

Silence fell. Thad looked increasingly conflicted. Michelle's heart went out to him. This was a very tough situation.

"One way or another, I am sure William will find a very good home with loving parents." *She would see to it.*

Thad nodded, his handsome face a mask of sheer male determination. "Initially, I was going to try to track down Candace Wright by phone. Now, I'm thinking our conversation should be done face-to-face."

"I agree," Michelle said. "And you should probably take William—and someone else with you—to witness the events. Just in case there are any questions later about what was said and by whom. It also might be a good idea to get Candace to give you a copy of her original surrogate contract, as well as an affidavit relinquishing any claim to custody, under the current conditions of William's abandonment, if that is still her desire."

"We couldn't just use the letter she left on my front porch?" Thad asked hopefully.

"We'll produce it as evidence of course, but a judge is going to want to see more than that."

"It'll have to go to court?"

"Eventually, yes, because we're talking about a change in whatever custody agreement was put in place prior to William's birth."

Thad exhaled. "This is getting complicated."

Michelle offered a sympathetic smile. "Surrogate arrangements always are." People were rarely prepared for the complexities involved.

"I'm beginning to think I should take legal counsel with us."

Michelle felt another give in the lock. Almost there.

"It's not a bad idea."

From the other room, they heard a whimper, then a full-throated cry. Thad disappeared. When he returned, William was snuggled against his chest, quietly looking around. Michelle could see Thad was already getting his hopes up that the baby would end up staying a member of his family. She didn't want to see him disappointed.

"Will you go with us?" Thad asked.

Aside from Michelle's law partner, Glenn York, there was only one family-law attorney in Summit. Tucker James was a good guy, but not one inclined to work weekends or take on matters that were unusually complex. If this situation turned out to be as messed up as it appeared, Michelle knew Thad was going to need a top-notch attorney experienced in surrogate arrangements. That would be Glenn. Unfortunately Glenn was already working all weekend on a messy divorce-and-property-settlement case that would be in deposition next week. Reluctantly Michelle volunteered. "I can help you out *temporarily*."

Thad smiled his relief, putting far too much stock in her abilities. "That would be great!"

"One thing, though," Michelle cautioned.

He waited, sandy eyebrows raised.

"No more kissing," she said firmly.

"Agreed." He grinned. "Unless you change your mind."

Oh, how she wanted to, Michelle thought. It had been so long since she had felt so wanted. So long since her body had hummed with distinctly female satisfaction.

But Thad did not need to know that, she schooled herself sternly.

She looked him in the eye. "I won't."

He went very still. Looking disappointed, but no less determined, she noted.

"Because…?" His low voice sent shivers over her body.

Once again Michelle pushed away the desire welling up inside her. She called on her cool-as-ice courtroom demeanor. "We're neighbors and we need to stay on good terms."

He searched her eyes with daunting intimacy. "And you think we wouldn't if we kissed again?"

I think I'd be devastated if I turned out to be one of your three-dates-and-it's-over women. Hence, better safe than sorry, Michelle thought, as she gave the lock one more nudge. It opened with a click. She lifted the lid. Inside were several insurance policies on expensive camera equipment Russell Garner owned, an old driver's license of his and a Summit High School class ring. There were no legal documents of any kind. Certainly nothing pertaining to a surrogate arrangement.

"I don't know where else to look," Thad said in frustration.

Michelle knew it wasn't the end of the road for getting the information he needed. Far from it. "The attorney who prepared the documents will have copies. Maybe we can find out who that is tomorrow," Michelle said.

Aware her reason for sticking around was gone, she stood. It was as difficult as she'd suspected it would be to leave the baby she had cared for all day. She forced herself to suppress her own deep longing for a child and look at Thad.

"What time did you want to leave tomorrow?" she asked casually.

"Seven in the morning okay with you?"

Michelle held Thad's gaze a moment longer, then touched William's cheek gently. "I'll see you both then."

MICHELLE HAD JUST changed into her pajamas and climbed into bed when the phone rang. Seeing it was Thad, she picked up the receiver and heard the loud, angry wails of an unhappy newborn.

"What's going on?" she asked, aware William hadn't cried that way when she'd been in charge.

More loud crying. "Help," Thad said over the din.

Michelle was already reaching for her slippers. "I'll be right there."

Grabbing her light raincoat, she slipped it on against the chill of the spring evening and headed across the street. Thad was waiting for her, the wailing baby in his arms.

"What's the matter?" Michelle asked, stepping inside.

The moment she spoke, the crying dimmed.

"You poor baby," she soothed.

The wailing stopped altogether.

William studied her with his long-lashed, baby-blue eyes.

"Is it possible he just wanted to hear your voice?" Thad said.

Michelle scoffed and shook her head. "I only wish I were that wonderful. So what's going on?"

"I was trying to give him his formula." Thad pointed to the full bottle on the table next to the sofa.

Michelle walked over and picked it up. She frowned. "It's cold, Thad."

He looked even more clueless. "Yeah, so?"

"You're supposed to heat it."

He held up a hand in expert fashion. "Actually that's an old wives' tale. Infants are perfectly capable of taking their formula cold."

Michelle narrowed her eyes at Thad. "Did they teach you that in medical school?"

"As a matter of fact," he told her smugly, "they did."

Unfortunately, Michelle thought, babies had individual quirks and preferences, just like adults. "Well, maybe that would be okay if he'd had it cold from the beginning. But he hasn't. I gave him warm formula all day. The bottle you gave him earlier this evening was warmed, too."

Thad appeared to think that over, but in the end refused to give ground. "Maybe he just missed you and wants *you* to give him his bottle again."

Michelle's ego liked the idea of that. Her maternal side had other ideas. "And maybe he just wants it warm."

Thad shrugged. "One way to find out." He handed William to Michelle.

She sat down in a chair, her raincoat still on.

His mouth quirked in barely suppressed amusement. "You can take off your coat and stay a while."

No way, she thought. She was in her pj's. No underwear. "I'm fine." Michelle settled William in her arms and offered him the nipple. He looked at her with absolute trust, started to suck, then got a taste of the cold formula. He pushed it out with his tongue and kept looking at Michelle.

"He's not crying," Thad noted.

That was because he was busy snuggling against the softness of her breasts, the way he had all day. Michelle continued making eye contact with the little cutie. It was odd how much she had missed him, so quickly. It wasn't as if he were *her* baby.

Perhaps she should remember that.

Aware Thad was still holding on to his med-school theory about not needing to warm baby formula, Michelle told him wryly, "The only reason he's not crying over cold milk is he's probably wondering how I got so dumb so fast. Right, little fella?"

William's tiny mouth opened slightly. He looked as if he wanted to talk, wanted to tell her what was on his mind, but just couldn't figure out how.

Michelle smiled, utterly besotted.

"Try the bottle again," Thad said.

Knowing a point had to be made here, Michelle did.

William took a taste, then again pushed the bottle away with his lips and tongue. Michelle tried once more. William once more refused it. "I think we should warm it," she reiterated.

"One problem." Thad walked toward the rear of the house. She followed with William and the bottle. Unlike her kitchen, his hadn't been upgraded in many years.

The cabinets were painted white, and the walls were covered with a yellow-orange-and-brown-plaid wallpaper. A yellow-laminate-topped breakfast set with padded vinyl chairs were so retro they were back in fashion. The appliances were similarly dated. Even the faded yellow curtain above the sink looked like it had been there since his mother was alive. The only new items in the kitchen were a toaster and a matching coffeemaker.

"I don't know how to warm a bottle," Thad continued.

"Let me guess. You've never done any babysitting, either."

"I've been around kids."

"Not the same thing."

"Apparently not," he conceded.

The silence was contentious. And veering dangerously toward flirtation again. It made her nervous. "Are you paying attention?" she asked.

"Close attention."

Okay, so he still desired her as much as she desired him. It didn't mean they were going to act on it. She gave him the bottle. Their fingers brushed. She felt the heat of his body all the way to her toes. Swallowed. "Actually, maybe you should do this," she told him. "That way it will be easier for you to remember."

All business now, he said, "Okay."

"They make bottle warmers, but we don't have one, so we're going to do it the old-fashioned way. There was a pretty bowl here earlier..."

"That belongs to Violet Hunter."

Why was Michelle not surprised?

"She brought me some chili in it earlier in the week and I keep forgetting to take it back. She called after you left, offering to come by and get it tonight, but I told her I'd bring it to her at the hospital. Now, if you want me to go out to my car and get it..."

Michelle shook her head. Best he return the bowl to the lovesick nurse as soon as possible. "Where do you keep your bowls?"

He opened a cupboard, revealing a mismatched assortment of dishes, and handed one over.

Michelle shook her head. "That's a cereal bowl. It's way too shallow." She paused. "Surely you've got mixing bowls."

Thad gave her the blank look of a man who did not know his way around a kitchen. Michelle tried a simpler approach. "Where do you keep your pots and pans?"

This he knew. He pointed to a lower cabinet.

Michelle handed William to Thad and knelt to see what was there. Plenty, as it turned out, although again, everything there was at least thirty years old. She took out a saucepan, carried it to the sink and filled it with very warm tap water. She set the bottle in the pan, so the water covered the contents.

Thad leaned in, over her shoulder. "And now?"

"We wait."

Thad edged closer, smiling down at the baby. "How will we know when the bottle's the right temperature?" he asked as he and the baby made goo-goo eyes at each other.

"We'll keep testing it. It should only take a few minutes."

"Hear that, William?" Thad gently caressed the little one's cheek. "Your dinner will be ready shortly."

Three minutes later, the formula was the right temperature. They returned to the living room.

Thad sat down to give William his bottle. William made a face and pushed the nipple right back out.

"*Now* what's wrong?" Thad asked.

Michelle could only guess. "Maybe William senses you're uncertain."

Thad didn't deny that could be the problem. "Maybe you should give it a try again," he said.

Figuring the little one had waited long enough for his feeding, Michelle sat down next to Thad on the sofa. He handed the baby to her. She shifted William so he was in a semi-upright position, resting in the crook of her arm. "We know you're hungry," she said, putting the nipple to his lips. William just stared at her, still refusing to drink. "You're not going to be able to go back to sleep until you take this bottle," Michelle said softly, gently rubbing the nipple back and forth across his lips. "So give it a try, little guy."

Still watching her, William opened his mouth, took the nipple and began to suck. Twenty minutes and two burps later, William had downed all three ounces.

"I guess he was hungry," Thad mused.

Reluctantly Michelle handed the baby back to him. She knew she shouldn't be getting this involved in something that was essentially not her problem, but she really wished she could stay right here with the two of them, or better yet, take William home with her.

Reminding herself that was not an option, Michelle stood. "He should be good for three hours," she said.

"Sure you don't want to stay the night? We could have a slumber party."

The image of Thad in his pj's was all she needed to throw her overheated senses into overdrive. She quickened her pace. "Nice try."

William in his arms, he followed her into the foyer. "What should I do if he starts crying again?"

Michelle paused, her hand on the doorknob. "Generally speaking, if William is unhappy, it's one of four things—he's wet, hungry, sleepy or in need of comfort and reassurance. Just go down the list, and if all else fails, just talk to him."

Thad said, a tender note in his tone, "He likes your voice."

And I like yours, Michelle thought, realizing how easily she could get used to being around Thad.

She smiled. "He'll like yours, too, if he hears it often enough."

"Thanks for coming over." Thad shot her a look full of gratitude. "For helping. For everything."

Unwillingly Michelle flashed back to another man, another time, and gratitude that had been mistaken for something else. She hardened her defenses, knowing she had to be careful. "Try to get some sleep." She opened the door.

"Can I call you in an emergency?" he asked as Michelle swept into the darkness of the cloudy spring night.

She nodded, throwing the words over her shoulder. "But *only* if it's an emergency."

MICHELLE HALF EXPECTED Thad to call her every three hours through the night. He didn't. Several times she got up and went to the window and looked across the street to his home. At eleven, two and five, the lights were on, and the rest of the time the house was dark. Which probably meant, she thought, that William was sleeping between feedings.

Telling herself that was good—Thad could easily handle parenting William on his own, after all—Michelle forced herself to go back to bed each time and try to get some sleep.

When the alarm went off at six, it was a relief. She skipped her usual morning run and headed for the shower. At seven, Thad and William were at her door.

Soon after, they were off, Michelle and Thad sitting in the front of his BMW SUV, William sleeping contentedly in the middle of the rear seat.

"So how was your night?" Michelle asked, opening up her briefcase. If she was going to protect her heart, she needed to stay in business mode.

"Fine, as soon as William and I reached an understanding."

Michelle heard the smile in Thad's voice. "And that was?"

"There was only one place he was going to sleep more than ten minutes."

She sent him a sidelong glance. "You held him all night?"

Thad nodded, looking as content as she had felt after spending all day holding William. "I slept in the reading chair and ottoman in the study, and he slept on my chest."

Michelle could imagine that was a very warm and snuggly place to sleep. She cast a look back at William, but couldn't see a lot, because the infant seat was facing backward. "I'm surprised he's been content in his car seat for as long as he has."

"It's probably the motion," Thad theorized.

As it turned out, he was probably right. William slept all the way to Big Spring, and continued sleeping as they followed the MapQuest directions to the address listed for Candace Wright.

The surrogate mother lived in a small yellow bungalow with a sparse lawn and overgrown shrubbery.

"Think one of us should ring the bell and see if she's home first?" Michelle asked.

Before Thad could reply, the front door opened and a slightly pudgy young woman stepped out. Arms crossed in front of her, her long dishwater-blond hair whipping around in the spring breeze, she stalked over to the car. Took a glance at the infant seat in back. Sighed. "Let's not do this on the street," she said, motioning at the bungalow.

THAD WASN'T SURE what he expected the surrogate mother's home to be like. Certainly not a wall-to-wall artist's studio, with beautiful landscapes stacked against every surface, and an easel with a half-finished canvas front and center in the room.

"I'm sorry I had to leave the baby like that," Candace Wright said as soon as introductions had been made, "but I was afraid you'd be like everyone else in this mess and refuse to take him."

"You're sure Brice and Beatrix Johnson don't want him, either?" Michelle asked.

"Apparently not." Clearly confused about the situation, Candace shrugged. "I'm as surprised as you are. They were thrilled about the baby until a couple of days before William was born. Then they started acting a little weird, almost like they were having second thoughts."

"Did you ask them about that?" Thad interrupted.

Candace shook her head. "I told myself they were just nervous about becoming parents. Happens to a lot of people, from what I've seen. Anyway, they came to the hospital and were there when William was born. As soon as they held him they seemed really happy again. We signed the papers. They took him home. Everything was great. A day later, Beatrix shows up at my door with the baby, completely distraught, and just hands him to me."

Thad and Michelle both did a double take, but it was Michelle who asked the question first. "With no explanation?"

Candace lifted her hands in helpless frustration. "Beatrix said a lot of things, but none of it made any sense, she was crying so hard. All I got out of her was that she couldn't do this right now…and maybe not ever… and that because I was his mom I had to take care of baby William…there was no one else. By then he was crying, too. Beatrix really started sobbing." Candace sighed and shoved a hand through her hair. "Beatrix mumbled something about her husband needing her, then she ran back to the car, jumped in and drove off, still crying her eyes out. I didn't know what was going on, so I called the lady lawyer who handled the legal stuff for the surrogate arrangement—"

"Do you have her card?"

Candace nodded and went to retrieve it. "She sounded as stunned as I was when I told her what had just happened, but she wouldn't do anything, or even talk about the situation with me."

"She really couldn't until she had spoken to her clients," Michelle explained.

"That doesn't make sense!" Candace complained.

"It's complicated," Michelle admitted. "But her first duty, as the Johnsons' legal counsel, is to them. Whatever is said to her is privileged and can't be shared with anyone else without their express permission. Otherwise, she could be disbarred."

"Whatever!" Candace scowled. "Anyway, she said she'd have to investigate and get back to me. I asked her to come and get the baby. She said not until she spoke to her clients. And then she asked me to sit tight and take care of the baby until other arrangements could be made." The young woman threw up her hands in exasperation. "I've got a showing in Houston next month. I'm already way behind in what I need to have ready, and I don't have time for this! So then I remembered that Russell had said he had a brother who was a doctor in Summit, Texas. I looked you up on the internet, got your address and dropped William off and ran before you could tell me you didn't want the responsibility for him, either. Not that any of this was supposed to be my problem, anyway. I only agreed to be a surrogate so I could afford to stay home for a year and concentrate on my art! I never wanted to become a parent. I *still* don't."

Thad wasn't sure whether to be grateful or annoyed that the surrogate was so emotionally distanced from William.

"What about the donor egg? Do you know where that came from?" Michelle asked.

Candace nodded. "There was a nurse the Johnsons knew at the fertility clinic. She felt sorry for them just like I did because they wanted a kid so bad, and it wasn't going to happen for them any other way. She's the one who donated the egg."

"Do you have the nurse's name?"

Candace sobered. "She died in a boating accident a couple months ago."

"Did she have family?" Michelle asked.

"No." Candace paused. "So that just leaves Russell as William's family. Since I can't find Russell, that means you have to deal with this, Dr. Garner! Because I can't!

And frankly," she finished wearily, "I shouldn't have to, since I was just the vessel that carried the baby. Nothing more."

MICHELLE AND THAD STAYED long enough to get an affidavit from Candace briefly explaining what had happened.

Michelle telephoned the San Angelo attorney who had handled the private surrogate arrangement and left a message, asking to meet with her as soon as possible. And then Michelle and Thad headed toward the Johnson home in San Angelo, William in tow.

Unlike Candace Wright's humble artist's lair, Brice and Beatrix Johnson lived in a very nice home that sat on several acres of land in an exclusive gated community. Thad drove up the paved drive and, as before, they'd barely gotten out of Thad's SUV when the front door opened. A woman Thad estimated to be in her early forties rushed out, overnight bag in hand. Her hair was wet—as if she had just gotten out of the shower and hadn't taken time to dry it. The little bit of makeup she did have on could not hide her red nose or the fragile puffiness surrounding her red-rimmed eyes. She stopped when she saw the baby cradled in Thad's arms. Her expression fell.

Thad took a chance. "Beatrix?"

She nodded, eyes still on little William.

Thad extended his free hand. "I'm Thad Garner, Russell Garner's brother. This is my attorney, Michelle Anderson. We need to talk."

As Thad had hoped, Beatrix Johnson acquiesced. Minutes later, they were all settled in the elegant white living room. Briefly, Thad explained how they came to have custody of William.

Beatrix continued to look a little shell-shocked. "I'm so sorry. This is all such a mess."

"So you have changed your mind about adopting William?" Thad asked.

Beatrix nodded, looking all the more miserable but no less resolute.

Michelle pulled a notepad from her bag and began to take notes. "And you started having doubts a few days before William was born?"

Beatrix reached for a tissue. If she was surprised at how much they knew, she didn't show it. "We found out I was pregnant—with twins. Due in six months. At first we were just so stunned. We didn't know if we would be able to handle three children born so close together, but then we decided we could."

William stirred and Thad cradled the baby closer to his chest. "So you took him home from the hospital."

Beatrix nodded. Fleeting happiness appeared on her face. "It seemed like everything was going to be fine." She paused for a breath and her expression changed. "And then the very next day my husband was in a terrible car accident. So I rushed the baby over to Candace and I went to the hospital to be with my husband and that's where I've been ever since. I just came home this morning to shower and get a fresh change of clothing. I was on my way back to see Brice when you arrived."

"Is your husband going to be all right?" Thad asked.

Beatrix's shoulders slumped in obvious relief. "The doctors think so, but he has a broken back and leg and months of rehabilitation ahead of him." Beatrix's lower lip trembled. "I can't handle a newborn, take care of my husband and be pregnant with twins at the same time. Even if we were to get help in, it's just too much!" She dabbed at her eyes. "I talked to my husband this morning. And as much as it breaks our hearts, he agrees. We have to do what is right for William and find him a home where he can get the love and attention he deserves."

MICHELLE WAITED UNTIL the three of them had stopped for lunch at a park on the outskirts of town before she asked Thad, "Are you okay? You've had a lot to try to absorb the past thirty hours or so."

Thad walked William back and forth while she added powdered formula to sun-warmed bottled water. His expression as sober as his thoughts, he turned his gaze back to hers and told her what was on his mind. "My brother's attitude I can almost understand. Russell likes to help people on the fly, and he never thinks things through. Candace Wright obviously needs money, and I think her heart is in the right place, too. She could have turned the baby over to foster care, or driven to the closest police or fire station and dropped him off there anonymously." He exhaled. "Instead, she drove him all the way to Summit and left him with me. With the only true family William has."

"You're right." Michelle shook the bottle vigorously. "The surrogate mother could have simply called 911 and let them sort it out. As for Brice and Beatrix Johnson—" This wasn't anything they had asked for. "They're really in a tough spot. My heart goes out to them."

Thad accepted the bottle she gave him. Still standing, he offered it to William and watched as the little boy began to take the formula. "I feel for them, too," Thad said. "This is a very difficult situation. Clearly, it's not easy for them to give the little guy up, but they are forcing themselves to be realistic, no matter how much it hurts, and do what is best for William under the circumstances. They're putting him first. Just as I intend to do."

Michelle caught her breath at the intent look in Thad's eyes. Although she wasn't supposed to be getting emotionally involved, this was what she had secretly hoped for. "What are you saying, Thad?" she asked cautiously, needing to be sure.

Thad stepped closer yet, steely determination in his golden-brown eyes. "I want to adopt William, Michelle." Deliberately, Thad held her gaze. "Will you help me?"

Chapter Four

"I know you mean well."

He guided her to the low brick wall that edged the grass surrounding the picnic area. Making sure they were out of earshot of everyone else, he sat down with William still in his arms and stretched his legs out in front of him. "But...?"

Michelle sat down, too, making sure there was a good distance between them. Which he promptly closed, simply by sliding toward her. "Adopting a child is not like helping out in an emergency. It's a lifelong commitment."

"You think I don't understand that?" He sounded faintly annoyed.

She turned so her bent knee was touching his rock-hard thigh. "I think you're acting in the heat of emotion because you feel responsible for this child in a way no one else seems to, and because you've grown to care for him." And it wasn't hard to see why. William was a very lovable little boy, cute and fragile in the way all newborn babies were.

"I'm not going to change my mind."

If he had other children or even a wife, Michelle might feel differently. But he was a bachelor, a man who'd never been able to settle on one woman. She sent him a level look, aware her heart was racing again. "You need to think about this," she insisted.

His voice dropped. "I have thought about it—all last night and today."

So had Michelle.

But five years' experience in family law had taught her to proceed cautiously. Decisions made in the heat of emotion were often the wrong ones. "I know this seems like a good idea now," she said gently, determined to remain sensible, "but you've only been responsible for William for the past thirty-some hours, and of that time, I was taking care of him for thirteen hours."

He acknowledged this with a slight nod of his head, his eyes never leaving hers. "I had him by myself all last night."

She pretended she wasn't playing with fire here. "And had help from me again today. What's going to happen when you and I both have to go to work tomorrow?"

He lifted his broad shoulders in an unapologetic shrug. "I'm off tomorrow and I traded my Tuesday shift, which means I don't work again until Wednesday. That gives me time to figure something out, after I get the legal issues taken care of."

Michelle tried not to make too much of his unexpectedly bold confession. She swallowed the knot of emotion in her throat. "You're really getting ahead of yourself here, Thad." Ignoring the warmth in Thad's eyes as he gave William his bottle, she said, "Brice and Beatrix Johnson haven't officially terminated their rights yet."

Thad waited until William had a good ounce, then handed her the bottle and moved William to his shoulder for a burp. As he patted the infant gently on the back, he said, "They will."

He was so confident.

Michelle's gaze drifted to the trusting way William rested his cheek on Thad's shoulder, his angelic face turned into the comforting curve of Thad's neck. They were so cute together, these two Garner guys, already looking so much like father and son.

"As far as the law is concerned, right now Brice and Beatrix Johnson are still William's parents. You have physical custody of the child *only* because they are allowing it."

Thad shifted William back into the strong cradle of his arms and offered the bottle again. Michelle watched as William suckled eagerly. It was as if at some point during the night the infant had decided he wanted Thad to be his family as much as Thad wanted William to be his.

"What do you think I should do next then—from a practical standpoint?" Thad asked.

"Get legal representation for yourself as soon as possible." More a friend now than counsel, Michelle put a gentle hand on his arm and looked him in the eye. "And in the meantime, you need to really think about this tonight, Thad. And make absolutely certain it's what you want to do." *Before you and William bond even more...*

"THAD GARNER IS on the line. He wants an appointment ASAP."

Michelle had already alerted Becky—her and Glenn's legal secretary—that Thad might be calling. She'd also talked to Glenn about the situation. "Ask him if he can come in at nine-thirty."

Becky relayed the information, then covered the

mouthpiece. "He wants to know if it's okay if he brings the baby."

Trying not to think how much she had missed seeing William during the night, Michelle nodded. "Of course."

An hour later Thad arrived.

Michelle knew he was there, because she could hear Becky oohing and ahhing even before he was formally announced.

Seconds later Thad walked in. He was wearing a light blue button-down shirt and khaki dress pants. He looked every bit the doting father, with William bundled up in his arms. He aimed a smile her way. "Good morning."

It was *now,* Michelle thought. She slipped back into a business frame of mind and returned calmly, "Good morning."

Looking as glad to see her as she was to see him, Thad walked over and transferred the baby to her arms. "William wants to say hello to you," he told her softly.

Michelle looked down at the sweetly composed little face. "He's asleep," she noted drily.

Thad's husky voice broke the silence of the room. He sat on the edge of her desk. "Not for long, if the current trend continues."

Michelle rocked back in her swivel chair. It felt so good having the little fellow in her arms again. Longing swept through her. If only he could be *her* child. "Long night?"

He traded glances with her, heaved a rueful sigh. "I couldn't put him down for more than ten minutes at a time without him waking and wanting to be held." Thad lifted a palm. "I know what the old hands at child-rearing would say, but...I don't think he could be spoiled yet. Do you?"

Michelle looked down at William. No way was this angel spoiled! "I imagine he's just trying to figure out where he fits in this world."

"Well, I know with whom." A mixture of determination and protectiveness laced Thad's low tone.

"Meaning?" she asked.

"I haven't changed my mind," Thad told her. "I still want to proceed with what we talked about yesterday afternoon."

"All right, then." Michelle reluctantly handed William back to Thad and pressed the intercom button. "Becky, would you please ask Glenn to come in."

Moments later Michelle's former law-school colleague and new law partner strode in. The thirty-four-year-old father had a mild-mannered look that was deceptive; he was an extremely effective litigator, and an even more acclaimed negotiator with a reputation for crafting solutions that made everyone happy, even in the messiest divorces and custody cases. The two of them had joined forces several months before to buy out two retiring Summit lawyers and take over their practice.

Like her, Glenn—and his family—were new to that area of Texas. "As I told you yesterday, Glenn does all the family-law cases for our firm. I'm going to meet with the two of you long enough to bring him up to speed, and then he'll be happy to help you."

To MICHELLE'S RELIEF, Thad did not press her to represent him but, instead, took the assignment of counsel graciously. She excused herself and headed to court. From there, she went to a meeting with a client, back to court for another hearing on a business dispute she was handling, and then back to the office to draft a will for yet another client.

Only when she had finished did she pack up and head home for the day. When she reached her street, she could not say she was all that surprised to see balloons tied to the mailbox, a big wooden stork sign and at least two dozen cars parked on the drive and on either side of the street. Thad Garner was having a party. Whether or not it was premature was too soon to tell.

Glad she hadn't received an update from Glenn regarding the progress of Thad's case but, instead, had stuck to her own clients' needs, Michelle grabbed her briefcase and headed into the house. She'd barely had time to kick off her shoes when the doorbell rang. Through the beveled glass in the front door she could see a familiar figure. She went to answer it.

Looking as happy as any father coming out of the delivery room, Thad handed her a bubblegum cigar.

"Celebrate with us," he urged.

Michelle lifted her eyebrows. "I don't know. Sort of looks like you have your hands full."

Doubtless Violet Hunter was there, too.

Not that she was jealous.

Thad clamped a cigar between his teeth. "It's a hand-me-down shower. Everyone brought stuff their kids no longer need." Sensing correctly that stronger persuasion was needed, he lounged against the portal. "Seriously, it's a lot of fun. And there are a lot of people from the hospital I'd like you to meet."

Michelle didn't deny she needed to get acquainted with more people in the community. In the three months she'd been in Summit, she'd been so busy working and meeting with clients, she'd had no time for socializing.

She tried to sound casual. "Where's William?"

Thad's mouth curved in a playful smile. "Back at the house, greeting his adoring friends and neighbors."

Did she really want to miss that, too? "What's the dress code?" she asked.

"Come as you are." He took her hand, drawing her close. "Which means you can come as you are."

In a suit and heels? She tugged back. "I'd prefer to change."

Impatience underscored his low tone. "Promise you won't take long?"

She fell victim to the seductive smile. "Five minutes."

"I'm going to hold you to that," Thad murmured with another lingering look, then he released her hand and headed out the front door.

IT WAS FIFTEEN MINUTES. Thad knew, because he was watching the clock and the door. The wait was worth it, though, when Michelle walked into the party.

She had changed into a pale yellow, V-necked sweater, black denim jeans and boots that made the most of her long and lean runner's body. She'd swept up a section of her gorgeous hair in a jeweled clasp. Her cheeks were flushed pink. From self-consciousness? he wondered. Interesting, because he'd never seen her ill at ease before. Unless you counted the aftermath of their one and only kiss. Then, she had looked much the same way. As if she'd wanted to be with him, and she didn't. As if she'd enjoyed kissing him, yet wished she hadn't fallen victim to the potent chemistry sizzling between them.

"You made it." Thad wrapped an arm around her shoulders and guided her into the throng of curious co-workers. "Let me introduce you to everyone…"

To Thad's satisfaction, Michelle warmed to the throng as much as they warmed to her. She especially hit it off with Dotty Pederson, which was good, Thad thought.

"Dotty has agreed to be William's nanny," he told Michelle.

Out of the corner of his eye, Thad could see Violet Hunter watching the two of them, an inscrutable expression on her normally cheerful countenance.

At the same time, Michelle looked as if she didn't know whether to be happy or concerned about Dotty Pederson's new position in William's life. Not sure why she'd object to the hiring of a nanny, Thad continued, "Dotty used to supervise the E.R. nursing staff. She retired last summer."

Dotty ran a hand through her short, white hair. A smile split her elfin face. "I'm sixty. It was time. But I've been bored, staying at home. This will be perfect, especially since Thad has agreed to let me care for William in my home while he's working at the E.R."

Beside him, Thad felt Michelle relax ever so slightly. "That does sound perfect," she said.

Still, Thad could see that something about the arrangement was bugging her. And he was even more sure of it when she slipped off toward the buffet table seconds later and lost herself in the throng.

By eight-thirty the impromptu party was winding down.

Guests began departing. When Michelle looked as if she was about to head for the door, too, Thad brought William to her. "Mind holding the little guy for a few minutes?" Thad said. He put William in Michelle's arms before she could formulate a reply.

That was all it took. Michelle melted visibly at the

sight and feel of the baby in her arms. She looked, Thad thought, like a natural-born mother.

The kind every kid would want and should have. And the kind William needed.

MICHELLE WASN'T FOOLED. She knew Thad had asked her to hold William in order to make sure she was the last guest to depart. She couldn't really say she minded. She hadn't had a chance to cuddle William since this morning at the law office, and she had missed him. And Thad. Which was ridiculous. She and Thad barely knew each other!

"So how are things going?" she asked Thad as soon as they were alone. She still wanted to stay uninvolved, but figured a few more minutes' conversation with Thad wouldn't hurt anything.

Thad put the plastic cups and paper plates in plastic garbage bags. "Glenn didn't tell you?"

Michelle swayed a surprisingly wide-awake William back and forth. "I haven't seen him. Although for the record, he probably won't keep me apprised of what's going on unless I'm called in, in a pinch, to handle something on the case."

Thad frowned. "I'm not sure I like that." He bent over to put a twist tie on the bag, then set it in the laundry room, just inside the back door. Then he rummaged beneath the sink and pulled out a roll of paper towels and some disinfectant cleaner. He spritzed the sticky places on the counter, then rubbed them dry with a paper towel. "Don't get me wrong. Glenn is a nice guy and he seems very competent."

"He is."

Finished, Thad wadded up the paper towel and threw it in the trash can beneath the sink. "I'll just feel better if you're involved, on some level." He turned to face her. "So what I want to ask you is this—will you sit in on all the lawyer-client meetings and conference calls, not as cocounsel, since you're clearly uncomfortable with that, but as my friend?"

THAD DIDN'T KNOW what Michelle's reaction was going to be. He knew what he wanted—her by his side. And not just in legal meetings or court hearings. Or for William's sake. But for his.

"Have you talked to Glenn about this?" Michelle asked finally.

Thad lounged against the counter, arms folded. "I asked him if he would mind if you remained involved on some level, and he didn't. So...will you be there as my friend?"

Michelle raked her teeth across her lower lip. "I guess you don't have anyone else you'd rather ask?"

Unsure how blunt to be, Thad said, "I trust you." *I want you.* "William trusts you. I just think you'd be a good person to be on our team."

She smiled faintly, then finally relented. "All right," she said. "I'll be there whenever the two of you need me."

Gratitude flooded through him. "Thank you."

Michelle crossed to him and settled against the counter next to him, so the wide-awake William could see both of them at the same time. "So bring me up to speed on what happened in your meeting with Glenn," she suggested.

"He contacted Beatrix and Brice Johnson's attorney while I was in the office. Their attorney confirmed that the Johnsons did want to terminate their parental rights, and since my petition-slash-motion to adopt has to be filed at the same time, they decided Glenn would file all the papers simultaneously with the court as soon as he gets the signed and notarized affidavits from the other attorney." He paused. "He's supposed to get them tomorrow morning and file everything with family court by the end of business tomorrow."

"Wow." Michelle looked impressed.

"I know. I'm pleased with how fast it's all happening, too."

She shifted to better see his face. "No second thoughts?"

Sensing she would understand, Thad confided, "I admit I'm a little overwhelmed with the logistics of becoming a parent, all the stuff that has to be done, but I feel good about having Dotty babysit William when I'm at work. She's an excellent nurse, as well as a mother and grandmother, so he'll be in good hands. And I had a lot of others volunteer to help out, too, so I know I've got the child care covered." He sighed. "The only thing that really bothers me is the waiting period, after the papers are filed with the court. Glenn said it could take thirty to forty-five days before we get a hearing and the adoption becomes final." Thad frowned, wanting Michelle's reaction. "It seems like a long time to wait."

She didn't seem to think so. "Why?"

Thad tensed. "I guess I worry someone else will come forward and want William, too. Or Brice and Beatrix will change their minds." And that would really suck.

Michelle raised her face to his. "What about you?" she said softly, searching his eyes. "Is there any chance *you'll* change your mind?"

It was an innocent question, bluntly put. Thad wasn't offended. Maybe because he knew she was only asking because she had come to care for William and wanted to see the little guy loved and protected as much as he did. "Not a chance," he said.

Michelle smiled.

"So," Thad continued, "will you be my backup on this?" *Legally and...otherwise?*

Michelle took the hand he offered. "It would be an honor," she said.

HAPPY EVERYTHING WAS working out for Thad and William so quickly and so well, Michelle gave William a bath and a bottle and rocked him in the rocker-glider someone had brought to the shower, while Thad took out the trash and finished cleaning up after the impromptu party.

By the time he had finished, William was asleep in her arms.

Thad carried the bassinet someone else had given him upstairs and placed it next to the bed in the master bedroom.

Michelle laid the snoozing William on his back in the cozy infant bed. He jerked his arms and legs. She placed her hand gently on his tummy, reassuring him. His movements quieted.

Acutely aware of Thad standing beside her, she stayed there a moment longer, then backed soundlessly out of the room and headed down the stairs beside him.

The house was quiet.

So quiet she could hear the meter of their breaths.

At the foot of the stairs she stopped and looked up at him. He looked down at her. The next thing she knew she was in his arms. His lips were on hers. And the world around them ground to a halt as emotion built upon emotion.

She wasn't sure what drew her more, the fact that Thad was such a decent guy or that he knew how to kiss like no one else.

One touch of his lips and she was on fire. The sweep of his tongue was even more electric. He tasted hot and male and possessed her with a kiss so intimate and sure she tingled all over. Wanted all the more. And did not know, for the first time in a very long time, if she ever wanted to stop.

THAD HADN'T MEANT to kiss her tonight, and certainly not like this, with no warning and no restraint. But when she stopped and looked up at him, her breath catching at the same time the air stalled in his chest, he knew it was kiss her then and there, or regret the chance not taken. So he had wrapped his arms around her, drawn her close and lowered his mouth to hers.

And once their lips had touched, there was no question—he had to give it his all. Had to discover again what she liked, how she kissed, how she tasted, at the end of a very long day.

Initially, she simply surrendered to the kiss, let him take the lead. But it wasn't long before she was venturing, too, tangling her tongue with his, increasing the pressure of her lips, opening her mouth to his all the more.

Heat and speed turned to languorous desire for them both. Then sweet, wild yearning. A passion destined to be fulfilled.

And that was when a furious, high-pitched cry split the air, drawing them apart.

"WILLIAM," THEY SAID in unison.

Michelle shook her head. "I can't believe he's awake again."

"Dotty suggested swaddling," Thad said, as the two of them ascended the stairs and headed for the master bedroom.

Michelle tensed. "I've heard of it, of course, but I've never done it."

"I've never done it, either." Thad picked William up and put him against his shoulder. In a replay of what had happened repeatedly over the past two days, as soon as he was picked up, William stopped crying and cuddled against Thad's broad shoulder, deeply content but also wide-awake. Doubtless knowing the lack of quality sleep couldn't be any better for the baby than it was for him, Thad asked, "Think we can find instructions on the internet?"

"I'm sure we can," Michelle said.

They went into the study down the hall. Thad's computer was already booted up, so it was easy to sit down and do a search.

"Problem number one," Thad said, after they'd perused the instructions. "We don't have a swaddling blanket."

"Are you sure?" Michelle asked him. "You've got those bags of used infant clothing down there. There might be one in there."

"Good point."

"You stay here with William. I'll go look," Michelle said. She returned with two shopping bags full of infant clothing, most of it for newborns, as well as half-a-dozen stretchy, waffle-weave receiving blankets. She held one up for him to peruse. "I think this is what they're talking about."

"Looks right," Thad said.

"Where should we do this?"

Thad shrugged. "My bed?"

Michelle flushed, despite herself. "Good idea."

She led the way into Thad's bedroom. Glad for something to concentrate on other than the man who slept in this very bed, she spread out the baby blanket on the mattress, then folded down one corner of it. Thad placed William on it, then together they aligned his shoulders with the top of the blanket. Next, they brought one side over and tucked it underneath him, just as the instructions had said.

"Now the other side," Thad murmured.

Last but not least, they brought the bottom point up and tucked it in the hem just under his chin.

William had been patient while all the wrapping was going on. When he realized he could no longer wave his arms and legs, his face scrunched up and he let out another lusty cry.

Michelle picked him up and looked down into his face. "Now, now, this is not so bad. Being swaddled like this is going to help you sleep."

William's lower lip shot out.

Thad laughed.

William looked at Thad, as if wondering what this was all about. Thad looked at Michelle. The two looked so good together. So perfect. Like mother and son.

She handed him over gently. "I think you should rock him now."

Thad frowned. "I'm not sure he's going to go back to sleep. He's had ten minutes."

Michelle gave them both an indulgent look. "I think he will if you rock him."

She was looking for an excuse to leave, Thad thought, before they found themselves alone and started kissing again.

"You just want a good night's sleep," Thad teased.

"Yep." Michelle pranced out of his bedroom and back downstairs.

Thad followed, William in his arms.

Michelle paused in the hallway to kiss William's cheek and look deep into Thad's eyes. "Seriously, I hope this swaddling thing works," she told him.

"I hope so, too," Thad said.

Otherwise it was going to be a long night.

Chapter Five

The next morning, Thad had just finished giving William his nine-o'clock bottle when the doorbell rang. He'd been up for hours. He hadn't had a shower or shaved yet. But maybe that was a good thing, he mused, if his early caller was yet another single woman hoping to rescue him from single fatherhood. Maybe she'd take one look at him and run scared.

Holding William in his arms, football style, he made his way to the door.

Michelle stood on the other side of the threshold. Unlike him, she was dressed for work, in a gray pin-striped suit, silky white blouse and conservative gray heels. A simple silver necklace rested just below her collarbone, in the open V of her blouse. She had her briefcase slung over one shoulder, her BlackBerry in her palm. She finished reading whatever was written on the screen, then looked at him, her expression grave.

Thad's gut tightened. There were times in his life when he kept waiting for the other shoe to drop. This was one of them. "Something up?" he asked casually.

As Michelle nodded, her silky hair brushed against her chin. Her eyes held his. "May I come in?"

"Sure."

Her heels clicking on his wood floors, Michelle followed him into the living room, where the gifts from the impromptu shower were still heaped in messy stacks. Thad knew he should be doing something with all the stuff, but right now he had no idea what to do with most of it. Although a few of the blankets and a couple of baby rattles had already come in handy.

The fragrance of Michelle's hair and skin sending his senses into overdrive, Thad reached down with his free hand and cleared a place for her in a club chair.

She flashed a too-polite smile, then gracefully moved to take the seat. "Glenn's in Fort Stockton this morning taking a deposition for another case, so he asked me to cover for him."

Thad moved past her and sat down on the sofa across from her. "What's happened?"

Michelle's eyes reflected the concern of someone left to deliver bad news.

"We just got word from family court," she told him matter-of-factly. "Your case has been assigned to Judge Barnes."

"That's bad, I take it."

Michelle hesitated a second too long for Thad's comfort. "Judge Barnes is something of a stickler."

Meaning, Thad thought, old-fashioned and sexist.

"He's really by-the-book," Michelle continued with obvious reluctance. "And he doesn't mince words. He tends to say exactly what's on his mind."

William snuggled against Thad's chest and, even in his sleep, let out a contented sigh. Thad tore his gaze from the baby's precious face. "And what is on Judge Barnes's mind?" he inquired warily.

Briefly worry lit her pretty green eyes. "We're about to find out. He wants you and William and your representative—which right now is going to be me—and the Johnsons and their attorney, Karin Hendricks, in his courtroom at 1:00 p.m. today."

"You don't think…" Thad swallowed around the sudden compression in his throat. "He's not going to order William into *foster* care, is he?"

From her inscrutable expression, Thad noticed Michelle wasn't making any promises. "Besides, I thought I didn't have to go to court for thirty to forty-five days."

"Generally, that's the way it works," Michelle allowed.

"But not in this case?"

Michelle tugged down the hem of her skirt, which had ridden up slightly on her thigh. She leaned forward. "There are unusual aspects to the origin of the agreement between you and the Johnsons regarding the adoption, as well as how you came to have physical custody of the child. It's appropriate for Judge Barnes to want to go over everything and make sure everyone is on the same page."

FOUR HOURS LATER Michelle met Thad and William just outside the hearing room in the Summit County Courthouse. Thad looked very handsome in an olive-green suit and tie. William was wearing a white sleeper with a satin yellow duck sewn across the front.

Had Michelle not known better, she would have thought Thad was William's father in every sense. Which made the stakes for this hearing all the higher.

As Michelle expected, Judge Barnes didn't waste any time getting down to the business of the hearing, once he was seated behind the bench. His penetrating stare was as no-nonsense as his close-cropped gray beard and thick, closely shorn hair. Gruffly he made himself known to all parties present, then he slid his black-rimmed bifocals down the bridge of his nose, and spoke to the attorney for the Johnsons. "As discussed, due to Mr. Johnson's hospitalization, I am waiving your clients' appearance today, but next time, I'll expect to have at least Mrs. Johnson present in this courtroom."

"Yes, Your Honor," Karin Hendricks said.

The judge turned to Thad. His assessing gaze rested on the baby cradled in Thad's arms, then he looked at the papers in front of him one last time.

The suspense was almost unbearable.

Finally Judge Barnes frowned and said, "Let's make sure I understand this correctly, Dr. Garner. This baby was left on your doorstep after the adoptive parents changed their minds about adopting him. They gave baby William back to the surrogate mother, and she didn't want responsibility for him, either. The surrogate mother tried to give William back to one Russell Garner, the sperm donor, who also happens to be your brother. She couldn't find your brother, so she left William on your doorstep with a note asking you to take care of the matter, and you've been caring for the little boy for the past three days."

Thad nodded. "That's correct, Your Honor."

"You and the attorney present, Michelle Anderson, have spoken to your brother, Russell, and he does not wish to reverse his prior termination of any and all parental rights to the child."

"That's also correct."

Judge Barnes slid his bifocals even farther down his nose. "And now you think *you* want to adopt him?" Skepticism rang in his voice.

"I don't think—I *know*," Thad said firmly.

Good, rock-solid answer, Michelle thought.

Judge Barnes rocked back in his chair, took off his

glasses entirely and set them on the desk in front of him. "Forgive me, son, for being blunt here, but you have no clue what you're getting into. I'm a father myself—and I do! Parenting is hard work, a lifelong commitment, not something you take on as a whim or out of guilt or some misguided sense of family. This would make a lot more sense to me if you were already married and had kids of your own, or at the very least had another family member at home who could help you out. But you don't."

Fearing the judge was about to remand William to foster care, Michelle cut in, "With all due respect, Your Honor, single people *can* foster and adopt."

Judge Barnes picked up his glasses and slid them back on. "Sure they can. When they've thought long and hard about it, and gone through all the proper interviews and home studies." He pointed to the papers in front of him. "None of that has been done here. And while I applaud Dr. Garner for stepping up and trying to do right by this child, in these very unusual circumstances, I also think reacting emotionally is not the solution. Therefore, I'm ordering social services to begin an investigation immediately, starting today. If the social worker assigned believes the home environment is suitable for a newborn, William can stay with Dr. Garner until such time as an adoption petition is considered by this court."

"Thank you, Your Honor," Thad said in obvious relief.

"Don't thank me." Judge Barnes glowered. "Just make sure you consider this carefully and do right by that child."

"YOU DON'T HAVE to worry about the social-worker evaluation," Thad told Michelle as she led the way out the rear entrance of the limestone courthouse to the parking lot. "I work with social workers all the time at the hospital. The people in the department know I'm a good guy."

Talk about naive, Michelle thought. Briefcase still in hand, she struggled to keep up with his longer strides. Not easy, considering the narrow hem of her skirt.

She curled a hand around his biceps, wordlessly slowing him down. "This isn't about whether or not you are a good guy, Thad," she told him grimly. "It's about what is best for William. Child Protective Services could easily decide that he would be better off in a home with a mother *and* a father. He's a newborn. There's no shortage of people waiting for a baby—people who have been waiting for years! People with little hope of actually receiving a child anytime soon, given how long the lists of available, approved, adoptive parents are."

"Those families aren't related to William by blood!"

For Thad and William's sake, Michelle wished that was all that counted. Unfortunately it wasn't.

She slowed her pace even more and broke the news to Thad as gently as she could. "Technically, from a legal standpoint, neither are you. Your brother, Russell, terminated his rights at the time he donated the sperm. So legally, he has no say in what happens to this baby. To get those rights reinstated would involve a long, complicated process." A reinstatement that Judge Barnes was, at least at the moment, unlikely to grant.

Thad stopped next to his SUV, the still-sleeping William in his arms. "You said a *private* adoption is possible, if the Johnsons agreed I could have William."

Michelle stepped closer to Thad to allow another couple to pass. "That's right. It is possible. And there *was* a chance," she continued, "had baby William not been dropped off on your doorstep after he was given back to the surrogate, that this petition of yours might have gone through without a hitch. But William *was* left on a doorstep. And it's possible that social services will decide foster care is the way to go for the moment."

Michelle's phone rang. She listened intently to the caller on the end. "Yes," she said firmly, not all that surprised at the speed with which everything was happening now. "He can be there. Fifteen minutes is fine with us."

FIFTEEN MINUTES FOR WHAT? Thad wondered, studying the concerned look on Michelle's pretty face.

She ended the connection and slid her BlackBerry back into the outside pocket of her briefcase. "Tamara Kelly, the social worker assigned to do the home study and make the evaluation, is on her way to your place."

Thad tried to recall if he had even done the dishes. He didn't think so. In fact, he was certain he'd left his cereal bowl, a couple of baby bottles, as well as assorted cups and glasses in the kitchen sink.

Upstairs, his dirty clothes were scattered across the floor. He hadn't had a chance to fold any of his clean laundry or do anything with the stacks of hand-me-down baby gifts in the living room.

Damn it. If only he'd had some advance notice. Even a half-hour warning would have been a huge help in getting ready for the inspection. But then, he supposed that was the point. They didn't want him to have a chance to do anything that hadn't already been done.

He looked at Michelle. "Tell me you can be there for this."

Michelle glanced at her watch, frowned.

He could see her taking an emotional step back already. She bit her lip. "It's not usually the case to have an attorney present for this."

Thad realized that. He also knew, if Tamara Kelly based her decision on how much laundry had been left undone, or the condition of his bedroom and bath right this minute, there could be a problem.

Normally he did household chores on a semi-regular basis. The past few days, since he'd been taking care of William, he'd let everything—but caring for the baby—go. Whether his bed had been made or his dirty clothes picked up off the floor hadn't mattered. Now, suddenly, they did.

Thad looked Michelle in the eye. "As Judge Barnes pointed out, this isn't a usual case." Thad did not want any more unexpected developments.

Michelle looked at William, then back at Thad. "All right," she said. "Let me call my office and reschedule a few things, and I'll meet you at your house."

By the time Thad got home, a small sedan was already parked in front of it. A tall, efficient-looking woman with frizzy, fading red-gray hair emerged from the car. She smiled at William, who was snoozing away in his car seat, then turned back to Thad and introduced herself as head of the Summit County Child Protective Services Department.

He shook hands with her. "It's an unusual situation," he said.

Tamara Kelly nodded, her eyes kind but impartial. "I understand you're trying to do the right thing," she said gently.

The fortysomething social worker just did not look or sound as if she felt that adopting William was it.

Thad was used to proving himself in his profession—E.R. doctors were constantly put to the test.

Not in his personal life.

Of course, there had never been this much at stake in his private life. Not since he and Sela ended their relationship three years ago.

Another car pulled up. Michelle's. She stepped out, looking calm and professional. She introduced herself to Tamara.

Thad unbuckled William from his car seat and led the way inside.

Tamara Kelly carried a clipboard and pen with her. She looked in every room of the house. Occasionally she asked a few questions. Mostly she just wrote things down. She wrote a lot of things down.

Thad was a confident guy. And with good reason. He had earned everything he had ever gotten. But the silence, the inscrutable expression on Tamara Kelly's face, the fact that she rarely made eye contact with him were making him nervous.

Michelle, for all her outward cool, seemed edgy, too, as they walked past Thad's unmade bed and the borrowed bassinet that now served as William's sleeping berth.

Thad had liked having William close by during the night.

He could see, though, that to the outside observer, he looked completely clueless when it came to setting up for a baby. As if he didn't care enough to do things right.

Finally Tamara made her way back downstairs to the foyer.

Abruptly she seemed more than ready to leave.

Thad looked at Michelle.

Michelle looked at the social worker and said, "We'd like a copy of the report as soon as possible."

"Certainly." Tamara Kelly flashed another officious

smile. "I probably won't have it typed up until tomorrow morning."

"Could we have a brief verbal assessment now?" Michelle persisted.

Tamara hesitated.

Thad cut in. "I know the place is a mess. Like most new parents I've been all about the baby for the past few days, but if there's something I need to fix, I'd really like to know about it as soon as possible."

Clipboard pressed to her chest, Tamara took another moment to consider. Finally she said, "Let's sit down, shall we?"

Bypassing the mess in the formal living room, they retreated, instead, to the formal dining room. The table had an inch of dust on it. Ditto the china cabinet. Thad made a mental note to clean those, too.

"Okay, first the things you have going in your favor," Tamara told Thad, her glance touching briefly on the newborn baby sleeping contentedly in his arms. "Baby William has obviously bonded to you. You have a home in a nice, safe neighborhood. A good job and a fine professional reputation, both at the hospital and with our department. There is nothing physically or fiscally wrong to prevent you from becoming a fine parent."

"Great!" Thad said with relief, figuring he'd heard enough to know he'd passed the test.

"And the cons?" Michelle asked, every bit the I-don't-believe-it-until-I-see-it-in-writing attorney.

Tamara frowned. "Your home is not baby-proofed, Dr. Garner. Baby clothes and gear are heaped all over the living room. There's no nursery, no crib set up, no food in the fridge, no spouse or other family member to help with child care."

"I have a babysitter lined up for when I go to work," Thad reminded her.

"And I made note of that." Tamara pointed to her clipboard. "But you've also never been married. Never reared a child. You have a reputation, socially, within the community as a man with a notoriously short attention span when it comes to relationships. The bottom line is you lose interest in a woman after a few dates. How do we know you won't lose interest in a child just as quickly?"

THAD HAD NEVER FIGURED, in his attempt to give every potential woman and relationship a chance to turn into something lasting, that he was making a mistake.

Now he knew better.

And so, apparently, did Michelle Anderson.

He waited until Tamara had left before he turned back to Michelle. "I feel like I'm being unfairly judged here." It irritated him. He was a private person. He didn't "kiss and tell," and he didn't feel—even in this instance—that he should have to explain why he and any woman he had previously dated hadn't been right for each other. It was enough that he and the women knew.

With the exception of Violet Hunter—who still seemed to have a crush on him—all the women he'd dated seemed to agree that they were just not suited for each other.

Michelle shrugged, not at all surprised. "People talk about this stuff—especially in rural communities, where not a lot else goes on."

"But she's a professional."

"Who is doing her job. You don't have a good track record with women here. If, for instance, you had ever been in a serious relationship…"

Figuring if he had to discuss his romantic past with anyone, it might as well be to one of the two lawyers representing him, he looked Michelle in the eye. "I dated a woman for five years, and Sela and I lived together for two after that."

Michelle blinked, stunned. After a moment she pulled herself together and continued in the same tone she probably would have used had she been a prosecuting attorney. "But didn't marry," she said quietly.

A fact, Thad knew, that wouldn't sit well with a stickler like Judge Barnes, either.

Thad went to put the sleeping William in the only available bed nearby—his infant carrier. He knelt to strap him in and tucked a blanket in around him, then walked with Michelle back to the dining room. "Only because Sela wasn't ready."

She stood, hands hooked over the back of the chair where she'd been sitting. "What happened?"

Suspecting Michelle was asking as much for her own curiosity as for the benefit of his case, Thad gestured for her to take a seat again.

When they were settled, he said, "Sela and I met in med school and started dating then. We stayed together until we finished our residencies, both in emergency medicine. Then we were starting to interview for jobs. I would have gone to Houston or Dallas or anywhere else she wanted to be. The big cities were more reasonable because they had a higher likelihood of us both finding positions at hospitals near each other." He paused, remembering the shock and the hurt. "Sela thought it wasn't a good idea, that our relationship had gone as far as it was going to go."

Michelle leaned back in her chair. "And you didn't agree?"

Thad had always wanted to be closer, to have the kind of relationship where they could finish each other's sentences. It hadn't happened. But that didn't mean he and Sela hadn't been happy, spending time together whenever they could. "I expected us to get married and have kids," he said finally.

Still listening, she leaned closer. "And?"

"Sela felt that while we had been a great support system for each other, we didn't have the kind of emotional intimacy necessary to build a future on, have a family. She thought it was better if we called it quits while we were still friends."

Compassion lit Michelle's eyes. "Are you still friends?"

Thad shook his head. "I couldn't go backward in the relationship and that's what it would have been, at least to me. So we ended it and moved on. For a while afterward, I shut down and didn't see anyone. Then I realized that wasn't good, either, so when I took the job in Summit, I decided to put as much effort into finding someone to settle down and have children with as I have everything else." He cleared his throat. "So I've tried to stay open to the possibilities. Not just dismiss women without getting to know them first. The trouble is," he explained patiently, "if you go into the getting-to-know-each-other-phase strictly as friends, you can't get close to each other the same way you would if you were romancing them, but if you're romancing them and it doesn't work out, it can be hard to go back to the possibility of being just friends."

Michelle heaved a commiserating sigh. "Damned if you do and damned if you don't."

"Exactly." As their eyes met and locked, Thad felt a shimmer of tension between them. Man-woman tension. "The thing is," he continued, "I'm not going to give up dating, because I still want to get married and have kids. I want to find that special someone."

And in fact, Thad thought, his spirits lifting, he was beginning to think he already had.

MICHELLE STUDIED THAD, aware once again that the situation had taken an unexpectedly intimate turn. And while, as a woman, as a neighbor, as a friend, she was glad to know that Thad wasn't the player she had thought, as the law partner of his family attorney, it put her in an awkward spot.

"I usually don't talk about my ex," he said.

Forcing herself to get back to business, she reached for the yellow notepad and wrote a memo for Glenn. "It's something the social worker should know." Something *she* had needed to know, too.

Thad grimaced. "Unfortunately Tamara Kelly seems to have formed an opinion of me, and it's the same one you had."

Michelle ignored the intensity of his gaze and kept on writing. "It's hard not to think that with the number of women constantly traipsing to your front door," she remarked casually.

"If you've noticed that, you've also noticed I usually manage to avoid inviting them in."

Playing devil's advocate, Michelle pointed out, "But you often sit on the front porch with them for a while."

"To be polite," Thad qualified, his frustration apparent. "I don't know how to discourage them without hurting their feelings."

Michelle joked, "Rudeness often works. But it'd be a heck of a time to start being rude, when you're trying to adopt a baby."

"Exactly. I need to appear more of a gentleman than ever." Thad met her gaze again. "But if you were interested in me—"

Michelle stopped him before he could go further. "I'm not," she fibbed as her heart kicked against her ribs.

Thad looked at her as if thinking the kiss the other night indicated otherwise. "Let's just pretend, for the sake of argument, you are," he drawled. "What would discourage you from making a play for me?"

That's easy. "If you were involved with someone."

Thad's lips compressed. "I've been dating someone before. That hasn't stopped the female attention aimed my way."

That was because he was such a genuinely nice guy. "It probably would if you were seriously involved with someone."

He ran his palm across his jaw. "You've got a point. I never had this problem when I was with Sela."

"See?" She studied the buttons on his shirt. "Easy."

Thad inclined his head. "Let me get this straight. The judge wants to see me in a lasting relationship. So would the social worker. And you think if I were to see someone seriously, I'd no longer have the problem with all the single women making plays for me. So, in theory, having a steady girlfriend would solve all my problems."

"*In theory* being the key words, Thad. You can't just... I mean you shouldn't...get involved with someone simply as a means to an end." People could get hurt. *She* could get hurt.

He continued to study her as if he was trying to figure something out. "You're right," he concluded. "If and when I do get involved with someone again, it has to be for the right reasons. Because I know even before we have our first date that it's going to work."

"Again that sounds fine in theory, but..."

"Easier said than done," he guessed.

"I think so." Another silence fell. "In the meantime, you have a lot to do." Michelle got up to leave.

"Yeah, I do," Thad agreed.

She packed up her briefcase, then paused to take one last look at the still-sleeping William. "If you need any help..." she murmured, her heart swelling with love for the abandoned baby boy.

Thad lifted his brow. "Are you available tonight?"

Chapter Six

"How did the depositions go?" Michelle asked Glenn. She was about to walk out the door. Her partner was just walking in.

Glenn set his briefcase on his desk. "I think it's going to take several more days before we finish." He removed his suit jacket and looped it over the back of a chair. "How did the hearing go with Judge Barnes?"

Briefly Michelle filled him in, finishing with the social worker's home visit.

"A bad initial report can be hard to overcome," Glenn warned.

But not altogether impossible.

Recalling she had promised Thad she would help out with the baby again that evening, Michelle said, "Between you and me, I don't think Thad considers failure an option in this situation. Which is why I wanted to talk to you. I don't think I should be representing Thad, even in a pinch. Any other one of your clients is fine— I'm happy to help—but I think it's a bad idea for me to get professionally involved with Dr. Garner."

Glenn eyed her with the wisdom of someone who had known her for years. "I thought your days of getting emotionally invested in cases were over," he stated.

So had she, but Thad had a way of drawing her in,

making her feel a part of his—and William's—life. "The thing is, we're neighbors. I don't want there to be any bad blood if things don't go the way Thad wants. It'd be too awkward, living across the street from each other."

"I understand." Glenn paused to peruse the extensive notes she had made for him. "You really think the court might turn down Thad's petition to adopt?"

"I don't know." She only knew she didn't want to lie awake at night worrying about it.

Figuring Thad had probably lined up an army of people to help him get his house quickly up to the standards of children's services, Michelle drove home. She was pleased to see a housecleaning-service van in front of the house. That meant Thad was taking the evaluation process seriously. It would help a lot to have everything sparkling.

She went inside and changed into jeans, sneakers and an old shirt, then walked across the street to see if there was anything else Thad and William needed. Looking incredibly handsome and relaxed, Thad answered the doorbell with William in his arms.

"Are we ever glad to see you!" Taking her by the wrist, he drew her inside the house, past the activity in the living room, dining room and foyer to the kitchen. Overflowing grocery sacks were scattered across the countertops and table. "William and I went shopping," he announced proudly.

His cheerful attitude was infectious. Michelle grinned. "I can see that." Just as she could see what a wonderful dad Thad was going to be.

"We got a lot of different stuff. I was going to put it all away, but the vacuum cleaner startled William and he started fussing, so…would you mind holding him while I heat a bottle of formula for him?"

Their hands and arms brushed as he transferred William to her. To distract herself from the tingling sensation, Michelle cuddled William close and looked around some more. Front and center on the countertop was a very handy gadget. "You got a bottle warmer."

"Yeah, it was in that stuff I got at the shower the other night. I found it when I was trying to sort through it all and put it away. Pretty neat." Thad demonstrated how it worked for her. "You just put a little water in the bottom, set the bottle of formula in the warmer, press this button and then wait for it to heat up."

Michelle smiled. If Thad kept improving his parenting skills at this pace, his next evaluation was bound to be a lot better. There was only one problem. She inclined her head at the groceries. "Are you really going to use all this?"

He looked puzzled. "Why?"

Michelle decided to be blunt. "Because if you don't, and you forget about the fresh produce and the meat and milk, and it ends up going bad in the fridge, that wouldn't look so good, either."

Thad's eyes glittered with undecipherable emotion. "You don't think I can cook?"

Was that a serious question? "Uh…no."

He came close enough for her to inhale the scent of soap and aftershave clinging to his skin. "Why not?" he taunted, looking very much like he wanted to kiss her again.

The damning part was, she wanted to throw caution to the wind and kiss him, too. "You don't have the kitchen of a man who cooks," Michelle said. He hadn't even known what a mixing bowl was.

He gestured toward the cabinets. "I've got pots and pans and dishes."

Michelle did not know what he was used to, but she was not afraid to go toe-to-toe with him. "And as of this afternoon, when Tamara Kelly was here doing her inspection, nothing but juice, coffee, bottled water, formula and milk was in the fridge. If you cooked—" she edged closer, further pressing her point "—you would have had eggs and flour and salt and spices, meat and veggies, bread."

He looked at her like he wanted to do a lot more than kiss her. "I had cereal."

She wanted to do a lot more than kiss him, too. "True."

He braced his hands on his waist. "I'm going to learn how to cook."

His nearness had her pulse racing. "Really?"

He nodded. "And I'm hoping you'll volunteer to teach me, starting tonight."

THAD WASN'T SURE what was more disconcerting, the stunned look on Michelle's face as she processed his request or the sight of her standing in his kitchen, cradling William in her arms. Was this what it would be like to be married and have a kid? He'd never felt as close to anyone as he did to the two of them at this moment. And they barely knew each other.

Thad continued casually, "I figure simple is better."

Michelle's pretty green eyes widened. "Don't you think you should slow down?"

"Heck, no." The light on the warmer went off, signaling the bottle was ready. Thad plucked it from the warmer, wiped off the moisture clinging to the bottom, and shook it well. He tested the formula on his wrist. Lukewarm. Perfect.

He waited for Michelle to settle in a chair, perpendicular to the kitchen table, then handed her the bottle. "I know how these things work. Surprise visits always follow the scheduled ones. I'm going to be ready next time. Hopefully with an apron on, looking very domestic."

Michelle snuggled William against her breast. "You're kidding."

Thad watched her slip the nipple into William's mouth. The baby began to drink almost immediately, looking up at her adoringly all the while.

Thad couldn't blame the little fella. He was pretty besotted with her, too.

"I'm kidding about the apron. Not about being ready." He started taking staples out of sacks. He'd purchased everything from canned green beans to dried barley. Salad stuff. Boneless chicken breasts. Fresh fruit. Potatoes. Soups. More cereal. Bread. Butter. Milk. Cheese. A dozen eggs.

"I'm serious about being the best dad ever," he said.

Michelle regarded Thad with new respect. "I'm impressed."

A feeling of accomplishment shot through him. "That's the general idea."

The vacuum cleaner stopped.

The cleaning-crew boss, a middle-aged woman in a uniform shirt and jeans, appeared. "You want to sign here, we'll be out of your way," she said.

"Every week from now on, right?" Thad said.

The crew boss nodded. "Every Tuesday, from three to six."

"See you next week, then."

"Yes. Thanks, Dr. Garner."

The sounds of workers packing up and leaving were followed by the closing of the front door. Thad turned back to Michelle. "Alone at last," he murmured.

"Not quite," Michelle said, looking down at their tiny chaperone.

"So what do you think we should have for our dinner?" Thad asked.

"You're really going to do this? Learn to cook?"

"With your help?" He nodded. "Absolutely."

"Then wait here." She shifted William and his bottle to Thad's arms. "I'll be right back."

Michelle returned a few minutes later with a book entitled *Kids Learn to Cook*. Thad figured the battered volume had to be at least twenty years old. She set it down on the kitchen table, where he could see. "This has everything you need to get started. Seriously—" she grinned when he glanced at it doubtfully "—even a third grader can follow the instructions. I know, because I started cooking with it when I was that old."

"Your parents gave this to you?"

"I wish." Michelle sighed. "No. My gran gave it to me, but she had to keep it at her house. My parents would have *freaked* if they'd seen it."

That sounded bizarre. "How come?" Thad asked. "Didn't your parents want you to learn how to cook?"

Michelle leaned against the kitchen counter. "My father thought it altogether unnecessary. He wanted me putting all my energies toward academic pursuits. My mother thought I should have one or two signature dishes to entertain with, so she brought in a chef to teach me how to make coq au vin and boeuf Bourguignon."

That sounded excessive, too. Thad began patting William gently on the back. "Why French food?"

"Because she taught college French, so it made sense that if I were going to learn to cook something, it would be something she might have taught me."

"Only she didn't."

"Neither of them were really into the whole parenting thing, except when it came to turning me into some sort of child genius." Michelle's lips thinned into a rueful line. "There, they excelled."

"Let me guess. Perfect score on your college entrance exams."

Sadness glimmered in her eyes. "That didn't please them. They were both professors at Rice University and wanted me to go Ivy League all the way. I wanted to stay in Texas and go to college with my friends. And since I had a full ride at University of Texas in Austin, I didn't need them to approve of my decision—or pay for it."

"A rebel."

She nodded self-consciously. "I guess."

"Surely they forgave you for that."

She looked uncertain. "To tell you the truth, I was never all that close to them. I was to others in my life— just not my folks."

His eyes returned to the cookbook with the kid chefs on the front. "Which is where the gran who gave you the cookbook came in," Thad guessed as William burped in his ear.

Smiling, Michelle watched Thad turn William around and offer him the last of his bottle. "I got to stay with my dad's mom whenever my parents traveled on the guest-lecturer circuit—which was practically every summer and during the semester breaks. Gran lived in Killeen, Texas, and was very down-to-earth.

She never really understood how her son changed from a humble kid to an elitist snob."

"Is that how you think of him, too?"

Regret flashed in Michelle's face. "Let's put it this way—I didn't have a typical childhood. While all my friends were going out to barbecue places and seeing movies on the weekend, I was attending lectures, going to museums, being tutored in five different languages. We dined out constantly. But only in five-star restaurants. The only time I ever got to go to an amusement park or eat at a fast-food restaurant was when I was on a school field trip." She sighed. "You know how they say kids rebel against whatever their parents want them to be? Well, I craved *normal.* I would've given anything to eat off the children's menu. Since that wasn't possible when I went out with my parents, Gran taught me how to make all the kid-friendly things—which I could only eat at her house. Mac 'n' cheese. Chicken fingers. Grilled cheese."

Thad could only imagine how tough that had been on her. "Did your parents know that?"

"They knew I ate kid-friendly fare when I was with her. I never let on she taught me to cook, though, and such pedestrian fare. I think that might have put an end to our visits."

Obviously the deception had cost Michelle emotionally. "Where's your gran now?" Thad asked.

Sorrow darkened Michelle's eyes. "She died five years ago."

Had Thad not been holding William, he would have taken Michelle in his arms and held her until she felt better. Unfortunately all he could do was tell her how he felt. "I'm sorry."

Michelle accepted his sympathy with a nod. "I had

a lot of good years with her. She taught me how to connect with people." Michelle paused, reflecting. "To see more than just someone's career potential or IQ."

"She sounds wonderful," Thad said softly.

"She was." Michelle smiled. "And she gave me this cookbook." She tapped the cover of the much-used instruction manual. "And now I'm lending it to you. So... good luck. Keep it as long as you need it. I know all the recipes by heart, anyway."

MICHELLE SLIPPED OUT the door before Thad could entice her to stay. She congratulated herself as she crossed the street to her own home. She'd been helpful, neighborly. But she hadn't gotten overly emotionally involved with one of their firm's clients.

Nevertheless, as the evening progressed, she couldn't help but wonder how Thad was faring. She was still wondering at 6:00 a.m., when she left the house for her run.

Half an hour later, she was back. Thad stepped out onto his front porch before she reached her mailbox, waved her over.

Acutely conscious of the way she must look, in her running shorts and T-shirt, the top section of her chin-length hair caught in a messy ponytail, Michelle sprinted up his sidewalk.

Thad flashed a smile that upped her pulse another notch. "Got something to show you," he announced proudly.

Michelle could have begged off. She had to shower and prepare for work. However, curiosity prompted her to step inside his house. Thad was dressed as casually as she was, in a pair of gray sweatpants and a white T-shirt. William was dozing in a canvas baby carrier strapped to Thad's chest. Something else that was new, which seemed very well suited to his style.

"That cookbook you lent me is great!" he said.

Michelle blinked. "You tried it out already?"

Satisfaction radiated from him. "Sure did. Grilled cheese sandwiches last night. Oven-baked eggs in muffin tins this morning." His grin widened. "I made enough for two."

He ushered her into the kitchen. The table had been set. A bowl of fruit salad and buttered toast sat on the table. The aroma of fresh-brewed coffee and baking eggs filled the air. "I cheated on the fruit salad," he admitted sheepishly. "Got that out of the produce section. But the rest I did."

Michelle checked her watch in amazement. "How long have you been up?"

"Since five. William decided he was done sleeping. I gave him a bottle, but he showed no signs of going back to sleep and fussed every time I put him down. Finally I put him in this—one of the nurses at the hospital recommended it. It works. Little guy goes right to sleep."

Michelle could see why. As she'd thought before, snuggled against Thad's broad chest, who wouldn't want to drift off to dreamland?

A timer went off and he pointed to the oven. "If you wouldn't mind…"

Michelle put the heatproof mitt on her hand and removed the eggs. They looked done to perfection.

Thad pointed. "Those two are yours. There might be a little shell in the other two. It took me a couple of tries to get the hang of breaking the eggs into those little cups." He winked. "Thus, if anyone lives dangerously, it should be me."

Gallant to the core, Michelle thought. She worked the

eggs out and slid them onto plates. "The social worker would be impressed if she saw how hard you're working. Although I have to tell you, it's not necessary to do all this. You just have to demonstrate the ability to feed your child. That could be by hiring someone to come in to cook…"

Thad shook his head. "I remember what it was to have our mom cook for us, versus our dad, who never did. Her way left us feeling pampered and loved."

"And your dad's way?"

The expression in Thad's eyes was bleak. "Russell and I felt like a burden to my dad. I'm going to make sure that William knows he is loved."

Michelle couldn't help it. She reached out and touched Thad's hand. "You feel a deep connection to him already, don't you?"

His fingers closed over hers. "It's funny," he confessed. "My whole life I've had trouble feeling as close to people as I'd like—it's as though I can get so close and no closer. But it hasn't been that way with William. From the first moment I held this little guy in my arms, there was something special. I know it sounds kind of corny…but I know I'm meant to be William's father in the same way that I knew I was meant to be a doctor."

Michelle was impressed. Moved. "You're very determined."

He shrugged. "I'm used to setting goals and getting things done." Thad held out her chair for her. He paused to study her expression. "I can see you still have your doubts, but I'm going to be the perfect father to this baby."

Thad moved around to sit opposite her. "Everything is going to be so well organized and run so smoothly there is no way the court or children's services can say I'm not qualified to be William's dad."

Michelle spread her napkin across her lap. "I admire your determination. I really do. I can see how much you want this."

Thad's glance narrowed. "I hear a *but*," he said.

Michelle instinctively reverted back to lawyer mode again. "But you need to prepare yourself for the fact that despite everything you're doing, Judge Barnes and Tamara Kelly might not see things your way."

Thad didn't speak, and Michelle went on, "I've had unforeseen events develop and seen clients disappointed before. When it comes to child-custody cases, anything can happen. Decisions are sometimes made by the court that don't seem fair."

"Which is why, to do this, I'm going to need someone to stand beside me." Thad leaned toward her. "You've already said you didn't want do to it as my lawyer. Will you stand by me as my friend?"

THAD WAITED WHILE Michelle considered his request.

"I'll be happy to help you, one neighbor to another," she said finally. "But I'd prefer not to get emotionally involved."

Thad dug into his eggs. "You really think my situation is that risky?"

She swallowed and concentrated on her breakfast, too. "It's not that."

"Then what is it?" he demanded.

Michelle looked over at him. "Situations like this heighten the emotions of everyone involved."

Exactly, Thad thought, why he needed a friend and a sounding board more than ever. To see him through it.

"We could become close to each other very quickly," Michelle cautioned.

Thad added salt and pepper to his eggs. "I can see you also have a problem with that."

She grimaced and tore off a small piece of toast. "It wouldn't be genuine intimacy."

"Says who?"

A pulse throbbed in the hollow of her throat, as she admitted in a low, hoarse voice, "Says someone like me, who's been through it and made that mistake before."

Thad wasn't surprised to learn she'd been hurt. He'd known something was responsible for her skittishness where he was concerned. He waited for her to go on. Eventually she did.

"Four years ago I had a client, Jared, whose wife, Margarite, died in childbirth. His in-laws held Jared responsible for Margarite's death because Jared had known about her heart condition when they married. The two of them had agreed they would not have children—too big a risk for Margarite—but she wanted a baby desperately and became pregnant, anyway. They all tried to talk her into terminating the pregnancy, but she wouldn't listen, so Jared did the only thing he could do—he supported his wife." A pensive look crossed Michelle's pretty face. "Unfortunately the doctors were right—it was too much for her, and she died in childbirth. The baby survived. Margarite's parents blamed Jared for their daughter's death, and sued him for custody of their only grandchild."

"That must have been awful for everyone involved," Thad said.

Michelle put down her fork and clenched her hands together. "That's an understatement. It turned into an ugly, protracted battle that went on for almost two years.

I not only represented Jared and his son, Jimmy—I fell in love with both of them. The day the court battle ended, with a verdict in Jared's favor, he asked me to marry him. I said yes. But as life returned to normal and the wedding day got closer, Jared realized that although I loved him…he did not love me. Not the way he'd loved Margarite," she reflected sadly. "So we broke up. And I promised myself never again would I put myself in a situation where a man I was attracted to could mistake gratitude for love."

Thad took a moment to savor the fact she had just admitted she was attracted to him. "I can see how that must have been difficult for you," he said after a moment.

Remembered hurt shimmered in her eyes. "Try heartbreaking."

"Our situation is different."

She lifted her eyebrows and got up to pour them both more coffee from the carafe. "Is it? You have an adorable baby to whom I'm already feeling emotionally attached. I'm here having breakfast with you, when I should be home getting ready for work."

Thad studied the conflicted look on her face. "This is about the fact I've kissed you and you kissed me back, isn't it?"

A blush pinkened her cheeks. She stood, restless now. "It's about the fact I can't stop thinking about the two of you and your situation."

Thad shrugged and, finished with his breakfast, stood, too. "Then we're even, because I can't stop thinking about you, either, in ways that have nothing to do with your expertise in family law or the gentle way you handle William."

Michelle lifted both her hands before he could take

her in his arms. "Look, I understand how much is at stake for you here. I wish you all the best. I really do. But beyond that," she claimed, "I can't put myself in that situation again—I'm too vulnerable. And you shouldn't put yourself there, either, Thad. Not under these circumstances."

MICHELLE WORKED LATE the next two days, not getting home until after nine. By then, Thad's car was already in his driveway, the lights on inside. Even at that late hour, there was a steady stream of women driving up and dropping things off—everything from congratulatory balloons to casseroles to festively wrapped gifts.

Often they were invited inside.

More often, they did not stay long.

Michelle figured that was not by the visitors' choice.

After all, who could resist sweet baby William? Or the handsome, eligible bachelor determined to adopt him?

Only her, of course.

Still applauding herself for her practical attitude, she headed to work Friday morning. Stayed unusually late at the office again that evening, not getting home until ten.

Curiously, even though she'd seen Thad leave for work just before eight that morning with William in tow and knew he got off at eight that evening, there was no car in Thad's driveway. No lights on. No sign of either Thad or William.

Michelle told herself she shouldn't be surprised. Friday was a date night, after all.

Thad was single and had made it clear he did not want to go through the adoption process without a supportive woman by his side.

He and William had probably accepted an invitation to dinner at someone's home.

It was none of her business where he was or with whom.

That didn't stop her from wondering—a little jealously, she admitted reluctantly—where Thad and William were as she took a long, luxurious bubble bath and changed into her favorite pair of white satin pajamas.

At midnight, when she finally slipped into bed, there was still no sign of them.

Minutes ticked by. Then half an hour. Another hour.

Michelle was no closer to sleep when finally, at one-thirty in the morning, she heard Thad's car.

Before she could stop herself, she had slipped from bed and moved to the window.

She saw Thad get out of the SUV. Shoulders slumped, he trudged toward the house, unlocked the door and moved slowly inside.

William was not with him.

Or was he…?

Without warning, Michelle recalled news stories of new parents who had become distracted and forgotten they had an infant in the safety seat in the rear of their vehicle.

Surely Thad—an emergency-room physician and determined new father—would not have made a similar mistake, Michelle told herself. A shiver of unease slid down her spine.

But what if he had?

What if William were sleeping soundly in the car?

What if he *wasn't?*

A raft of possible disaster scenarios filling her head,

Michelle put on a pair of driving clogs, grabbed her raincoat out of the closet and ran outside.

Shivering in the brisk air, she headed across the street.

Chapter Seven

Thad had just polished off a slice of cold pizza and uncapped a beer when he remembered he'd forgotten to bring in the day's mail. Wearily he went out to the foyer, set his beer down on the table, looked outside, then stopped in astonishment.

Michelle, hands cupped around her eyes, was peering into the back of his SUV.

Curious now himself, he quietly eased the front door open.

She was definitely snooping. Though what she could want with the back of his BMW, was anyone's guess.

"Can I help you with something?" he asked drily, trying not to notice how good it was to see her again after several days' absence. He was fairly certain she'd been taking great pains to avoid running into him.

Michelle jumped at the sound of his voice.

Just for the hell of it, he reached inside and switched on the porch lights.

Michelle stood there, looking ridiculously beautiful in the glow of soft yellow lamplight and backdrop of dark night sky. Her hair was delectably tousled, her lips soft and bare, her cheeks a becoming pink. She was clad in her raincoat, which fell only to mid-thigh and which was open to reveal a pair of white satin pajamas that elegantly draped her slender form. It was clear, from the imprint of nipple against the silky fabric, that she was cold.

Desire sent an arrow of fire to his groin. Desire, he told himself, he did not want to feel.

"Well?" He arched a brow, waiting. "For someone who eased so deliberately from my life three nights ago, you sure are nosy."

She flushed guiltily. "I'm sorry. I was worried. I was trying to see if by chance you'd accidentally left William in his car seat in the back. But—" she paused and wet her lips "—there's no car seat."

"I leave it with Dotty when I drop him off in the mornings, in case she needs it."

"Oh."

Silence fell between them, more awkward than ever.

Aware she wasn't the only one getting chilled by the brisk mountain air, Thad said, "Anything else you want to know you'll have to find out inside."

Too tired and cold to stand on ceremony, he walked past her to the mailbox, grabbed the few letters and magazines there, then headed back into the house. As he suspected—or was it hoped?—she followed moments later. The first thing he noticed was that she had buttoned—and belted—her raincoat.

She wrung her hands. "I'm really sorry for snooping."

Thad set down the stack of mail. He picked up his beer and took another swallow. It had been a hell of day and appeared not to be over yet. "Are you finished?"

Politeness would have dictated she murmur another apology and leave.

The attorney in her continued with the investigation into what he figured was his overall fitness as a parent.

The fact he had done nothing wrong prompted him to make her work like hell for any further information.

"Is William all right?" she asked finally.

Thad turned and headed for the kitchen.

Deciding a second beer wouldn't hurt, he went to the fridge and pulled out two icy bottles. He uncapped both and handed her one.

After a moment's hesitation, she took it.

Eyes on his, she waited.

"Why wouldn't he be?" Thad said.

Michelle sipped her beer. Still holding his gaze, she shrugged. "Because he's not here with you."

"He's still at the sitter's."

"Oh."

Something dark and disapproving glimmered in her green eyes.

Thad scowled, making no effort to hide the fact that he was disappointed—in the way the evening had gone, in her.... "I couldn't pick him up at eight. I didn't know when I would be done at the hospital, so I talked to Dotty and we decided it would be better for all concerned if William spent the night at her home. I'll go get him first thing tomorrow morning, since I'm off tomorrow."

"Oh," Michelle said again, but this time her expression was one of relief.

Obviously, Thad realized, she had jumped to the conclusion that something dire had happened to William.

Sighing, he carried his beer into the living room. She followed him and watched as he sat down on the center cushion of the sofa and worked off his boots. Slouching down until his shoulders were lined up with the back of the sofa, he stretched his legs out in front of him.

Days and nights like this had him wishing he had someone to come home to, someone to unwind with.

Because both club chairs were filled with neat stacks of baby gifts Thad still couldn't figure out where to store, she took the only available other seat, one in the corner of the sofa next to him.

"Must have been some night at the E.R.," she murmured sympathetically.

"Not the kind I ever want to have again, believe me," Thad responded.

"What happened?"

He looked at the way her knee was bent between them. He wished he could go back and erase the whole day for all concerned.

"There was a head-on collision on the highway outside of town. A drunk driver hit a family of six." And that wasn't the worst of it, not by a long shot. "None of them were wearing seat belts."

"Oh, God."

"Both parents and the drunk driver were killed instantly. The children, ranging from one to eight, were all seriously injured."

Her eyes instantly filled with tears, and her compassion reached out somehow to envelop him in a way that words could not. She covered his hand with hers and asked softly, "Are the kids going to make it?"

"I don't know." Thad accepted the comfort of her hand even as he took another long pull on his beer. "We airlifted them to Children's Hospital as soon as we got them stable, but it's not looking good for any of them."

Michelle turned ashen. She tightened her fingers on his and edged closer to him. "I'm so sorry," she choked out.

Thad ran a hand over his face. "If they do make it,

at least they've got family in Houston, already on their way to the hospital." Which wasn't, Thad knew, always the case.

Michelle continued staring at Thad. She shook her head, seemingly at a loss as to what to say or do to make things better.

Experience had taught Thad there was no way to do that. "I shouldn't have laid all this on you," he said gruffly. He shook his head, turned away.

"I don't know how you stand it," she blurted. "It breaks my heart when I see a kid that's hurt or sick."

Mine, too, Thad thought.

"You must be exhausted," Michelle said finally.

He was. "That doesn't mean I'll sleep. Too much adrenaline."

Michelle paused, then asked, "How do you usually work it out of your system?"

Thad knew how he wanted to work it off—tonight. He looked at her and said nothing.

She blushed. "Oh."

"Which is why," he told her candidly, wishing he could just haul her into his arms and kiss her, "maybe, you should head on home."

YES, SHE SHOULD, Michelle knew, as they both stood. If she stayed, she would end up in Thad's arms again.

But maybe that wasn't such a bad thing. Just for this one night. Maybe if they made love once, she would be able to get him out of her system. Stop obsessing over his comings and goings, stop thinking of him day and night. Maybe, if they explored the attraction between them, she would be able to walk away. And so could he. Maybe. She hoped so.

"I'm up for it," she said quietly.

He stared at her, as if not sure he'd heard her correctly. "Up for what?"

"You." Her heart racing, Michelle stepped closer. "Me." She wrapped one arm around his neck, threaded the other hand through the hair on the nape of his neck. "This."

Their lips met halfway in a searing connection of heat and need. Wonder swept through Michelle, along with the knowledge that chemistry like this was something to be savored. So what if this pleasure was going to be meaningless and short-lived, she thought, as he swept a hand down her spine, urging her closer. Her breasts were crushed against the hardness of his chest. Lower still, she felt the depth of his need for her.

Thad kissed her like a man who'd been as starved for intimacy as she. He held her as if he never wanted to let her go. And the truth was, she didn't want their passion to end, either. Not without seeing where it led.

Sifting his hands through her hair, he kissed her temple, her cheek, the corner of her mouth. "I want to take you to bed," he said softly.

Feelings ran riot inside her. "Just this one time," she whispered against the encroaching pressure of his mouth.

His eyes darkened with an emotion she couldn't identify, then he was taking her by the hand, leading her up the stairs. They paused on the landing to kiss, and then again as they made their way down the hall. When at last they ended up in his bedroom, he slowly untied and unbuttoned her coat, kissing her slowly all the while. She trembled as he took it off. He paused, then moved to turn on the bedside lamp.

She wanted to hurry; Thad wanted to take his time. Kissing her, even as he unbuttoned her pajama top, one button at a time. By the time the fabric fell open, her breasts were aching for his touch. He eased the fabric down her arms, baring her to the waist.

"Incredible," he murmured, rubbing his thumbs across the dusky crowns. He cupped the weight in his palms. "So incredibly beautiful," he whispered.

Through his eyes, she felt beautiful. Sensual. Ready and eager to please. And she wasn't alone.

He guided her backward, toward the bed, bracing her against his arm. Ever so slowly, he lowered her till she was stretched out on her back, then he kissed his way from her lips, to the nape of her neck, the V of her collarbone, the valley between her breasts. She trembled, her arms clinging to his shoulders and neck. She watched, as if in a languid dream, while his free hand explored every curve and hollow of her breasts. Her skin heated. She had never felt this way before. "Thad..." she gasped.

"I know," he murmured. "I'm getting there."

Claiming her lips again, he eased his hand beneath the waistband of her pajama pants. Tenderly caressed her stomach, moved lower... And still he kissed her, over and over, as if this chance would never come again. He knew exactly how to touch and engulf her in pleasure. How not to rush. Silken brushes of his fingertips alternated with soothing strokes of his palm. Almost before she knew it, she was free-falling over the edge. His breath rough against her cheek, he held her until the quaking stopped, then finished undressing her and joined her—naked—between the sheets.

Lost in a world of undeniable pleasure, inundated with the touch, smell and taste of him, Michelle surrendered to the desire flowing through her. Indulging in her most secret fantasy, she took her time exploring his body, too. His skin was warm satin, his muscles hard. Lower still, she found him hot, hard, demanding. Patient enough to wait until she had stroked and loved every inch of him, too, until there was no more holding back. Finally, he was parting her thighs and positioning himself between them.

She trembled as he slid his hands beneath her and lifted her to him. They kissed lingeringly, and then she arched to receive him. The merging of their bodies was as electric as the joining of their lips, the need to explore supplanted by the yearning for satisfaction. Together they reached new heights—until there was nothing but the two of them, this wild yearning, this incredible passion...this sweet moment in time.

THAD HELD MICHELLE CLOSE. They'd barely finished, and already he wanted her again. Not just physically, but emotionally, too. And that was definitely worth noting. He wasn't used to being this attached to anyone this soon. Aside from the feelings he had for William— feelings of connection and closeness that had seemed to be there from the very first—he'd never felt as close to anyone as he felt to Michelle in this moment.

And that was something, given they'd barely known each other a week.

He kissed the top of her head, drinking in the orange-blossom fragrance of her hair and skin. Face pressed against his chest, she snuggled against him. "I can't believe we just did that," she murmured.

Thad threaded his hands through her hair, tilted her face up to his. "I can." He looked into the emerald depths of her eyes. "I've been wanting to make love to you since the first time we kissed." He grinned, amending with rueful honesty, "Actually, sooner than that."

Excitement mixed with satisfaction in her husky tone. "When?"

Thad stroked his fingers through her hair. "Even when you wouldn't even give me the time of day." He kissed the smooth curve of her shoulder, the nape of her neck, her high sculpted cheek. "When did you realize you wanted me?"

She kissed his shoulder, the V of his collarbone, the place above his heart. "I don't know."

He wasn't buying the evasion for one second. "Yes, you do," he insisted playfully, stroking a hand down her spine.

She quivered at his touch. Against his bare chest, he could feel her nipples beading. "The first time I saw you mowing the yard."

Aware he was getting hard all over again, he lifted a brow.

She shifted, and he felt the softness of her thighs against the hardness of his. "What can I say?" She shrugged, offhand. "I liked the way you looked pushing a mower."

He laughed. "You're serious."

"Oh, yeah." She smiled dreamily. "You're one attractive guy." She patted the center of his chest with the flat of her hand. "But then you know that." She started to get up.

He caught her wrist and drew her back down beside him. "Not as attractive as you."

She flushed. "I wouldn't bet on that." Her gaze sobered. "Which is why we really need to pull back and think about this."

He rolled onto his side, propping up his head on his palm, draping his thigh over hers.

With her tousled reddish-blond hair, she looked like

an angel. "There are times for thinking—" he traced her lower lip with the pad of his thumb "—and times for not." This was, he decided, the latter. He bent to kiss her.

"You're making it very hard to argue," she whispered as their kiss deepened.

Feeling her tremble acquiescently, he kissed his way lazily down her body. "That's because I don't want you to argue," he said.

She sighed as he found her center. "One more time then," she assented, closing her eyes and giving herself over to him. "One...last...time..."

HOURS LATER, MICHELLE awoke, to find herself cozily ensconced in Thad's strong arms, her head nestled against his chest, her legs draped over one of his. Daylight was filtering in through the closed draperies. She heard a car start up and rumble down the street. With effort, she forced herself to open her eyes. Seven o'clock!

She yawned, extricated herself from the warmth of his limbs and sat up. She shoved the hair from her eyes. "What time were you supposed to pick up William?"

"Seven-thirty." He glanced at the clock and sat up, too.

Michelle rubbed her eyes. "I guess we fell asleep," she said. After the fourth time. Prior to that, they couldn't get enough of each other. Every time she'd even thought about leaving, he'd reached for her. And once she was in his arms, it had been so easy to succumb. To tell herself pleasure was fleeting and she'd had so little of it in her life lately, she deserved at least one night of all-out passion.

Now, in the light of day, she wasn't so certain it had been a good idea. Instead of satisfying her curiosity and getting Thad out of her system, she had only drawn him deeper into her. That couldn't be good for someone trying to maintain a professional distance. And she was trying hard not to get involved with Thad while his petition for adoption was being considered by the court....

Thad kissed the back of her hand and rose. "Want to come with me to pick William up?"

Michelle looked at him in surprise. "Wouldn't that look…"

"Like we were involved on some level? Yeah. Probably."

Thad did not care.

Michelle did.

She didn't want to give anyone, least of all herself or Thad, the wrong impression. "I don't think that's a good idea."

Feeling suddenly shy about her nakedness, she clasped the sheet to her breast. Then she looked at her raincoat and pajamas still scattered on his bedroom floor. She bit down on an oath. "I can't cross the street in that."

He grinned. "Guess you'll have to stay here all day, then."

"Seriously." Michelle dreaded the thought of encountering one of the neighbors wearing only satin pajamas and a raincoat!

"You want me to go over to your place and bring something back for you to wear?"

"That'd probably be worse if someone saw you going in and out."

She couldn't believe it. She was thirty-two years old and about to do the walk of shame.

Thad opened up his closet, rummaged around, emerged with a pair of stretchy, black running shorts and a gray

T-shirt. "Put these on, and wear your coat over them, and it'll look like you've been out jogging."

"In someone else's clothes." Michelle ran her hands through her hair. "This is ridiculous."

"My offer to go over to your place still stands."

They heard another car start nearby and drive down the street.

"No." Michelle sighed. "The longer we wait, the more likelihood there is I'll run into one of the neighbors. I'm just going to put on the pajamas and my coat and go home."

"You can always carry a cup of sugar with you. Now that I actually have some in my pantry, you can pretend you came over to borrow some."

"Very funny, doc."

Still not taking this dilemma as seriously as he should, Thad smirked and disappeared into the bathroom.

Michelle used his absence to get out of bed and slip on her pajamas. She ran her fingers through her hair and put on her clogs. She was in the process of picking up her coat from the floor when the doorbell rang.

Michelle turned to Thad, who had just walked out of the bathroom, in the same clothes he'd worn to work the evening before. Morning beard rimmed his jaw. He smelled like mint toothpaste. "Expecting anyone?" she asked, feeling trapped.

Thad shook his head. "Stay here. I'll go see who it is."

Michelle perched on the edge of the bed while he walked downstairs. The doorbell rang again, more insistently this time. When Thad opened the door she cringed when she heard the familiar voice....

THAD STARED AT the social worker standing on his door-step, aware her timing could not have been worse. "I'm here for a second inspection of the premises," Tamara Kelly said briskly.

Not sure what would happen if Michelle were to come downstairs, clad in her pajamas and looking as if she'd just spent the night with him, which of course she had, Thad tried a diversionary tactic instead. "William's not here."

Tamara lifted the glasses on the chain around her neck and peered at him through the lenses. "Where is he?"

"At the sitter's."

"Already?" Tamara glanced at her watch, noting it was seven-twenty.

"He spent the night there. I didn't get out of the E.R. and home until almost one-thirty."

She nodded cryptically.

"I was on my way to pick him up," Thad continued. "So if you'd like to accompany me, you could check out the place where he stays while I'm at work. I think you may already know his sitter—Dotty Pederson. She used to work in the nursery at the hospital."

"I do. And I probably will pay her a visit at some point, but right now I need to have a look around here."

For the first time Thad lamented the lack of a back staircase in his home. "I probably should go upstairs and tidy up first," he said.

"Actually you shouldn't." Tamara brushed by him, on a mission now. "It's important I see things just as they are."

If it had only been a messy bedroom, Thad wouldn't have cared. But there was no way around the fact that Michelle was up there.

Or not, he thought, as Michelle appeared at the top of the stairs, her jacket buttoned and belted over her white satin pajamas.

"Hello, Tamara," Michelle said pleasantly, descending the stairs as if her presence was nothing out of the ordinary.

Tamara's eyebrows shot skyward.

Whatever she was thinking was definitely not good, Thad noted.

"Counselor. I'm surprised to see you here so early this morning."

"It is early, isn't it?" Michelle smiled and continued coming down the stairs.

Tamara turned to Thad, with disapproval. "Tell me this isn't what it looks like—that you didn't dump the baby at the sitter's so you could...entertain a guest overnight."

Chapter Eight

Michelle knew that making love with Thad—even for one night—would lead to trouble. She just hadn't figured it would be *this* kind of trouble. She took a deep breath. "This wasn't planned," she explained.

"But I'm not sorry it happened," Thad cut in.

Tamara frowned. "Then you acknowledge that the two of you are now...?"

"Involved," Thad confirmed. "And I'm not ashamed of that."

Michelle only wished she could say the same. She hadn't felt this mortified since she'd been caught making out with her first boyfriend when she was fifteen.

"I see." Tamara made a note on her clipboard.

"I'd like this...situation to remain private," Thad said.

Tamara made another note as she walked through the living room, her gaze on the empty beer bottles they hadn't bothered to discard. "You'll have to take that up with your attorney and let him take it up with the court."

Michelle looked at Thad, explaining quietly, "There's no point in fighting this. It'll be in her report. And her full report—not just the selected excerpts she wants him to see—goes to the judge."

"Why?" Thad asked, clearly irked. "What does you

being here this morning have to do with my adopting William?"

"It goes toward your fitness as a potential parent," Tamara explained.

"Then I would think it would help," Thad insisted, "for Judge Barnes to know that I am serious about a woman of such fine character."

Tamara's eyes widened.

It was all Michelle could do not to groan out loud. Gently she laid a cautioning hand on Thad's forearm. "I don't think Ms. Kelly needs to know the specifics of our relationship, Thad."

"Well, I do," Thad countered. "I can see what you're thinking, Ms. Kelly, but this is no one-night stand!"

THE MOMENT THE social worker left, Michelle turned to Thad. "I want to talk to you." She pushed the words through gritted teeth.

"Good," he said, wanting nothing more at that moment than to rid her of her embarrassment, "because I want to talk to you, too."

"But I want to do it at my house." Michelle lifted a palm impatiently. "I need to get some clothes on."

Thad thought she looked pretty good in her white satin pajamas and trendy little raincoat, but sensed she did not want to hear that. "I still have to pick up William. I should have been there twenty minutes ago."

She nodded, looking almost relieved she would have some time to get over the shock of the social worker's unscheduled visit and pull herself together. "Go ahead and get William. Then come on over."

They parted company. Thad got in his car and drove the short distance to pick up William, who'd just been fed. "He'll probably fall asleep before you get him home," Dotty warned.

Thad smiled. "That's okay. I've gotten the knack of removing the baby carrier from the car seat without disturbing him. He sleeps pretty well in it."

By the time Thad reached Michelle's house fifteen minutes later, William was indeed sound asleep. Thad unlocked the carrier from the base, lifted it out of the car and transferred it and William to Michelle's front porch.

The door opened before he had a chance to knock. She had been waiting for him, it seemed. Hair caught in a ponytail, she was dressed in yellow-and-blue running gear. She looked adorable.

She motioned soundlessly for Thad to put William's carrier on the dining-room table, then turned and moved quietly out of the room and around to the kitchen. She waved Thad into a seat at her kitchen table, where a glass of juice was waiting.

An empty glass sat on the counter. She remained standing.

Not a good sign, Thad thought.

"I know you were trying to make the best of a very awkward situation, but you shouldn't have told the social worker that our relationship was serious," she said in the dispassionate lawyerly voice he was beginning to know so well.

Thad rocked back in his chair. He wished she would sit down. "Why not?" he countered, mirroring her faintly contentious tone.

Her green eyes glowered at him. "Because it's not true."

Thad thought about the way they'd made love over and over again. She might want to deny it now, in the light of the day, but in the comfort of his bedroom, she had wanted him every bit as desperately as he had wanted her. "So," he said, "you're saying…?"

Her mouth tightened. "Last night was about sex and loneliness and pure animal attraction."

It had been all that, Thad admitted, but a lot more. And it was time she owned up to that, whether she wanted to or not. He pushed his chair back, stood and closed the distance between them. "I wouldn't have made love to you," he said, "if I hadn't been seriously interested in you, Michelle."

She lowered her gaze. "I know you think that now."

He cupped her shoulders, holding her in front of him, when she would have run. "I'm not your ex. I didn't turn to you out of gratitude."

She shut her eyes against his searching gaze and reminded him in a low, strangled voice, "I know you think that, Thad. I also know that this is a confusing, highly emotional time."

"No argument there," he agreed.

"I know how much you want to adopt William."

Not *want,* Thad corrected silently. "I *am* going to adopt William."

Doubt flashed in her expression. "The court has to agree that it's in William's best interests."

She was sounding like a lawyer again—a worried one. Thad tensed, despite his effort not to let the recent turn of events derail him in any way. "You think they won't?"

"I think the situation is suddenly a lot more complicated than it was," she replied soberly. "And I'm sorry about that. I know better."

Thad could see the emotional wall going up around her heart as surely as if she was erecting it in concrete. He tightened his grip on her shoulders. "I'm not going to apologize to anyone for making love to you last night. Even you."

She extricated herself and turned to face the window over the sink. "You could tell the court it was a mistake, that it won't happen again."

He looked at the lovely line of her back. "Then I'd be lying."

She whirled. "You plan to let this happen again… with William in the house?"

Thad lounged against the opposite counter, hands braced on either side of him. "That's right. But let's stick to the facts, shall we? William *wasn't* in the house last night."

Michelle gestured helplessly. "He easily could have been."

Thad shrugged. Last night had shown him how much he wanted Michelle in his life. Irked at the roadblocks she kept throwing up, Thad stated, "Even if he had been there with us last night, he's way too young to be aware."

"That won't always be the case." Once again, Michelle took on the role of devil's advocate. "And Judge Barnes is old school. He thinks a couple should be married. At the very least deeply committed to each other."

Thad scowled. "Who says I'm not committed?"

MICHELLE HAD KNOWN Thad was going to be difficult. What she hadn't expected was the tumult of her own emotions. She tried again. "I understand Tamara Kelly's poorly timed home visit has backed you into a corner. But we can still turn this around."

"How?" Thad challenged. "By getting married?"

"That's not funny."

He shrugged his broad shoulders affably. "Who's joking? Seriously, if I need to be married in order to adopt, then I'll take that leap. But only," he clarified in a low, husky voice that sent shivers down her spine, "with you."

The notion of the two of them walking down the aisle wasn't nearly as disturbing as it should have been. Michelle drove her hands through her hair. "You're missing the point!" she cried.

Thad crossed to her. "That *is* the point." He wrapped his arms around her, draping her in warmth. "Last night meant the world to me, Michelle. And if you were honest, you would admit it meant everything to you, too."

Before she could do more than take a breath, his lips were on hers, arguing his point, staking his claim, making sure she knew that the chemistry between them was as potent as ever. And as much as Michelle wanted to deny the passion and, more important, deny Thad access to her heart, she couldn't. When he held her like this, when he brought her so close and kissed her so sweetly, so ardently, all her inhibitions melted away. All she wanted was this moment in time, with this man. If William hadn't chosen that exact moment to wake up, fussing, she was pretty sure they would have ended up in bed again.

But their tiny chaperone did sound the alarm. And it was perfect timing, Michelle thought, as she showed the two of them the door and then went out herself for an extra-long morning run. She had a lot of thinking to do before she made any more impulsive mistakes. And the rest of the weekend in which to do it.

Like it or not, for the next two days, Thad and William were going to be on their own.

"MICHELLE?" GLENN YORK appeared in her doorway on Monday morning. "I need to talk to you in my office for a minute, if you wouldn't mind."

Surprised by the grim note in her partner's tone, as well as the request, Michelle rose and walked into Glenn's office.

As soon as she saw who was already there, she knew the reason Glenn had been so cryptic in his request.

Figuring the staff did not need to hear any of what was about to be said, she shut the door behind her. Gave Thad—and the baby in his arms—a brief, assessing glance, then turned back to Glenn.

"What's going on?" she said, knowing it had to be something dire, otherwise Glenn would not have called her in when she had requested not to be involved.

He gestured for her to have a seat in the chair next to Thad. "I had a phone call from the social worker on Thad's case a while ago."

Thad cut in glumly, "Among other things, Tamara Kelly doesn't like the fact I had to leave William overnight with the sitter while I was at work."

"She fears it could be a harbinger of the future," Glenn said. "Given that he's a single parent and has such a demanding job."

Heat moved from Michelle's neck into her face. "Anything else?"

"She wanted to warn us that Judge Barnes is probably going to want to speak to you about your, uh, relationship with Thad." Glenn cleared his throat, looking like he wished he were anywhere but there. "I've already requested the conversation be in chambers, but it's going to be on the record, as will the social worker's written report."

Great, Michelle thought. Well, what had she expected? She'd known, going in, that spending the night with Thad was a mistake.

"As the attorney of record," Glenn continued reluctantly, "I need to know what you're going to say."

The problem was, Michelle thought, she didn't know what she was going to say.

Both men continued to look at her.

Finally, she shrugged. "That it was a..."

"If you say 'mistake,'" Thad interrupted, "I'm done for."

Her law partner put up a cautioning hand. "Not necessarily."

"It'll look like it didn't mean anything, and it did," Thad insisted, not backing down.

Michelle grimaced. She felt like she was sinking. Taking a deep breath, she tried again. "The thing is, it's private. I don't...discuss that aspect of my life." She met Glenn's eyes. "With anyone."

"As a friend, I understand," Glenn returned. "As Thad's lawyer and a fellow member of the Texas Bar Association, I'm telling you that you don't have that luxury. When Judge Barnes asks you that question—he wants to see the four of us and Tamara Kelly in his chambers at four-thirty this afternoon to discuss the suitability of William remaining in Thad's custody until a decision regarding the adoption petition can be made—you're going to have to be prepared to answer it a lot better than you did just now."

THAD KNEW THAT Michelle did not want William to go into foster care, even for a brief while, any more than he did. He also knew that she'd been steadfastly avoiding him since they'd parted company Saturday morning and wouldn't misrepresent anything she felt to the court.

Unfortunately, before they could discuss the situation further, the clients for her ten-thirty appointment arrived, and she excused herself to meet with the elderly couple.

Glenn looked at Thad. "It'll be fine," the lawyer said.

Thad hoped so.

Judge Barnes's severe expression when they entered his chambers six hours later was not as reassuring.

"Well, seems we've had some developments since this time last week," the conservative jurist said, leaning back in his chair. "For one thing, Dr. Garner isn't the only one who wants to adopt this child."

Thad cuddled William close to his chest.

"I came over Saturday morning to tell you that," Tamara Kelly admitted, "before things took an unexpected turn."

"We'll get to that in a minute," Judge Barnes said gruffly. "Meantime, you should know, Dr. Garner, eleven other families have approached social services and, by extension, this court, and volunteered to adopt William."

Thad couldn't say he was all that surprised.

Word had gotten out. Everyone in the county knew how and why William had been left on Thad's front porch. Hearts had opened up all over the place, which always happened when an abandoned baby made the news. But none of those wanting to help were family.

"They have no blood claim," Thad said. He remembered what Michelle had told him—that from a legal standpoint, in his case, blood didn't matter—but felt he had to play all his cards.

Judge Barnes shrugged. "In your case, Dr. Garner, it's not applicable."

"I beg your pardon, Your Honor, but in this case it is," Thad shot back. "William is my nephew. Initially, yes, it was a shock, finding him the way I did. Even more of a jolt, discovering how he'd come about and been abandoned, first by my brother—who'll never have any idea what he's missing in not raising this child—and then Brice and Beatrix Johnson, who went to such lengths to make his birth happen." His voice cracked. "But I never had any doubt what the right thing to do was, and that was give William a home and the family he deserves."

"Which is exactly what we're talking about," Tamara Kelly inserted gently.

All eyes turned to her. The social worker continued, even more kindly, "No one is saying your heart isn't in the right place, Thad. We all know you want what is best for William."

"And that might be," Judge Barnes intoned, "a mother and father who know what they are getting into and are equipped to care for the child in a more traditional sense."

Glenn broke in. "Judge, the babysitter is a former pediatric and neonatal nurse, who is now retired and has brought up children of her own. William could not be in better hands during the time Dr. Garner works at the hospital."

"That's true," Tamara Kelly said.

So what was the problem? Thad wondered.

Judge Barnes looked at the notes in front of him, then over at Michelle. And Thad knew it was crunch time once again.

MICHELLE HAD THOUGHT she was ready for the inquisition by the notoriously finicky judge. Suddenly everything she had been prepared to say, about her private life being her own and not germane to this case at all, went out the window. She looked over at Thad, at the infant ensconced in his arms, and knew what she had to do—for all their sakes. "I care about William, too, Judge Barnes," she said quietly.

The judge waited for her to go on, one craggy brow raised in silent query.

She knew what he wanted to know, what everyone there wanted to know. "It's true that Thad and I have really gotten acquainted only recently, but there is something between us that is, well, unique."

"Unique," Judge Barnes repeated.

"We're not teenagers." Michelle tried again. "Sometimes, yes, things happen quickly and unexpectedly. You fall in love with someone, a child, or a…a potential mate, and it goes against all logic, and yet…" She glanced at Thad, looking so strong and virile and loving as he held the baby to his chest. "You know if you don't open yourself up to the possibilities being presented and allow yourself to feel these emotions and become involved, that you will always regret it."

"So you're as serious about Dr. Garner as he is about you?" Judge Barnes asked finally.

Michelle locked eyes with Thad.

There was no pressure in his gaze. Instead, she picked up on myriad other sentiments. Interest. Affection. Want. Need. The struggle to understand. She swallowed and looked to the truth deep in her heart. "He and I have found something unique." *Something she had been looking for her entire life and could not walk away from now.* "I plan to see it through and be there for Thad and William…whenever they need me."

Thad's eyes darkened with an emotion that far surpassed gratitude.

She felt connected to him. On the brink of falling

for him, head over heels. And he looked as if he felt the same.

Minutes later the session behind closed doors ended. William was still in Thad's custody.

"Good job in there," Glenn said as he walked Michelle and Thad to their cars.

"We're—Thad—isn't out of the woods yet," Michelle said awkwardly.

Thad shifted William to Michelle's arms while he unlocked and opened the door of his SUV and let some of the sun-warmed air out. She held William close, breathing in his sweet baby scent. Beside her, Thad's expression was solemn.

"Michelle's right," Thad told Glenn with a sigh. "I need to work harder to prove I'm the right parent for him."

Glenn did not disagree.

"What more can you do?" Michelle asked.

Thad shrugged. "I can even the playing field with the other families who want to adopt William."

Michelle's heart began to race. "How are you going to do that?"

"By finding a good mother for him," Thad stated seriously. "A smart, loving woman who would agree to co-adopt William and bring him up with me."

"WERE YOU SERIOUS?" Michelle asked moments later. Glenn had just headed off to his car, leaving Thad and her, still with William in her arms, standing there.

"As a heart attack," Thad said.

Michelle looked into the strong, indomitable lines of Thad's face. "What makes you think Judge Barnes would go for two unmarried people adopting a baby together?"

"He might not. Then again," Thad said, "if the judge's only arguments are that William should grow up with a mother—which is something I happen to agree on, having lost my own mother as a kid—and that I'm having sex outside marriage, then maybe I should just get married and knock off two objections with a single 'I do.'"

Michelle thought it had been wrenching to learn that Jared had confused gratitude with love and asked her to marry him for that reason. But that misstep was nothing compared to knowing that Thad was contemplating marriage for purely practical considerations. Yet she could tell by the expression on Thad's face that his heart was in the right place.

As was hers. There were bigger, more important things at stake here than their own egos. In particular, a child's well-being. "You'd really do that for William?"

"And more. I love him, Michelle. Like my own child. And I know what I said, about him being of my blood, but to be honest, it's not so much that or even the connection I feel with him—the same connection I feel with you—it's the fact that he needs me. He needs you. Look into his eyes. Feel the way he snuggles against you, like you're the only mother he's ever wanted, and tell me you don't feel the same way."

"I admit that…" Oh, what the hell, Michelle thought, swiping a tear from her cheek. "I've loved this child from the very beginning." Working to get a handle on her out-of-control emotions, Michelle swallowed around the tightening of her throat. "But you and I are not in love with each other, Thad."

Thad regarded her steadily. "We could be," he said softly, "given a little more time."

The deeply romantic part of Michelle felt that way,

too. Especially given how she'd felt when they'd made love, how happy she was to see him whenever their paths crossed, and most important of all, how often he was in her thoughts these days. And yet…the lawyer in her who'd had years dealing with family-law catastrophes had a much more pragmatic view.

She looked at Thad, as William curled his fist around her little finger and held on tight. "What if what we feel now is as good as it gets? What if we never do fall head over heels for each other?"

Thad shrugged. "What if we don't?" His voice dropped to a soft murmur. "We're sexually compatible. We live in the same town. We both have jobs we enjoy. We both want to be married and have kids and it hasn't happened. Maybe we've been waiting for perfection, and perfection is never going to come along. I, for one, am not getting any younger."

Neither was she.

"William needs us now," he said fervently.

Thad was beginning to make far too much sense. "How do you know another family wouldn't be better?" she asked.

He grimaced. "William's already been rejected and passed off twice. He's settled in with me and he's started to settle in with you, too. Do you really want to see him taken away from us and carted off to a fourth home, in less than—" Thad did the calculation quickly "—two weeks?"

Did she?

MICHELLE THOUGHT ABOUT what Thad had said the rest of the evening and all through the night.

By dawn Tuesday morning, she knew what she had to do. Seeing the lights on over at his house, she showered, dressed and walked across the street. Thad answered the door as if he'd been expecting her. "I take it you have an answer," he said.

Michelle nodded. "And the answer is yes." She held up a palm before Thad could interrupt. "But there are some stipulations."

He ushered her inside. "Okay."

Michelle paced his foyer restlessly. "We have to do a trial run."

His eyes narrowed. "In what sense?"

"I want to try out being a mom, the same way you've been trying out being a dad. I want to spend as much time as possible with you and William."

"Judge Barnes is not likely to go for that if we're not married," Thad said.

"And maybe he will," Michelle replied quietly. She was as determined to protect this baby from future heartache and disappointment as she was resolved to shield herself. "If we can demonstrate that together you and I can provide a mother and father's love, a sense of family and all the love William will ever need or want—*without* getting married first."

Chapter Nine

"Michelle's right," Glenn told Thad as the three of them met in Glenn's office a few hours later. William was snuggled in Michelle's arms. "What the two of you are proposing is not without precedent. In fact, it happens all the time. A biological parent abandons the child and/or signs away all rights to avoid being stuck paying child support. And someone else—usually a new girlfriend or boyfriend to the remaining parent—will step in to adopt the child, even if the two of them aren't living together and have no desire to do so."

"And the state allows it?" Thad asked.

"Most judges rule it's in the best interests of the child to have two people legally responsible for the welfare of the child, as long as custody issues are agreed upon and worked out in advance."

Thad's brows lifted. "Custody," he repeated in concern.

Glenn nodded. "You and Michelle are going to have to decide if you want to split the care of William fifty-fifty, with each of you having equal say and equal time with him. Or if you want Thad to have sole custody, and Michelle visitation rights. Then there are monetary issues, as well. To what degree will each of you be fiscally responsible for William's needs? And most important of all, Michelle is going to have adequate home studies done, so that social services can determine her fitness as a parent."

Which meant, Michelle thought, she would need to have a nursery set up, too.

"What about the relationship part of the arrangement?" Thad asked.

"Don't try to hide anything from the court—or social services," Glenn warned. "Be clear about whatever it is. And be prepared to talk to Judge Barnes about it again during your next court date—a week from Monday."

What if, Michelle thought, *we* don't know what our relationship is?

"Meantime, I'll notify Tamara Kelly that you are petitioning to adopt William, as well, and get her started on your home study," Glenn promised Michelle.

"Thanks, Glenn."

"No problem." Her partner smiled. A devoted family man himself, he clearly wanted this to work out for them the way they wanted.

Yet he was skeptical, too, probably because she and Thad hadn't said they were in love or planned to get married. Michelle had seen it in the brief hesitation in Glenn's actions when they'd first told him why they had asked to meet him at his office.

Michelle, William and Thad left and headed back to Thad's SUV. "I was going to drive to Fort Stockton today to purchase a crib and a changing table. Interested?"

Michelle had already rescheduled her appointments for the next few days. "I'm going to need some baby gear, too." And after that, they could start working out some of the details of their baby-sharing arrangement.

"Wow," Michelle said as they wandered through the furniture store geared exclusively for kids. Thad was carrying William now. "I had no idea they had so many different kinds of cribs and kids' beds."

"Amazing, isn't it?" Thad stopped in front of a wooden crib painted fire-engine red.

Michelle looked at a similar one in white. Then one in mahogany.

She looked back at Thad. "Do you think we should both get the same kind of crib and bedding? Or mix it up a little?"

"Good question." Thad smiled at a red-white-and-blue chenille rug shaped like a dump truck. "The same bedding would make him feel at home wherever he was."

"But it could get a little boring, too."

"I guess different, then," Thad said. "If you don't mind, I'd like to go with the mahogany, and get this car-and-truck sheet set."

"I'll get the white crib, changing table and glider rocker with the animal-safari sheets."

As they went off to find a salesperson, Thad stopped in front of a bed shaped like a boat. He grinned. "Things have sure changed since I was a kid."

Michelle nodded as they passed a very pregnant woman and her husband, along with two toddlers, debating over a train table and easel.

The woman looked up and smiled at Thad and Michelle and the baby in Thad's arms, obviously thinking they were just another family.

The surprising thing was, the three of them *felt* like a family.

"How was your bedroom decorated when you were little?" Michelle studied a vivid display of wall art.

Thad moved in close to make way for a woman with a double stroller trying to get through the aisle. "It changed. I remember something about a train when I was in kindergarten, and then when I entered elementary school, everyone was really into spaceships. When I outgrew that, my room was more of a mess than anything else. What about you?" He shifted William as they waited their turn at the sales desk.

"I never had a kids' room. My parents believed that traditional little-girl themes—like princesses and kittens—lowered the intellect of the child. So my bedroom was decorated with Renoir and Monet prints, the bed linens were Egyptian cotton. The study desk was really nice, though."

"I bet." His gaze roamed over her silk sweater and slacks. "Were you ever allowed to get dirty and messy? You know, climb trees and ride bikes and all that stuff."

"I was taught how to ride a bike and swim. My mother and father thought those were necessary skills. Beyond that, the only time I was allowed to run free on a playground was at school recess."

"What kind of childhood would you like to see William have?" he asked.

"If I could wish one thing for him, I'd want him to be free," Michelle said. "Free to explore and just be whatever he wants to be." She studied Thad's generous smile. "What about you? What kind of childhood would you like to see William have?"

"I want him to feel loved and wanted, secure in his place in our family and in the world."

They were in the BMW and almost back in Summit when Thad's cell phone rang. The road was treacherous, twisting, with no place to pull over. He inclined his head toward the holder clipped to his belt. "Would you mind grabbing that and just hitting the speaker button? I'll take it from there."

Flushing a little, Michelle did as directed.

"Thad Garner," he said.

"Hey, Thad. It's Violet Hunter. I just saw your message. And I think I might be able to help you out."

Thad kept his eyes on the road. "Actually, Violet, it's not a good time to talk. I'm driving back from Fort Stockton. I'll get back to you later," he said.

"I'll wait for you to call," Violet said cheerfully.

Thad hit the off button. As the road straightened out, he shifted and slid the phone back in his belt clip.

Michelle knew that whatever Thad wanted to talk to Violet about was none of her business. It shouldn't even matter that Violet still had a crush on Thad. Still, it bothered her. By the time they reached Summit, Michelle knew what she had to do. She turned to Thad as they got out of the car.

"If you wouldn't mind, I'd like to have William by myself for a while this afternoon. See what it's like to be a mom, instead of just a family friend."

Thad thought for a moment, then said, "Good idea. I've got some work to do on the nursery at my house. It'll go a lot faster if William is with you."

HOLDING WILLIAM IN her arms, Michelle walked through the house and tried to see the place as a social worker would.

Her home was definitely the abode of a single woman. The downstairs living room had cream-colored furniture, elegant lamps and beautiful framed prints on the walls. The television was hidden in a stylish armoire. Even the coffee table was an elaborate creation of glass and wood. There wasn't a toy or piece of baby gear in sight.

The dining room was formal, the kitchen outfitted with every gourmet-cooking appliance imaginable.

The second floor of her cozy Arts and Crafts house was just as elegant—and the reason she'd bought the house. The previous owner had raised the ceiling to the attic rafters, ripped out the second bedroom and turned it into a sumptuous master bath with a huge, built-in closet. There was no place for a nursery on either floor.

But there was plenty of room in her heart, Michelle thought as she carried William back downstairs and settled with him on the sofa. If only she hadn't fallen in love with a child before, to disastrous result, she thought, resting her cheek against the downy softness of William's head. Maybe then she would feel a little more confident that it was all going to work out. That Judge Barnes would see she was the mother this little boy wanted and needed.

As an attorney, she knew it was up to her to make sure he did. Feeling empowered, now that she knew what she had to do, Michelle headed back across the street.

Thad answered the door. He was dressed to work—in an old T-shirt, jeans and sneakers. He had a smudge of navy paint across his jaw, another across his cheek. Perspiration clung to his forehead and the back of his neck. He looked at the baby dozing in her arms. "Everything okay?"

"We need to talk," Michelle said.

HE NOTICED WILLIAM was swaddled. "I forgot to give you something for William to sleep in, didn't I?" he said.

"It's okay. I forgot, too." Michelle was already heading for the Moses basket in the corner. She gently lowered William into it. He stirred, as if trying to wake up. Spreading her palm across the width of his chest, she touched him lightly, all the while shushing him softly.

After a moment he seemed to settle. Then he was asleep. Michelle backed away quietly.

Figuring he might as well get her opinion on something while she was here and happy to postpone whatever it was she needed to tell him, Thad motioned her up the stairs. "Where'd you learn to soothe him like that?" he whispered, impressed she'd managed to keep the baby from waking up during the transfer from arms to bed.

Michelle shrugged. "I figured it out on my own. He sleeps best when reassured—by touch—that he's not alone."

Or been abandoned again.

"That's why the canvas baby carriers work so well."

"Ah." Thad led Michelle into the room that had once been his office. And was now—thanks to some marathon clearing out and transferring to the garage—soon to be William's nursery.

"I went to the paint store and got this child-safe, fume-free color, but once I started to put it on…" Thad looked at the wall he'd painted. "What do you think? It's too dark a blue, isn't it?"

Hands on her hips, Michelle stepped back and regarded what he had done. "To do the whole room in? Yeah, it is." She tilted her head to one side. "Unless you want it to always feel like nighttime in here."

Thad sighed in frustration. The color was good for sleeping, not playing. "Not exactly the look I was going for."

Michelle tossed him a reassuring smile. "All isn't

lost. You could use it on the lower third of the wall and then paint a lighter blue above that. I'm sure William would like that."

Thad exhaled in relief. He was trying to be superdad here, but decorating really was not his thing. "I want to get this done today, so I can at least get his crib up before the next unannounced visit from Tamara."

"Just make sure you get the same undertone in each shade," Michelle cautioned.

Thad blinked. "Say that again?"

Michelle checked her watch. "Tell you what," she said, making note of the color shade written on the can. "I'll run to the paint store now. Anything else you need?"

Thad shrugged. He hadn't a clue. "You tell me."

Michelle looked around again, seeming to miss nothing, regarding his amateurish attempt. "I'll be right back. And, Thad, I know the manufacturer said no fumes…"

Thad knew where she was going with this. Before, it had been just him. Now, William was in the house, too. "I'll open all the windows on this floor," he promised.

Thad kept an ear out for William as he measured the wall into thirds and penciled in a line. He even went down and checked on William once he'd taped off the areas to be painted. To his amazement, the little guy kept right on sleeping.

There was a click behind Thad as Michelle let herself in the front door.

She had changed into an old T-shirt, sneakers and a pair of worn, paint-splattered jeans. She set down the paint can she'd bought and tiptoed over to where he stood. "Guess we wore him out with our shopping trip," Thad whispered.

Michelle nodded and leaned in for a closer look. "There was a lot to look at," she whispered.

He followed her back to the foyer, picked up the five-gallon can and sack of supplies she'd purchased. They headed up the stairs.

She knelt to pry open the can. Thad took a look at the coordinating pale blue shade. "That's nice."

She'd also bought an extra pan and roller.

"How about you take the top and I'll take the bottom? Since you're tall and I'm not."

"No problem." Their fingers touched as he handed over the roller, already saturated with the dark blue paint. Relishing how good it felt to be working side by side with her on this, Thad asked, "So what did you want to talk to me about earlier?"

Without warning, she seemed to be holding him at arm's length once again. "I was thinking we should sit down as soon as possible and work out our custody arrangement." She sounded practical, matter-of-fact. "You know—what nights I'll have William, when you'll have him…and then we'll draw up a plan."

"Alternate holidays," Thad joked, thinking how much this sounded like they were splitting up, instead of coming together.

Michelle tensed. "Yes," she said slowly, concentrating on her painting now, "I suppose that, too."

That wasn't what Thad wanted. He had no qualms about making his opinion known. "Do we really have to be this regimented about it?" he asked. He had envisioned a much looser arrangement. One that had them popping in and out of each other's homes, at whim.

Michelle painted the same way she made love, with slow, thoughtful strokes. "The court will want to know,

Thad." She focused on her task. "And I think it's best. This way we'll avoid any misunderstandings."

"Like what?" Thad countered, feeling as if they were on the verge of their first fight.

Finished with the spot she was in, Michelle shifted several feet to the left. "We should split the cost of William's babysitter. Whoever is off first should pick him up."

Thad used a brush to paint along the trim line. "That seems reasonable."

Michelle pressed her lips together. "That way he won't have to be with the sitter more than three or four days a week at most. As for nights…that's a little trickier. I'd like to have him fifty percent of the time, if that's okay with you."

Wow. She *had* thought this out. Though Thad knew it was only fair she enjoy her share of nighttime feedings, since those were the times when William was likely to be most in need of rocking and cuddling.

"What else?" He tried not to think about the evenings he wouldn't spend looking after William anymore. Funny how quickly the little guy had become a major part of his existence, to the point Thad could no longer imagine his life without him.

"My home," she said, "is not set up for a separate nursery. I can put the crib and changing table in my bedroom for now, but eventually, I'm going to have to hire an architect and put a two-story addition on if I want a room for William upstairs next to mine. Which I do."

"Okay," Thad said, not sure what she was getting at.

"And it could take a while to get the construction completed. In the meantime, I really think he needs the comfort and stability of his own nursery."

His hopes for a more congenial arrangement rose.

"You want to stay with us on the nights you're the responsible parent?" He could go for that.

She looked at him as if shocked he would think her so presumptuous. "I want us to do what some divorcing couples do when they share custody and want to give the kids the reassuring comfort of their own space, in their own home. It's called 'bird-nesting.' The kids stay in the same place—it's the parents who come in and out, when it's their turn."

"So on your nights, you'd sleep here…"

Michelle nodded. "And you'd sleep at my house, in my bed."

Thad could easily imagine trekking everything back and forth, but to sleep in her bed—and have her in his? How would he be able to do that and not think about making love to her again?

But then, maybe that was what this was all leading up to. Maybe she just needed him to slow down in the romance department while they figured out how to co-parent. All Thad knew for certain was that he wanted to be with Michelle as much as he wanted to be with William.

A spot of color appeared in Michelle's cheeks. "It would certainly keep us from having to duplicate everything—in the short term. Until the adoption goes through, officially. And then, as William settles in and I get a place set up for him in my home, we could gradually transition him into spending half his time with me and half his time with you."

"Sounds…complicated," Thad said. Almost as if she already had one foot in the door and one foot out.

"Not really," Michelle said, not meeting his eyes. "This is actually going to be easier for us in the short term. And it's not like William would never be at my place with me. He would be. At first, like now, for small periods of time. For afternoons. Naps. While I'm also doing laundry and things like that. But once the construction starts, you know as well as I do that it'll be too noisy and disruptive for him to be there."

She had a point there. The sound of nail guns and hammers drove him crazy, Thad thought, and he was an adult. Just the sound of the vacuum cleaner had awakened and frightened the little guy the other day.

Michelle knelt to refill her paint tray. "The bottom line is, we have to be as proactive and consistent as possible in what we do where he is concerned."

"And here I thought we'd just parent by the seat of our pants," Thad joked.

Michelle lifted a censuring brow and rolled the last of the dark blue paint on the lower walls.

Thad had seen women lose their sense of humor when it came to issues like this. He'd hoped Michelle would not be one of them. He cleared his throat. "Seriously, I see your point. Although I don't think William is all that aware of his surroundings."

"But he will be," Michelle predicted. "He's getting more and more alert every day."

"Speaking of which…" Thad finished applying the light blue paint and set the roller in the tray. He glanced at his watch. It had been nearly four and a half hours since the last feeding. "William should have been awake half an hour ago."

Alarm flashed in Michelle's eyes. Thad knew exactly how she felt. Usually William let them know when it was time to feed him.

"I'll check on him." Michelle was out the door like a shot.

Thad was hard on her heels.

They bounded down the stairs and into the living room, over to the Moses basket, where William was sleeping.

Eyes open, he had worked one arm out of his blanket and was lying quietly, looking up at the ceiling. Although he wasn't making a sound, Thad noted his cheeks looked a little pink.

"Hey there, little fella," Michelle said, reaching down to pick him up.

She frowned as she held William. "Thad? I think he feels a little warm."

Chapter Ten

"Thanks for meeting us at your office," Thad told his colleague Sandra Carson forty-five minutes later.

"No problem." Sandra switched on lights as she went. The forty-two-year-old pediatrician was dressed in jeans and a T-shirt bearing the name of her youngest daughter's T-ball team. "The game was just over when you called and the kids were going out for pizza with their teammates. My husband will bring them home." She winked. "As well as a little dinner for me." Sandra paused to wash her hands at the sink, then looped her stethoscope around her neck. "So what's going on?"

"William woke from his nap with an elevated temperature." Thad laid William on the examining table. The baby began to cry. Beside him, Michelle looked about to tear up, too. Realizing for the first time what it was to be the *parent* of a kid in this situation, instead of the doc in charge, Thad swallowed around the unaccustomed lump of emotion in his throat. "I know what I think it is, obviously, but I wanted an expert opinion."

"Well, you've come to the right place." Sandra unsnapped the knit sleeper. Her expression intent, she listened to William's heart and lungs, then gently palpated his abdomen, checked him for any stiffness, looked into his throat, ears, nose. "There's an enterovirus going around—usually lasts around three days—but I want to do a little blood work to confirm."

Thad had expected as much. He began to relax. "We've been seeing it in the E.R., too."

"It's that time of year," Sandra said sympathetically. "My kids had it week before last. They weren't feeling very well, but they were happy to miss school."

Michelle and Thad both chuckled.

"If you'll hold him, I'll do the prick," Sandra said.

Michelle winced as William let out an enraged wail. Empathetic tears slid down her face.

"I'd like to get his temp again, too, when he calms down," Sandra said before slipping out of the room.

Not sure who needed comforting more, Thad handed William to Michelle. The moment the little guy was wrapped in her arms, he stopped crying. "Guess he knows who his pals are," Thad said.

He reached for the thermometer. While Michelle continued to hold William, Thad took his temp again, as unobtrusively as possible. By the time Sandra came back in, the thermometer had beeped. Thad read the results out loud. It was a degree and a half above normal.

Sandra made note of it on William's chart. "Not too awfully high, but you'll need to keep an eye on it." She looked up. "The blood test showed it's not bacterial. So the treatment, as you know, is going to be acetaminophen, fluids and a lot of TLC. He may get a little worse before he gets better. Most important thing is to keep him comfortable, well-hydrated and his temp down." Finished, Sandra held out her hand to Michelle. "I'm sorry. We got down to business so fast, you and I haven't been properly introduced. I'm Sandra Carson, William's pediatrician. And you are...?"

"Michelle Anderson, Thad's neighbor..."

"And William's mom," Thad finished.

THAD'S COLLEAGUE LOOKED like she could have been knocked over with a feather, Michelle thought.

"We're both petitioning to adopt him," she explained.

Sandra looked at Thad. "I didn't even know you were involved with anyone."

"He's not. I mean, we're not," Michelle said, aware that even as she spoke the words felt untrue. Because they *were* involved, more so with every moment they spent together. Just not the way people expected.

"It's complicated," Thad said.

Michelle pretended an ease she didn't feel. "A friends-becoming-family thing."

"Michelle will be every bit as involved in William's care as I will be," Thad stated casually.

Sandra blinked. "That's great. Congratulations. William is one very lucky boy."

"You okay?" Thad asked, when they were back home and getting William out of the back of his SUV.

Michelle nodded, though in truth she still felt a little shaky. It was always upsetting when a little one was sick. And with William barely two weeks old... She swallowed. "I know it's supposed to be my night to take care of him, but I'm thinking...under the circumstances...that we should do it together at my house."

Noting William had drifted off to sleep again on the short drive home, Thad left the baby strapped in the car seat and lifted the infant carrier out of the base. "Agreed."

Trying not to think how nice it would feel to be with Thad all the time, Michelle walked slowly toward his front door. "One of us will have to sleep on the sofa bed."

A warm spring breeze drifted over them. "No problem," Thad said.

She studied the gentle, respectful light his eyes. He had such an easygoing attitude. "You sure?"

Thad nodded. "With him sick, I wouldn't be comfortable away from him. And as William readily demonstrated in Sandra's office, he needs you, too. So what do you say we gather up everything we need and then head across the street?"

Relieved they were on the same page, Michelle said, "Sounds great."

They walked into the house. Michelle noted that the red light on Thad's phone in the foyer was blinking. "Looks like you've got a message."

Thad set the baby carrier down on the living-room floor, well out of any draft and away from any noise. He came back and punched the play button. A female voice floated out from the machine. "Hey, Thad, it's Violet. How come you haven't called me back? I thought you really needed my help ASAP but—"

Thad punched the end button. "I'll listen to the rest of that later." Guilt flashed across his handsome face as he studied her stricken look. "I know what you're thinking. It's not what it sounds."

That was good, Michelle thought grimly, because it sounded like he was two-timing her—or would have been, had they been dating. Which, Michelle reminded herself firmly, they were most definitely not.

"It doesn't matter," she said.

"It does." Thad caught her by the shoulders and turned her to face him.

Michelle held on to her dignity by a thread. Aware

she'd already inadvertently revealed far too much of her feelings, she said as nonchalantly as possible, "Look, you're free to date whoever you please, whenever you please. I am, too."

He let her go. Stepped back. Studied her face, his own expression impassive. "That's really the way you want it?" he asked. She noticed that his voice was a bit hoarse.

She avoided his gaze. "We're both adults, with needs and…and desires. Simply put, this is the only way this arrangement of ours is going to work."

MICHELLE'S VIEW ON how their parental partnership should be conducted did not change Thad's mind about where he wanted their relationship to go. But figuring his agenda could wait until after William was well, Thad did not pursue the issue. Rather, he said simply, "No matter what, Michelle, I want us to be friends."

"I do, too."

"Good. So, on to getting what we need for the evening ahead…"

While William continued to sleep in the baby carrier, Michelle collected clothing, blankets and diapers. Thad got the bottles, formula, baby first-aid kit containing acetaminophen and his medical bag. They heaped everything into an oversize laundry basket and took William across the street to her house.

Since the things they had purchased would not be delivered until later in the week, Thad returned for the portable crib and Moses basket. Realizing belatedly they probably needed the baby bathtub and assorted baby lotions, cleansers and wipes, he returned to get those, too.

When he came in, Michelle was in the kitchen, a

fussing William in her arms. A half-made bottle of formula sat on the counter. "Need a hand?" Thad asked.

She nodded, her relief palpable. "I don't know how single parents do it."

Neither did Thad. He needed Michelle tonight, as much as William did.

Quickly he finished preparing the bottle and handed it to her. Michelle leaned against the counter and gave William the bottle. He drank a small amount, then started to drift off to sleep.

Michelle looked at Thad, a question in her eyes.

"We have to get more fluids than that into him," Thad said.

Michelle shifted William to her shoulder, jostling him enough to wake him. She patted him on his back. He looked around, seeming listless and out of sorts. "I feel so bad for him," she murmured.

"He'll get through it," Thad promised.

When William burped, Michelle tried again.

William sucked on the bottle without much interest. It took quadruple the amount of normal coaxing to get two ounces into him. Finally he pushed the nipple out of his mouth.

Thad touched the back of his hand to the little guy's cheek. It was cool. The acetaminophen they had given William in Sandra's office was doing its job. "Maybe we should put him down for a while and try again in two hours, instead of the usual four," Thad suggested, knowing they were likely to have a long night ahead.

"SURE YOU HAVE everything?" Michelle asked Thad some five hours later. Thad looked at the sofa bed she'd made up for him in the living room. It was outfitted with cream-colored sheets, the same hue as the sofa, and a matching quilt. The pillows looked luxurious.

William was already settled in the mesh-sided portable crib upstairs next to her bed. Pushing aside the yearning to take her in his arms and give her a proper kiss good-night, Thad said gruffly, "I'll be fine. Let me know if you need me."

"I will." Looking for a moment as if she wished he would kiss her, she gave him one last, grateful glance. "And thanks for staying over."

"Nowhere I'd rather be," Thad said.

Michelle smiled and slipped upstairs. Thad heard her moving around on the second floor as he went into the guest bath to change into a clean T-shirt and jersey sleep pants. By the time he'd climbed beneath the sheets, all was quiet again. He turned off the light and lay there, thinking about the day they'd had and the many more ahead of them. The next thing he knew Michelle was standing next to the sofa bed.

"There's something wrong with William, Thad!" She shook him roughly. "Come quick!"

He leaped from the sofa bed and raced up the stairs after her.

William was still in the portable crib. He was lying on his back, trembling and uttering a weak, distressed cry. Thad didn't even have to touch him to know he was burning up. Calmly he lifted William and carried him over to the rumpled covers of Michelle's bed. Although his adrenaline was pumping, his actions were measured as he coated the rectal thermometer with petroleum jelly. "Fill the baby bath with lukewarm water. Get a towel ready, and a clean diaper and change of clothes. I'll be right in."

By the time he entered the bathroom with a naked, still-whimpering William, Michelle was ready for him.

Thad eased the baby into the tub, holding his tiny body in the palms of his hands. Being careful to keep the little guy's face and neck above water, Thad said, "We need to lower his temperature as quickly as possible."

Michelle edged in, her expression one of maternal distress. "How can I help?"

"Sponge him down with that washcloth."

Michelle gently did as directed. "How high is his temp?"

Thad noted she was shivering, too. Probably from anxiety, since the interior of the house was warm and draft free. "One hundred three point eight—almost three degrees above normal."

"When do we worry?"

"If it goes any higher, but it won't. I just gave him another dose of acetaminophen. That, plus the bath will help."

William's wailing approached a normal pitch.

Over and over, Michelle gently sponged him down. "He really doesn't like this," she murmured to Thad.

"I know," Thad said, cradling the infant in his hands. "But he'll feel better soon, I promise."

Together they worked on cooling William's fevered skin, both of them reassuring him with touch and soft words. William continued to cry. Finally Michelle began to sing. She had a lovely voice, clear and lilting. As the sweet sound filled the bath, William's cries lessened, then eventually stopped. As his body temperature fell to normal, he looked up at Michelle, with a mixture of wonder and what Thad could only describe as love. And the most incredible thing of all was that Thad felt it, too.

IT WAS ONLY LATER, after they'd diapered, dressed and fed William half a bottle of formula once again, that Michelle realized the front of her satin nightshirt was all wet. For modesty's sake, she'd left her bra on. It wasn't doing much to hide the shape of her breasts.

Blushing, she turned away as Thad settled William in his crib once again.

William's eyes blinked sleepily, then finally closed.

Thad stayed there, hand spread lightly across William's chest, waiting until their baby's breath was deep and even.

Slowly he straightened.

He and Michelle looked at each other, as wide-awake and filled with adrenaline as if they'd just started a 10K race.

When she went into the bathroom to clean up, she shivered. By the time she'd dumped the contents of the baby bathtub and set it in the shower to drain, Thad was behind her.

"Sorry if I kind of ordered you around," he said after a moment.

That wasn't why she was upset. "Are you kidding?" Aware she was trembling all over, she released a nervous breath. "I would have been beside myself had you not been here." She paused, dropped her gaze, nibbling anxiously on her lower lip.

Then, on impulse, she looked up into his eyes and confessed. "Oh, who am I kidding? I *panicked*, Thad. I saw William like that and I knew he was sick and…all I could think was I had to get you as soon as possible."

Thad leaned on the edge of her bathroom sink. "That makes sense. I'm a doctor."

She threw up her hands in frustration. Helpless tears

stung her eyes. "But if I'm going to be his mother, I should know what to do!"

"And next time," Thad countered implacably, "you will."

Michelle was not so certain. She shut her eyes. Another shiver went through her. The next thing she knew Thad's arms were around her waist. He stood and pulled her into the strong, reassuring cradle of his arms. "It's okay," he whispered, his breath warm and tender against her ear. "I was scared, too."

Michelle sniffed. "You couldn't have been."

"Oh, yes, I could've." He tucked a hand beneath her chin, lifted her face to his. "I see much worse in the E.R.—but none of those patients are my own kid. I have to tell you, what happened just now, the way I felt... the way we *both* reacted, gives me new insight into the way parents of patients behave. It *is* scary when your kid is sick. I don't care what kind of medical expertise you have. The feeling of helplessness—our inability to keep this from happening—is overwhelming."

Thad's confession prompted an admission from her. "I love him, Thad," she whispered, her voice thick with tears. "I know we haven't had him all that long, but I love him so much."

"I love him, too," Thad said.

"If anything were to happen to him..." Her voice broke. She began to cry in earnest.

"I know," Thad said in a low, choked voice. He stroked her hair. "I know."

Michelle tilted her face up to his, needing the reassurance of his gaze as much as she needed his warm, strong arms around her. Thad stared into her eyes and tilted his head. The next thing she knew his lips were connecting with hers, his kiss brimming with all the compassion, comfort and security she needed.

Michelle hadn't expected to make love with Thad again. She'd told herself she wouldn't fall victim to such impossible yearning again. But suddenly she needed to draw on his strength. She knew they weren't in love, but when she was with him like this, she felt loved. She felt secure in this moment, in her life, in a way she never had before.

Thad let her be who she was, gave her the space she needed, and his acceptance made the years of crushing expectations and narrow parameters of behavior fall away. When she was with him, she was free to go after what she wanted, free to express herself in any way she pleased. And what she wanted tonight, she thought, as his hands found her breasts and their kiss deepened, was Thad.

Thad knew Michelle was overwrought. He was, too. It was hard as hell seeing their son sick. The doctor in him knew William was going to be okay in another day. That didn't make it any easier to see their baby boy run a fever so high he trembled, was robbed of his appetite. It broke Thad's heart seeing William so miserable. And it was just as hard seeing Michelle upset, knowing that despite the temporary reprieve that had William fever-free and blissfully asleep, they had another twenty-four hours to go.

Instinct had him seeking comfort in her arms, the same way she was seeking comfort in his. The need to make her his had him unbuttoning her nightshirt, slipping his palms inside.

And once he felt her surrender, felt her body molding to his, there was no stopping with just one kiss. Her nipples budded against his palms. Her silky flesh warmed. He stroked, he kneaded, he caressed, until she surged against him, threading her hands through his hair, kissing him back eagerly, tongues melding in pleasure. Needing more of her, he slipped his hand beneath the hem of her nightshirt, smoothing his palm across her thighs.

She moaned at the new, deeper intimacy and shifted her hips, moving back slightly, giving him access. Throbbing with the need to possess her, he eased a hand beneath the elastic of her panties and found her to be just as soft and womanly as he recalled.

"Don't stop," she murmured, arching against his touch.

Thad groaned as she found him with her hands, too. "I don't intend to." He stepped free of his sleep pants at the same time she kicked off her panties. Moments later, he lifted her up onto the bathroom counter. Need pouring through him, he stepped between her spread thighs. Still kissing him ardently, she hooked her legs around his waist. The intoxication accelerated. And then there was only the touch and taste and smell of each other, the feel of their hands stroking as they gave and received, over and over. She was coming apart in his hands. With a soft moan of wonder, she whispered his name, then, "Now."

"Now," Thad agreed.

Hands beneath her buttocks, he pulled her to the edge of the marble counter, lifted her slightly and ever so slowly entered her, became a part of her. She shuddered and wrapped herself tightly around him. "Thad," she whispered again, still kissing him ardently, making him feel, want and need in a way he never had before.

Their mouths and tongues began to play the same age-old rhythm as their bodies. She gave him every-

thing, demanding more. Sensation built on sensation,
pleasure on pleasure, conjuring up passion and surrender, until all control ended, and together, they soared
into white-hot oblivion. Stayed, suspended there…and
then floated slowly back to reality.

MICHELLE HAD NEVER felt anything like this before.
Never wanted anyone as intensely as she wanted Thad.
And suddenly she knew it didn't matter how many times
they made love, she was always going to want him in
her life in exactly this way. And that scared her more
than she was willing to admit.

She had given her heart away before, to disastrous
result. She did not want to make the same mistake twice.
Nor did she want to walk away. The thought of never
making love with Thad again was impossible to bear.
Which left her, she admitted ruefully, in a quandary.

How could she continue to make love with Thad,
spend time with him and not fall head over heels in
love with him?

His body still a part of hers, Thad cupped her cheek
in his hand. "We don't have to figure it all out tonight,"
he said quietly.

A small gasp escaped her lips.

Leave it to Thad not only to see the private worry she
would rather have kept hidden, but address it. "You're
right." She forced herself to be practical, too. "Our primary objective tonight is taking care of William."

His eyes darkened at the off-putting sound of her low
tone. Something in his gaze shifted, grew less intimate,
too, even as he made no move to disengage their bodies.

"And to that end…" Michelle continued, but now
there was a telltale rasp in her throat. She trembled
at the realization of the resurgence—not dwindling—

of Thad's desire, the rekindling of her own. "We, uh, should figure out how we're going to do this."

Thad flashed the grin of an unrepentant sinner. "I'll tell you how we're going to do this." He lifted her against him—her legs were still wrapped around his waist—and he leaned down to whisper in her ear. "We're both going to sleep upstairs in your bed tonight."

Her breath caught halfway up her windpipe. She hadn't known it was possible to be so thrilled and reassured both at once.

"We're going to check on William, and make sure he's still all right, and make love again. And then," Thad whispered, "we're going to go to sleep wrapped in each other's arms until he wakes up again."

Chapter Eleven

William awoke three more times during the night. Once immediately after she and Thad had made love again, and then at four, and again at six. They continued to give him formula each time he woke up, though he wouldn't take much. And acetaminophen every four hours. He was still running warm to the touch at eight-thirty in the morning, when the three of them got up again, so Michelle held him across her lap, soothing him with gentle strokes, while Thad readied the thermometer.

"What is it?" she asked when he'd finished.

"A hundred and one point five, which is just above normal."

Michelle finished diapering William, then went to dispose of the diaper and wash her hands.

Because the tiny boy seemed content for the moment lying there on his back, she stretched out next to him on the bed. She took his little fist, kissed it gently. "I think his cheeks are less flushed, too."

William looked up at her with big eyes.

Thad joined them, stretching out on the other side of William. "He does look better," Thad decreed. "More interested in what's going on around him."

Thad reached over and got a rattle. He put it in front of William.

William's cherubic mouth dropped open in a soundless *O* of wonder. Reveling in the intimacy of the moment, Michelle smiled, too. "You think he'll run as much fever today as he did yesterday?"

"Typically, temperatures spike in late afternoon and into the evening, possibly through the night. He should be okay for a while this morning." Thad looked over at her, as relaxed as she had ever seen him. "Why don't you go for a run?"

It was Michelle's turn to mouth an *O* of surprise. He wanted her to leave? "Now? Are you serious?"

Thad shrugged. "You usually run every morning, and you didn't get to go yesterday. You've already told your office you won't be in for the next two days. It's a beautiful morning." He reached across William and covered her hand with his own. "Why not take a much-deserved break?" He smiled gently. "I'll stay here with William."

Michelle had to admit she was yearning to stretch her limbs. Running relaxed her the way nothing else could.

Still, she hesitated. "You really wouldn't mind?"

Thad brought her hand to his lips. "Parenting solo would be my pleasure."

The brisk breeze of the late-April morning caressed Michelle as she sprinted up and down the hilly streets of Summit. Flower blossoms were interspersed with the vibrant green of the grass and trees. The granite mountains rose majestically in the distance as the climbing sun lit up the cloudless, Texas-blue skies.

Spring was here, all right, Michelle thought dreamily. When she'd been younger, spring fever had hit her with tsunami force. Somewhere along the way, that force had dwindled, and the past couple of years, had finally gone altogether.

Now it was back again, fiercer than ever. And Michelle knew why.

It was because she'd found a town that felt like home. A child who made her realize just how much she wanted and needed to be a mother. And—most important of all—a man who respected her independence and treated her like an equal.

Life was good.

So good it scared her.

But, like Thad had said last night, they did not have to figure everything out at once.

They would put the adoption first and let everything after that slowly fall into place.

What counted right now was the joy she felt in her heart as she jogged up the street toward home, and the feeling of family waiting for her in her house.

Michelle slowed her pace as she hit the drive, walking the last thirty feet. She paused beneath the kitchen window to stretch her muscles. Hands splayed against the cement-board siding, she leaned in to stretch her Achilles tendon, and that was when she heard Thad's voice, coming through the partially open window.

"Thanks for the offer, but I'd rather not. Michelle?" Thad paused, sounding surprised. "Actually she's been of enormous help…. Yeah, she's still running as much as ever. She's out right now, as a matter of fact." Another pause. "You're right—that *is* one way to burn off excess energy…" Thad chuckled politely, as if hearing a quip he didn't particularly like. "Thanks, Violet. Like I said, I appreciate you going out of your way for me like this. Okay, catch you later."

Violet?

Michelle leaned against the side of the house, her heart pounding. More from what she'd overheard than from the exercise.

Why was Thad talking to Violet Hunter again?

Was that why he'd been so intent on sending her on a run this morning? Because he wanted to make a call he hadn't wanted her to know about while she wasn't around?

Fighting feelings of jealousy, Michelle strode in the back door. What she saw stunned her. Thad was standing at the stove, William strapped via canvas baby carrier to his chest. The little guy had fallen asleep again, silky lashes resting against his soft cheeks.

The junior cookbook she had loaned Thad was in the cookbook stand on the counter. The kitchen table was set for two. Thad looked so at home, so right.

This could be her life. And suddenly Michelle knew what she had to do. And the first order of business was not asking what Thad had going on with Violet. She spied the golden slices of bread sizzling on the griddle. "French toast?"

"It's actually not that hard to make," Thad said. Using the shaker she kept in the cupboard, he sprinkled some confectioner's sugar atop a stack of French toast that was ready to eat, added a pat of butter and a drizzle of maple syrup.

He winked. "I should've gotten one of these cookbooks a lot sooner. It's right at my level—beginner. Explains everything, including what a mixing bowl and measuring spoon is."

He sure wasn't a beginner in everything, Michelle thought, recalling the expert way he'd made love to her. Sensation sizzled through her, and with it, the desire not to screw things up unnecessarily.

Everything she knew about Thad thus far said he was an honorable man. She needed to trust that he was. Michelle smiled. "It looks wonderful." She appreciated the trouble he'd gone to. Glasses of milk sat on the table, along with a big bowl of strawberries. The aroma of fresh-brewed coffee filled the room. Surely he couldn't be up to anything significant with Violet. Then again, she'd never had a guy cheat on her. What would she know about infidelity?

And was it even that? Given the fact they'd never said they wouldn't see other people, not even when they'd been making love…

Oblivious to her tumultuous thoughts, Thad said, "Have a seat." He brought another plate over and sat down opposite her. "So how was the run?"

Michelle spread her napkin across her lap. "Nice." *Until I came home and heard you talking on the phone.* "Invigorating." To the point her heart was racing. And not from the exercise.

"Good."

She cut into her breakfast and found the toast tasted every bit as delicious as it looked.

"I need to talk to you about something," Thad said.

Michelle's mouth went dry. Pretending an ease she couldn't begin to feel, she looked at him and waited.

"As long as we're both petitioning to adopt William," he said, then paused to wrap a protective hand over the baby strapped to his chest, "do you think he should carry both of our last names?"

"I'M TRYING TO be fair," Thad continued. He watched Michelle's cheeks go from pale to pink. Taking in her distracted expression, he said, "I like William as his first name. It suits him, don't you think?"

Michelle let out a breath. Whatever she'd been expecting him to say, Thad noted, that wasn't it. "Absolutely," she said.

"And Garner his last name." Thad hoped she agreed, because he felt strongly about that.

Looking even more relaxed, she took a long, ladylike sip of juice. "Right."

"But—" this was the tricky part "—we could make Anderson his middle name. That way, we'd be carrying on your family name, too."

Michelle swallowed the bite of food she was chewing. "I think it would be great to have him both an Anderson and a Garner."

"Then it's settled. We'll talk to Glenn tomorrow, ask him to amend the petition, or do whatever it is he needs to do."

Michelle nodded, obviously concurring.

"And there's something else," Thad said hesitantly. He hated to do this. But he had responsibilities he couldn't ignore, much as he wanted to today. "I was supposed to work eight to eight today. I got someone to take my shift this morning, but his daughter is in a performance at school this afternoon..."

Michelle didn't hesitate. "Of course you should go in to the hospital."

Still, Thad did not want her to feel abandoned. "I wouldn't go if I didn't think William would be fine."

"I know what to do for fever now," she reassured him.

Thad knew that was true. Still, he felt this odd, powerful reluctance to be away from them. Intellectually it didn't make sense. He knew William would get well without him. Emotionally, though... He knew what it was. That parental urge to hover. He'd witnessed other parents of sick kids doing just that when their offspring were admitted to the E.R.

It was time, he knew, to do what he had advised countless other needlessly worried moms and dads: go do what you have to do; your child's in good hands. Nevertheless, he couldn't help but add, wanting to be sure Michelle knew he was not deserting them the way his dad had often deserted him and his brother, "The hospital's only a five-minute drive away."

Michelle gave Thad the same look he'd given her when he'd encouraged her to go for a run. "What time are you going in?" she asked almost too casually.

"I need to be there by one."

"No problem." She began to eat her breakfast with single-minded concentration.

"You're sure you don't mind? You don't feel I'm running out on you?" Thad said. Something subtle had shifted between them and it wasn't to his favor, he was sure of it. Whatever it was had happened while she was out on her run. Had he been wrong in pushing her to go? he wondered. Had she somehow taken his consideration for her well-being the wrong way? Seen it as an invitation to put up the walls between them again? "Because if it seems too much to handle," he persisted, wishing they could go back to the mood they'd shared when they'd first awakened this morning and found William feeling much better... "I can make some more calls—"

She lifted her hand. "If I'm going to be William's mother, then I need to care for him when he's sick, too. And honestly? With him feeling the way he's been feeling, there is nowhere else I'd rather be."

Thad felt the same way. Unfortunately there was a shortage of E.R. doctors in the area. Getting someone in to cover a twelve-hour shift on very short notice was a real problem.

"We're going to be fine, really," Michelle insisted, practically pushing him out the door when the time came.

And that, Thad found, was that.

MICHELLE HEARD ABOUT the salmonella outbreak at the community volunteer picnic on the evening news. By 6:00 p.m., one-hundred-fifty people had been taken to the Summit hospital emergency room for treatment. More were expected, since nearly all of the three hundred or so guests had eaten the tainted potato salad.

Not surprisingly, Michelle did not hear from Thad until nearly eleven. "I'm on my way home," he said, sounding exhausted.

"Rough day?"

"And then some. How's William doing?" They hadn't talked since around four, when the first wave of sick people had started coming into the E.R.

"His temperature has been running a degree above normal, whenever the acetaminophen wears off. So I give him another dose and his temp returns to normal. He just had a bottle and he's sleeping right now."

"You must be tired, too," Thad said gently.

She was. But it was a good kind of tired. The kind you felt after accomplishing something important. And nursing William through his first illness was extremely significant to her. The crisis, short-lived as it was, had let her know she was more than capable of being a good mother to this little guy. Michelle glanced fondly at the infant sleeping in the portable crib next to her. "I'm okay."

"I missed you today," Thad said huskily. She could

hear the sound of his steps moving briskly across concrete, the engine starting on a nearby car.

"I missed you, too."

"Where are you right now?" he asked, his voice still husky.

She smiled. The come-on in his voice thrilled her. "Upstairs," she responded flirtatiously.

"In bed?" Thad persisted. The ding of a car door opening sounded in the background.

Michelle shivered, recalling the way they'd made love the night before. "Yes."

She could almost feel the heat of Thad's body over the phone. "I'm going to go home and shower and change clothes," he said in a low voice that sent her senses into overdrive. "Then I'll be right over."

Michelle snuggled more deeply into the covers. "See you soon, then."

They said goodbye and she hung up the phone.

The next thing she knew the phone was ringing. She looked around in confusion and picked up on the second ring. Thad's sexy voice rumbled in her ear. "You fell asleep, didn't you?"

Michelle looked at the clock, realizing only fifteen minutes had passed since they'd last spoken, but she had been dead asleep. "Afraid so." She yawned.

"Going to let me in?"

"I'll be right down." Michelle rose, padded barefoot down the stairs and opened the door.

Thad stepped inside. He'd shaved. His hair was still damp from the shower. He smelled of soap. And looked good enough in the gray jersey pants and white T-shirt to be in an ad for athletic clothing.

Upstairs, they heard a full-pitched wail.

Thad dropped his overnight duffel on the floor and,

as they both ascended the stairs, said, "I'll get him. You go on back to bed."

Michelle wanted to protest. He'd worked all day, too, in the E.R. But one look at his besotted expression as he bent over the crib and hefted William in his arms made her realize that Thad had missed William, too. "I'll put him back to sleep," he said.

Michelle was too tired to argue. "Promise you'll wake me if he doesn't go right back down?" she said.

A now silent William cuddled against his broad chest, Thad bent and brushed a kiss across her temple. "Promise." He hugged her with his free arm, then guided her down to the bed. "Now sleep."

The next thing Michelle knew, it was morning. Sunlight was streaming in through the open curtains. And her house was quiet and still as could be.

She hadn't set her alarm, figuring William would wake her at the crack of dawn. Instead, there was no baby sleeping in the crib beside her, no Thad in bed next to her.

Pulse picking up, she climbed out of bed and tiptoed downstairs.

Thad had opened up the sofa bed in her living room again. He was sound asleep on one side of the mattress, one arm folded behind his head. On the other side of the mattress, toward the center, was the Moses basket.

Michelle crept close enough to peek inside.

William was sleeping contently next to Thad. His cheeks weren't flushed. She touched his forehead—fever-free. Two near-empty baby bottles on the table beside the sofa indicated he'd eaten twice, three ounces each time. Which meant his appetite was coming back, too.

She was still debating whether to let Thad sleep or put the coffee on when the doorbell rang.

TAMARA KELLY STOOD on the other side of the portal. The social worker's swift, assessing glance took in Michelle's white cotton nightshirt, bare feet and sleep-rumpled hair. "Sorry to wake you. I thought, it being a Thursday, you'd be up, getting ready to leave for work."

It was after 8:00 a.m., Michelle noted.

"I was looking for Thad and William, and I thought you might…"

Realizing this was Thad's final surprise inspection before a formal report was presented to Judge Barnes, Michelle ushered Tamara in. "They're both here," she told Tamara quietly. "But William's been sick with a virus since Tuesday and they're sleeping, so—"

Too late. The doorbell and now whispers had been enough to rouse Thad. He sat up and blinked as if trying to make sense of the scene in front of him.

Recognizing Tamara, he lifted a hand in greeting.

"Mind if I have a look around?" Tamara asked Michelle.

Michelle gave her immediate consent. After all, she knew that since she was petitioning to adopt William now, too, she was subject to the same scrutiny as Thad. "The master bath and bedroom are upstairs, if you'd like to start there."

Clipboard in hand, Tamara toured Michelle's home. By the time she came back downstairs, Michelle had managed to slip into the guest bath and brush her teeth and run a comb through her hair. A sweater plucked from the drying rack in the laundry room and a pair of slippers from the basket next to the back door made her feel a little less exposed.

Maybe it was because he was a guy, or perhaps it was because he'd grown up without the same stifling set of expectations that she had, but Thad hadn't even bothered to comb his hair before he strode into the kitchen. Wordlessly, he gave Michelle's shoulders a quick, reassuring squeeze. As she smiled up at him, he smiled back and brushed another kiss across her temple.

Just that easily, some of the tension left her body.

"William still sleeping?" Michelle asked, realizing how wonderful it was to wake this morning and find Thad and William in the house with her, even if they had been downstairs.

Thad nodded and set about making some coffee with the familiarity of someone who knew his way around her kitchen. A fact that did not go unnoticed by Tamara Kelly when she entered, making notes right and left.

"Can we offer you some coffee?" Thad said.

A buzzing sound rumbled through the house. It sounded like something was drilling through the wood floors. They all knew what it was. "Excuse me while I go get my pager," Thad said, "It's on vibrate."

Just that quickly a wail pierced the air.

Michelle rushed to go pick up William while Thad grabbed his pager.

As always, the infant stopped crying the moment she touched him.

Aware that Thad was now on the phone with the hospital, Michelle carried William back into the kitchen.

"He looks pretty good this morning," Tamara noted.

Michelle told the social worker what William's pediatrician had said, concluding, "This particular enterovirus only lasts forty-eight hours, so he should be absolutely fine by this afternoon."

Thad walked into the kitchen. "That was the E.R. I

was supposed to be off today, but there's another wave of salmonella patients coming in. Seems everyone who didn't come to the E.R. yesterday for treatment is in there asking for care this morning. They want me to come in ASAP. So—" Thad looked at Tamara "—can we reschedule?"

"Certainly," Tamara said pleasantly.

Thad turned to Michelle. "I don't know what time you're planning to go into the office today—"

"Actually I'm not. I've arranged to work at home today and tomorrow."

"If either of you are worried about the impact on the department's evaluation if you have to go to work as scheduled," Tamara cut in, "don't. We have no problem with you carrying out your other responsibilities as long as adequate care is provided." She smiled. "William's sitter is a retired registered nurse with years of neonatal experience. She has no other children in her care. It would be perfectly fine for him to go to the sitter today."

"I'm his mother." The words rushed out before Michelle could stop herself. "At least I hope to be if the court accepts my petition." Her voice filled with emotion. "I think one of us should be with him until he's been completely clear of fever for twenty-four hours." Until they knew for certain that he was well again. "And since Thad has to go to the E.R. this morning, I think I should be here."

"I feel exactly the same way about our baby," he stated.

Our baby. Thad's words brought a thrill to Michelle's heart.

His emotional admission did not go unnoticed.

Tamara wrote on her clipboard.

Thad's gaze settled on Michelle. "So you'll call me if there are any problems?" he asked softly.

Once again the world seemed to narrow to just the two of them. Michelle found herself in perfect harmony with Thad. Her heart warmed. "I promise," she said.

Chapter Twelve

Tamara agreed to stay and have a cup of coffee after Thad left for the hospital. Because it was also time for William's bottle, they adjourned to the living room to talk. Acutely aware of the sofa bed where Thad had been sleeping, Michelle gestured for Tamara to take a wing chair, while she pulled up the porch rocker that was now doing double-duty inside and settled into it.

For the first time in nearly two days, William latched on to the nipple hungrily. Michelle made sure William was comfortably situated in the crook of her arm, then looked over at Tamara as the social worker spoke. "I had an email from Thad's attorney stating that you are joining Dr. Garner's petition to adopt."

"Yes."

"As William's mother?" Tamara prodded.

"Yes."

"But not Thad's wife."

Now came the hard part. The part Judge Barnes—and even Tamara Kelly—might not understand. "That's correct."

Tamara made another note on her clipboard. "What exactly is your relationship with Thad Garner?"

"Right now? I'd have to say co-parents."

Tamara wrote something else down. "Are you dating?"

No, but we are sleeping together.

Not trusting her voice to be even, Michelle shook her head. "If I had to characterize it," she said eventually, when it became clear Tamara expected her to reveal something about the specific nature of her relationship with Thad, "I'd say we are friends."

Tamara's glance slid to the sofa bed where Thad had been sleeping. It was clear she recalled the morning she had seen Michelle at Thad's house when the circumstances hadn't been so platonic in nature.

Tamara lifted one eyebrow in mute consideration. Finally she said, "Are you planning to date each other?"

"Dating" seemed a little redundant to Michelle, given the way she and Thad seemed to be so quickly and seamlessly blending their lives. "Probably not, under the circumstances," she returned.

"But you don't know for certain," Tamara pressed.

Noting that William had slowed down on his feeding, Michelle removed the bottle from his mouth and sat him up on her lap to burp. Holding his chest with one hand, she gently patted his back with the other.

"I don't think either Thad or I want to do anything that could undermine the sense of family we'd like to build."

"And dating would?" Tamara held her pen aloft.

"Dating could make things difficult later if it didn't work out." Although not impossible, Michelle amended silently, since she knew plenty of divorced couples who had overcome their romantic history for the sake of the kids. She looked Tamara straight in the eye. "Uppermost in our minds is what is best for William."

"I can see that." Tamara smiled as William let out a healthy burp.

Michelle smiled, too. "We both love him dearly." She situated the infant so he could resume his feeding.

The mood in the room turned overwhelmingly tender. "I can see that, too."

Contentment flowed through Michelle as she watched William latch on to the bottle again. She offered him her little finger, and he promptly wrapped his fist around it and held on tight. Michelle gazed into his sweet, baby-blue eyes while continuing her conversation with the social worker. "Thad and I want William to have everything he needs, and we both feel it's better he have a mother and a father even if the mother and the father aren't married to each other."

Tamara sat back. She took off her glasses and let them hang from the chain around her neck. Finally she said in slow, measured tones, "Judge Barnes always reads the social worker's report, but like the maverick he is, he doesn't always go with our department's recommendation. He prefers to make his own decisions, and as a judge, he has that right." Tamara's glance dropped to William, who had stopped sucking on the bottle and was staring up at Michelle adoringly.

Tamara continued with a sigh, "I won't lie to you. We have a dozen families waiting in the wings—families who've either already adopted, have been fostering or have been on waiting lists for a child for months. Families who know the story and are offering to give William a home, too. We're duty-bound to report that to Judge Barnes, too, since—under Texas law—he'll be making his decision based on what is in the best interests of the child, period."

"What's in the best interests of William," Michelle

said firmly, upset at the mere suggestion they could conceivably lose physical custody of this little boy, "is for him to stay with me and Thad."

"I can see how much you and William and Thad have all bonded. I can see how much you and Thad love this baby." Tamara slid her glasses back on. "But I also need to understand how this is all going to work on a practical level."

MICHELLE HAD NEVER felt any sympathy for a woman who complained—after the fact—that a relationship wasn't working when she had never told the man in her life what she wanted.

Yet when Thad showed up at her door that evening, she found herself curbing her first impulse—which was to take him in her arms and give him a meaningful kiss. Instead, she ushered him inside and over to the Moses basket, where William was sleeping blissfully.

Together they gazed down at William. Tenderness welled inside her.

"What's his temp?" Thad asked quietly.

"Normal for the past five hours, even without acetaminophen."

Thad wrapped a companionable arm around Michelle's shoulders, showing her the kind of affection she'd always wanted.

"Looking at William now, you'd never know he'd been sick," Thad mused.

Michelle relaxed against Thad's body. "Amazing, isn't it?" she agreed. "How fast babies can get well."

"And sick," Thad said.

Michelle recalled how frightened she'd been when their little guy had first spiked a fever, how reassuring and strong and kind Thad had been. Not just to his son, but to her, as well.

He was an excellent father. A solid man and good friend. And a tender and passionate lover. Only one thing was missing in their equation. And unfortunately, according to Tamara Kelly, that was the ingredient Judge Barnes was going to be looking for. She decided it was time to put herself out there, take a risk. She'd do it while they ate dinner. She looked at Thad. "Have you eaten?"

He shook his head.

"Me, neither. Want to order in some Chinese food?"

He grinned. "Sounds…just what the doctor ordered."

Thinking how easily she could get used to this kind of camaraderie, she made the call while he went home to shower and change. By the time he'd returned, the deliveryman was at the door. Assured William was still dozing peacefully, they took their order into the dining room. "Candles," Thad noticed, pleased.

And the good silver, china and crystal. Michelle took another leap of faith. "I thought we should celebrate," she said.

Thad's gaze locked with hers. "We do have a lot to be thankful for."

Indeed.

"So how did the rest of the visit with Tamara Kelly go this morning?" he asked as they munched on spring rolls.

Aware this was where it could get sticky, Michelle stirred sweetener into her tea. "She went ahead and conducted the formal interview for my home study."

Thad paused, chopsticks halfway to his mouth. "And?"

Wishing she didn't have to be the one to tell Thad,

Michelle drew a bracing breath. "She had a lot of questions about our arrangement."

Thad leaned back in his chair and gave her a once-over that had her heart pounding. "I have a lot of questions about our arrangement."

A whole gamut of emotions radiated from her voice. "Me, too."

Suddenly Thad's mood became as cautious as hers. "Ladies first."

"Well." She forced herself to do what she did in every difficult legal situation—revert to the facts. Concentrate on what could be proved. "Okay, we're not in love with each other, but we do have a lot going for us."

Something flickered in Thad's eyes, then just as swiftly went away.

"Like?" he prompted, a hint of worry in his low, gravelly tone.

Michelle drew another bracing breath. Forced herself to look into Thad's eyes. "We're a great co-parenting team," she stated honestly, knowing that could not be disputed.

One corner of Thad's mouth lifted slightly. "Agreed."

Mentally Michelle went down the list she had made, since the social worker's visit. "William has bonded to us both—to the point that Tamara noticed and commented on it. So I know that will be in her report to Judge Barnes."

Thad looked pleased. "That's good."

"But—" finding she had lost her appetite, Michelle pushed the food around on her plate "—Tamara Kelly remains concerned about how this arrangement of ours is going to work on a practical, everyday level."

Thad's expression stated he had similar questions. "What did you tell her?"

Michelle shrugged. "The truth. That we intend to continue to live across the street from each other, even if it means I have to put an addition on my house. That we're friends. That we intend to be a family in every way that William needs."

"Without the wedding rings," Thad ascertained, a funny look on his face.

Michelle wondered if he was beginning to feel more than just a friends-with-benefits thing for her, too. But there was no clue on his handsome face. "Unfortunately that raised other questions for Tamara."

Thad's glance narrowed. "Such as?"

"She wanted to know if we were going to be dating other people, carrying on independent romantic relationships."

He went very still. "And you said...?"

Michelle tensed, too, despite her earlier decision to remain cool, calm and collected during this conversation. "That we'd have to get back to her on that."

Thad studied her in silence, his demeanor calm. He leaned toward her, searching her eyes. "Are we going to be dating other people?"

"I'll be honest." Michelle cleared her throat. "I would prefer we not. I know—" she held up a hand, as if taking a solemn oath "—it's selfish of me." She leaned toward Thad, too. "But our relationship with William is too new. We're still trying to figure things out and get in the groove. And to add another man or woman to that would be..."

"Messy," Thad concurred.

Michelle gulped. Inexplicably, joy began to bubble up inside her. "And difficult."

"Way too complicated," he added. His hand covered hers.

Sinking into the warmth of his gentle touch, Michelle had to force herself to go on. "I also know that you're a healthy adult—with needs—and I'm a healthy adult. And we're sexually compatible."

Thad grinned. He stroked the inside of her wrist with the pad of his thumb. "Very sexually compatible."

Achingly aware that all she wanted to do was make love with Thad—right here, right now—Michelle knew for both their sakes she had to stay on track.

So she continued with lawyerly calm, "Well, what I am proposing is that we become sexually and romantically exclusive. We can tell the court that we're not seeing anyone else but each other, and that, as William's parents, we are in a committed relationship."

Thad nodded enthusiastically. Still, he countered, "You know what Judge Barnes is going to ask. He's going to ask us why we don't just get married."

Was it her imagination? Or did Thad want to know the answer to that, too?

"We'll tell him we're both a little too independent for that, that we like having our own space. So—as I told Tamara today—to avoid confusing William with that, we're planning to do the whole bird-nesting thing."

Thad appeared as if he had forgotten completely about that. "Right," he said after a moment.

Once again Michelle forced herself to push on. Just because she wasn't getting what she wanted—Thad, wildly in love with her and asking her to commit to him for all the right reasons—did not mean they could not be happy. Because the past few days they had demonstrated that they could.

Michelle withdrew her hand from Thad's and resumed eating her dinner. "Of course to really make that a viable option, we've got to finish the nursery at your house as soon as possible and start implementing our whole nesting process."

Thad resumed eating, too. "Anyone ever tell you that you sound like a lawyer?" He helped himself to more *moo goo gai pan*.

She added brown rice and lemon chicken to her plate. "I'm serious, Thad. We have to demonstrate that we can make this work on a practical, everyday level before we go back into court next Monday. So to that end, I'm taking off work tomorrow, as well."

"Well, you're in luck there, because I'm off, too."

"Now for the bad news." Michelle drew a breath. So much to do. So little time. "William and I went over to your house earlier today. And while the paint fumes are completely nonexistent, the color is a little splotchy in places, which means the walls in William's room are going to need a second coat." She paused, hoping to enlist his cooperation. "I was thinking I could do it tonight—if you'll stay here with William."

IT WASN'T THE WAY Thad wanted to spend the evening. He also knew what was at stake. They needed to get this done in advance of the hearing with Judge Barnes on Monday. So she worked all evening finishing up the paint job, and then came home and collapsed in bed next to Thad, too exhausted to do anything but sleep. Early the next day she and Thad tackled everything else that had to be done. And while they were at it, Thad worked on a very special errand of his own.

"Hey, Thad," Hannah Callahan Daugherty, the proprietor of Callahan Mercantile & Feed, said when Thad entered the general store the next morning. She walked out from behind the coffee bar. "Violet Hunter said you'd be coming by."

Thad nodded, relieved everything was going according to plan. "I assume Violet filled you in?"

Hannah beamed. "She did indeed and your secret is safe with me. How's the little one I've been hearing so much about?"

"He's well and home with Michelle. How are Isabella and Daniel?"

"Great." Hannah beamed. "Adopting them was the best thing Joe and I ever did! But you're not here to listen to me go on about my deliriously happy family. Come on back to the storeroom. The item you ordered is in a box back there. You're going to love it." She pushed open the swinging double doors and led him to an oversize carton. "Both Violet and I adore ours. And speaking of Violet— you're aware she may have taken your request for help on this issue the wrong way, right?"

Thad knew Violet had gone all out to get the information to him. "What do you mean, the wrong way?"

Hannah shook her head in mute remonstration. "You men can be so dense sometimes! Violet still has a crush on you."

Thad frowned, irritated to be going over the same ground again. "We tried dating. It didn't work."

Hannah shook her head. "For you, it didn't. For her, well…"

Thad sighed. "So Violet thinks…"

"You asked her to help find this—" Hannah pointed to the box "—as a way of getting close to her once again."

Minutes later, still swearing silently over the misunderstanding, Thad loaded the bulky carton into the back of his SUV, then drove the short distance home. He was surprised to see Violet's car at the curb. He parked in the driveway, left his purchase where it was and rushed into his house.

Michelle was seated on the sofa, folding a load of freshly laundered hand-me-down baby clothes and blankets. Violet was sitting opposite her, still in her nursing uniform.

Their polite conversation stopped the minute he walked in.

Violet stood. "May I have a word with you?" she asked Thad.

Michelle looked upset. Not a good sign.

Figuring first things first, Thad turned back to Violet. "Sure," he said.

Violet murmured a polite goodbye to Michelle, then walked outside. By the time Violet had reached her car, tears were shimmering in her eyes. "Why didn't you tell me that Michelle was adopting William with you?" she demanded.

Thad hadn't made a secret of it. "I thought you knew."

"Well, I didn't. I thought—"

Thad cut Violet off before she could say anything else. "I consider you a friend. You know that."

"Right." She bit her lip.

"I want us to be friends," Thad continued. "I've always wanted that."

"Well, it's not what I want." Violet composed herself with effort. "I'm looking to get married again, Thad. I want my little girls to grow up with a father."

Thad didn't know what to say to that, except, "You're a terrific woman, an excellent nurse and a wonderful mother."

Tears rolled down her cheeks. "Just not the woman for you."

Thad's heart went out to Violet, but he refused to feel guilty. He had done nothing wrong. Instead, he gently reminded Violet of ground they had covered before. "Violet, we don't love each other. We never did."

"But you do love Michelle, don't you?" Violet guessed.

Thad didn't know what to say.

THE CIRCUMSPECT ATTORNEY in Michelle knew she should mind her own business. The emotionally involved, possibly two-timed woman in her had to go to the window and see what was going on out there.

Whatever it was, it wasn't good. Violet appeared to be both crying and ticked off as all get-out. Thad had that dumbfounded look men got on their faces when they were truly clueless about what was happening.

Finally Violet appeared to tell Thad what he could do with his good intentions and stomped around to the driver's side. Thad watched her drive off, then turned and headed up the walk.

Michelle rushed back to the clothes she'd been sorting.

Thad opened the door and walked in.

He looked over at the Moses basket, only noticing now that it was empty. "Where's William?"

For once Michelle was glad the little guy wasn't there with them. "Dotty called right after you left. She missed William and asked if she could see him. Once she was here and saw we were trying to get the nursery finished, she offered to take him back to her house for a few hours." She finished sorting the bibs and started on the Onesies. "It was clear William was as glad to see Dotty as Dotty was to see him—she's the closest thing he has to a grandmother—so I said okay."

Thad folded his arms across his chest. He did not try to conceal his irritation. "What time are we supposed to pick him up?"

"Six-thirty," she said through her teeth.

He inhaled the delicious aroma permeating the entire downstairs. "Are you cooking dinner?"

It was supposed to have been a surprise for him. Now she was regretting it. "Coq au vin."

His eyes widened in interest. "That's one of your signature dishes."

She lifted one shoulder. "Used to be."

He came closer. "How long was Violet here?"

Michelle folded another Onesie and set it on the stack. "Long enough," she said flatly.

Thad exhaled and ran a hand through his sandy-brown hair. "I'm sorry she had the wrong idea."

Michelle lifted her chin, angry all over again. "It's not surprising she did."

Thad's eyes narrowed. "What do you mean?"

"All those secret phone calls and messages that have been going on between the two of you!"

Shock reverberated through him. "If you thought there was something going on, why didn't you ask me about it?"

Michelle flushed. "Because it was none of my business."

He shot her a condescending look. "You preferred to jump to conclusions, instead."

She watched him just as steadily as he watched her. "It's no secret how she feels about you. Everyone in town knows!"

"Wait here." Thad walked out.

This time, Michelle did not go to the window to

see what he was up to. She stayed on the sofa, folding clothes.

A couple of minutes later Thad opened the door again and hefted a big, bulky carton inside. It had a big red bow on it.

His mouth thinned as he brought it closer and dumped it at her feet. "I was going to give this to you tonight," he said. "But I think you need to see it now."

Michelle stared at the information printed on the side of the carton. "A jogging stroller!" she gasped.

Thad planted one hand on the top of the box. "It's your New Mom's gift," he explained patiently. "You know, what a husband typically gives his wife after the birth of their first baby. Usually it's jewelry, but I didn't know if that was appropriate in our case, and I've never seen you wear a whole lot of jewelry, anyway." He shrugged. "Then I figured you're a practical woman, so why not be practical and get you something you can really use? So I got you this jogging stroller. When you want to go for a run, you can take William with you."

"How does Violet fit into all this?" Michelle asked weakly.

He crossed his arms. "I asked Violet to help me because I knew she liked to run as much as you do and had tried out a few different brands of jogging strollers until she found one she really liked. So I called her to find out what the brand was, and she promised to get back to me right away with the information."

An array of emotions crossed Michelle's face as Thad finished telling all the details.

"But I couldn't write the product information down in front of you because that would have ruined the surprise," Thad continued slowly. "Instead, I waited until you were gone to call Violet again. Once I had the right model number, I ordered the stroller online and had it delivered to Hannah Callahan over at the mercantile, because I wanted to give it to you personally."

Never had Michelle made such a horrible mistake. "I am so sorry." She got to her feet and moved around the box to examine the picture on the label and peruse the long list of features. Then she touched the top of the box almost reverently. "This is such a wonderful gift, Thad, I hardly know what to say."

His gaze gentled in the way she loved so much. "I want you to have it," he told her gruffly. "You deserve it and so much more for everything you've done." He stopped her before she could interrupt. "And I'm sorry that my asking Violet for help gave her the wrong idea. Just to be clear—I set her straight a few moments ago, and I'm pretty sure she now hates my guts. Which is probably a good thing. She needs to find someone worthy of her, someone who will love her for the good woman she is. It's just not me."

Michelle knew that, too. "You were right to be honest with her, even if it hurt. As for the rest—" she released a pent-up breath "—I don't know whether to laugh or cry."

Thad wrapped his arms around her waist. "You were jealous," he said in satisfaction, looking down at her.

As much as Michelle wanted to deny that, she couldn't. "I don't want to think of you with another woman."

He hauled her close. "Well, that makes us even, because I don't want to think of you with another man."

"Then what *do* you want?" she whispered, thinking she already knew.

"You," Thad replied, "and only you."

Chapter Thirteen

Up to now Michelle had promised herself that she could make love to Thad without actually falling *in* love with him. She'd vowed she wouldn't let her feelings grow to the point she would be heartbroken if Thad didn't return her feelings.

But when his lips captured hers, she knew she'd been fooling herself.

She did love Thad, with all her heart and soul. It was apparent in the thrill coursing through her whenever he was near. The loneliness she felt whenever he was not. It was in the complete and peaceful way he made her feel at times like this. As if there was no problem, no difficulty, no complication they could not handle as long as they were together.

Rising on tiptoe, she wound her arms about his neck and returned his kiss. He tasted so good, all mint and man, and felt even better, the hardness of his chest and thighs pressing against her. She could also feel the hard evidence of his desire. She moaned softly as he clasped her to him and drew out the kiss until it was so wild and reckless it stole her breath.

He slid his hands down her arms, beneath the hem of her T-shirt, to lightly caress her back. His lips forged a tantalizing trail across her neck. Then he kissed her on the mouth again, deeply and irrevocably, until she thought she would melt from the inside out.

She moaned again, her need for him surpassing everything else. The next thing she knew she was being shifted upward until her weight rested against his middle and her legs were wrapped about his waist.

Her pulse raced at the heat and intimacy of their contact. "Thad..."

He kissed his way down her neck, then back to the shell of her ear. "I want you, Michelle," he whispered, taking a sensual tour of her lips once again.

Desire shuddered through her. She felt her nipples beading beneath her bra, the strength of his forearm beneath her hips. "I want you, too."

His lips twisted mischievously. Then he headed for the stairs with her. "Hold that thought."

By the time they reached his bedroom, everything she felt—everything she'd once wanted to deny—she saw reflected in his eyes. He set her down next to the bed and held her face with both his hands. "Now where were we?" Slowly, deliberately, he lowered his mouth to hers.

His lips were hot and sensual, possessive and protective, tempting and erotic. She gave back as good as she got, running her hands across his shoulders, down his back.

"I think you were about ready to take my clothes off," she murmured, aware she'd never felt such power as a woman.

"And here I thought we were still at the kissing stage." He tilted her face up and kissed her again, and it was as masterly and dangerous and uninhibited as before.

Michelle reveled in the seductive demand of his

mouth on hers, the erotic sweep of his tongue. She had never felt so wanted, so needed. The sudden unsteadiness of her body had her clinging to him, wanting more, more, more...

And he was just as hot and bothered as she was, his skin burning through his shirt, the proof of his desire almost scorching through the denim of his jeans. And still he kissed her, until Michelle thought she would drown in the tantalizing give and take of his lips. And only when she was pulsing with need did he shift his hands to the hem of her shirt and ease her T-shirt over her head. Her lacy bra followed.

The air between them reverberated with excitement as he took in the silky curves of her breasts and the jutting nipples. The world fell away and the last of her inhibitions fled. Wanting only to be his, she let him look his fill, let him bend her backward over his arm to kiss and caress the sensitive undersides of her breasts before settling on the sensitive tips. His caress was electric, filling her with erotic sensations unlike any she'd ever known. Pleasure flooded her in great, hot waves. Michelle swayed against him helplessly and let out a whimper she couldn't restrain.

Eyes filled with desire, he lowered her to the bed and took off her remaining clothes, except for her lacy red thong. "Beautiful," he murmured, and then that was coming off, too.

His lips drifted lower, past her navel, across her hip. Nothing had ever felt as right as the hot moistness of his mouth on her skin. Her eyes drifted shut as Thad parted her thighs and moved between them, creating ripples of need. She caught her breath as the sensations spread—until the aching need was almost more than she could bear. He held her right where he wanted her as her body arched. And then there was no more holding back. Passion swept through Michelle, her body now shuddering and coming apart.

And yet she still wanted more, wanted to explore the need pooled deep inside.

She shifted so that he was beneath her, then began the process of undressing him, too, uncovering hard muscle and satin skin. Taking her time, she showered him with sweet, sure kisses and slow, tender caresses. Until the fire flared out of control, and need had them shifting again, so he was lying on his back once more and she was astride him.

He reached into the nightstand and found the condom. She sheathed him, protecting them both. Then he cupped her bottom and lifted her toward him, his hands spreading her thighs farther.

Michelle opened herself up to Thad and he took her with a masculine ease that had her whimpering in pleasure. Everything about their joining felt wickedly wonderful and intensely sensual. Hands guiding her movements, he took her slowly, sweetly. Her heart soaring, she wrapped herself around him, taking him deeper and deeper. Their mouths meshed in powerful kisses.

And then there was no more holding back. The love she felt for him dissolved in wild, carnal pleasure. She cried out his name. Thad gasped out hers. They were lost. Free-falling into ecstasy that warmed her body and sated her soul.

"That was spectacular," Michelle murmured.

Thad rolled onto his back, taking her with him, holding her close. "More than spectacular," he agreed contentedly, sifting her hair through his fingers.

He also knew it hadn't been just about laying claim

to the woman who wanted to be William's mother. Or finding some much-needed physical gratification for them both.

Making love had been a way to channel their feelings into the relationship without the burden of words. Or expectations.

If he had his way, of course, he'd already have them going down a much more conventional path—moving in together, instead of trying to figure out how to continue to keep one foot out the door while they got inevitably closer. He'd also have the legalities all wrapped up. The petition to adopt would already be granted. William would be his son officially. Michelle would be William's legal mother. And the three of them would be bonded together from this day on.

Unfortunately they were only days away from the next court hearing. Nevertheless, there was no doubt the three of them were a family.

And no doubt, from the way she was cuddled up to him with the aftershocks still coursing through her, that Michelle wanted to be with him every bit as much as he wanted to be with her.

The two of them were meant to be together, Thad thought, smiling at the realization that her legs were still wrapped snugly around one of his a good five minutes after they had climaxed.

They had time for one more bout of damn fine love-making, too, before he had to pick up William from the babysitter. Thad tumbled Michelle onto her back, slid between her thighs. "And speaking of spectacular..." He loved the rising excitement and passion in her eyes. He kissed his way down her throat, his body already hardening.

She arched against him as he made his way to the

sweet ripeness of her breasts. "You can't be ready, Thad. We only—"

He took the tantalizingly aroused peak into his mouth. "Just watch me."

"BEING A FATHER agrees with you," Dotty noted when Thad arrived to pick up William an hour later.

"What makes you say that?" Thad held William while Dotty gathered up baby things and put them in the diaper bag.

"I've known you since you were a kid. I've never seen you looking so happy."

Thad *was* happy. And for more reasons than just the infant in his arms. For the first time in a very long time, he felt part of a family. Felt as if all things were possible. And if his instincts were correct, Michelle felt the same.

By the time he and William returned to his house, Michelle had set the dining-room table for dinner. Working like a well-rehearsed team, Thad gave William his bottle while she put the finishing touches on the coq au vin and tossed a salad. She lit the candles. He situated William in his infant seat, next to them. The meal seemed like a harbinger of many wonderful evening meals to come.

"I have to say," Thad praised as they dug into the expertly prepared chicken and mushrooms in wine sauce, "all those cooking lessons you took as a kid paid off."

Michelle grinned and handed him the basket of crusty French rolls. "You're not bad in the kitchen yourself."

She looked pretty in the candlelight. Content, just hanging out with them. Thad wanted to make love to her all over again. "I'll be better once I graduate from the junior-cookbook level," he promised.

Michelle chuckled and held up a hand. "You don't have to be good at everything, Thad."

"I want to be—for you."

Their eyes locked. Michelle looked as caught up in the raw sentiment of the moment as he was, and Thad knew life was good. Better, in fact, than he had ever dreamed. And when they took William upstairs to see his finished nursery for the very first time, his cup truly ran over.

Together, Thad noted, he and Michelle had done an incredible job of changing the former study into every little boy's dream nursery. A chenille rug covered the wood-plank floor. The linens in the mahogany crib were brightly colored. A matching border in the same car-and-truck motif separated the two tones of blue on the wall. A dresser that doubled as a changing table was fitted with a cozy, terry-cloth-covered pad. A rocker-glider sat in one corner. Cloth-lined wicker baskets held diapers and toiletries. A collection of toys and books filled the low bookshelf.

William looked around as they readied him for bed. When he was dressed and swaddled, they set him down in his crib.

"I think he likes it," Michelle said softly.

Thad wound up the music box on the colorful mobile attached to the crib rail. The sweet sounds of "Brahms' Lullaby" filled the room. Thad reached over and squeezed Michelle's hand. "He knows we're as lucky to have him as he is to have us."

By the time the music had stopped, William was fast asleep.

Michelle and Thad turned on the baby monitor, then went downstairs.

"Social services should definitely be impressed on

their next unscheduled visit before the court date," Thad remarked.

Michelle's mood sobered. Thad knew she was likely thinking like a lawyer again and pondering all the things that could conceivably happen next. As a doctor, when waiting on the lab results that would allow him to diagnose and treat a patient, he often did the same thing.

He also knew that second-guessing what the experts were going to recommend was pointless. He and Michelle were already doing everything they possibly could—save one last thing—to make sure their joint petition to adopt William was approved.

Michelle frowned and stepped away from him. "Speaking of which…we need to talk about a few things," she stated.

Talking was the last thing Thad wanted to do. Especially when she was looking so on edge.

Knowing that what seemed unworkable at night after a long and tiring day often seemed quite manageable in the morning, Thad tried to buy time. Leaning against the counter, he studied the pink flush rising in her cheeks—the one that always appeared when she was on the brink of getting upset.

Telling himself there was no need to panic—Michelle was not trying to hold him at arm's length again but was just worried about the social services evaluation and Judge Barnes's decision—he asked gently, "Can it wait until morning?"

Words were not likely to help right now. Making love to her, holding her while she slept would.

Michelle shook her head. "Tamara could be here by then." She shoved a hand through her hair, pushing it away from her face. "We have to figure out our regular weekly schedule, figure out who's going to be taking William to the sitter when, and so on. Once we do that, we need to get the schedule typed up so we can give it to them."

"Can't we just make some general rules and take each day as it comes?"

Michelle's chin jutted out in the stubborn way he knew so well. "It's always better to have everything in writing," she said, sounding more lawyerly than ever. "And besides—" she gestured vaguely "—we need to figure out who is sleeping where tonight."

Thad had figured they would be sleeping together. He crossed the room to her side and wrapped his arms around her. "My bed is plenty big enough."

Her body stiff, she splayed her arms across his chest, wedging space between them. She looked up at him in frustration. "We're supposed to be doing this whole bird-nesting thing, remember?"

Thad regretted ever agreeing to such a ridiculous plan. Although at the time, it had made sense, he admitted reluctantly. "We made that decision days ago," he countered. "We weren't making love then, and regularly spending our nights together. Now we are." Now everything had changed...

She was becoming upset. "We only started doing that because William was sick."

Thad was beginning to see where this was going. He didn't like it. "It doesn't matter how or why we got close to each other, Michelle, just that we are." He didn't want to lose that.

"That's where you're wrong," she claimed.

"Tell me you're not comparing me to the situation with your ex-fiancé."

She was.

"I learned the hard way. It doesn't matter how wonderful it feels at the time." Michelle's eyes gleamed resentfully. "Traumatic bonding doesn't last."

"It could in our case," he said, "if we want it to, and I do." Knowing that the only way he could convince Michelle to see things his way was by being exceedingly practical, forthright and analytical, too, he gathered her in his arms. "I don't want to figure out which nights we're going to spend away from each other, Michelle. I want us to be more than a family of three. I want us to be a couple."

He paused, then decided what the hell—it was time to take yet another leap of faith. Time to convince her how truly committed he was to their future together. "I want us to get married," he blurted.

MARRIED! MICHELLE STARED at Thad, feeling as if the floor had dropped out from under her. She couldn't deny she wanted to be with Thad all the time, too, but the thought of marrying him for practical reasons that had very little to do with the kind of romantic love she felt for him had her reeling.

She had been down this road before. Been with a man she loved, but who—in the end—did not sincerely love her back. She couldn't do it again. Couldn't risk her heart. Couldn't risk their entire future, because now William was involved, too. "I'm not playing around here, Thad. This is serious," Michelle said quietly.

"Damn right it is," he responded with genuine feeling. "Think about how much easier it would be. Think about all the benefits. We wouldn't have a disadvantage over all the other families who'd like to adopt William, too. There would be no misunderstandings—with Violet or anyone else—about what we mean to each other."

His voice dropped a seductive notch as he continued persuasively, "No more women chasing me. No other men chasing you! No more awkward run-ins with the social worker. We could go to Judge Barnes next Monday as husband and wife and prove to him how committed we are—not just to William, but to each other and to our family."

Disappointment and disillusionment mingled inside her. "You've thought this all out, haven't you?" Michelle couldn't help it—she was beginning to feel a little used.

Thad's eyes darkened. "We have something special," he coaxed, linking his hands with hers. "An attraction that will last."

A physical attraction, maybe, Michelle conceded. As for love... Thad may have acted as if he loved her and made love to her as if he were crazy about her, but he hadn't ever actually come out and said he loved her.

Michelle had no doubt that if she were to make that a condition of marriage, he would dutifully utter whatever time-honored phrases she wanted. The only problem was, empty words and rote phrases weren't what she wanted, either. She wanted the kind of enduring love that had been lacking in her life thus far. She wanted a foundation of love for their family. Not just friendship. And certainly not just lust.

Because lust alone would not last. And when it faded, where would they be? Headed for divorce court?

The thought crushed her spirit.

She knew how hard divorce was on kids. She couldn't—wouldn't—put William through that.

So it was back to keeping one foot out the door.

"Listen to me, Thad." Injured pride brought a lump to her throat and she disengaged her hand from his. "Everyone who takes the plunge and gets married—for

whatever reason—thinks they will make it. And believe
me, as someone who practiced family law for five long
years, I've heard every imaginable motivation for saying *I do.* But I'm here to tell you, only the couples with
deep, abiding, real love have even a hope of making it
for the long haul."

And the long haul was the only way she'd ever want
a marriage.

"Michelle…" Thad began, reaching for her again.

She held her ground. "We can't do this for appearances, nor can we do it to enhance our chances of adopting William. Because if we go into that courtroom and
what we say doesn't ring true, Judge Barnes will know
it. Trust me, he'll ticked off." She sighed. "And if that
happens, I can almost guarantee you we won't have the
outcome we want where William is concerned."

Thad grimaced in exasperation. Clearly he was very
disappointed in her for not going along with his plan.

Unfortunately that changed nothing.

Moving away from him, she persisted doggedly, "We
owe it to William to stay off—not go down—a path that
could potentially lead to heartbreak." Or, if they were
very lucky, lifelong bliss. "We need to focus on what
we know to be true—that we both love William with
all our hearts. Everything else that has happened has
been wonderful. But you and I don't need to *rush* into
anything. Not when we can remain lovers and friends
and co-parents and leave it at that. At least for a while.
Till the initial excitement of adopting William passes
and we can be sure our feelings for each other and the
overwhelming passion we feel right now *won't* fade."

Thad looked at her as if she were a complete stranger.
He clamped his arms in front of him. Stood, legs braced

apart. "That's a very convincing argument," he countered in a low, silky smooth tone.

And one, Michelle thought too late, he'd heard before, to heartbreaking result.

"But I don't believe a word of it." Thad stepped closer. "This has nothing to do with what is practical and what is not. You're just afraid to love, afraid to believe in us and our future."

The ache inside Michelle intensified. She had no reply for that. Because Thad was right. She was afraid of putting it all on the line, the way she had before. She'd much rather hold on to what they had than risk wanting too much and losing everything in the process.

Thad shook his head in silent admonition. "You know what's ironic about this?" He threw up his hands and stepped away. "All along, I was worried that I was the one who couldn't make an intimate connection with someone. Well, guess what?" he said, his anger spilling over. "I was concerned about the wrong person!" He leveled a lecturing finger her way. "You've had one foot out the door this whole time, and you still do. You're the one who won't allow yourself to take the risk."

Michelle turned wounded eyes to his. "That's not true!" she cried, just as upset. She clenched her fists at her sides. "I'm committed to being a mother to William, and a companion and lover to you."

"Just not a wife." Bitterness tinged his voice.

She traded contentious glances with him. "We have to be practical," she repeated. "Marriage without love won't work. The rest of it will."

Thad's jaw hardened at the implacable note in her tone. His handsome features frozen in a blank mask, he countered with a willfulness of his own. "I'll co-adopt William with you, because I think he needs you as his mother, but as for the rest of it, I think we should go back to being just friends and co-parents. Nothing more."

The unexpectedness of his rejection was like a slap in the face. Wanting to be sure she understood what he was saying, she said numbly, "Not lovers."

Thad's muscles had turned to stone. "*Definitely* not lovers." He pushed the words through clenched teeth.

Tears stung her eyes. They had taken care to be so practical, to protect their hearts, their hopes, their future. How had it come to this? "That's really what you want?" she asked in a disbelieving voice, aware she had never felt more abandoned.

Thad turned away, a stranger to her, too. "It's the way it has to be."

Chapter Fourteen

"Thanks for coming in on such short notice," Glenn said the following morning.

Catching the veiled concern in the other man's eyes, Thad shook hands with his attorney and took a seat on the other side of the desk. "You said you wanted to talk to me about the adoption."

Glenn nodded and rocked back in his swivel chair. He rested his elbows on the arms of the chair and steepled his fingers in front of him. "I wanted to go over the specifics of the nesting arrangement."

Thad eyed Michelle's law partner warily. "Shouldn't Michelle be here for this?"

Glenn frowned. "I spoke to her earlier. She's already conveyed her thoughts on how it should go."

Or in other words, Thad thought sullenly, she did not want to see him.

Glenn opened the folder in front of him. "She would like each of you to parent three twenty-four-hour periods a week. And then every other week, you'll each have an extra day."

Trying not to think about the last time he'd kissed Michelle and held her in his arms, Thad shrugged. "Sounds fine."

"She'd like to care for William on the days you are

working at the hospital. So if you will provide her with your work schedule via email, she'll mark off her calendar, as well."

Struggling to contain his disappointment, Thad said, "Sounds…efficient." Which was just like Michelle. Only now she would be using that same preparedness to avoid him whenever possible.

"When she is in residence at your home, she would like to sleep downstairs on the sofa—and she requests you do the same at her home, when you are in residence," Glenn continued.

The thought of sleeping in Michelle's bed where they'd once made love and never would again was unbearable to Thad. It was understandable she wouldn't want any reminders of their failed romantic relationship, either. "No problem," he said tersely.

"She would like the nesting schedule to begin today. And since you had William last night and are at the hospital until eight this evening, she'd like to pick William up at Dotty Pederson's when she leaves work this afternoon."

Thad thought about the way William fixed his gaze on Michelle's face whenever she was near. "I'm sure he'll love that."

Glenn scrutinized Thad closely. "Are you okay?"

Thad did not know how to answer that. Yesterday at this time, he'd thought he had everything he had ever wanted. Now…if Judge Barnes approved their joint petition to adopt, he and Michelle would have a son to love, their homes and the satisfaction of their careers, but that was it. There would be no big romance. No sense of family, at least not the one they'd almost had within their grasp. And damn it all, he still didn't know why Michelle had broken it off. The truth was, he might never know. "I've had better days," Thad admitted finally.

"So has Michelle," Glenn confided. "I saw her this morning before she left for probate court. She looked like hell, too. Still gung-ho on being a mom, but otherwise...completely shut down."

Thad exhaled sharply. "I get the feeling you're trying to tell me something."

"I don't know what's been going on between the two of you except that lately she's been happier than I've ever seen her. And it wasn't just because she finally has a chance to become a mom. It was something more—and now that's gone." Glenn paused. "What did you do to make her feel so blue, Thad?"

"I HAVE TO BE honest," Tamara told Michelle during her last unscheduled home visit later that same day. "I didn't think this whole nesting arrangement was going to work."

Michelle moved around Thad's kitchen nearly as easily as she moved around her own. Doing her best to disguise her broken heart, she set a cup of hot coffee in front of the social worker and offered up an efficient smile. "But now you're a believer."

"Hard not to be!" Tamara broke apart a freshly baked scone. Beside her, William was seated in his bouncy chair, batting awkwardly at the arc-shaped toy bar in front of him.

"The baby is thriving. The nursery upstairs is beautifully done—he's obviously very comfortable there. Plus—" Tamara tapped the typewritten pages in front of her "—you and Thad have the scheduling thing down pat. I wish all our single moms and dads were as cooperative with their parenting partners as the two of you are."

Arranging the details of William's care via email and text message was an easy task. Figuring out what she and Thad were going to say to each other when they finally came face-to-face with each other again was not. Thus far, she and Thad had managed to avoid an actual physical encounter by doing the exchanges at Dotty's house. But Michelle knew that wouldn't continue indefinitely. Sooner or later she and Thad would have to parent together...

Wary of the wellspring of emotion within her, Michelle sat across from Tamara and sipped her coffee.

She had come to terms with the fact that she would always love Thad.

What she couldn't accept was the fact that he didn't love her back. Because if he had, he would have given them the time they needed to make sure their feelings for each other were more than just a reaction to bringing William into their lives.

She swallowed. Forced herself to go on. "Thad and I both want what is best for William, no question. That's a powerful bond." So powerful, in fact, that Michelle had let herself forget all common sense and get swept up in a fantasy that couldn't possibly come true.

Tamara nodded, understanding. "I sensed that from the first," she said, then paused meaningfully. "I also thought the two of you might...well, have something more intense going on."

Michelle shrugged and felt her cheeks heat. She never had been able to hide her deepest feelings, which was part of the problem. Aware Tamara was still waiting for a reply, Michelle rationalized, "Adopting a child is pretty intense."

Tamara lifted a brow. "You know what I mean."

Silence fell.

Michelle ran her fingers around the rim of her cup.

"Would you mind a bit of advice?" Tamara asked eventually.

It couldn't hurt. Michelle swallowed around the growing lump in her throat. "Please," she croaked.

"If there is one thing I've learned in my years as a social worker, it's that every day, in every situation, we have an opportunity to construct one of two things—a bridge…or a wall." Tamara stood and patted Michelle's shoulder gently as she prepared to leave. "Make sure what you're constructing will get you where you want to be."

MICHELLE SPENT THE rest of the weekend taking care of William, all the while thinking about what Tamara had said. By Monday morning she knew what she had to do. Risk her feelings once again and talk to Thad face-to-face.

Unfortunately he didn't come across the street until it was time to leave for the courthouse. He looked incredibly handsome in a starched blue shirt, dark suit and tie. His hair had been recently cut, and the tantalizing fragrance of his after-shave clung to his jaw. Michelle was inundated with so many memories, all of them good. Thad seemed equally pensive. And in some ways, unapproachable. As if he were ready for the adoption decision—and little else.

"Would you like to drive separately or together?" he asked, towering over her while she knelt to strap William in.

She thrilled at the low sound of his voice, the expectant look on his handsome face.

A bridge...or a wall.

The choice was simple.

Pretending to feel a lot more self-assured than she did, Michelle handed him the infant carrier holding William. "I think we should go together."

His eyes softened. "I do, too." Ever the gentleman, he escorted her down to the car, snapped the infant carrier into the base of the car seat.

"What do you think Judge Barnes is going to say?" Michelle asked nervously while Thad drove the short distance to the courthouse.

Thad took a deep, even breath. He kept his gaze straight ahead. "I know what I hope he'll say."

"Me, too." Michelle fell silent.

The next few minutes were consumed with finding a place to park, extricating William from his car seat, grabbing the diaper bag and heading inside.

Glenn York, Tamara Kelly and the court stenographer were inside.

They all sat down. The bailiff called the courtroom to order, and Judge Barnes strode in. As usual, the no-nonsense judge wasted no time getting down to business.

Tamara Kelly was up first. "I've read the reports," he told the social worker. "For the record—what is your recommendation regarding the minor child, and why?"

Tamara referred to her copious notes as she spoke, her clear voice laced with respect. "Although William is an infant and thus way too young to understand what blood ties are, there will most likely come a day when he is older when he will want to know his biological family, like so many other foster and adopted children do. Thad Garner can provide that essential link. In addition, it is clear that William has bonded emotionally with both Michelle Anderson and Thad Garner. They have worked well together to ensure that all of William's emotional and physical needs have been met." She looked the judge square in the eyes. "But what impressed me the *most* was the creative problem-solving used to address even the smallest concerns."

Tamara proceeded to describe their nesting setup in depth before continuing her assessment. "I have no doubt that Michelle Anderson and Thad Garner both love William very much and will make an excellent mother and father to him. Therefore, I am recommending to the court that their joint petition for adoption be approved."

Judge Barnes looked through the written report. He asked a few more questions. Stroked his chin thoughtfully. Finally he smiled over at William and said, in his usual gruff, irascible tone, "I was prepared not to like what I see here today, but it's clear this is one child who already has all the love and family he will ever need." Judge Barnes banged his gavel. "Motion for adoption is granted!"

MICHELLE WAS STILL a little teary-eyed and disbelieving as she and Thad left the courtroom, William in tow. Together, they accepted the congratulations of lawyer and social worker, then headed back to Thad's car.

"Big day," Thad remarked, his voice sounding a little rusty.

Michelle's throat ached with the effort to hold back happy sobs. She nodded, not trusting herself to speak.

"What do you say we forget about going home for a moment and take William for a stroller ride in the park instead?" Thad asked, his eyes as suspiciously moist as her own.

Michelle couldn't think of a better place to be on a beautiful spring day. And this time, she did find her voice. "I'd like that."

Thad got the brand-new jogging stroller out of the back of his car. Michelle helped settle William in the seat and strap him in, then the three of them crossed over to the green. The gardeners had been out, and the air was filled with the scent of fresh-cut grass and blooming flowers. Birds sang in the trees. Sunshine filtered through the trees. Children ran about on the playground in the distance. But on the path where they were standing, they were blissfully alone. William, lulled by the motion, was already asleep again.

Thad parked the stroller in the shade, then turned, took both of Michelle's hands in his and looked deep into her eyes. "I want us to celebrate today," he said, looking ready to make all her dreams come true and then some.

"I do, too."

"But first—" he raked her with a glance that was both tender and seductive "—I have a few things I want to say."

"Thad, I—"

He wrapped his arms around her and said in a rough voice laced with all the affection she had ever wanted, "I was wrong to try to rush you into marriage and walk out the way I did. You had every right to be cautious, given what you've been through."

"And you had every right," Michelle countered, with equal understanding, "to want more from me."

Thad tucked a strand of hair behind her ear. "The point is I should have backed off because I know that you deserve so much more than what I've given you so far. Not just time for us to get to know each other better and become a couple, as well as a family. But things like romance and flowers and candlelight dinners."

He wasn't the only one willing to sacrifice. Tears of happiness pricked her eyes. "Oh, Thad. I don't need any of that." *I just need you. And William and the three of us.*

With the pad of his thumb, he brushed away the tears trembling on her lower lashes. "Yes, you do," he insisted, the passion he felt for her gleaming in his eyes. "We both do." He pressed a kiss on her temple and then wrapped his arms about her waist, bringing her even closer. "I don't want to bypass this phase of our relationship. I want to savor every single minute of it."

Relief rushed through her. She laid her head on his shoulder and cuddled close, drinking in the warmth and strength of him. "I want that, too," she murmured.

He paused to kiss her, then threaded his hands through her hair. "Remember when I told you that I felt this immediate connection with William?"

Michelle nodded as hope rose within her. She splayed her hands across his chest. She could feel the thundering of his heart; it matched her own.

"What I didn't tell you," Thad continued, "was that I felt it with you, too, right from that first morning when we found William on the porch. And that scared me," he admitted. "Not because I was close to you, but because that felt better than anything else I've ever felt in my entire life. I was scared because I worried I wouldn't be able to figure out what you wanted and needed and I'd let you down. And what do you know?" he reflected bitterly. "I did."

It was her turn to confess. "Only because I wasn't honest with you," Michelle said gently, gazing into his eyes. "Because you were right, Thad," she conceded softly. "I was afraid to take a chance on us." The words rushed out before she could stop them. "Afraid that my loving you wouldn't be enough to hold a marriage together."

Thad paused. "You love me," he said after a moment, looking absolutely dumbfounded. And ridiculously pleased.

Michelle swallowed, knowing that now was the chance to lay it all on the line and hope that with honesty and time, they could make everything come out right. "Yes, I do. I love you with all my heart, Thad." The tears she'd been fighting spilled over her lashes and rolled down her cheeks.

Once again Thad was looking a little misty.

He flashed her a crooked grin. Eyes glistening with emotion, he bent to kiss her. "I love you, too," he professed, his possessive hold telling her every bit as much as his heartfelt words. "That's why I asked you to marry me. And that's why I want us to start over—" he paused to kiss her "—so this time we can take our time. And do it right."

Epilogue

One year later...

"It's a bold move," Thad said to Michelle as they toured a rambling Arts and Crafts home located three blocks from their existing residences.

While William relaxed in Thad's arms, Michelle and Thad looked around the second floor, with its half-dozen bedrooms and three full baths. All were in need of serious updating, as was most of the first floor. But structurally, the place was sound. It had two great porches, front and back. A yard big enough for a sandbox and a set of swings. And best of all, it had a study downstairs with a separate entrance, so she could work—and meet clients—at home.

Michelle squeezed Thad's hand, then leaned over to kiss William's cheek. "We're up to it," she promised.

Thad bussed the top of William's head, then her temple. He wrapped his arm around her shoulders. "Then let's do it." He grinned.

They proceeded to talk terms with the Realtor. By the time the sun set that evening, their bid on the new place was accepted. Their other two homes had For Sale signs out front.

The three of them had dinner together. Then she and

Thad bathed William, read him stories and gave him his bedtime bottle. Minutes after he was tucked in, he was asleep.

They walked back downstairs, and Michelle stepped out onto the front porch.

A lot had happened since the previous spring. All of it good.

Thad lifted a brow. "Not much chance of us spending the night together tonight, I guess."

Michelle shook her head. He knew what tomorrow would bring. "This is one time-honored tradition we're keeping." She stood on tiptoe and brushed her lips across his cheek. "I'll see you in the morning," she promised.

BRIGHT AND EARLY the next day, she got up and put on her running clothes, just as she had one year before. At seven o'clock, the anniversary was upon them, and she went across the street.

As they had planned, Thad met her on the porch in the clothes he had been wearing the moment their lives became irrevocably intertwined.

William would no longer fit in the outfit he had been wearing that fateful morning, but he had on a similar white sleeper, with a blue sailboat embroidered on the front. "Dada! Mama!" William shrieked, waving his arms exuberantly as he played around the Moses basket he'd been left in. "Hi! Bye!"

Michelle and Thad chuckled. "Hi! Bye! William!" they echoed.

William grinned, happy his newfound powers of speech were being understood. Still babbling, nonsensically now, he lifted his arms high, letting them know he wanted to be picked up. And that, Michelle noted silently, wasn't all he could do. He had just started taking a few steps on his own. He was attempting to feed himself. Insatiably curious, he had the sunniest, sweetest disposition they had ever seen. "Our little guy really is thriving, isn't he?" Michelle murmured to Thad.

He wrapped his arm around her shoulders and pulled her close. "We all are," he whispered, pressing a kiss to her hair.

Having had his snuggle with Thad, William reached for Michelle. "Mama!"

Grinning, Thad handed their baby over to her.

Right on schedule, four cars pulled up and stopped at the curb.

William snuggled contentedly in Michelle's arms while Tamara Kelly, Dotty Pederson, Glenn York and Judge Barnes walked up the steps onto Thad's front porch. All had been part of the process that had welcomed William into their lives. All were clad in casual, Saturday-morning clothes.

Judge Barnes looked at Thad and Michelle and shook his head. "Young people are crazy these days," he complained in his usual crotchety tone, but there was an unmistakable twinkle in his eyes.

Michelle grinned. There had been a time when she was afraid of being more than co-parents to William, and family—in the loosest meaning of the word—to Thad. No more. The past year had shown them all just how strong love and commitment could make a family. Their baby boy had done more than just bring her and Thad together. Bringing up their son had shown her and Thad contentment unlike anything they had ever dreamed. And now, at long last, it was time for the next big step.

"Thanks for agreeing to marry us," Michelle told Judge Barnes. "Especially in such an unorthodox way."

"About time you two tied the knot!" the judge declared with a teasing smile.

"I couldn't agree more, so let's get started," Thad said, the promise of a life to be lived happily ever after in his eyes.

Her heart brimming with joy, Michelle handed William to Dotty.

She turned back to Thad.

Lovingly, he took her hands in his. They said their vows in clear, strong voices, and at long last, their journey as husband and wife began.

* * * * *